A DUBIOUS HOPE

ELLEN L. SAUNDERS

SLIMHORN & WREN, LLC

This book is a work of fiction, in case sentient tardigrades weren't enough of a clue. It is the product of the author's imagination. Any similarity to live or dead humans, other fictional characters, places or events is coincidence.

For more information:

Slimhorn & Wren, LLC

www.slimhornandwren.com

or email staff@slimhornandwren.com

Michael Brugger's website:

https://michaelbruggerarts.com

Jordan Walker's website:

www.jordankwalkerart.com

CONTENTS

CONTENTS

ONE
BILQUIS REBORN

EARTH YEAR 3410 CE
NEW HOPIAN YEAR 712
HEAVENLY GANGES aka THE MILKY WAY

A star whirls in sapphic dance with another in the vastness of the Milky Way. She is massive compared to the star that still warms Earth, perhaps twenty times larger. Give her a number or call her Bilquis—she is indifferent to labels. Like all stars, she and her companion have been slowly consuming themselves. She creates helium in raging storms of quantum explosions, fusion on a colossal scale that releases enough energy to easily outmatch the crushing gravity of her substantial girth.

But lately her infernos have been dimming. Too little hydrogen remains. Outward pressure from her billowing plasma weakens.

Gravity is implacable, unforgiving.

When the tipping point is reached, she falls into herself. The collapse takes mere seconds. Her once vast gaseous edges slam solid, tense. Chain reactions transform helium. She is weighed down with heavier elements, each giving her less and less in return

—carbon, oxygen, silicon—until finally, she creates the one that takes but does not give: iron.

Iron suffocates her shrinking core in the blink of an eye.

Bilquis inhales herself. Crashes inward like lava forced into lead-filled lungs, like an asteroid belt sucked to a planet's core. She implodes with unspeakable force and speed. Atoms compress to the screaming point. Gravity forces electrons to violate their boundaries, squeezes them into protons; boson or fermion, their charges gone. Bits shear off. Nothing about this process is voluntary.

It is too much. Everything too near, too hot, too—

Bilquis explodes.

She has spent an eternity fusing her core. In microseconds, she flings much of it away, expanding as rapidly as she had collapsed. Shockwaves reverberate at pressures and speeds reminiscent of her own birth. She creates again, briefly: nickel, silver, tin and every element in between. Her possessive gravity clutches, seizes, clings; succeeds in holding her together.

When the maelstrom subsides, she spins faster, burns hotter. Her magnetic fields have increased by orders of magnitude. Her traumatic near-death has pulled her companion star within reach. Bilquis reels in outer layers of its plasma onto her own unsettled, roiling surface until again, it is too much.

Jets erupt from opposite sides of Bilquis' superheated form. The brief flare is a brilliant light show as gorgeous as it is vicious.

Stars are seldom immortal. Lucky Bilquis has become a phoenix. Reborn a pulsar, she is a rare jewel in the night sky.

Whipped by an unstable magnetic field, the superheated plasma she ejected into space rockets through the cold vastness that is mostly but not entirely empty. One of those beautiful, deadly particle streams strikes a planet humans dubbed New Terra a mere 900 years earlier. The earth-like sphere's magnetic field is no match for the blast, which doesn't even slow as it strips away New Terra's atmosphere and incinerates everything it touches on the planet's surface.

New Terra may phoenix someday as well, but it will take eons, even with terraforming. Its ability to support mammalian life is gone.

EVEN LIGHT HAS ITS LIMITS, such as speed. It takes time for the brilliance from the rebirth of Bilquis to travel to areas that are populated with minds. When it finally arrives, it is, like all information, interpreted differently depending on the motivations of the viewer.

One powerful being, fascinated by what they learn looking through others' eyes, lacks the ability to sense starlight. So Bilquis's flare does not stir their insatiable curiosity, though its consequences will reverberate through their orbit for millennia.

Also unaware is a brooding female beneath the surface of planet Vasom. She only has eyes for her unusual lover. He watches with satisfaction as she takes a sip of the green beverage he has offered her. That swallow will have as many ramifications for the solar system's residents as does Bilquis' rebirth.

Elsewhere on Vasom, a couple celebrating in a dark bay delight in Bilquis' short-lived brightness in their sky. They twine teal tentacles tight as they float in the cold water, sharing joy and raw mollusks under the stars. Perhaps their children will investigate. They've just convinced their spaceships to begin wider exploration, beyond the known planets.

Far away on planet Taequa, a servant hurrying over the cobblestones through the blessedly cool pre-dawn air glances up, sees the flare among the stars, and sinks her talons into her fur. Is this yet another ill omen for her people?

MUCH LATER, an insomniac astrophysicist on the generation spaceship *New Hope* gazed in wonder at the brilliant light, thinking about the studies he can do with the captured data. It took him an hour to think to check the pulsar's path. When he did, he fell to his knees, swearing. Vomited bile. Checked his math and the many instruments trained on the fried planet. Finally, he woke the head of planetary research and the ship's captain.

Seven hundred and thirteen years after its launch from Earth, the *New Hope* hurtled onward toward New Terra.

TWO
HOPE, SHATTERED

ABOARD NEW HOPE
NEW HOPIAN YEAR 713
SECOND MONTH'S FIRSTDAY
REMEMBRANCE BREAKFAST DAY

Five hours after the captain's rude awakening, the non-hibernating residents of *New Hope* began their day.

In the noisy cafeteria kitchen, Harriet Pangea broke apart freshly extruded cutlery and chatted with the dishwasher, using her volunteer shift to recover from the morning's spat with her husband. Why could he not leave their youngest alone? Some days she wished they'd not had children at all; they'd been so happy alone.

The mission requires sacrifice, Harriet thought, and sighed.

The air carried the clattering, sizzling, slapping sounds of food preparation, and mouth-watering smells; spice-coated fried 'hoppers, simmering congee, frying tortillas, sautéed mushrooms, and piles of berries. A generous meal to break the fast of the First Month's final weekend.

In the insulating spaces of the hull, something flexed its tendrils and fed.

In the large meeting room, six-year-old Lethabo fought to keep his empty stomach quiet during the closing ceremony for First Month's final weekend. He and others have spent the weekend fasting while learning about, remembering, and grieving lives lost to ethnic genocides. A thoughtful child, Lethabo was more somber than usual. This weekend he learned why so many New Hopians participate in this tear-filled memorial. Roughly three hundred ship years prior, *New Hope's* mission had nearly been destroyed by racist ideology pushed by a charismatic sociopath. It took them two generations to recover. New Hopians, descended from every member country of the United Nations of Earth, cannot afford to forget what happens when community is ruptured for personal gain, exceptionalism, hubris, or religion.

Last night, young Lethabo had decided to honor the suffering of his ancestors by skipping the evening snack allowed the elderly and the young. He did not quite regret that decision, but he was now motivated to ensure no one else endured this horrible sensation.

The event concluded with the reciting of the whole of the Community Accord. Lethabo added the words he knew into the flow, "...all are of equal value. ... differences ... exist, but we honor and support ... We find roles of service for all. ... We value the gift of every individual ..."

The audio of the ceremony was broadcast across the ship. Back in the kitchen, a tinny communicator shared the closing ceremony's audio. Clanking spoons and conversation stilled so all could hear, and join in the final words of the Accord:

"Given our ancestors' harrowing experiences, we disavow the label 'human.' We are Spacers. We live and die together."

When it is over, crickets chirped a raucous symphony in the protein ranch, Harriet's regular work station, while her colleagues walked among their plexiglass containment areas, checking larvae for diseases.

Volunteers and agriculturists in the neighboring vegetable fields gave an impromptu concert in the row crops, singing the working call and response, " Ivinda ya Mbua," as they harvested the lunch and dinner greens: purslane, collards, mâche and others.

Near the center of *New Hope*, a sweating mentor answered questions posed by Marfa, an energetic seven-year-old on a neighboring treadmill. Marfa wanted to learn about the ship's recycling process and the problems contamination could pose. The mentor took the opportunity to reinforce a lesson the child's fathers had requested, "That's why we wash our cutlery before we melt it to be re-used." She rocked her fist forward to show she had heard, though her wrinkled nose made it clear what she thought of that chore.

In the Quartier Vivant, neighbors greeted each other with, "The hull is secure!" or, "May you never thirst!" in at least a dozen languages, sharing tea and other drinks at tables lining the wide hallway. A vivid, multicolor mural on the table side of the wall included the words, "Hydration is love." Gossip, snatches of song, and laughter filled the air.

Behind one of the still-closed doors in the neighborhood, two women discussed their coming day, their calligraphy projects, and the challenges faced by their new mentee.

In a Quiet Quarter hallway three floors below, a teenager in a leg brace quietly sketched next to an open door while a friend plaited his hair. They listened to the teen's parents singing songs of passage in the crowded apartment inside, where the family sat in vigil for an elderly uncle. The uncle had declared his regrets and made his fond goodbyes the day before. Now his thoughts slipped into dreams of his deceased wife, meaty mushrooms and immortality. His breath rattled to a stop.

The tendrils stopped feeding and flailed, overcome to their basal filaments by grief.

ABOARD NEW HOPE: QUIET SECTOR
NEW HOPIAN YEAR 713
SECOND MONTH'S FIRSTDAY

FIVE DOORS in from the bedside vigil, nine-year-old Opal Pangea sat at the family table, biting her lip to stay focused as she created letterforms.

Opal carefully laid her pen to the side, and scanned for any smears or drops in her work. She rubbed her right palm with her left fingers, easing cramped muscles. She'd been gripping her new pen too hard. Her knees hurt, too, from kneeling on the hard chair so she could reach the table. She unbent and rubbed them. She should have gotten a cushion, but her angry brain-bees had been loud this morning, pushing her to "Hurry, hurry, hurry!"

Her new mentors had told her that with practice, focus would soothe her brain-bees. Told her to never rush. Told her, "True craft takes patience and time."

Time Opal understood. Mère and Père's weaving could take months.

Patience was harder. Patience was something her red-headed mother did not possess, although Père had plenty for them both. Unfortunately, his patience often took the form of waiting for days to tell Opal that she'd started something wrong and would have to do it all over, adding, "Maybe you'll remember not to screw up next time."

It wasn't like she could have inherited his patience; she tried to reassure herself. Like her sister and about half the children on board, she was a creche-child, created from the conservatory of Earth eggs and sperm. But she didn't seem to be learning patience, either. Or much of anything that mattered to Père. That thought caught in her throat, stung her eyes. She made herself stop thinking. She read aloud what she'd lettered in her family's language, French. She bent back over the paper.

"*Inspire.* Breathe in. Find something blue. Hold the breath and appreciate one aspect you like about that object." She and Mère had dyed a large batch of recycled fiber a pale blue two years ago. It had been a hard project, and a long one, but the two of them had worked together in an easy companionable rhythm that involved several songs. It was one of Opal's favorite memories.

"Exhale. Think of something soft. Hold the exhale while you imagine softness." The congee in the community kitchen this morning had been filling and soft.

"Inhale. What was your favorite meal last week? Hold. What did it taste like?" That was easy, last night's fried termites. The cooks had come up with a new spice mixture that was kind of like five spice, only more woody-green. Everybody had raved about it.

"Exhale. What music relaxes you? Hold. What sound is the most comforting?" Vocalists or drumming, because string and brass instruments sometimes set off her bees.

"Inhale. What can you smell? Hold. What's your favorite scent?" This ink smells a little like sulfur, she thought. Her favorite scent was the dusty musk of rice husks, because that meant a full harvest and she liked rice the best of all the starches.

Opal had just finished inking "l'odeur." The rest was lightly traced. "Exhale. Look around you. Hold. Name three things you see." She looked up, turning away from the clutter of her parents' loom-filled weaving studio, which in another dwell would be a family's living room, instead seeking objects in the more calming, spartan kitchen: the portable burner, Père's heirloom blue-white tea jar, their framed wedding knot.

Her personal litany against anxiety was nearly done.

Opal planned to hang it on the wall of the cluttered room where her sister was currently swearing and flinging clothing around. Opal smiled. Adamantine would strut out soon, all poised and stylish, sleek black hair gorgeous. That was just who she was.

Her smile faltered. She was not Adamantine. She was not confident. She was short and dull and pale and a panicky disappointment with dishwater brittle hair who hadn't been allowed her own hobby until her tenth anniversary.

Thanks to Mère, she'd gotten it three weeks early, but it still rankled. Most of her cohort had been allowed personal hobbies from near-infancy. Terri, whose anxiety was arguably the worst on board, had four. Mère and Père said they always needed Opal to help with their weaving. But it was pretty obvious that Père just didn't trust her to do anything unsupervised.

And still didn't.

Before Père had left for his research office, he had told her he would inspect her calligraphy when he got home. "Prove to me you should be allowed such luxury," he said.

"Obert," Mère had said. "That is her mentors' job, not yours." Her tone carried the electricity of a previous argument, her cheeks reddening.

He stiffened, dark cheeks like broken stone, and snapped, "I have a meeting." He had left without agreeing with her.

He was still mad that Mère had agreed to the mentors' barter without him. He didn't think much of calligraphy. Or of the calligraphers. Opal couldn't tell.

Probably just because calligraphy was her choice. Her shoulders slumped.

Père was brilliant, and respected, and had high standards. Opal was proud to be his daughter and tried to live up to his expectations. That had gone from hard to impossible as she got older. Nothing was ever good enough.

She looked back down at her work. She could see every shaky serif, every less-than-perfect curve. Was this going to be good enough for Père?

It would look better without the under-tracing, she thought. She should finish so it would be dry enough to erase them before he got home. She grabbed her pen and dipped into the squat pottery vial. In her rush, she forgot to drag the loaded pen across the lip.

A big drop of ink fell from her pen as she pulled it over the paper. She jerked her hand left and away, but a huge splotch splashed down onto the left margin.

"Non!" she cried out. She set the pen down on her scratch paper and burst into tears. She'd ruined it. Père would take her pen away. This tiny bit of freedom, gone. Why was she so stupid, so clumsy, so bad at everything?

"Petite sœur, qu'est-ce que c'est ?" Adamantine danced out of their shared sleeping chamber. She leaned over Opal's shoulder, giving it a gentle squeeze, and sat Gengi, the stuffed tardigrade she'd made Opal as a comfort toy, in her sister's lap.

Opal grabbed him and kneaded Gengi's comforting soft body between her fingers.

"Fantastic! It didn't land on your lettering." Adamantine could see beauty in an overflowing toilet if she wanted to, or make a hangnail utterly destroy a joyful day. "How would your mentors fix it?"

Opal took a ragged breath and tried to think of the finished works they'd shown her. Images of weird hybrid creatures, starry fields, fancy patterns came to her. "Oh. They would draw something to cover it up. An Earth animal, or a pattern, or a person climbing out of a flower. Something weird." Something Père would hate, she thought, because it wouldn't make sense.

"Do that, then!" Adamantine wrapped her arms around her sister. "You can do well. We want Père to be proud of you."

Mère's words. Opal missed Mère's hugs. She couldn't remember Père hugging her. She forced herself to be present, to hug Adamantine back. She calmed in her sister's arms.

"I have dance now. Until later." Adamantine pulled away and skipped around the table.

"Until later. Merci, grande sœur." Opal stuffed Gengi into her pocket and turned back to her litany. She wiped her nib clean, staring at the splotch for the time it took for Adamantine to cross Mère and Père's weaving studio in the neighboring room and go out into the Quiet Quarter's central hallway.

The blob of ink seemed less massive now, with five arms

spreading out in symmetrical curved lines. Like a galaxy. Opal took a deep breath and set her dry nib down between two of them and pulled, adding another curving line that spiraled in the same direction, but longer, ending in a fancy curl. She added four more, one between each of the original splash lines.

Now it really looked like a spiral galaxy. The lines she'd drawn sucked much of the excess ink away, making the drop less heavy, but it was still wet. Opal added distant stars up and down the left margin, using the blotch like an ink pot. In one place the star didn't look right, so she turned it into another, smaller galaxy.

She'd never had the chance to draw anything permanent before. And this was just for her. It felt like a luxury, a gift. The bees in her head quieted, and a sense of contentment grew. Maybe this was what her mentor meant.

ABOARD NEW HOPE: RESEARCH SECTOR
NEW HOPIAN YEAR 713
SECOND MONTH'S FIRSTDAY

A DOZEN planetary scientists entering the meeting room near their offices groused about the short notice they'd gotten for this morning's meeting.

"I couldn't even get into my office!" one complained as they entered. "My door was security locked! Tate better have a good explanation."

Exobiologist Obert Pangea glared at the man's back as he followed the group through the doorway. Whatever was going on was probably this man's fault. Nothing involving the research of a planet they wouldn't reach for four more generations could possibly be urgent, and this morning's summons had interrupted his focus on a particularly complicated weaving pattern Harriet had strong-armed him into, all for his idiot offspring's unnecessary calligraphy mentorship.

Obert and Harriet wove for the family's luxuries on the barter market, and as far as he was concerned, those trades should be limited to goods and services for the three family members that mattered. Sitting on that deeply held belief frustrated him. They'd spatted again this morning over something Harriet believed their pasty youngest had expressed an interest in. *Idiotic.*

Opal was too stupid to do anything on her own. In truth, the girl should be iced for the good of the ship's genetics. Not something he could say aloud; if he loosed his tongue to the wrong person, he could be iced himself. He'd faked his way this long, but that damned Accord was going to kill him.

Obert flung himself into a seat and pinched the bridge of his nose, doing his best to nonverbally communicate, "I have a headache, don't talk to me."

The door to the room clunked shut, followed by the click of its interior lock. Obert looked up in surprise.

"We're all here, finally." Tate Dorofandu, the director of planetary research, turned back from the door panel. "Disable cameras. Stop any audio recordings. Absolutely no record of this meeting. Everything said in here from this moment forward is a shut-it." He sat back down, pointing his heavy black fingers at several personal devices on the table with an emphasis that bordered on rude.

"A shut-it?" Obert echoed in disbelief. *Utterly bizarre.* What in their work could possibly require a death-vow-sworn secrecy?

He and his colleagues glanced at each other, bewildered. Exobiologists, chemists, physics experts, exogeologists, distance-sensing researchers and others, they'd researched, discovered, and debated together their entire careers. They commonly shared details they learned or confirmed about their future home with their fellow passengers. The group's sole focus was research about the planet the United Nations had chosen as their destination. No one alive shipboard, save the Earthborn floating in their hibernation pods, would set foot on New Terra, yet even the most mundane detail the research group discovered about their descendants' future home could be the focus of ship gossip for days.

Obert reveled in that attention. He rarely bothered arguing with Tate, a precision-focused community builder, but he chafed at the nebulousness of this demand. "Maybe you could explain why first?"

"I will explain. But the explanation is the shut-it." Muscles bunched on Tate's forearm as he clenched and unclenched his fists, something he did when deeply stressed. "Shut them off."

He looks exhausted, Obert thought. *Or terrified?* A ripple of anxiety ran up his spine and he mentally stomped on it. That was Opal's problem; she wallowed in such weakness. He would not indulge in it.

"Tate, do we need to sing for you?" someone asked.

The director snapped his fingers in negation and began to rub his temples.

Their communications tech bounced up and manually turned off the ship's recording camera in the corner. Grumbling, people began to turn off their personal devices.

Obert was among the last to comply. *The mission comes first*, he reminded himself. He remained deeply annoyed.

Tate glanced around and verified their privacy was assured. Then he slapped his palm on the table. "New Terra lost its atmosphere in a gamma ray burst we recorded at two hundred and fifty-five-minutes ship time. It is completely uninhabitable." Each word was clear but sounded ripped from his throat. His eyes closed.

A moment of silence, and then the room erupted into noise: decibels of shock, denial, horror, and protests about such a macabre joke.

Obert froze, fighting nausea. His belief was instant. Tate was not a joking man when it came to his life's work, where he did not tolerate mistakes. *Everything I've identified, my life's work—gone.*

Eventually people took Tate's heavy silence as a cue. When

they quieted, he provided the proof. Several pieces of equipment had been live and caught the moment of contact. Tate had cobbled together a quick, crude model that illuminated the brutal impact of the stripped atmosphere all too clearly.

Soft swearing punctured the tense silence as they took in the imagery, the abrupt shift in biosignatures.

"All that life, gone," one of the women said brokenly.

"It'll be thousands of years before the surface is habitable again," another breathed.

"And it will remain in the path of a pulsar," Tate snapped. He took a deep breath. "I'm sorry. I only found out a few hours ago, and I've been vibrating from the possibility that someone—else— could have gotten to the instruments first. I've locked down all the equipment."

His elision of the words "someone less circumspect" was clear, at least to Obert.

Tate continued, "All our research efforts will entirely shift, obviously. We must find a new destination. Captain Ximena has been included in the shut-it and, if you're wondering, requested it. You cannot tell the community. You cannot tell your partners or your mentors, and certainly not your children and mentees. The panic that would result from this—"

Shouted objections drowned out his words. Several people slammed back into their chairs, protesting. A few leaned forward, imploring. All were arguing some version of, "You can't expect us not to share this with—"

Obert closed his eyes and tuned them all out.

A perfectionist by nature who devoted his hobby hours to weaving, Obert did poorly in situations he could not plan in minute detail. He preferred problems he could fix by pulling threads and reweaving, or repeating measurements and re-running calculations. Now, his future, his family's future, his mission's future had abruptly and irrevocably spun out of his control. He was simultane- ously adrift and filled with a pure, unfocused fury.

Saira Keo's soprano tones cut through his focus. His rage ballooned.

Saira's son Rupert was the boy Obert should have had. A mathematics genius who understood physics concepts well beyond his years. Egotistical, as he should be. Obert reserved special contempt for the part of the Accord that insisted everyone was valued equally no matter their intellect. Nonsense! Anyone who could not do the necessary math, the science needed for research, was simply not as important as he was. Brilliance should be lauded!

Saira frequently tore her boy down in the name of humility, out of a superstitious fear of sociopathy, all supported by the community Accord. *Ridiculous.* She took ancient ship history and applied it to her son. Rupert was too smart to attempt a ship mutiny.

Obert had been quietly bolstering Rupert's ego for years. Well, he wouldn't hide that effort any longer. He straightened. Requiring genius to be humble resulted in mediocre pablum. He'd simmered for years, unable to convince anyone else of this, not even his wife.

Harriet. His fiery, beautiful wife would never forgive him for keeping this news from her. But he would not argue with the demand for a shut-it. Harriet kept silent only if the secret mattered to her, and his daughters had precisely the kind of personalities his team could not trust.

He doted on his talented eldest, Adamantine, but he was aware of her manipulative drive to ferret out people's secrets. She would share this news to evoke reactions without understanding the consequences. He smiled. Adamantine's quirks entertained him even as he acknowledged he could not allow it in this case.

So the mission was doomed. It shouldn't be a shock. *New Hope* was failing; he'd overheard a mech privately admitting they were nearing the end of their replacement parts after the last debris cloud they'd plowed through. They'd even had to repurpose the metal from some inner walls. Not much was left to use. It had been questionable that the mission would succeed as it was. Now? They would have needed to find a new location two generations ago to make a safe direction shift.

Vaguely, he heard the familiar melody of a grieving song; his colleagues working their way towards catching up with his acceptance of reality. *Very apt.* His life, the entire mission was a wasted effort. Just as he and his wife had wasted their second opportunity to breed. The second daughter he still thought of as their lab mix-up, the fragile disappointment who should have been his son. Hearing this news, his timid youngest would just fall apart, crack like the fragile gem his father-in-law had named her for.

It would be a relief to not have to coddle her any longer.

"Obert? Pangea!"

He opened his eyes. Everyone else had a hand in the air, and several stared at him with a compassion he found distasteful.

"If you are ready," Tate said. "We're swearing the shut-it."

Obert raised his hand.

Tate referred to his pad; he'd drafted the oath in advance. "We each swear or affirm that we shall keep all information about New Terra's suitability for life among ourselves and ourselves only until we find a new home planet. We will die before betraying this oath."

Until our purposeless deaths, then. Obert droned with the rest of the team, "I so swear."

ABOARD NEW HOPE: QUIET SECTOR
NEW HOPIAN YEAR 713
SECOND MONTH'S FIRSTDAY

THE OUTER DOOR OPENED. Adamantine must have forgotten something.

Opal called out, "I fixed it, sœur, it's working!"

"Fixed? Just what have you broken now?"

Opal froze. It couldn't be Père. Père wasn't due home for hours.

But it was. He must have come home early to weave. Maybe she could clean everything away before he saw it. She quickly stoppered the ink vial, wiped the pen clean, and shoved both next to Gengi in her pocket.

He didn't linger in the weaving room, though. He stomped up to the table. His hand slashed down and ripped her litany off the table.

"Non!" she cried out, taking in the torn edges still adhered to her work surface, then up at the litany, already crumpled in his hand. "You tore it! You ruined it before you even looked at it!"

Père had always been severe, harsher than any of the other parents on board. It was because he had higher standards, Mère would say, with a slight smile on her lips, an unfocused look in her eyes. She usually interceded when he got too loud or too angry with his daughters.

But Mère was not home. And Père was angrier than Opal had ever seen him, his forehead one solid mass of muscle, his normally dusky skin glossy, as if he had run back from his meeting. He'd been angry coming in the door.

"This monstrosity is what you've spent all those hours on? What a waste." He ripped the paper in half, watching her as he did it, a smile growing on his face. That malicious smile was familiar. He looked just like Terri's brother, who faked anxiety so he could be privy to everything they said at support group, who delighted in making them both miserable. Who hated Terri, who hated—

Père hates me.

Opal had spent every day of her life trying to please her father, and he still hated her. Her brain-bees screamed, and something else, something deeper, howled in pain, in anger. She'd been proud of that litany. The inside of her chest hurt, like a rib had broken. "You're not being fair!" It came out a scream, the way Mère would reply to him during one of their fights.

"Fair? Fair would be me having the son I deserve instead of," he looked her up and down with contempt, "you."

The howling paused, startled. Her thoughts froze for a moment, silent. Opal stared at him. Her brilliant, demanding, perfectionist Père—all this misery he'd inflicted on her was because he'd wanted a *child with different parts?*

The weight of years of trying to appease him, of constantly failing to be what he wanted, dropped from her shoulders as if flung. It was too ridiculous, and so sideways of her fears about him and herself that her astonishment spilled out.

She laughed, a short bark. "That's so *stupid!*"

His entire body locked up.

One did not laugh at Père. Or insult him.

"How dare you," he hissed as his muscles thawed, became liquid malice. "What did you even attempt to say to me?"

Scary as he was, Opal hated him back. He'd made her miserable for a dumb reason. And she wanted her litany back, even if it was in pieces. She slid off the chair, landing awkwardly, and straightened. She faced him, gut churning. "Give me my project and I'll tell you."

Terri had successfully pulled this trick on her brother last week.

But Père was smarter. She'd just told him the calligraphy mattered to her. He stared at her, tearing and wadding up the pieces. His smile was gone. "We will recycle this."

"That paper will ruin the recycling. Which will ruin your weaving fiber." Opal's mind was clearheaded and cold, her bees silent. *Maybe this is why Père spends so much time angry. It clears his mind.*

"Like that matters now."

"Now that you've suddenly realized I'm a girl?" she said acidly. In the back of her mind, she was stunned by her own audacity. "The recycling *always* matters. My mentors told me the ink should never be recycled. And they will want to see what I've done."

He looked startled, then his face tightened again, voice hardened with contempt. "You misheard them, and your output will never matter to anyone."

It fueled her indignation. She shrugged as if she didn't care and shuffled closer.

Père flung the wads into the recycler's hopper. He turned, took two steps to its edge, and leaned over to hit the button on the side.

She snatched the wads back out and hurried around the table, heading for her bedroom.

He snapped upright, face boiling with rage. "What are you doing! You will recycle that!"

Opal had told people—neighbors, mentors, a well-meaning counselor—that Père had never hit her.

"Yet," one neighbor had replied, adding, "Never hide violence. Ever."

As Père moved toward her, she knew *yet* had arrived. She was alone with a man who hated her, who seemed to want her dead or at least gone. Her bedroom wasn't safe enough.

Her brain-bees screamed. *Run!* Opal bolted, dodging looms and baskets of fiber. As she neared the outer door, she yelled, "Open! Fast open!" She squeezed between the spreading halves into the quiet hall beyond.

"OVERRIDE! CLOSE!" he yelled. The sharp snap of the closure silenced his swearing.

Opal would have laughed again—doors on *New Hope* wouldn't open for five minutes after an emergency override closure—but she saved her breath. She needed to get to her mentors and then find a place to hide. It would be hours before it was safe to go home.

If it ever was again.

THREE
DECISIONS

**ORBITING PLANET SEM
SEMU YEAR 1140
(NEW HOPIAN YEAR 713)**

It was the phren Voice's first meeting of the minds, and excitement kept raising waves that rippled through his roan fur. The passengers and staff of the blinkship *Hematite's Hoard* had been remanded to their sleeping or eating quarters, so he sat alone on the floor of the control room with the only active exterior port open.

Gazing upon the sight of Planet Sem was an honor that thrilled him. The fact that the meeting had been called primarily due to a threat to all of semqu did little to chill that excitement. He kept himself quiet and tried to still his thoughts so they didn't interrupt anyone or bother Hematite, his semqu companion, who was intently following the telepathic debate.

Periodically, his excitement would spike and threaten to spill through Hematite into the flow of discussion. His patient semqu would calm his mind. Hematite seemed only mildly irritated by his lack of attention to two items under simultaneous discussion: Trye9's routine request to move, and the more serious topic.

The phren was young and needed to move constantly. Hematite had often encouraged him to take indoor runs and do gymnastics or dance, but today that was not possible. As the morning conversation tipped into the midday and finally sunset on Sem, the youth's attentive posture went from sagging to writhing on the hard floor, trying to find a comfortable position. He cast longing glances toward the captain's chair. His fur generated static that could damage the modeel, however, so he stayed where he was.

Privately, he told Hematite, <I used to say the phren choir could sing a subject to death, but semqu take it to another level.>

<We must be thorough,> they answered, clearly distracted. <We have benefited from and yet also suffered much from decisions made in haste.>

Shortly afterward, the telepathic flow went silent. That was unusual. There must be a third, secret topic being discussed. Hematite's Voice was curious, but the semqu also deserve privacy. Besides, he was far more interested in learning about any new resident on Trye.

The silence was comparatively short. Most of the ensuing conversation was about who would coordinate with the Krufrugaan about the investigation into this new threat and its source—not a task this Voice was suited for, so his mind wandered again. He was startled when the aged aupoin Voice for Sem asked, "We are agreed?"

The young phren scrambled on all fours into a formal attentive position again, and started combing his fur, asking Hematite, <All topics, then?>

<Yes, we agree,> Hematite replied, focused and calm.

The telepathic semqu had no need of such a vocal roll call, of course, but Voices couldn't communicate with each other telepathically over much distance. It had become tradition to do a vocal litany of agreement ordered by age of semqu contact; Sem's Voice first, then the Voice of the oldest-contact planet, and down to the youngest blinkship's Voice. It had a soothing feel of elder-respect, order, and rightness that Hematite found deeply satisfying.

The phren tried to appreciate it in the same way, but he was still self-conscious.

"We are agreed," said the modeel Voice for Vasom39, his hard-case swathed in a violet contented aura. Amusingly, he was the youngest Voice present, so the eldest contact's proclamation came in adolescent tones.

Hematite's Voice rolled his eyes; of course they'd agree. Vasom39 had brought up the fraught subject, the knowledge of this dangerous substance. Though, he conceded, how that knowledge was to be dealt with had been an open question.

"Boredom, gratitude to be complete here. We are agreed," said the always blunt larsivian Voice for Ylas20.

"We are agreed," a grouchy older peqe said, for Taequa6.

Hematite relaxed a bit. This peqe had argued the most, and mostly for their own people, rather than for their semqu, which had deeply irritated the others.

The roll went on through the planets and then the blinkships. When it was the phren's turn to speak aloud for Hematite, he said proudly, "We are agreed." The instant he'd given his answer, and before the next ship's Voice spoke, he asked Hematite, <Does Trye9's request mean a baby semqu?>

Gentle amusement buffeted him. <Yes, Voice, it means a baby semqu on Trye, though not until Tyre9 finds a suitable home. Once they are braided, we can visit and say hello if you like.>

<I would!> Infant semqu were fun.

<It could be a long time in your reckoning. We should arrange to visit your own people on Iyam more often. I think you miss phren babies more than you admit,> Hematite said.

Memories of tumble-and-chase made them both warm for a moment. <I would not say no to visiting my nieces and nephews more often. But it is always a mixed blessing.> They always wanted him to stay, which he could not do. And he'd never have his own pyle, his own lovers, his own children. It was a soft ache, even now.

<I am sorry you have regrets.>

<No one gets all they want in life,> the phren said. <I enjoy your company, and I am more happy than many on Iyam. I am content.> Contentment met contentment. Then a wave of excitement buffeted him from his companion.

<You should say nothing about this,> Hematite said. <But we may have many new babies in Se Collective soon.>

<What? How?>

<We've encountered something new!>

Excitement, curiosity, and acquisitiveness poured from Hematite on their mental connection. Voice's fur stood on end. Among phren, acquisitiveness was considered a deeply dangerous emotion, sometimes more dangerous even than resentment.

<I have worried you, and I have not meant to.> Hematite almost seemed wounded. <I will tell you more when I can.>

Fur smoothed, emotions calmed. <I trust the judgment of semqu,> the phren said. <And I trust yours. Whatever it is, I am sure it will be good for Se Collective, for us all.>

ABOARD NEW HOPE
NEW HOPIAN YEAR 713
SECOND MONTH'S FIRSTDAY

OPAL RACED down the main corridor, clutching the balls of paper to her chest. It was the mid-morning break; she had to dart between neighbors talking about shift change and sharing gossip and hobby tips. She ran past the first neighborhood gathering room and its sounds of Ukrainian conversation practice, and the second room's Swahili. Some young dancers were showing each other steps in the hallway in line at the first corkscrew tube. Her sister was not among them.

Homophones. What would she tell Adamantine? *Think about that later.* The wait would be too long here. Père could catch up to her. She'd have to take the second tube. She veered around them and jostled the end of a chain of four people braiding each other's hair.

"Sorry!" she called back.

"Shh!" was the only response she got. She wasn't sure if it was aimed at her or a group arguing farther down the hall. One of them yelled, "I'm telling you, blaseball was a bigger thing than fantasy football!"

The second tube's entrance was unoccupied. Opal jumped through the opening and found her footing on the moving staircase inside; it slowly spiraled her upward with the scent of sweat and blooms. The pollinator crew must have taken the lift before her. She clung to her paper wads tightly so the rising air wouldn't pull any free, the need to hurry fighting the reality that she couldn't go faster than the tube. She lurched out three floors up, bumping against the frame, which slowed the coil. The alarm bleated and then cut off.

"Désolée!" she called again. She turned right, dashing through a wide hallway lined with tables and people playing board games. Her brain insisted on identifying each language, right or not: Yoruba. Tagalog. Hindi. Mandarin.

A drum circle sprawled across the entrance to the Quartier Vivant. Chest heaving, she slowed to weave through without banging into people or their instruments.

"Be easy, sister," one of the drummers said, his ink-dark skin gleaming with sweat. "The hull is secure."

Several musicians joined her in the traditional response, "and nothing else is worth worrying about." Her brain-bees hummed. No one needed to know she was running from Père, that would look bad. She bowed as well as she could to the thoughtful drummer and hurried on, trying to take slower, deeper breaths.

Nearly all of the twenty doors she passed were open, the people inside calling hello, which required her to call back politely, twenty different variations: salut, hallo, skol… it felt endless and took air she didn't have. When she reached the intricately decorated door of her mentors' apartment, she allowed herself to look back down the hallway. Lots of people, but no Père. Maybe the door hadn't released him yet.

No one living in the Quartier Vivant with any desire for privacy had working verbal commands on the entrance to their homes. She stared at their door, lost about how to attract their attention. Her fingers were full and cramped from clutching all the pieces. Finally, she leaned forward and rapped the surface with her forehead. It hurt.

No sound from inside. What would she do if they weren't home?

Her brain went sideways, snapping the way it did sometimes, brain-bees exploding into a spiky cloud, ominous enough to override her fear of Père. Footsteps approached, finally, but it was too late; she was shaking, her teeth chattering, by the time the door irised open.

"I'm so sorry, désolée, I'm so sorry," Opal babbled to Léa Delvaux, the elderly calligrapher who answered the door. Opal tried to bow without dropping anything.

Léa said something, but Opal couldn't hear it, couldn't understand, couldn't stop saying she was sorry. Eventually, the woman reached out and tugged Opal inside, placed a firm, wrinkled finger on her lips. Opal managed to close them.

Père was not there. Yet as the door shut behind her, the walls of the densely packed room seemed to squeeze in on Opal. Her ears filled with music of a type she didn't recognize, something full of many different instruments, loud. Artworks competed for wall space; embroidery, paintings, punch-work, a priceless ancient photo, and many calligraphic images all crammed next to shelves full of books and scrolls and a surprising number of plants. Every horizontal surface, including the floor and two visiting chairs, had piles of more of the same, with the addition of a few cups and plates close to the slanted calligraphy desks that were the primary furniture in the room.

When Opal had visited before, the apartment had seemed so welcoming, so different than the still air and minimalist decor of her parents' home. Today it was too much. Too much color, too much sound. She didn't know how to explain, so she just whimpered and held out her hands.

"What is it, Opal?" Léa asked.

Her partner looked up from her desk and frowned. The elder of the calligraphers, Tem Chie Charna exuded a sense of peace that Opal had always longed for; one of the reasons she'd asked these two, rather than any others, to mentor her. There was nothing of Père's temper or Mère's fire in either of them. Grey-haired with a broad sepia face, Chie looked at her now with a watchfulness that Opal found unbearable.

Opal pushed her burden toward them. "Please." Her squeaked plea sounded pathetic.

Their expressions softened to worry.

Chie moved toward her, both urgent and gentle. The two women had to gently pry her crabbed fingers straight. Bits of the calligraphy paper fell to the floor. She bent to help the pair pick them up, fingers still like claws.

"She needs tea," Chie said softly.

Léa left them, turning the music down as she went. A bit of the pressure squeezing against Opal eased.

Chie took a piece of hardboard and covered what she was working on, carried Opal's wads to her desk. Opal handed her pieces and watched Chie flatten them and puzzle the page back together. As the woman worked, the spiky storm in Opal's head slowly receded.

Chie traced Opal's calligraphy with a forefinger before speaking. "This is fine work. Why is it in pieces?" she asked gravely.

Opal sagged, relieved by the lack of censure in her tone. She blurted, loud, "Père tore—" the calligrapher winced. Opal stopped. She sounded hysterical. She tried to start over twice more, dropping her volume each time. "Père tore it up. He said I ruined it." Opal pointed to the blotch.

"Haiyo. He ruined it, not you. You did well. The spirals are a lovely idea. Arms of a creature, or a galaxy. Beautiful. Calligraphy has a long tradition of making mistakes into art."

"But it's ruined now." The spikiness grew, and she forced words out. She had to talk, she had to explain while she could. "It took me forever! And I liked it!" Suddenly she was crying, and that made everything worse. "When he tore it up, he threw the pieces in the recycler!"

"Burnt rice and bitter tea." Chie slapped her hand flat on the paper. "Did any—"

"I got it all. He—he didn't believe me! I ran—" Her throat closed; he would make her pay for that. She swallowed, trying to contain her outrage, her tears. Being angry at Père was suddenly terrifying. "He said it didn't matter."

"He had no right to do that," Chie said firmly. "To not take your word is a breach."

Léa, coming up behind her, said, "He abused your creativity, Opal."

A wave of conflicting emotions crashed into her. Opal dissolved, sobbing. She covered her face in her hands and fought to pull herself back from the edge. Père hated her, but she could not shame him. Mère would not stand for that. Mère was all she had left.

She'd said too much already, and Père would be coming here.

Or would he? No. Père would not bother. She had never seen him display his anger outside the apartment walls. Any time she had messed up in public, he'd waited until they got home to yell at her. She wiped her face, apologized.

"Tears are healthy, Opal," Léa said, handing her a square of cloth. "Crying releases tension."

Opal took the cloth, wiped her face, and handed it back with thanks.

"You may come here for your hobby hours," Chie said. "That way no more damage will happen to your work."

"Oh! Thank you." A tiny window of hope opened in her heart. She slammed it shut immediately. She and Père had fought over her calligraphy. He would not honor the mentorship bargain. Miserably, she added, "But I do not think that will work."

Chie's lips compressed and she leaned back, looked at her wife.

"Where was your mother?" Léa asked.

"At the grasshopper ranch." Harriet was an agricultural tech; her hours were as long or longer than Père's, sometimes as long as six hours a day.

"Would she have stopped this?" Léa gestured to the destroyed litany.

"Probably." Opal shrugged. She was so tired. "He would not have—" she stopped herself. She felt them waiting for her to finish the sentence, but she was worried now, wary, teeth resting on her tongue, staring at the floor. A thought raced through her mind— Père's obsession with gender was like the mind police's contagion. If he was deemed ill, he could be removed from the family. Mère would not forgive her for that.

"Does she also scream at you?" Léa asked.

"No." Opal risked a peek up at Léa.

Léa's eyes had narrowed, her lips tight, her expression full of suspicion and anger that softened to concern when she caught Opal's glance.

Opal's brain static went sharp and noisy again. She did not want them to focus on her parents. "Père has never gotten that angry before. It is not his fault. I am a problem." The words sounded clunky. It was getting harder to catch air. She wasn't running anymore. It should be easier.

The two adults exchanged glances. "We will speak to your parents' mentors."

"Oh! Oh, no. Please no." That had happened once before, when Opal had unthinkingly complained about some harshness of Père's to another adult. Her chest muscles tightened; her fingers tingled. A panic, she finally admitted. She should go, she didn't want to burden them, not after all this. They'd been so kind. But she couldn't have a panic in the hallway, either. Especially not with Père out there somewhere, still angry at her. She sucked air against clenching ribs. "That won't be necessary," she said, aiming to sound formal, calm, adult. She sounded squeaky and scared even to herself.

"Opal. Listen to the words of the Accord," Chie said. "'We swear and affirm to value each other and the health and thriving of each member and the whole of the community. We honor the privacy and autonomy of each individual as long as they do not endanger themselves or others.'" She emphasized the last phrase.

They were words Opal had heard many times before. "But also," she said desperately, "'We require consent before crossing boundaries.'"

"Yes. Which your father did not do. He is harming your ability to thrive," Chie said. "We do not do this for you, we do this for him, and for the community. It is our responsibility."

"Please, no! It won't help." She turned toward the door. Her throat was starting to tighten.

"Do you fear he will harm you if we speak to his mentors?"

"No." Her reply was automatic, even as Opal's mind flashed to Père's contorted face, his fury. But he'd been angry with her before. He would calm. "He has never hit me," she said. "I should go. I should not have bothered you. I should not have brought my woes to you." There were gasped spaces between each sentence.

"You did not bother anyone," Chie said. "I appreciate your trust, Opal. I am glad you came. It was the right choice."

"I made tea. Will you sit and drink with us?" Léa asked.

Was her vision going dark? It was hard to stay standing. She couldn't pass out in the hallway. She slumped to the floor. "Yes."

"You were out of breath when you arrived," Léa said.

"I ran the whole way." She'd forgotten to bring a gift for them, for inviting her into their home—did that apply in an emergency like this? Was it still an emergency? Was it ever? Had she just over-reacted? The spikes in her head were greyer, and louder, and more menacing. Dimly, she heard Léa ask a question.

"With your little friend in your pocket?"

Friend? "Oh! Gengi." Opal pulled the stuffed tardigrade toy out of her tunic pocket. The ink vial and pen came out with him, and she carefully set them aside on the floor before she pulled Gengi to her lap and mashed his segmented body in her fingers.

"He's so colorful. Is he soft?" Léa asked.

"Yes." Her sister had made him from recycled scraps of her parents' weaving projects.

"Even his eyes?"

"No, they're hard." Buttons for eyes. "Black like my sister's." Beautiful, talented, smart Adamantine, who was everything she was not. Opal's eyes were a green that Mère insisted was lovely. Opal thought they looked weird. Most people she knew had brown eyes. Adamantine's were so dark you could barely see her pupils.

"Does he make a sound?"

"Just... rustling, maybe?"

Léa handed her a small cup, warm, not hot. Tea. A barter luxury, to have tea at home, not in the cafeteria. They honored her with such a gift.

Opal bowed her thanks for their generosity and sipped.

"Is it sweet or bitter?" Chie asked.

"A little bitter. Very good."

She knew what the calligraphers were doing; leading her

through the sensory details that could help keep her grounded, hold the panic at bay: touch, hearing, sight, smell. The litany from her support group, the litany she'd rendered in ink. The one Père had destroyed.

Panics were a sign of weakness, Père said, a symptom of a useless burden, a waste of food and oxygen, a *human*. A spacer should be better evolved.

Adamantine and Terri said she wasn't a burden, and these skilled women, her mentors, didn't act like she was one. The support group had helped her; when the adult leader was there, she was better able to function. They all had panics too. Well, all but Tiani.

Père was important; the work he did mattered. She was still proud to be his daughter, even if he wasn't proud of her. Surely, he was right about the panic attacks? She just had to be stronger, rely more on herself. Maybe she could try being a boy for him. She almost laughed. What difference was there between boys and girls except body parts? If she wove or felted herself a penis, would that make Père like her? *No.* This was something she couldn't fix.

She dried her tears and sipped. Chie resumed her calligraphy. The music played softly. The space still seemed overwhelming, but more interesting and less threatening. The storm in her mind subsided and coalesced into the normal cloud of bees.

The door opened and closed. She jerked and looked up.

"Just Léa," Chie said. "On an errand, and to the cafeteria."

"Not to his mentors? Please?"

"We often eat at home; she is picking up our meal."

Chie hadn't answered her question. They were principled women who valued the Accord in ways Père did not. They would go to his mentors. She needed to accept that and deal with it. How much worse could it get? A lot, probably. Spikes flashed; she couldn't imagine what would happen. Whatever it was, it was her fault, again, she was the one who'd started this—*no.*

No. She believed Chie and Léa about that part.

Père was wrong. It was hard to wrap her brain around, to wedge into her view of her perfect father, but his furious confession helped. She managed it. He could be brilliant at work but stupid about her gender, and sure of himself about both.

How was she going to cope? Her personal vibrated; probably her friend Terri. She ignored it; she couldn't help anyone else right now. A plan began to form. Slowly, the spiky fuzz retreated. Her breathing began to return to normal. "I should go."

Chie cocked her head to one side, watchful. "Where will you go, Opal? I have been told your parents discourage you from visiting your neighbors. Is your father not still at home, still angry?"

"Adamantine is at dance. I'll go watch her." She pushed confidence into her words; she wanted Chie to believe she was no longer afraid. And she did need her sister's advice right now.

"Ah. That is a good plan. You can return here if you wish, Opal. Remember that?"

She promised to remember. But they were hurting her, too, as they tried to help, even if they did not understand. Opal formally thanked Chie for her mentorship as she left, asked her to thank Léa for her. She left behind her ink and pen. She did not expect to touch them again.

ABOARD NEW HOPE
RECREATION SECTOR, QUARTIER VIVANT
NEW HOPIAN YEAR 713
SECOND MONTH'S FIRSTDAY

ADAMANTINE DIDN'T WANT her at dance practice, and she was surrounded by possessive friends. It felt like forever before Opal could get close enough to whisper, "It's Père, and it's bad."

Adamantine pulled her into a corner, waving everyone else away. Opal explained as best she could.

"He tore it up?" Adamantine was horrified and broken-hearted. "Are you sure he was really going to hit you?"

Opal nodded, feeling like she was destroying her sister's life. "I didn't tell them that part. But they said they were going to talk to our parents' mentors. About Père."

Adamantine swore, then paced for a moment, biting her nails. Then she grabbed Opal's hand. "We need to hide you while he calms down. I know just the place."

To her surprise, her sister headed back to the Quiet Quarter. Adamantine had Opal hide in a neighbor's doorway as she went into their apartment, then waved Opal inside, hustled her into their bedroom, and started flinging clothes around.

"You ran out. He saw you leave. They'll never look for you here," Adamantine explained. "Especially not in my dirty clothes. And you'll be able to overhear anything they say." She gestured to the clothing nest she'd made on the closet floor.

"I—"

"It will work, petite-sœur. Get in."

Opal obeyed. Adamantine tucked Gengi next to her cheek and carefully covered her with a few shirts.

"Perfect; you look just like a pile of my clothes. Now. I'm going to go back out and find out what's going on if I can. I'll leave the door partly open. Stay here and stay quiet. Even if Mère comes home first. Promise?"

"Promise."

It was quiet and dark and comfortable in the closet. Her sister's scent lulled Opal into a sense of safety, made her realize how exhausted she was. Not long after Adamantine left, Opal drifted, half-asleep. She snapped alert when Mère came home, had to dig her fingernails into her palms when Mère called out, "Anyone home?" and came to the door of the bedroom. "Opal?" Mère sounded stressed.

Opal felt guilty for not answering, but she kept her promise to her sister.

Mère walked away. There was a scrape, chair legs on the floor. "Ah, Obert, my love, my everything. What have you done?" Mère swore, sharp and loud. Was she crying? It sounded like she was crying. "Why must you always blame her? She's a child! It's not her fault!"

Not my fault. Not my fault. Opal curled her body around Gengi and wrapped her mother's words tight around her heart.

Mère quieted. Later, Opal heard the outer door, then Père shouting, "Do you know what that useless brat has done? Those mentors of hers claim I've violated that idiotic fucking Accord!"

A person unable to live in accord with the Principles of Community could be asked to choose between vacuum-death or hibernation. This was not Père's first warning, and everyone knew were no more hibernation pods available.

Opal's breakfast slammed into her throat. She fought the urge, counted breaths. She couldn't throw up on Adamantine's clothes.

"They needed to get your attention," Mère yelled back. "What were you thinking, shredding her art like that?" Another door closed, muffling their conversation. They must have gone into their sleeping chamber. The ensuing argument was unnerving because she could only make out a few shouted words.

"Useless," from Père.

"Idiot," from Mère.

Opal couldn't take it. She pushed the clothes aside, tiptoed to the outer door and slipped out again. She ran to the tube and up two levels to her friend Terri's apartment. Standing at the door, hand raised to knock, she could hear raised voices inside.

Was everyone having a horrible day?

Interrupting a family dispute was rude. But where else could she go? She was too upset to eat, to go to the cafeteria. Her parents had made it abundantly clear that she was to only talk to her professional mentors about the subjects she was to learn. She couldn't go back to the calligraphers. Anyone else she could talk to would want her to leave her family. Terri understood.

There was a lull in the shouting. Opal took a chance and knocked.

Tiani, Terri's slim brother, answered. He glared down at Opal, and her stomach clenched. She tried to remember how she'd felt, facing down Père.

"Called one of your so-called friends, did you?" Tiani turned to Terri. "You'll still have to do your algebra later."

Terri huddled at the table, her curly brown hair haloed around her head, pale against her darker forearms.

"You have to get better at math," he said. "'We acknowledge that our sciences keep us alive. We will ensure our sciences are kept alive, added to, and *understood*,'" he quoted with a smirk.

Opal pulled on what courage she had left. "Are you sure you understand our sciences well enough to teach?"

"Opal!" Terri jumped up.

Out of habit, Opal tocked quietly so Terri could find her easily. Her weak vision seemed to worsen with stress. "Mentoring to someone's best possible contribution does require the mentor to know their subject and want their student to learn," she said.

"Ooo, listen to the shaker!" Tiani stalked toward his sleeping chamber.

Terri's thin arms wrapped Opal in a humid hug that smelled of star anise. Opal inhaled deeply. When they cooked, Harriet and Père only used herbs, never spices. Opal followed Terri into her bedroom.

Her friend closed the door, sinking against it. The skin under her eyes was three shades darker than her cheeks. "Thank you for coming, finally."

Guilt stabbed Opal. During the past week, Terri had messaged Opal every day to come visit. But Terri often forgot that other people had problems, too, and sometimes helping Terri triggered

Opal's own panic attacks. She didn't want to tell Terri that. "I didn't want to burden you with what's going on with Père," she said. "But after this morning—I have to talk to somebody."

"Let me tell you what's going on with Tiani first. I'm about to kill myself."

Her heart sank. Terri talked about suicide about twice a year. Opal's worries shrank as Terri shared hers. Tiani was smarter than either of his parents, and he'd outwitted them repeatedly, turning them against four mentors who might have done him some good, and taking out every setback on his sister. This week he'd been particularly awful because he'd talked their parents into letting him mentor Terri in all her subjects "as a test."

At least Opal had Adamantine in her corner.

Two hours later, Opal hadn't even mentioned Père, and she was deeply worried that Terri might try to end her life.

Terri's mother came home and insisted Opal go with them to the cafeteria for the evening meal, chattering endlessly the entire walk. Opal tried to get a word in about Terri's misery several times but was shut out each time. Her mother insisted Terri only take half a portion, until one of the cooks noticed and refused to short her, and then Tiani sat between Terri and her parents.

It was a miserable meal. Tiani monopolized the conversation, telling his mother how horribly Terri was doing with her previous mentor and how much progress he'd made with her today. Terri's mother hung on every word, praising him for his devotion to his sister.

"Liar," Opal muttered.

Terri's mother compressed her lips. "We have family time planned this evening, Opal. You'll need to go home now."

It blindsided her, and she flashed with an unsettling fury that immediately shifted into that cold clarity she'd had earlier in the day. *If I'm going to die at Père's hand tonight, I should do what I can for Terri now.*

Opal leaned forward. "You know that everything he just said is a lie, right? Do you hate your daughter so much you want her to kill herself? Is that why you constantly leave her alone with him? He abuses her all the time!" She was not quiet. She saw a man's back stiffen at the next table. Tiani spluttered.

Terri gasped and squeezed her hand.

Opal hugged her. "I want you to live." She looked at Tiani, who glared at her, furious. "We'll all know it was Tiani's fault if you don't." She stomped off, his protests squawking behind her as she left. His mother was defending Tiani when Opal stopped in the doorway. "Your parents should never leave you two alone, ever," she shouted. The whole cafeteria heard her.

Opal lost the bulk of her dinner in a communal bathroom on the way back to the apartment. One of the adults from the cafeteria caught up to her and helped her clean up. She demanded details, which Opal gave. At least someone would help her friend.

"It sounds like we have failed both you and Terri," the woman said.

Opal locked up. The weight of what she'd done crashed in on her.

This was what the calligraphers had tried to do for her. Would it make Terri's life worse? Would Terri hate her now? Terri was her only real friend. Neighbors and community members had gotten so kind about not triggering her social anxiety that they ignored her for the most part, unless they were trying to protect her from Père, which never ended well. Opal could feel lonely and alone no matter how many people surrounded her.

"If your father does anything in retribution, you must tell an adult. Any adult. The entire ship is supporting your family. Normally we would move the parent from the home, but in this case, our next step is either to move an observer into your home or move you to a more supportive family. You have that choice."

What? Opal finally recognized the woman as the ship's new

therapist. She couldn't remember her name. "We don't need that. I don't want to leave my family. Mère, Adamantine…"

"We will give you that choice. But you need to come talk to me weekly, okay?"

"Okay."

They talked for a bit longer, arranging a time, and then Opal walked home in a bit of a daze. She stood outside her own door for a long time.

"Do you need a song, or a meal, Opal?" It was a neighbor couple, a kind pair whose intelligence Père often insulted, at home.

Opal gestured no, not trusting herself to speak.

"Your Père is a cruel, mean, stupid man," the man said, softly.

She was shocked. Her eyes watered. "I—He—"

The woman patted her shoulder. "You are loyal. He does not deserve you. You never have to put up with abuse." Anger radiated from her, so different from her normal demeanor that it stunned Opal. Her voice softened as she added, "We respect your wish to stay with your parents. But we would happily welcome you as a daughter."

"I... you are kind, but—" Opal gestured no, unable to say the word out loud, not wanting to hurt them for their kindness.

"Just think about it," the man said. "Our door is always open to you." They glanced back at her as they went into their dwell. His eyes looked wet.

Her community valued her. She'd always known that, but it was good to be reminded. Opal took a deep breath, steadying herself in the quiet of the hallway. Then she asked her door to open.

It parted. Père and Mère sat inside, weaving. His lips tightened as she forced her feet forward, but he didn't look up.

Mère didn't ask where she'd been, didn't smile when she looked up from her work. "You don't need to help us tonight, daughter," she said. "You can stay in your room."

Opal hustled to her bed and wept in relief. She had feared that

Mère would choose Père, tell her to find another family. But she hadn't. Not yet.

Père was stupid about the boy thing, and she hated him for destroying her litany. But he was still her father. She still had a family. She had a supportive sister. Her entire community supported her; she had places she could go.

Life could be worse.

**ABOARD NEW HOPE
PLANTING AND GROWING SEASONS OF NEW
HOPIAN YEAR 713**

PÈRE DIDN'T SPEAK to her the next day, nor for the rest of the week. He didn't show up for dinner the night of her tenth anniversary fête, and Mère acted like she didn't expect him.

Weeks of compressed lips and evaded glances became months.

Neighbors and others took turns stopping Opal to chat. It startled her at first. Then she recognized a pattern in their conversations and guessed that the therapist or her father's aged mentors had requested the conversations. But the interactions helped her feel less invisible, more a part of a larger community. She did her service and mentorship hours with more confidence.

Given the sudden and near-constant support she met in the hallways, in her meetings with her vocational mentors and in the cafeteria, Père's silence could have been a blessing. Instead, Opal was constantly on edge. She had nightmares where Père would look at her and the floor collapsed under her feet. She'd fall, bouncing past every mistake in her life all the way through the hull to the icy vacuum outside.

She didn't know if it was better or worse that the silence extended only to her. Adamantine suddenly benefited from an unusual outpouring of generous warmth from Père in everything from affection to listening to gifts. He'd certainly learned that he didn't have to snarl at Opal to make the distinction in how he felt about his daughters perfectly clear.

Mère's lips would tighten at his profuse praise, and the way he would fall silent if his eyes happened to land on Opal, but she never addressed it. She would talk to both daughters, stressing their equality, but she never spoke to Opal about Père. Opal tried, once, and Mère cut her off. She didn't try again.

Opal went to the therapist weekly, and then monthly, for some time. She managed to keep her conversations with the therapist short and limited to her panic attacks. She could honestly say Père had said nothing mean to her when the therapist or others asked. She said no more, because she wanted to believe that Père was, in his own bizarre way, trying to change for her benefit.

Terri didn't see it that way. She and Adamantine were the only people Opal allowed herself to be completely honest with. Terri was living with a new family. She rarely messaged Opal anymore. She was as full of "everything is wonderful" as she'd once been with "everything is miserable," and there was little room for Opal in either conversation, except criticism of Père, who Terri hated. She never talked about Tiani or her original parents. It was as if Terri blamed Opal's father for her own broken family.

The more Terri attacked him, the more Opal found herself defending him.

She missed calligraphy but did not want to risk evoking that horrible day or making anything Père might judge. Instead she took up reading as her hobby. She spent hours buried in fiction, biographies of all sorts, even technical manuals about wastewater treatment and infrastructure on Earth, mining and drilling, which were fascinating and read like fiction. Oceans and continents were pure fantasy to her. She could not imagine the vast reserves of soil and rock the books' subjects implied.

One day the therapist leaned forward and said, "Opal, do you think there is anything else we need to talk about?" When Opal shook her head, she added, "You are free to come talk to me anytime. But I don't think you need to come see me on a set schedule anymore. You should be proud of the progress you've made."

Opal left, her smile fading as soon as she turned the corner. She had skills she didn't have before, but she didn't feel proud. She felt like she'd narrowly escaped something dangerous: getting her father killed.

ABOARD NEW HOPE
NEW HOPIAN YEAR 715
TENTH MONTH'S TWENTY-FIFTH DAY

On the day of Adamantine's fifteenth anniversary, the family dinner was tense for Opal and a celebration for the rest of the family. Their parents gifted her elder sister an elaborate red and black embroidered dress that must have cost them three massive rugs in trade.

That cheered Opal a bit. Things must be going better, she thought. Père even teared up during his toast at dinner. Opal succeeded in not making a single noise during the meal, other than clapping when Adamantine made her wish. Père didn't look at her once.

She gave Adamantine her gift in their room, afterward: a small needle-felted black cat, shaped as well as Opal could into a panther, Adamantine's chosen avatar.

Adamantine turned the gift over in her fingers, expressing her delight. But then she leaned over and said, "I ask a boon for another present, if you'll give it!"

"Anything you want, sœur," Opal naively answered.

Words that would haunt her.

"It hurts how different Père treats us. I want to get Père to love you again. So, for the next year, we're going to work on you!"

"Me?" Opal protested. "Why not work on Père?"

Adamantine stared at her for a moment, and she stared back. The absurdity of her question hit them both. The two sisters started to giggle, and then Opal snorted, and then they were both howling with laughter.

Mère came in, reprimanding them both for making too much noise, and they stifled their giggles under their blankets.

"Seriously, though," Adamantine said later, as Opal drifted off to sleep. "We're going to start tomorrow."

Two weeks later Opal thought, "Hell is a sister who loves you."

Adamantine's method of "fixing" her was to become worse than Père. She tried to direct Opal's every waking moment, treating her as a personal programmable robot with corrective orders parroted from Père.

At the table, "No, don't sit like that. Sit up straight."

About a personal preference, "Answer the question asked, not the question you think I'm asking."

Folding laundry. "Do that over, it's not perfect.'

Following her in dance lessons, "Try to keep up."

Always in Père's harsh tone. Her beloved supportive elder sister had vanished, replaced with a clone of her father, who detested her. Opal cried herself to sleep more often than not. Her sister's face wasn't dry, either, but nothing Opal could say would get her to stop.

One twelfth month day, Opal huddled in a gasping ball on their bedroom floor, muscles locked in a full-body panic attack.

Adamantine paced nearby. "I know you can do this!" her sister snapped. "Why do you keep falling apart?"

"Adamantine." Mère stepped into their bedroom. "Go help Père."

"I'm working with Opal," Adamantine said.

"You push your sister into a panic attack, and you call that help-ing?" Mère said. "We've talked about this. Obert is not a role model for how you treat Opal. If this happens again, I will move you into our bedroom and forbid you from spending any time with Opal at all. Go."

Adamantine whined and sniffed, but she left.

After that, she waited until Mère was at the insect ranch before "helping" Opal. And she stopped before she pushed Opal over the edge. But just before. Opal spent most of that year anxious, looking over her shoulder, constantly on the verge of a breakdown.

FOUR

INTRODUCTIONS

**ABOARD THE LIMONITE'S LEAP
SEMU YEAR 1141
(NHY 716, SEVENTH MONTH, LASTDAY'S EVE)**

Khosmek and his pals were taking a joyride with their parents' blinks, skipping from asteroid to asteroid, and getting a little mining in on the side. These rare trips were the only time he got to play at his dream job, being a miner-extractionist. His parents had other plans for his future. He was raptly watching his visual display, where the extractor arm was picking up chunks of iron ore, when the Voice who seemed to live in his mother's ship hurried into the spacious command center.

"We have an emergency," she said, her encircling biofield violet-serene as always. "We need you to contact an alien ship."

"Alien?" Khosmek was twenty-five in modeel years, barely an adolescent in the way modeel track emotional development, so he was fascinated with creatures from other planets. But one rule he'd had burned into his synapses as a squirt of spacefaring parents: he was never to initiate contact.

"First contact is a job for diplomats," he quoted his mother. "My father would smelt my case into slag. So, I—"

She interrupted him. "We must."

Shock flashed red in his biofield, reflecting off her hard case. Khosmek was not accustomed to being interrupted by staff. But she wasn't truly *his* staff, was she? *Voices can be dangerous and should be listened to and always treated with deference.* A lesson from parents and tutors he'd never had to apply.

"It's an emergency," she repeated. "The semqu will reward you."

That got his attention. "What kind of reward?"

"A rich vein. We need all three ships for a variety of reasons, chiefly that children as spokespeople will be seen as far less threatening."

"I'm hardly a child," Khosmek protested. "What's the emergency?"

"The exact nature I do not know," the Voice said. "Although it appears to be a survival issue."

He swore. System law required any blinkship to help others in survival distress. Khosmek recalled the extractor arm and locked it in place. "Do they even speak Fugrast? Modeel? How am I supposed to communicate with—"

"We've attempted communication for long enough that I can translate simple sentences. We just need you to distract them for a short period. Let's say we're trying to ensure they're telling the truth."

Not tell the truth to semqu? Were these aliens insane?

Khosmek sensed a flash of shock from behind him. He turned a recorder toward his staff's hard suits, a mixture of lower-end models with limited sensors and appendage options. All were lit by their encircling biofields in hues of red and white: a morass of shock, fear, and dismay. One betrayed tiny bubbles of laughter, quickly quenched.

These were his mother's employees, and most were afraid of

both these aliens and the Voice. He didn't dare allow them to know he was afraid. That would breed insubordination. The one who laughed—was he laughing at Khosmek's fear of his father?

He'd been speaking far too freely. As much as he would enjoy being a miner, he needed to remember himself. He would be a diplomat one day. He could not risk being undermined by an underling's distrust.

Khosmek imagined himself as successful; rewarded handsomely by the semqu and lauded by his peers and parents. He was delighted when his biofield followed his lead, and lit a rich brown. It buoyed his confidence. He forced it to add a curl of admiration for the Voice's audacious suggestion.

"If the semqu require assistance," he said, "I'm your model."

He hailed his two friends. With eighteen arms among them, and the Voice's quiet suggestions thrown in, they quickly hashed out a plan. They'd all take turns talking and appear to be competing with one other for the best trades with these new potential customers.

Glee and anticipation flushed through their fields and his own.

"Let's do this!" Khosmek said. He cut visual contact with them to catch his first glimpse of an alien ship. Wary of his crew's reaction, he suppressed his own nerves.

Behind him he sensed colors of surprised admiration that abruptly shifted to the pale salmon of travel-nausea. When Khosmek's recorders resumed sending visual detail, he clattered in surprise. On his screen, a massive, ugly morass of metal slid by. *Do these brackwater rubes just push themselves through space?*

Khosmek swore again, turned to his crew and issued his first situational order. "Figure out what communication technologies they use, fast. Then open up a method we can use to talk to these uglies." Inspiration struck him. "A bonus for visuals."

They did it, matched a frequency the hideous ship was broadcasting. He made a mental note; such efficacy should be rewarded. By his parents, of course.

He needed the reassurance that the aliens also wanted to talk. Watching the massive ship roll by was rattling his nerves. Did it never end? What kind of mentality could beings who constructed something so huge and ugly possibly have? How big were they?

Khosmek's screen spluttered and fuzzed as his staff connected. One of his friends clanked a message.

"Are you seeing that glow around their ship? Is that emotion or will they attack us?" she asked.

"They protect themselves," the Voice said. "That's an asteroid shield."

A field that protected from space debris? That could be useful. Khosmek considered the possibility of actual technological trade. His mother would love that. He made another note.

His visuals screen filled with the image of a room occupied by about a dozen bipeds, vertically oriented, flat-faced creatures. Their torsos were covered with what looked like soft, flowing static-generators, and only had two arms. Their bulbous heads, topped by a sort of fur of varying lengths, sat on a short stalk and contained forward-facing, unprotected eyes. They displayed no emotion, no colors at all. Were their biofields inactive—or did they lack them?

Khosmek shivered. They looked incredibly vulnerable. He'd never been so happy to be in a hard suit in his life.

"I am Khosmek, merchant squirt of trader Khosleb and industrialist Tirdjraz, of ...of Vasom," he said, making a sudden decision to shorten the traditional lengthy introduction in the hopes of finding out more about these strange beings. "We are delighted to make your acquaintance. Have you need of ore? Meats? Beverages? Of fruits and vegetables, perhaps? Or we have many finished metal items we can provide you—"

He paused, letting the Voice translate for him. The language she used was incomprehensibly weird, soft like their tiny mouths— which were in their heads, under their eyes! Did these beings watch each other eat? He fluttered inside his hard case. He quickly suppressed his revulsion, barely preventing it from reaching his aura.

His friends jumped in, offering the trade items they supposedly carried, and Khosmek interrupted them from time to time. It was fun, but he found himself growing irritated. He wasn't getting any information about who or what these aliens were, and he wanted to know.

"They ask where we came from. We have been here long enough; we have our answers," the Voice said.

Slag. This was just getting interesting. "The planet of Vasom, of course! But have you not encountered our kind before?"

"Their captain says not," the Voice translated.

"Nor ... the semqu?" Khosmek forced anxiety into his synapses until his field fluttered with yellow spikes.

When the Voice translated the aliens' negation, her field carried the complicated coloration of complete sincerity. Khosmek was impressed; he'd been unaware that Voices had any capacity for manipulation. He'd have to pay her more attention. But now the four of them had to play their agreed-upon part and leave.

"We have no right to trade with you, then. We express much dismay and disappointment," Khosmek said. He burned with a desire to learn more about these creatures. "What do you call yourselves?"

"We are spacers," the captain said.

Khosmek tried out the odd-sounding name. "Well, spacers, welcome. The semqu will contact you properly soon." A shock of nausea hit him. His visual screen returned to the asteroid he'd been mining. He felt disappointed. These aliens were bizarre, so ugly they were almost ... no, not cute. Fascinating. Ore was boring by comparison.

"When can we talk to them again?" he asked the Voice.

"I thought that was a diplomat's job?" She could have been mocking him, but she didn't seem to be, just curious.

"That was incredible!"

"I am glad you think so. What reward do you seek?"

He didn't hesitate. "I want to be known as the first modeel to ever speak to a spacer." Surprise pulsed around the room. He ignored it, adding, "I will enjoy life as a diplomat if it involves missions like that." He didn't have to fake his sincerity.

"This was a once-in-a-lifetime service event," she said.

He pulsed with pride; his parents would be ecstatic to learn that he had achieved a lifetime service so young.

"However, you may get your wish." The Voice continued, "It is possible Vasom will soon need diplomats who want to work with these spacers."

ABOARD NEW HOPE; AG SECTOR
NEW HOPIAN YEAR 716
EIGHTH MONTH, TWENTY-FIFTH DAY

OPAL LEANED on the mural outside the rice fields, fingers flying over her communicator, pretending to send a message. The thirteen-year-old was stalling, hoping someone would use their code to unlock the door so she could hide in the rice fields.

She was running from Adamantine again. They'd had a few great weeks early in the year, but with only two months left on her year's project, Adamantine was getting more and more determined to succeed, harder to please.

Opal had given up hoping their relationship could go back to when Adamantine was nice to her; all she wanted at this point was a less predator-prey relationship. She'd had to settle for the occasional block of sister-free hours.

After what had happened with Père, she was terrified to complain to anyone outside the family, so she couldn't explain when she begged or bribed their neighbors to not tell her sister where she was. Not that it did any good. A graceful, accomplished dancer, Adamantine was practically a celebrity; people sought her out to help them with dance steps and to teach her their family's dances. Adamantine was better at *people.*

People were confusing.

Neighbors would quietly tell Opal that they found themselves telling Adamantine things they hadn't intended to say. Adamantine adored secrets. She had learned young how to manipulate anyone, even Père, to tell her what she wanted to know. Few people liked that, but a surprising number of adults found themselves powerless against it.

"Her mentors will train her out of it eventually," they would reassure Opal.

Eventually didn't help her now.

Opal couldn't count the number of times Terri had apologized to her because Adamantine had once again dug a piece of information out of her that Terri had promised not to share, including Opal's hiding places.

In desperation, Opal had pushed herself out of her comfort zone; she began to explore the work and agricultural spaces. She'd been waiting in this corridor for half an hour, listening for her sister's footsteps. Her breathing was getting tight, anxiety ramping up. If someone didn't come soon, she'd have to visit Mère in the insect ranch again. Adamantine had found her there last month and Mère, engrossed in her work, had insisted her daughters leave together.

The fever of gossip about a possible alien contact event last month had distracted Adamantine for several blissful weeks. But yesterday had been a twelve-hour marathon of orders that had ended with Opal in another full-blown panic attack. Adamantine had panicked herself. Opal had promised not to tell Mère, but only after she'd gotten Gengi back.

Opal brushed her pocket to reassure herself the comfort toy was still there. Her sister had made Gengi for her. Why did she keep trying to take him away?

Footfalls bounced behind her, heavy and fast. Opal glanced back. A tall, solid man in a workman's tunic hurried toward her, talking heatedly on his communicator.

"Why yes, thank you for finally hearing me. That's why I'm worried." He halted at the door and punched in a code. His umber skin gleamed with sweat. Perhaps he had been exercising to work off his frustration. "No, I'm back at the field. I explained my findings in the report, at which you clearly have not looked."

He added a rapid sentence in Korean. All Opal caught was the word "read."

Even adults try to avoid work, she thought; who enjoys reading reports? The barn door parted, and he rushed through, catching his left hip on the moving edge. He swore in Yoruba.

Her communicator vibrated; probably Adamantine. Opal followed the man quietly, sniffing the humid air with pleasure. She pivoted right to avoid the field camera and hurried along the front wall.

Behind her, he said, "What do you want?" He was back to speaking English, this year's ship language, and raised his volume sharply. "Youth, please answer me."

She turned. He'd pocketed his communicator. His posture was stiff with annoyance.

She quickly bowed to him. "Oh! I'm sorry! I didn't realize you were talking to me." What could she say that would get him to ignore her and let her stay?

"English. No relationship signifiers." He seemed aggrieved at the language, not at her.

"So annoying," she agreed.

"I am the agriculturist for this field, and I must know who is in it, and when." He was intense again, glancing at the nodding heads of grain.

She introduced herself quickly, adding, "I am very happy to serve, if you need help. I was hoping for a few moments—" She couldn't think of a good lie. Her communicator vibrated again. Her shoulders slumped in failure, "without my sibling."

He grinned, suddenly; tension melted off his heavy frame. "Good hiding among the grains," he said. Then his face turned grim again. "Don't go in past the tenth row. We...there might be a fungus at the far end."

A fungal infection? In the rice? Opal's concerns about her sister evaporated into a far deeper fear. Failed harvests meant food rationing. She wished there were hibernation pods available; she could volunteer. It was far from the first time she'd had the thought. One fewer mouth to feed during food rationing would be appreciated. Even Père would have to honor the sacrifice of that; it would reflect well on the family. A sharp pain pierced her heart.

His hand slapped over his eyes.

She must have shown too much on her face. Had he not intended for her to understand the ramifications so clearly? He probably had thought her younger. Her small stature often confused adults. She knew two eight-year-olds who were taller.

"I will not repeat that," she said. "And I will stay near the front. Is there anything I should look for that would help you?"

He dropped his hand and considered her, his light brown eyes alive with curiosity. She wondered what he saw. The baby-factory her sister claimed she would be? The pale beauty her sienna-toned mère insisted she was? The panic attack-stricken failure Père detested? Or the youth with the mechanically oriented mind her mentors praised sometimes but more often complained about? She slumped further. She was too much work for everyone around her.

"People, plants or piloting?" He meant her training. Maybe he just saw a young New Hopian. That would be nice.

"Infrastructure and safety, primarily," she said. "My mentors searched a long time for my talent, but schematics and blueprints seem to come alive for me."

"They took a while with me, too, because my family wanted me to have different skills than I have," he said, pronouncing "family" slowly and meaningfully.

"Oh!" That hadn't occurred to her. Her parents had consulted long and hard with her occupational mentors, and had been grudging about her recent training. She should have considered that Père would have objected to anything she enjoyed or might be good at. Her brain fizzled with light for a moment, and her shoulders relaxed. "Thank you."

He seemed pleased. "Watch for yellowed spots on the rice leaves, especially any with dark brown borders. Do not touch, you will spread it. Tell me, only me."

"Report any yellow spots, which I am not to touch, to you and only you," she repeated, in English and then, glancing at the language badges on his tunic, in Korean, the other language they shared.

The agriculturist nodded, apparently pleased, and gave her an adult's formal bow, honoring her maturity of behavior.

She proudly returned it. She'd never been given such an important community service task.

Then he sped off, disappearing down the walkway in the middle of the field of waving stalks.

She followed, then turned right between the first and second rows, admiring the beautiful stems arcing from their trays of growing medium. They blocked her view of the walls immediately. It was near harvest, and the heads were heavy with grain, some draping toward the fish tanks below. Fins and tails snapped as she walked past.

She had fond memories of this field from helping with previous harvests, and she wondered again how different it would have looked back on Earth. Rows upon rows of rice growing in—mud, was it? Or on the banks of small ponds? She tried to imagine looking up from a field to a far-off horizon, maybe a mountain, something no one on *New Hope* had seen in more than seven generations. She shuddered and glanced up at the ceiling to reas-

sure herself it was still there. She was glad she'd been born too early to be planet-bound. She liked living on the generation ship. She had no complaints a little distance from Adamantine and Père wouldn't fix. She winced at the disloyalty of the thought and then shook her head. She wasn't wrong.

But a planet? Planets just seemed so wide open. Insects flying everywhere instead of being carefully contained in fields like this one, or in the protein habitats. Predators hiding who knows where. Electrical storms and volcanoes and tsunamis—vast oceans one could drown in! Those in addition to wars and other nation-state conflicts were all historical artifacts to her, as unreal as fiction.

Her parents and civics mentors had taught her that ethnicity and language were valuable traditions; nationality was dangerous. Two mutiny attempts early in the journey had taught them that. Their language badges had once been nation-state flags, which made no sense to her. So many languages shared nations, while many nations hosted multiple languages! *New Hope's* communication badges were now hand-embroidered, artistic renditions of the word "language" or "tongue" in the language depicted, color-coded by proficiency level. Black Tongue, an ancient disease, was now a compliment: a term of respect for those who had mastered five languages or more. Opal hoped to be a Black Tongue someday.

She walked slowly, scanning the tall slender leaves for patches of yellow. Being surrounded by plants and fish was peaceful at first, but she was relieved to reach the wall and its reflective, light paint. She brushed her fingers across it lightly, reassured by its lack of motion, then took a deep breath and started down between the second and third row.

Not far in, she noticed a patch of white—not on the rice, but under a fish tank. It was as long as her arm. Surely not fungus that massive, this far from the back, and on the floor. A forgotten shirt, maybe? An old shade for a fish tank? Maybe she should take it to the recyclers.

She squatted down. The white seemed to shimmer. Her eyes

couldn't focus on it. Definitely not fabric, not even felted fiber. The rice leaves above were a vivid healthy green, the grains thick and golden. Maybe this wasn't a problem? The agriculturist's warning not to touch anything had been strong, so she leaned over and stuck her nose close.

It was a white mat of thin branching threads, its edges in constant motion. A fantastic scent rose, earthy and spicy and fragrant. She inhaled deeply, feeling the scents tickle her sinuses. It didn't smell like any mushrooms she'd ever eaten, but her mouth watered. This was fungus of some type. That meant it had spread a lot. Her heart rate spiked; this could destroy the entire harvest, maybe even infect the fish!

Her throat constricted, suddenly scratchy. No, no, no! She couldn't have a panic attack here. Not now. She reached into her pocket and clutched Gengi. His soft fabric bunched between her tense fingers.

"We need to find a way to tell him where this is, we need to— oh, number, there's a number, there are numbers on the tanks." The repetition and the solid detail slowed her thoughts. The fish tank above the patch was number 258. "Two-five-eight." She stood up, repeating the number. "Now, what's the fastest way to find—" A wave of vertigo slammed into her, sending her back to her knees. "Non, non, non. Aide-moi, Gengi! Not here, not now!"

The tiny stuffed tardigrade pulsed in her fingers as a seizure shook her, and she landed heavily on her side. Dimly she realized this was not a panic attack; it was something much worse. She'd never had this kind of all-over muscle cramping, this complete lack of control over her own body, not in this way. She rocked, side to side, or rather her body did. The sensations were so new, so unusual, that she didn't quite panic. Her heart kept beating and her lungs kept pumping air. Her brain kept telling her that, and it helped.

Her muscles, however, refused to do anything she wanted them to do. "Haugh!" came out as a yell, not quite voluntary. Would the agriculturist hear that over the water pumps? She punched and kicked the air. She tried but couldn't yell again. Her knees bent, feet pushing against the floor, she inched backward. Her hair got stuck underneath her, pulling her neck at an awkward angle. Terror built; would she break her own neck? Abruptly, her legs went limp and she had some control again. She managed to roll back and forth until her hair was free, then collapsed on her side, exhausted, feeling like a meat puppet.

Adamantine's machinations were nothing compared to this. The thought made her want to laugh, but she couldn't even do that; another seizure shook her, then another.

Waves of odd thoughts followed each seizure. Her mind was being ransacked and judged. She began to see bizarre and terrifying images; nightmares she'd forgotten? But they included sensations she knew she'd never experienced, like heightened feelings of heat and water pressure and taste. They had to be dreams. Curiosity grew as she tried to figure them out. She focused on sensations that seemed to be Gengi's, or at least what Gengi would have experienced had he been a cave dweller the agriculturist's size.

Her panic attacks usually ended when she went unconscious. She got no such relief this time. She had flashes of conceptual insight that felt like huge epiphanies but were all stupidly obvious facts. She was young. She was bipedal. She was a mammal. She (only!) had six senses. She was part of a community that valued service and autonomy and survival and each other.

Her family was perfect, her mother thought, because between the four of them they had four different eye colors, personalities, skin tones, and hair types, a near-perfect capsule of their species, unlike those "parochial" families that chose eggs and sperm (These species with only two reproductive sexes! How limiting.) for cultural or visual similarity.

The Pangeas each pursued different careers, so they could serve the generation ship in different ways. Where Opal saw a complete lack of common ground and, in her sister and Père, zero compassion, Mère saw strength and collective power. (This one values service. Excellent.)

Not all of the epiphanies made sense. One was essentially, "Only one stomach and no mandibles and still, they warred with one another!"

None of that was news to her. But her brain insisted on exclaiming over each obvious thing as if it was brand new, or relearning something it still struggled to accept. She was losing her mind, that was what was happening. Her father was right. She was broken.

Opal had settled on a self-diagnosis of mental breakdown by the time the agriculturist found her. She didn't hear him approach; he was just there, kneeling next to her, looking worried.

"Opal! Are you injured?"

Her lips wouldn't obey her. She couldn't speak. Maybe she was having a stroke? She could move her fingers, so she used the first language every *New Hope* child was taught, safety sign.

"Can't move, can't talk," her fingers flew, over and over and over and over.

He took her hands, enclosing her fingers. "I understand. I will help you. Can you hear me?"

Her fear ebbed a bit. He let go, and she rocked her fist.

"Good. Stay calm." The agriculturist called a harvester and lifted her onto it, walked beside it, talked calmly to her as the robotic cart carried her to the nearest medical clinic.

The staff there seemed puzzled, but not worried. A new wave of fear swamped her. Were they not taking this seriously because of her age? Was she going to die?

Such strong emotion; annoying, dangerous and unnecessary. A flat calm swept over her. That was better. Very weird, but better. That sense seemed to echo in her head, like she was feeling it twice.

"Would you like me to tell the staff to keep your sibling out?" the agriculturist asked her quietly. His tone was gravely calm, but his hands trembled as he patted Gengi and her forearm.

Adamantine would make this so much worse. She rocked her fist, repeating twice for emphasis, adding, "Please." Then she remembered the white patch. She grabbed his hand to catch his attention. She let go and pointed between her eyes and his, and then gestured the tray number, 258.

His eyes widened, and he ran out. She'd upset him. But she'd also done her duty, warned him. She'd served. Why did she feel uneasy, instead of pride or satisfaction?

A sense of curiosity that didn't feel like her own stirred in her brain, along with a sluggish concept-question, images and words that she finally sorted into, <Sibling means same-level family? One generation?>

It was an odd, childish thought. The words that clunked into place with the images were all in a different language, but still it seemed like a question to her, in her own brain. Opal's panic attacks had accustomed her to talking to herself in odd ways. This was different.

<Oui.>

<258 is sibling identifier?> Another multi-language mélange, obviously not her own thought.

<Sibling identifier is Adamantine. Adamantine's number would be negative.> That should be funny, but she was too weirded out to be amused. <258 is where I found that...weird white fungus.>

Flailing, then. Upset, but not her own.

Schizophrenia did not run in her genetic line. Or at least it had been absent from the encoded records of her egg and sperm donors. She was certain of that; Père would have mentioned it had it existed. But if she had to address any loss of mental stability, better here, with the clinic's gently indifferent medical staff conferring inaudibly across the room, than in her family's chambers.

So, she asked, <Who are you?>

A wave of pleasure, not her own. <Ah! You can differentiate me now, good. I am a semqu. I am sad to have caused you distress,

although you may have just caused me much pain because I did not move fast enough. We semqu can only talk through others. Will you be my Voice?>

It wasn't that clear—at first just a jumbled mess of images and words in different languages—but it repeated, getting more refined, until Opal stopped it. <Voice? Semqu? What.>

<Voice is translator. For me and my kind.> Translator was easy; Voice was more complicated. As Opal understood it, a Voice took thoughts and turned them into vibrating air for those incapable of mind-connection; those who needed air to communicate. Like spacers. That made sense as translation duty. The rest did not, just a jumble of images she couldn't parse.

Her brain leapt to the ship gossip: the three alien ships that had shown up the previous month. They'd said, "The semqu will contact you" and vanished, without explaining who the aliens themselves were, what a semqu was, how they were able to communicate in Earth languages, or anything else.

The crew who'd been in the command center swore the aliens gave the impression of being a group of teenagers on some kind of trading joyride until they realized it was a first-contact moment and fled. The entire ship went on high security alert for two weeks, and then the subject was dropped.

Adamantine had run down every detail possible and shared them with her. Mère had declared the story a practical joke. Opal, like her sister, had wanted it to be true.

She was curious what her brain thought the aliens had meant. Intuition could be interesting. <What is a semqu?>

Images of walls and locked doors; danger warnings, then, a sense of overwhelming belonging, of unity, that made her heart ache. <It is secret, much of what we semqu are. I am able to tell you more if you accept. You spacers value free will. I ask instead of demanding.> A sense of regret washed over her.

The regret was definitely not her own. She'd not been asked

what she wanted to do for a long time. The respect buoyed her. <I thank you for asking.>

No one in her family would allow her to do something so outside of their concept of service, of her field-in-training. Was this her brain's way of saying she didn't want to study infrastructure anymore? Her mentors would be disappointed. But her sister had no aliens in her plans for Opal, which included a boyfriend of Adamantine's choice and children Adamantine could raise and play with. She was probably just having a bit of an escape fantasy.

A nurse leaned over her and patted Opal on the forearm. "We're concerned about your heart rate and this paralysis, Opal. We're going to let you sleep while we run some tests."

She felt a light prickling in the back of her hand. A needle. She closed her eyes.

<We have no time for sleep,> the other protested.

It was too late. A wave of darkness swept over her, and she fell unconscious.

Her dreams were immediate, lucid and bizarre. She seemed to be exploring without sight or any sense of hearing, but with other senses and abilities she could barely comprehend. She could transport herself places without walking, understand the composition of plants and minerals by tasting them.

Curiosity was in every one of the dreams.

In the first, she was blind, groping, yet spreading assertively in three dimensions with a clarity of purpose she found breathtaking. She was flooded with a sudden awareness of being moved, of being aided, then with the question, "Who moves us?" A connection, then, with another creature who wove roots into meaning and tactile beauty on the walls and ceiling and floors of their underground homes. A sense that this was an old, old memory, beyond ancient. Those root-weavers called themselves aupoin, the agriculturist-sized Gengi-clones she'd imagined earlier, and they experienced the world in fast-time.

Real time was measured in the preferred way—slow. Whether

that meant eons or decades Opal couldn't tell, but her dream-self deeply preferred slow, and was bothered that everything involving other creatures had to be done in fast-time. Was anxious about something important that needed to be done, soon, in very fast-time, and whatever that agriculturist was doing—

The dream abruptly shifted to hitching rides on beings who could see and hear. The first creature who swam was a revelation, as was the first creature who sensed light through eyes; the first creature who flew. Ah, flying! Her comprehension grew by leaps and bounds as she borrowed the senses of others to understand their worlds, which were weird and complicated.

Pain snapped her awake, pain that didn't feel like her own.

She was scared. If these were the semqu's dreams, if the semqu was a real thing, then they were not just harvest-infection, but brain-infection. That fungus had infected her, might infect the agriculturist. Could she infect her fellow spacers? Was she a danger to her community? <You are parasites!>

<Incorrect. Parasites weaken those they enter. We borrow one individual to communicate—a service that individual provides for its community—and then we aid the entire population.>

<Why?> In Opal's reading, she'd learned that some driven spacers might claim a desire to serve, like her father, but once they gained power, they wanted everyone else to serve them. Were these aliens like that?

<Learning is growth, growth is learning. We make the most progress in both when we meet a new species. This is an exciting time for us, to meet creatures from so far away.>

Dreaming or awake, her hitchhiker was there, distinct in her head.

Opal began to accept that something singular had happened. Her mind wasn't broken, but it had been infected. Or contacted. Changed. She was broken, useless; why not let this thing infect her if it would protect the rest of the ship? <If I do this, do you promise to not infect my people? You will leave our food supply alone?>

Its reassurance was sharp and detailed and took some time to understand. She began to better appreciate its process of communication with her. There were mind-maps, a synthesis of concepts spacer and alien, overlaid occasionally with word-concepts, all with the edge of being downloaded into her brain by a harried computer.

Spacers and semqu did not share a food source.

They only needed one individual.

This one sought her consent.

The idea of being chosen was heady. Being asked for her permission was huge. It warmed her. She thought about providing her Broken Litany, as she thought of it, the list of everything wrong with her that she started every conversation with a new mentor with, so they wouldn't be disappointed in her inevitable screwups. She held back; she wanted this thing to choose her, not anyone else.

<Can I agree temporarily? Like an internship?>

The semqu clearly did not understand internship but did not wait for an explanation. <No. This is a lifetime choice. You cannot ever stop being a Voice. It would be your job until death. Some Voices serve even after they die.>

That sounded morbid and overwhelming. <I want to understand more before I agree.>

<The best way to understand is to do,> the semqu said. <Wake up now. We need you to explain something to your people in very fast-time.> It seemed worried.

ABOARD NEW HOPE
MEDICAL SUITE FOUR
NEW HOPIAN YEAR 716
EIGHTH MONTH, TWENTY-FIFTH DAY

THE NURSE WAS STARTLED when Opal sat up and alarmed when she tried to get out of bed. She decided not to fully explain;

they might medicate her again. "I remembered I have to make an announcement at lunch," she said. "It's important, my mentor insists." The nurse hurried off to confer with the rest of the staff.

Opal picked up her communicator. Terri had messaged her with a terse, "Call me." Then, "Please!"

Terri had recently moved back in with her birth family, a decision that bewildered Opal. Calming her down would take an hour. Opal typed, "I can't right now, I'm so sorry—Jasmine?" hoping Terri could call the new support group lead. Then she messaged the weekly organizer for an announcement slot during the community time meeting at the mid-day meal.

It took her some time to talk her way free of the medical staff, who ran her through a number of tests she'd apparently failed just an hour before, and couldn't believe the new results. They insisted on sending a nurse with her. He walked next to her, glancing at her often, as they headed for the main cafeteria where the mid-day gathering was happening.

The semqu did not tell her what it wanted her to say. <It is urgent but complicated. I am still working out how to explain so you can understand.>

That should have made her nervous, but Opal focused on the fact that she didn't have to obsess over the right words. All she had to do right now was make it to the cafeteria without running into a wall. That she could do.

The meeting had already begun when she and the unhappy nurse walked in. Her family was there, spread out at various tables. They all looked happy, in their own way. Her breath caught. Would they listen to her?

Her sister jumped up the instant they came through the doors. The nurse raised his hand in negation, giving her a "don't you dare" look. Adamantine sat down, lips compressed in a tight line. Opal's shoulders slumped. Every rebuff seemed to make her sister more determined to remake Opal in her own image. She was not going to react well to Opal's news. Because Opal was growing more and more certain that this was something she needed to do for her community.

About sixty people, including many guild leaders, were listening to Captain Ximena Bobbie give her quarterly report. Good for the semqu's purposes; it was happy to see a large gathering. But Opal had never spoken to such a large group. Anxiety bubbled up, acid and familiar. The minute it hit, though, that strange calm rose up and wiped it away.

I could get used to this, Opal thought. Her worries about her family's reaction felt muted too.

The nurse pulled a chair near the door and insisted Opal sit. He whispered that he didn't think she should eat yet and hurried off toward her parents.

Opal sat. She was not hungry. The nurse had put Gengi in her hands, and she traced the fuzzy tardigrade's seams. She didn't need its comfort. It was so odd.

Captain Ximena was wrapping up. "And in the best news so far, we are on track to use only 45 percent of our annual allotment by mid-year. That means we are adding five percent to the mission reserve as we had hoped." Snaps and applause, and a few questions followed. She answered them holding her tall body ramrod straight, the long black plait down the center of her back barely moving.

Opal had always envied Captain Ximena's ability to stay calm in the face of conflict, her way of speaking confidently in apparently any setting, and her thick, strong hair. Her entire body radiated competence, reliability and trustworthiness; even her deep brown hands were solid and broad. She inspired poetry and respect.

Mère had once commented on Ximena's prominent nose, saying it was a classic Mayan feature, so Opal privately assumed Captain Ximena was, like her, a conservatory-child. She would never ask, of course. That would be unforgivably crass. The conservatory of eggs and sperm from Earth were intended to keep the ship's bloodlines fresh and provide healthy DNA should radiation cause problems during their long journey, so asking implied the parents were infertile or defective in some way.

Opal had no idea where her own genetic material was from. Anytime she or Adamantine asked, Mère would say sharply, "Nations don't matter anymore."

After the captain sat, someone stood to ask for volunteers for a song circle and baby-helpers for a new mother having postpartum issues. Then another person broke into a song of gratitude for the cooks and kitchen crew, and Opal joined in on the cheerful, bouncy chorus. Partway through, she relaxed, enjoying the harmony and sense of community. Similar support from others had buoyed her during her worst weeks with Père, and it was nice to give back—a sensation that seemed doubled, as if the semqu appreciated that too.

She hadn't expected that connection from an alien. It soothed her. The song ended. Opal took a deep breath. <It's nearly time.>

<I am ready.>

Opal stood, ready to speak. To her dismay, the prayer bell rang, and the room fell silent, allowing those with religion to thank their deities privately.

<Now?> the semqu asked.

<NO! We have to be quiet until this part is over.>

The silence for prayer seemed to go on forever. Eventually the bell rang again, and the attendees joined in the interfaith gratitude to "the soil, the fungus, the insects, the pollinators and plants, the spark that breaks the seedcase, and the Hope that houses us all."

<Oh. I like that,> the semqu said. Its delight was contagious, and Opal grinned. The community organizer nodded at her.

<Good. So, we can talk now. What do you want me to say?> But abruptly, her throat was jerking harshly, and she was speaking aloud with no conscious concept first, words all jumbled, visceral and wrong. <What are you doing?> She gripped Gengi to her chest. She had a sharp image of *New Hope* approaching a blockade of alien-looking spaceships. Between that and the sense of being a

puppet, she couldn't make sense of the sounds coming from her own mouth.

Adamantine growled. Everyone else traded bewildered or worried looks; the nurse headed back toward her. A few people repeated phrases in various languages.

The negative reactions from her community irritated the alien presence that had invaded her body and mind. <What are they having trouble understanding?> the semqu asked.

<I don't even know what I said! Why did you not let me talk? Why did you take over that way?> Opal thought. <Why are those ships out there?>

<You have not yet accepted my request, and I did not want you to lie to them.>

<Why would I lie?> she demanded.

<New Voices sometimes do not understand.> A sense of betrayal, disappointment tinged with incomprehensible images rippled through her. It shared something with her—the final thoughts of several spacers, echoes of decisions that were clearly a choice to end their lives rather than live with the alien in their heads, while hiding that decision from the semqu until it was too late.

Oh. <They were honor-bound. They had all sworn shut-its, and you cannot keep a secret from someone in your own mind.>

<I did not know this about your people.> The semqu grieved their lost lives.

It made her feel better, that this alien had not intended to cause harm and felt bad that it had. People were getting up, complaining about the ravings of a child. The nurse gently put an arm around her shoulders.

"Let's get you back to the clinic."

"No." She held her ground. *They really really need to under-stand.* From what little she'd learned, these semqu were incredibly powerful. And now she definitely didn't want it to take over anyone else. "This is about our loss of speed and_"

The captain spun toward Opal. "How did you know about that? That's a shut-it!"

The room silenced. The nurse stepped back, clearly shocked. Breaking a shut-it was an unforgiveable offense.

"The semqu have contacted me," she said. "They used my body to share that message to you. They want me to serve as their translator, their Voice. Was I not enunciating clearly?"

The last was her family's go-to phrase for "What is wrong with my communication," stripped of her mother's burning condescension. She'd forgotten her sister was in the room. Adamantine, of course, heard it in their mother's tone regardless.

Adamantine leapt up, stalked toward her. The fifteen-year-old reminded Opal of a vibrating ribbon of steel. Opal was surprised she didn't feel compelled to shrink away. "How dare you! You disavow us, you claim knowledge of aliens, and you embarrass us in front of everyone with some word stew?"

"Let her talk!" the captain snapped. She tapped her communicator. "Navigator. We may have contact."

"You're believing this?" Adamantine asked incredulously. Several others apparently agreed with her.

The nurse interjected smoothly, "It would be helpful if you picked a single language, Opal."

The semqu inside her head *jerked*. The alien being that had connected to her brain, that had clearly attached itself to many of her synapses, that had connected her to a massive presence far beyond her capacity to comprehend—had made a mistake. Had caught itself in a mistake, was angry at itself about it, and was rapidly trying to fix it. She would have laughed, in relief and terror, had she still possessed the emotional capacity to do so. She did not.

<You use more than one language?> it asked.

<Hundreds,> Opal replied. <We pride ourselves in keeping alive many of the languages of our former world. I know parts of twelve, and you mashed them together. Only *babies* do that.> She

used Mère's condescension on the last sentence, and it apparently translated.

The semqu flailed. It was an odd description for something inside her brain. The impression she got was of many appendages, all moving at once. Like crickets in a cage. It amused her.

That amusement died as it occurred to her that the knowledge that her people used many languages might have been a safety protocol for dealing with aliens, not that they'd met any before, and probably should be a shut-it. She wasn't the first spacer this alien had chosen, and somehow those spacers had kept their multiple languages a secret.

But her community would figure out that if they spoke in a language Opal didn't know the alien presence couldn't overhear. Could it? No, it must not be able to.

The flailing stopped. Now she felt a lifting, a lightening, and a shifting in her brain. That brought her back to the present, fast. It also allowed her to review what she had said, with some dismay. The only phrase she had spoken in a single language was "The semqu require; Opal Pangea is no more." All the rest, a carefully reassuring speech, was lost in a hodgepodge of the dozen languages she spoke. *Oh, fiery, fiery silent consonants.*

Her eyes caught movement, her sister's hands flying upward, burying fingers into her tightly coiled black hair. "You idiot. Are you losing your mind?" Adamantine had just spoken in French. The nurse spoke English. She hadn't even noticed that until just now.

"The semqu did not realize we use more than one language," she said aloud, in English. It was hard, the words difficult to find, scrambled in her head. <What did you do to my brain!?>

<I'm fixing it. Ask them for time.>

"Patience. I need a moment. The semqu is working in my brain." She repeated herself excruciatingly slowly in three languages, mostly to reassure herself she still knew them as separate, but also to show the semqu what she needed to be able to do.

An announcement came over the intercom. "Captain. We are approaching multiple unknown spacecraft."

Images of massive nautilus-shaped craft that could move in the blink of an eye flitted into her mind. "They're... called ... blink-ships," Opal said, carefully choosing words in one language.

"What can you tell us about them, Opal?" the captain asked.

"They are friendly. Made by modeel, like the ones you met last month. Three young squirts and their crews." Opal was certain about that, but she wasn't sure she spoke in one language.

Captain Ximena's eyes widened but she didn't look reassured.

More flailing, more mental lightening. So heavy, that presence had been before! And yet it wasn't like the load was any lighter, just shifted. That worried her. What part of her brain was it taking over instead? But she could still move and breathe and speak, and that was better than the first few minutes of contact in the field, when she thought she would die. She stroked Gengi, and waited, surprised she didn't feel more anxious.

Her compatriots were not reassured.

"Is this some kind of joke?"

"We're supposed to believe this mysterious semqu is inside a teen who carries a baby toy?"

"Do you need us to sing or to dance for you, Opal?" It was the kindest offer, and it made her smile despite it all.

"Singing and dancing later," she managed.

A few people hurried out of the cafeteria. Some moved to the room's viewports to try to see the alien ships. Speculation raced through the room in multiple languages. She strained to understand, and her straining distracted and disconcerted the semqu.

<Calm them.> The phrasing it suggested was blunt.

She hoped the flat affect would convey it was not her wording. "The semqu ask, how have you traveled seven hundred years across the galaxy and learned nothing of patience?"

The rudeness from someone well-known as a polite youth silenced most of the room, but not her sister. "You've lost your mind! My sister! I can't stand that loss, I won't tolerate it, you will get help, you will fix yourself—" Adamantine hurtled toward her. Opal braced herself.

"Stop." The snapped order froze Adamantine in place. An older woman—*my mother*, Opal thought, shocked into stillness by how distant she felt, how little power Mère held over her. It forced her to accept that the semqu had truly changed her.

Harriet Pangea marched up to Adamantine. "You dare speak of your loss? As if you were the wounded party here? *You?*" If Adamantine was a ribbon of steel, Harriet Pangea was a foundational girder. She was slightly shorter than her elder daughter now, but husky enough to throw the girl over her shoulder. The expression on her broad face made it clear she'd do that if necessary, despite her arthritic fingers and the grey hairs dulling her auburn red.

How had she not noticed her mother's aging before?

"She is my sister!" Adamantine yelled into her mother's stern face.

"Yes." Harriet reached up as if to cradle Adamantine's cheek. She grabbed one earlobe with one freckled hand and buried the pale gnarled fingers of her other into Adamantine's hair. Opal winced in sympathy, remembering the pain of mother's fingernails digging into the tender edges of her ears, but it seemed like an echo, not a memory.

Harriet forced Adamantine to her knees. "And if she had not been trying to escape you, she would not have been in the rice fields. She would not have had those seizures. I told you to leave her alone, repeatedly, and you did not. Whatever is wrong with her is your fault." Her face showed no pain, only a twist of anger that came and was gone. "You will sit, and you will be silent." Clearly not trusting her elder daughter to do either, she pulled Adamantine along behind her as she returned to her seat, and forced her to sit at her feet, like a child.

Mère actually stood up to her for me, Opal thought. It had been a year since Harriet had intervened between the sisters; she'd ignored her daughters to focus on Père since the suicide of one of his team members. Opal should have been elated, or at least relieved. There was nothing, other than a mild contentment. But reality was reality. Such treatment, in front of others, would be pure humiliation to the proud teen.

<Adamantine will never forgive me for that,> Opal thought. <We should be careful around her.> An Adamantine early-warning system struck her as very useful. Could the semqu do that?

<Not forgive you for what? Her own behavior?> The semqu was still busy, but calmer now, and curious again.

It wasn't her fault? Opal blinked. Adamantine's behavior had triggered mother's reaction?

<You asked for something you needed. She refused to give it. And your mother blames your sister for her own failure, does she not?>

That sparked memories, connections, spiraling back into child-hood. <Oh. I had not.... Oh *homophones*.>

<...What?> The semqu stilled when baffled; that was good to know. She was too unnerved to be amused at having stymied the alien presence a second time, so soon.

"Opal, if you know something about these ships?" The captain had moved near the door, very close to her. "It would be good to know *now*."

Opal bowed to her. "Yes, of course." <Explaining will require slow-thought-talk. We should quick-communicate to others now.>

<Good. I am done.>

She took a deep breath and shifted into the high formal mode of address that members of the generation ship used to convey some-thing deeply serious. "Fellow members of my community, let me begin again. Please translate for any who need it. I have heard your concerns. I reassure you that I am still in control of my thoughts, if not entirely in control of my body. Semqu require a translator—

they call them Voices—to communicate with others. They have chosen me."

Her mother made a low moaning noise. She waited until it ended and did not look her mother's way again. "You should know that I cannot hide anything in my mind from the semqu, so they are familiar with several of our languages." She slid her hand down her row of language buttons, listing the languages she spoke for those too far away to see.

"I am young enough that I have been entrusted with no shut-its, and I am grateful to not have betrayed my people in this way, else I would have otherwise been honor-bound to suicide. This is the reason behind several losses in the past year. I was not the first Voice chosen." Her words vibrated a little, grief coming through despite the alien's calming effects. She named those whose final thoughts the semqu had shared with her. There was a rustle as many in her audience shifted uncomfortably or exclaimed aloud. The mutter of gossip and side conversations died away entirely.

The semqu inside her stilled entirely, and an unsettled, prickly feeling washed over her.

"Semqu cannot speak to any species directly—"

A derisive laugh from one of the older spacers interrupted her. "Oh, and pray tell me how many *species* there are?"

"That's an excellent question," Opal said. "One moment."

<All of them? I suppose we have a tally—> The alien sounded aggrieved. Opal got flitting images of hundreds of insects, birds, fishes, and creatures she could not begin to categorize.

Into the flow, she asked, <Sapient ones? The ones you need translators for?>

<We have translators for all! But—oh, you also categorize creatures that way. How interesting.> The images shifted. Tall, terrifying praying-mantis creatures, two distinct furred dinosaur-like beings, a massive furred predator, the robot-like creatures she'd heard described from the encounter last month, other images too

quick to process. <For varying definitions of sapience, you'd be the tenth in Se Collective. There may be 13.>

Opal repeated the last two sentences verbatim.

There was a stunned silence, and then an uproar.

"You are a childish lot, aren't you?" That came out against Opal's will, with a flat affect that made her feel like a robot.

<I really hate it when you do that, and it freaks them out.>

<Get them to calm down. We have a lot to say.>

Bemused, Opal asked, <Are you in a hurry for some reason?>

<We need to move you to your new home. The sooner we get this done, the better.> It was odd to feel someone else's anxiety in her own mind.

Captain Ximena moved in front of her, and she could see the woman's tension. "The ships, Opal."

Opal blinked. A sense of two planets arose in her mind—one fried and lifeless, its protective atmosphere stripped away; the second lush with food, seen through non-semqu eyes to have oceans, lakes, continents and islands thick with plant life. *It's so beautiful!*

Information pressed against her, an offer they were not being allowed to refuse because the semqu and modeel had run out of time. The *New Hope* was about to pass beyond their reach.

"OH! They are here to move us. New Terra is no longer compatible with life," Opal said. "It has lost its atmosphere."

"You useless prat!" Père leapt to his feet. "How the hell did you know that? Have you been eavesdropping?"

She stared at him, stunned. It was the first time he'd spoken directly to her in years. He looked and sounded as angry as he had been back on that horrible day.

And she felt ... nothing. No shame. Just a sense that this broken, mean man had rudely interrupted her and accused her of something she'd not done. Again. He was just another noisy mammal. What had this alien done to her? A blip of fear, and then a wave of gratitude. What freedom, to not be hurt because he didn't understand.

One of her father's colleagues grabbed him from the side, was shaking him, screaming. "You told your family?"

"We told her. That one has not spoken to his child for much time," Opal heard herself say, in that mixed-language medley again, only this time with fewer mixed-up words. "I ran across that as I was settling in and thought how odd it was. Do human parents not talk to their children?"

There was a stunned silence of a different sort. Spacers did not refer to each other as "human" except as an insult or reprimand. Père and his colleague stared at her, both open-mouthed. Mère yanked him back down into his seat.

Opal took a deep breath. "There is a gorgeous planet where we can live—nearbyish?—in the way they determine distance. They'll take us there."

"Oh, no," a man moaned. "Not another case of planet fever."

Opal ignored him and the murmur of agitated chatter about New Terra. "We'll share the planet with another species that lives underground. We will be expected to take care of the surface and its capacity for life, to be good stewards, because this solar system is already populated. This is the only planet we'll get. We normally would be given a choice, but they have had a hard time contacting us. It has taken two generations. They have no more time. They need to move us the instant we're between the ships. Which will be too soon for a spacer decision; they know how long that takes."

Someone laughed. Decisions that impacted everyone shipboard could take years.

"They apologize for making this choice for us. We can leave if we do not like our new home. They hope we agree. I hope we agree, it is ... there is no suitable word in English. It is incontournable, must-see." The word also meant inevitable, which was also true, but she didn't think that would help her case any. "You will love it."

"Planet fever," a woman across the room said, nodding.

<That was perfect,> the semqu said. <You were so much more concise than I could have been. We will work well together. Do you accept this?>

Opal was not accustomed to unfiltered praise. "Translator to alien" was beyond anything she'd ever envisioned for herself. It should be fascinating. And she'd be entirely out of her family's control. This was her choice, alone, the biggest choice she'd ever make.

Elation filled her, then flattened to calm. She knew she should fully understand a job before making an occupational choice, but her body flooded with excitement at the thought of having more control over her future than she'd ever envisioned, starting now, today. This was a choice only she could make. Her choice.

<Yes. Yes, I accept.> An easy equanimity filled her.

<Good. Now warn them to brace themselves and prepare your own body. We move.>

Opal said, "Everyone, brace yourselves, we're being moved—"

Clapping interrupted her. The man who'd first accused her of planet fever rose to his feet. "Thanks for the show," he said. "Now let's get you to the med bay so the rest of us—"

The intercom blared. "Captain, those ships! They've jumped, they're encircling us!"

"Right there!" someone yelled.

Out the viewport, she caught a glimpse of the curved wall of one of the ships she'd seen in her mind. A weird sensation hit Opal, as if every individual cell in her body was being turned inside-out. Given the cries from around the room, she wasn't alone in experiencing it.

The entire ship lurched. People swayed; several fell. Pots clattered and someone in the kitchen crew screamed, and then it sounded like the entire room was swearing or yelling or crying. Captain Ximena and the nurse both reached out and steadied Opal.

Concepts flooded her brain. She understood what had happened. Opal took a deep breath and pitched her tone to carry over people's cries of alarm. "We are now in orbit above the planet Trye. It circles a star the peoples of Se System call Serium. Welcome home."

Emergency beacons and sirens came on, blaring loudly.

"That's one hell of a case of planet fever," someone said.

Several people laughed, one a near-hysterical bark.

A child at the viewport yelled, "Ayi! A big ball! An asteroid, right there! Is it going to hit us?"

There was a surge toward the viewports, and much yelling. "It's a planet! It's really a planet!" was repeated in many languages. The noise went on in waves for some time.

Opal rested with her eyes closed, head between her knees. She did not remember sitting down. She would look later. She already knew where they were, and she was bone-tired; the semqu shared its exhaustion with her. The move had cost the alien, dearly. And— it had been poisoned?!

Non! <The agriculturist must have used fungicide where you found me in the rice fields,> Opal thought, horrified. <I'm so sorry. I am a broken, unworthy thing—>

<Voice. You acted to protect your people's food. That was a right-thing. I had to allow the poison to work, so he would not connect me to it. No spacer can ever know our true nature. Only our Voices are trusted with that information. Do you understand?> The words were scrambled with images, but the intent was a sliver of glass, sharp and clear.

<Yes.> So the semqu had shut-its as well. <I understand.>

<I will be weak for some time, but this will not kill me. Thank you for explaining. Your trust is valued.>

That made her feel a bit better.

Adamantine shrieked, "Are you telling me my sister's not crazy?"

She was so tired. Could she sleep in the same room as Adamantine after this? *No.*

The sirens stopped screaming. Opal saw several people sit down, apparently in shock. Mère dragged Adamantine to a viewport, and they silently stared out together. Across the room, Père was being hugged by his weeping colleague. Père seemed dazed but still angry. Around the room, people were excited or confused, afraid or limp with disbelief, like the nurse. Someone yelled out to him, and he left Opal to tend to an older adult who'd fallen.

Children ran by her, arguing excitedly over who was going to get to tell their mentors they could live on a planet now.

Eventually people were talking instead of yelling. When she didn't have to shout, she set Gengi on the floor next to the chair. She petted it, thanking the tardigrade toy for its years of comfort.

She stood. "Opal is no more. I now answer to Voice. And… right now I need a very long, uninterrupted nap." Captain Ximena was in the doorway, trying to re-enter the room from the hallway, impeded by people yelling or arguing or just desperate for her attention.

Voice swayed slightly, caught herself on the chair and bowed to the ship's leader. "Captain, under the circumstances, I request an adult's private accommodation."

"Non!" Adamantine screamed, a frustrated sound that cut off abruptly.

Captain Ximena pushed through the crowd of now-silent questioners who stared at Voice, and returned her bow, a full adult's bow with no irony to it. "Yes, of course. That makes sense, Op— Voice." She spoke into her communicator. "Berthing. I need an empty furnished dwell for our … our translator to the semqu. Our Voice. She's exhausted. Make it happen, now."

Voice followed her out of the cafeteria, hands empty. She didn't mind the stares and had no urge to look back. She was translator to beings so powerful they could move an entire generation ship in seconds. Beings who had just given her people hope and a new home. She could serve her community in a way no one else could. She would be able to finally repay them for the care they had given her.

Her days of anxiety and fear were over.

FIVE

A HATCH OR HARVEST EVENT

**PLANET TAEQUA
HOUSE POISTE, ZISSOKOT (CITY)
YEAR TWO OF ATTARC ACHLEOT'S COMMUNION
WITH THE GODDESS
NEW HOPIAN YEAR 716**

The news that Se Collective had new residents who not only had been gifted a planet but would undoubtedly gain a seat on its Council landed unevenly across the Known Planets.

On Taequa, in the city of Zissokot, the news interrupted a contentious Matriarch meeting on an exceptionally hot day, one most participants would have preferred to spend in their compounds at siesta, fanned by servants.

But Matriarch Nyshoof had once again raised the argument to outright dissolve the annual apiquai payments, on which rested Zissokot's entire economy, and every Matriarch from all six tiers, as well as representatives from every outlying ranch and hunting household, were crammed into Matriarch Poiste's inadequate gathering room for the discussion. Each Matriarch hummed and chirred, determined to have her say.

Crests burned, fevered with the sensation of so much body heat, adding to attendees' existing irritation. Serrated teeth clenched; nares flared. Talons, some carved with Temple glyphs and others with inlaid gems and precious metals, slid in and out of sheaths, creating a just-audible, unnerving susurration. Cheeks bulged as protective fighting kote pulsed full beneath the glittering eyes of single matrons who were already on edge, hungry to duel. Husband-choosing season was underway.

Matriarch Poiste sat slightly off-center. Her rectangular chamber forced an oval rather than circular seating arrangement, and the swarms of daughters at the edges gossiped about the implications of it, their eggling fingers flying so as not to interrupt their elders with speech. Poiste's servants anxiously waited in the entry for space to serve drinks or disperse cooling sprays.

The instant opening rites concluded, First-Tier Matriarch Nyshoof rose from her sling seat to begin her arguments. Nyshoof's thin roan-and-malachite fur glistened with scented plant oils from her arm-long jaw to her ankle-boot-clad toes, showcasing the strong muscular build she maintained moving the large blocks of stone required by her purpose-occupation, construction. She was only of average height, but her lengthy Goddess-blessed crest rose rigid high behind her head, its stiffened topaz and malachite filaments adding a meter to her stature.

"We should never have agreed to such a centralized structure," Nyshoof said, all ten of her nares flaring in emphasis. She paced an inclusive circle, eyeing each Matriarch quickly enough that her turned back gave no one reason to take offense. "It gives Temple Piertoc too much power over the city. How do we know they are giving us all we deserve of the proceeds from off-planet trade?"

Declaring one's purpose-occupation, or apiquai, was both a right and an obligation. Each matron had a singular choice about how they served, declared in a public adulthood ceremony that ended their civic adolescence. Temple-distributed payments to each House were based on the number of daughters who had declared their apiquai-right. The fact that a sixth-tier Matriarch with five daughters could earn more than a first-tier with only one had long rankled Nyshoof, whose bloodline seemed cursed with thin shells.

A servant, her temple mareet of blue and white streamers stained by sweat, raced through the open doors. "Matriarchs!" She took one look at the tension-filled room, slid to one knee, and disgorged her news before her throat could be taken for interrupting. "The Goddess' prophecy has come to pass! The Semqu have brought a new people into Se Collective! Travelers from across the galaxy! The Semqu have gifted to them the entire planet of Trye!"

A cacophony of whistled surprise and outrage swelled to drown out anything else she might have said.

The Matriarchy had learned that they were not alone in the Goddess' creation a mere two hundred years prior. Their egos had not adjusted well to that information, nor the reality that they were in fact far from the most advanced beings in existence.

Some had stubbornly clung to complete denial and the Old Ways, believing they were the most superior beings, as their beloved crests proved. Some had turned for comfort to a new cult of the Goddess, swelling its ranks and its influence until Temple Piertoc had become not only the primary religion, but a source of political power that had upended their lives. The entire population relocated when Zissokot had been built, replacing City Five as the hub of peqe life on the planet. No apeqe in the room had been alive for that brutal relocation, and none cared where the old city, fast fading into mythic status, was located.

And yet both warring faiths allowed Zissokot's leadership to continue to believe they were uniquely elite, superior, all-powerful. Any act by the Semqu was brutal on that denial. Having one's Goddess predict that act did not help, not the width of a single tooth.

The messenger scanned the noisy crowd, seeking the hosting Matriarch. She shouted into the first waning of the uproar, desperate to keep the assembled city leaders listening instead of lashing out. "These new creatures, they are flat-faced mammals. They have lived in a ship, but not a blinkship, one that travels extremely slowly, for generations. They call themselves spacers." She gulped a breath. "Attarc Achleot has charged me to return to the Temple to await more information to convey to you. Have you any questions for her?"

"Should it surprise us that the Temple is in charge of this news and its timing?" Matriarch Nyshoof snarled, furious at being upstaged by a szipeqe.

"We Matriarchs did agree that no one Household should be in charge of the off-world communicator the Semqu gifted us," said Matriarch Guettarch, whose Household claimed ancient authorship of the apiquai economy. "The Temple has been a trustworthy steward of that as well as the apiquai system."

They would have continued to argue, but other Matriarchs surged to their feet, and the room boomed with questions.

"They GAVE them an entire PLANET? Why?"

"How many of these spacers are there?"

"Why did the Semqu bring them here?"

"What kind of mammals? Rodents? Grazers? Carnivores?"

"What use are they?"

"What do they taste like?"

The messenger got to her feet and made a show of counting questions on her bound talons, bowing to each Matriarch who yelled at her. She slid one backward step toward the door, still seeking the hostess with some urgency.

The Matriarch of House Izhdench spoke. "Such a hatch or harvest event," she said, as if discussing a nut crop so unexpectedly heavy that Houses had to be discouraged from harvesting their own trees: news that could be taken well or poorly. "How can we turn this decision to our favor?"

Across the crowded room, matriarchs clicked teeth together, considering. Izhdench's old crèche-mate Matriarch Saena purred nearby, "That is an excellent question."

Hands gestured assent, and sheathed talons ran along jaws in gestures of thoughtful agreement. This framing suited their need to feel in control.

The messenger gulped a breath, having finally located Matriarch Poiste. She bowed deeply to the two elder Matriarchs and then knelt toward Poiste, gesturing thanks for aiding the Temple in sharing urgent news. "With your permission I will take your questions to the Attarc. I will convey that some of you wish to consult with her."

Poiste, wishing to be rid of the interruption, gestured her assent.

The szipeqe fled, racing back out into the sun-blasted day with her throat intact. She was too well-trained to show relief, and none of the assembled Matriarchs save perhaps Nyshoof thought about her again.

"We should kill them," Izhdench's daughter, Vassat, growled at her side.

Matriarch Izhdench frowned. Her eldest daughter Vassat was her House apiquiit, the first granddaughter, and would someday be Matriarch in her own right. Tall and deft for her age, Vassat had declared her apiquai in the physical arts as a mere eight-yearling. She should have been with a swarm, a servile group of second-born matrons her age, not sitting next to her Matriarch like a servant. Something had ruptured her swarm recently. Vassat would not explain, saying only she preferred to be alone.

"Vassat," Matriarch Izhdench said quietly. "Your spirit is strong, and fierce, and all admire your body's skills and what will surely be your dueling prowess. But you have much to learn. Do not fail to develop your mind-brain as you hone that of your body. You will have a House to run and the city to help govern. You may refuse the advice of your peers, but do not fail to learn wisdom from your elders."

Vassat looked up at her mire with one skeptical eye. "How is killing invaders not wise?"

Matriarch Izhdench lowered her long jaw alongside her daughter's head to ensure she was not overheard. She and the Attarc were old friends; Achleot often blessed her with sacred information. "Because if they are the Semqu's invited guests, they do not invade. If we attacked them, the Semqu would wipe us from the face of Taequa. Never let your ego nor that of others get in the way of reality, apiquiit. The Semqu do not tolerate those who attack their decisions. Our own—"

"This ludicrous blathering must not derail the important choices we have before us!" Matriarch Nyshoof shouted.

While her daughter looked askance at her, brooding, Matriarch Izhdench raised her head, blew a soft sigh through her lower nares, and gave the speaker her attention.

Rumors roared through the city in the following days and weeks. A popular one was that the aliens had been intercepted by the Semqu because they were headed to Taequa itself. Months on, a new rumor flew, this one with staying power, as it was seeded with a nut of truth. A spacer, a mere male, had dared insult the Matriarchy's representative. He compared her to one of their animals, a creature called a dinosaur.

By the end of the year, most of Zissokot's inhabitants, from the central temple to the horax ranches far beyond the sixth tier, were incensed by the spacers' very existence.

PFFTSLOSSLOSSYCK BAY, PLANET VASOM
SEMQU YEAR 1142
(NEW HOPIAN YEAR 716)

THE SEAWATER EDDYING through the rocky tidal nook and between the old friends bobbing there was already scented with negativity and anger, Waatoos Hecht noted. It might be a long afternoon. Her skin tinged with impatience.

She'd not seen any of these childhood friends during her long training. Some of them she'd not seen in a decade. They'd all aged well and grown; delightfully muscular tentacles on a few of the females, impressive dexterity in the males, every one of them sporting braincases bulging with training and use. A few had done well enough financially that they had been allowed to apply for mate-rights.

She had fond memories from their time together as squirts and had looked forward to reconnecting. She would be of mate-choosing age soon and had thought of this group first. She had high hopes; the hobbies they had been lightly discussing were all acceptable; music, poetry, some amazing new multimedia art, a few sports she could learn to be interested in.

Then she had been badly disappointed.

Physically, they were a lovely cohort, she couldn't have asked for better. Emotionally, however, they had not changed. All nine of them were immature, frill to beak to tentacle. Nearly stunted. It was appalling.

It was the conversation about the new residents on Trye that had cracked the shell for her. She should thank them for saving her, Waatoos thought wryly. Five minutes in, and she was so deeply unimpressed she was starting to lose patience with hiding it.

"Tar and slag and frost!" Bioluminescent stripes of red and black rippled down Foele's torso. "We'd surveyed Trye! It's ripe with ore and metals! We'd started negotiating with the aupoin there to start mining for us!"

The majority clearly agreed. Several turned dark with frustration and pheromones of rage poured into the water, churned by agitated frills and tentacles. "Years of work wasted," someone spat.

A school of squirts exercising in the open brine on the other side of the nook had been attracted by the commotion. A few fearful ones jetted away, pink and white, as the pheromones reached them.

It will take two days for the currents to wash this inlet clean, Waatoos thought. "Immoveable objects," she snapped. "We move forward."

Cablu surprised her with a pragmatic take. "Our time was not wasted. We know where many valuable ores are. They don't. We can negotiate if we trade well."

Foele jetted upward several meters, breaking the surface, and then sank back down to snarl, "Negotiate for what? What do they have that we need?"

"Well, they're competent metalworkers, obviously." Cablu said. "They could make our space-faring suits there. Let them deal with the waste products."

Foele spluttered. Others drifted closer, shifting jade-green-curious.

"I don't mean end our business," Cablu added. "We would finish the suits here. I doubt any of us want the spacers to know we need those suits, or that we'd be helpless in space without them?" Cablu enjoyed irritating Foele and making the others uneasy.

Their manipulation made Waatoos tired. "We long ago agreed we don't want any species other than the semqu to know that, and their Voices make me nervous enough," Waatoos snapped. She was proud that the lie in her second sentence didn't show on her skin. She rather liked a number of the Voices she had met. "I certainly don't want a species whose history includes war," she shuddered, "to know that."

One of the braver, more curious squirts had swum close enough to understand her. "What is war?" she asked.

There was a long silence.

Waatoos expelled water in a long sigh. "Something the semqu loathe and do not allow," she said.

She was not allowed to explain that the spacers' home planet apparently teemed with creatures; their populations were said to be larger than that of all the larsivians on Ylas. Large enough to disconcert even the semqu.

No one wanted them to call for reinforcements.

"But what is war?" the squirt persisted. Her siblings and friends crowded closer, some sixty of them now, jade green predominating, all repeating the question.

Their teacher, who'd thought they were following him across the inlet, began to jet toward them. He was not going to reach them in time.

Her old friends pulsed in the water, none of them wanting to answer. Some of them were probably as ignorant as the squirts. Waatoos cooled; her skin turned the color of education, the charcoal-green of healthy kelp. "You have played team games, yes?"

"Yes!"

"You win, you lose, you develop friendships and easy rivalries; you might play with your foes next week. It is a game, one that might come with bragging rights, but your rivals might have them next week."

The squirts swam various colors of confused now, and several of the adults as well. This was not how any of them would have explained it, Waatoos knew, but they could have stepped in and didn't. She had, so she would explain it her way.

"Sometimes people take games too seriously; they fight, and real feelings are hurt. You have experienced this, yes?"

The squirts all agreed they had.

"Now imagine instead of teams, one bay against another, you have... sharks. Sharks against squirts." It was not the best example, but it would do.

Most stilled, many of them flashing stripes of pink. Two jetted toward their teacher.

"That is not a game, is it?"

"No."

"Now imagine that sharks had intelligence, drive and culture as we do. And they wanted not just one meal, but all that we have. Wanted our bays, our creation spaces, our land-based cities, our blinkships. And tried to kill us all to get it. We would have to kill them to defend our families, our lives. That is war. It is ugly and rapacious. The semqu consider war an infectious idea, an ideology that is evil."

"But sharks do eat us!"

"Yes. And on occasion we kill sharks who get too comfortable feeding near our bays, to protect you." Waatoos forced her skin to stay kelp green as she lied. Killing singular sharks was difficult. Squirts who fed sharks because they swam too far were considered teaching examples for those who survived. Only the rare greedy sharks who hunted adults were considered worth the trouble to eliminate: a brutal cultural truth Vasom parents hid from their young. "But we do not wipe sharks from the sea. They serve a purpose."

Foele's skin turned black-brown with yellow splotches—hatred and fury. He would be happy to wipe all sharks from the sea. *Good to know.*

"Sharks do not attack us for anything other than a meal," she continued. "Mass murder for resources or territory or power is wrong."

"It's wrong to defend ourselves?" another squirt asked. Two of its arms had chunks of flesh taken out. Others had been picking on them by biting their arms and trying to eat them.

"No," Waatoos said. She remembered such harsh games and suddenly wished anyone else had answered the first squirt. "But choosing the right defense can be difficult. It takes maturity and calm to know how best to respond to an attack. You may never know if you've made the right choice. If you respond in anger, you might overreact. Even kill another and be judged a murderer."

"You might not survive if you don't," the squirt said.

"A bitter truth." One she had never heard acknowledged by an adult when she herself was a squirt. Her adult companions were various shades of uneasy. *Emotional cowards.* She regarded the bitten one more closely. Their conflicting emotions led her to believe that either this squirt or at least one of their bullies would not survive to adulthood. Maybe not the next season. She decided she would wager on this one. "I am both sorry and glad that you understand that."

The teacher had finally arrived, waves of pink unease rolling around his skin, arms around the scared squirts who'd fled to him. "These new aliens know war?"

Waatoos was grateful for the interruption. "They had a history of war on their old planet. Just as we had, though we do not speak of it now."

All of the adults paled, with jagged lines of disapproval and fear betraying deep discomfort. Waatoos was speaking aloud about erased knowledge.

It was past time they learned of her new profession. They needed to start taking her more seriously. Perhaps it would even help them grow up. "Spacers have renounced such acts."

The yellow-orange of nausea flashed to her right. The teacher, at least, knew what she was. He swiftly herded the squirts away, then jetted back to apologize with deference.

"Be calm," Waatoos said. "All of us, even squirts, need to learn that war must be prevented at all costs. This is semqu law." She said it with certainty. It evoked in her old compatriots that complicated brownish green steaked with white: fear-respect.

Truly, hadn't she earned it? She wanted to preen, but no. *Remain humble.* She could not let hubris corrupt her behavior.

Anyone with sense feared the Krufrugaan, the enforcers for the semqu. Even fellow Krufrugaan.

FRUITING BELLY OF THE FIFTH WEAVING NEST, PLANET VASOM

SEMQU YEAR 1142
(NEW HOPIAN YEAR 716)

THERE ARE Aupoin on each Council planet, and they are intimately familiar with the semqu. Semqu are immutable, essential, a source of housing, food and purpose, and the system-wide decisions they made rarely impacted the daily lives of any individual aupoin, most of whom nest communally underground.

So Aupoin were largely indifferent to the news of the discovery of yet another species, even an alien one. Such an aupoin was E-uuui-i, who had spent her larval years in the fifth weaving nest on Waatoos Hecht's planet of Vasom.

Flush from the joy of her adulting ceremony, E-uuui-i was helping the day-crew harvest in the blessedly dark fruiting chamber. She used two of her eight arms to slice mushrooms free and place them in the woven baskets. Someone rushed in, disrupting the quiet by snorting and stomping.

"There you are!" O-eee-u trumpeted.

E-uuui-i shivered with irritation; he was too loud. A few of the elders said as much; he ignored them, weaving around her fellow harvesters to trot to her side. Why had she ever let him imprint on her scent? She had been young and stupid.

"Have you heard?!" he blared. "A new people have come to Se System!"

"If you have nothing better to do than gossip, young one, you can help with the harvest," a nearby elder said. O-eee-u ignored him, too.

She had not heard, not that she cared, and he seemed oblivious to the fact that she was angry with him. "That's nice," E-uuui-i said. She sliced one of the mushrooms she was harvesting in half and had to recut the base properly.

"Nice? It's fantastic! It's the most exciting thing to happen since... since... since I don't know how long! They're going to Trye! We can go work there!"

"Enjoy the journey," E-uuui-i said. "If you had bothered to attend my adulting ceremony today, you would know that I'm already committed to Aun."

"Aun! That frozen planet? Why would you do that? I don't want to go there! We could never go outside. It'll be cold and miserable!"

"It is a quiet, tight community. They take their weaving seriously. They have fantastic community patterns. I enjoy connecting with the semqu," she said with practiced tact, because she knew this was a sensitive topic for him, "and their semqu is old and established. The kertueon leave them alone. Unlike our modeel," she said, more bitterly than she intended.

"Our modeel are great! You just haven't gotten to see their good side. We'll tell the organizers you've changed your mind; you'll have great friends when we move to the surface—"

She had reveled in her adulting rite and the respect of her elders. It was fresh in her mind, and yet O-eee-u still treated her like a child. Her anger surged. "I am not living on the surface. Nor am I moving anywhere with you."

"E-uuui-i, stop it. You've been joking like that for months," he said. "You're my mate for life. You would have talked to me before—"

"No. I am not." It upset her that he was making her be so rude in front of elders, but he was being unspeakably rude himself, ignoring her stated wishes. "I am not making a joke. Our collectives have already sung the agreement, at the rite you could not be bothered to attend, and the semqu there welcomes me."

"You can't trust—" O-eee-u broke off.

Her bristles stiffened; he had just stopped himself from saying something horrible.

O-eee-u had never melded with Vasom4 as a child. No one had ever been able to fix his connection; he seemed afraid of her. Afraid! Of the semqu who fed them!

Certainly, disconnection happened before, if rarely; sometimes pups were hatched who could not connect. But O-eee-u had baffled the collective; they'd never had anyone with such a ruptured relationship.

It was as if O-eee-u deliberately sabotaged all his relationships, she thought. He seemed to have done the same to her, all while claiming to want her partnership.

"I will sing in hope that you connect well with the semqu of Trye," E-uuui-i said.

"I don't want that!" O-eee-u blared.

"There are many other avenues open to you, youngster." The elder next to them had been paying attention, despite E-uuui-i hoping he was not. "You can be an emissary for the semqu, you can join the surface workers and be a liaison to modeel, or with these new people on Trye if you like. My cousin could not connect to the semqu; he works on blinkships now. The galaxy is open to you, if you wish to be a traveling one."

"I want E-uuui-i!"

E-uuui-i wilted away in horror.

"She has said no, and that is final." The elder gusted with irritation. "Youth, you are like a rustling winged beetle, noisy, in motion, never returning to the same spot. E-uuui-i is a rooted plant. There could never have been any hope of a future between two so different. How could you be so blind to both your qualities?"

"You're just ashamed of me because I'm not a Semule," O-eee-u said.

To confuse healthy connection with a mindless worship of semqu was insulting. O-eee-u sounded ridiculous, "anger rolling through every segment," as an adult would say of a larvae-youth.

"What kind of nonsense is this?" The elder asked.

E-uuui-i allowed her scents to fully convey her frustration. "He acts like this every time I tell him no."

"Enough! This will stop!" the elder blared, and the others in the room took up the cry. They crowded around O-eee-u, their bulk blocking him from view, and physically herded him from the room.

E-uuui-i continued the harvest with relief and gratitude. The elders' support confirmed her feelings; she was done with O-eee-u's immaturity. He claimed to have feelings for her but couldn't be bothered to attend the most important rite of her life. And then didn't apologize for missing it! She trusted in the wisdom of her elders; they would ensure he was sent far from her new nest.

O-eee-u's afternoon emigration was announced at mealtime, along with the news about new residents on Trye, travelers from many suns away who had been invited to join Se Collective. E-uuui-i had not been the only nest member to have trouble with O-eee-u. His exit evoked a general feeling of relief that bled into the hive's opinion of their new neighbors. Contentment, trust. The semqu rarely made mistakes.

Two days later, she herself left for Aun.

ABOARD NEW HOPE: QUARTIER VIVANT, VOICE'S CHAMBERS
NEW HOPIAN YEAR 716
EIGHTH MONTH, TWENTY-SEVENTH DAY

VOICE WOKE FROM A VIVID, complex dream to a persistent tapping.

She sat up, aware she wasn't in her own bed. Or her family's dwell. Had parts of her dream been real? Was she in a mental holding room? She remembered a dream from earlier in the night; the entire colony ship had been moved in the blink of an eye after she'd been infected with a telepathic alien who'd showed her how to fly and changed her name.

She climbed out of the weighted sleeping wrap and opened the covered viewport in the wall. Light from the closest star she'd ever seen glimmered off the surface of water on a blue and white orb below. She glimpsed swaths of green and brown through breaks in what her brain insisted had to be cloud cover.

She was looking at a planet.

How much of my dream was real?

<Parts of it,> her mental companion said. It sounded as groggy as she felt. <Spacer dreams are fascinating. I tried to teach you Fugrast while you were asleep, but the places your brain took us kept interfering.>

<Lucid dreaming takes practice,> Voice said. Why was she not freaking out about this alien in her head? More of the actual events reasserted themselves, as did her bladder. After she took care of her body, she was more fully awake, and she thought to ask, <Are you okay? You were pretty worn out.>

<I am still exhausted, and weak, and angry with myself for panicking,> the semqu said.

<You? You panicked? Why?>

<It's complicated. Part of it was the poison, I think.>

A wave of exhaustion flowed over her. Voice sat back down on the bed.

<I had to let much of my body die.>

The conversation about fungicide reasserted itself in her mind. <I am so very sorry.>

<You did not know. You are not to blame,> the semqu told her. <And you cannot share that.>

<I will remember,> Voice thought. <Will you be okay?>

<I will recover. Your body needs to eat, and hydrate. Your people are worried about you; you have slept long. And the others are practically beating on your ship's hull to talk to your leaders. I've held them off until this afternoon; two bells in your time-keeping scheme. Additional rest will wait until tonight.>

<Can you not rest while I'm awake?>

<Not fully; but some of me can. We live on a much longer, slower time frame than you do.>

That tapping began again. Someone was knocking on her door. Voice padded out into an open, spacious living room, with chairs and a writing desk, an actual living space where guests could feel welcome.

A wave of pleasure washed over her. She now had her own space, where no one could tell her she could not make a mess, or to put a project away as soon as she'd started working on it. She could leave a book open on her desk and not come back to find it closed.

She stopped at the door, unwilling to share this new sanctuary with anyone else before she'd explored it properly herself. "Who's there?"

"Opal? Finally! What have you been doing?" Her mother's outrage was unmistakable. "It's been two days!" Voice imagined Harriet bustling in, deciding what furniture she needed, cleaning up, telling her she'd only been here for two days and look at this mess—

"No. I mean, I'm fine, but my name is Voice now," she said firmly.

Captain Ximena added, "Voice, we're worried about you. Can you open the door?"

She shouldn't refuse the captain. Voice tapped the pad. The door slid aside with a slight groan. Captain Ximena and Harriet stood side by side, the first looking like an unhappy royal who'd rather be anywhere else and Harriet like a firefighter on a mission. Opal could not have faced two more imposing women, and yet her knees felt firm.

A young man in an officer's tunic stood against the wall near Captain Ximena, his back to Voice. Between his arm and the wall, she saw Adamantine peeking out from a doorway. Hiding from Harriet, not Opal. "You okay?" her sister gestured.

Voice rocked her fist at hip level, gave her a tentative smile. Could they start over now?

Harriet, oblivious, took a step forward.

"I'm not ready for visitors," Voice said. It was Harriet's phrase, one she used to stop people from coming into their dwell during a fiber-arts day.

Harriet halted, mouth open in silent shock.

"I've been sleeping," Voice said. "The transition was hard on my body and—" She started to say, "The move was tiring for the Semqu," and discovered she couldn't move the necessary air.

<Omit my weakness from your conversations.>

<Of course,> she thought. <My apologies.> She wondered at her swift agreement—had she replaced one controlling master with another? But she should have expected freedom would have come with a price, shouldn't she?

"And?" her mother prompted.

"And I needed to rest," Voice said. Mère was holding a small pile of clean clothes. "OH! Thank you, Harriet." She saw her mother flinch at the informal use of her first name. "I'll need these today," she said with a slight bow, and reached for the clothes.

Harriet released them reluctantly. "I thought I'd put these away for you."

"No time, and that's my job anyway." She had an irrational worry that her mother would never leave once she got in the door. "Captain, I understand that you need my translation services today. We have new neighbors who wish to discuss trade with us."

"We do?" Captain Ximena asked. She looked stunned.

Harriet's mouth dropped open slightly and then snapped shut.

"We do," Voice said. "In lieu of a ship meeting for a representative, you are our decision-maker, yes?"

"I suppose," Captain Ximena said uncomfortably. "But I should discuss this with the council."

"Call an emergency meeting, then," Voice said. "I need to clean up, and eat, and the representatives are on their way, in a blinkship. Tell me which of the large meeting rooms you'd like to greet them in—"

"Wait, they're coming here? They can't do that, we don't know if they carry diseases, if our atmosphere needs are compatible—they could exhale pathogens that could endanger the entire ship! We'll likely be carrying viruses or pathogens they've never encountered!" Captain Ximena was normally unflappable, but her eyes were wide, and her palms faced Opal, flat, the gesture for stop.

Everyone has an overwhelm point, Voice thought. A counselor had told her that once, and she hadn't believed it.

The semqu said, <This is a common and understandable concern. It has been addressed. When they arrive, they will carry nothing that can harm you. You will carry nothing that can harm them. Pick a room whose air you can flush after the meeting if you do not believe me.>

Voice repeated that, with slightly more cheerful phrasing, for the captain's benefit.

Captain Ximena responded sternly, "You're asking me to trust the lives of everyone on this ship to the judgment of this alien."

Voice blinked at her. "Captain, with all due respect, if they didn't want us alive, they wouldn't have gone to all the effort to move us to a habitable planet."

The captain's expression softened. "Do you think they understand us well enough to make this call?"

"I think they categorize every life form they encounter, from viruses to slime molds to creatures I don't want to think about living on my skin, so, yes. Yes, ma'am. What time is it?"

"Eleven bells."

"Homophones." Voice's shoulders sagged. "They'll be here in three hours. Pardon, I don't wish to be rude, but I need to change. I'm afraid I slept in this tunic—for two days, really?"

"Really," Harriet said, full of disapproval.

The captain cut her eyes to Harriet but simply nodded.

Voice discovered she didn't feel in the slightest chastised, but she wanted to seem normal, so she said, "I didn't mean to worry anyone."

Harriet said, "Well, you did." The captain tapped her with the side of her shoe. "Ah. Do you need anything, Opal—Voice?"

Her mother was trying to adjust. The strain in her tone triggered an ingrained response; she had done something wrong. She would normally have been overwhelmed with a need to figure out what Mère was upset about and fix it.

But she was Voice now. Fixing Harriet's emotional upset was no longer her task. Her job had changed with her name. It was an epiphany and a relief. What a burden that had been!

"I don't know yet," Voice said. "I'll tell someone when I do."

Various emotions flickered across Harriet's features, pausing on stunned. Then her cheeks reddened, and her eyes narrowed.

Captain Ximena intervened. "Let's get you fed. I'll check in with the council. I'm going to assign you a minder for the time being—someone who'll ensure you get to eat and not be hounded to death with questions and demands." She motioned the young man forward.

Voice recognized him as a fellow Quiet Quarter resident a few years older than herself, a teen in his first adult position. He'd been a determined weightlifter until he'd broken his leg, and then he'd switched to art with a vengeance. She'd rarely seen him without a sketchpad. His portrait of his mother in a decorated top had been honored in the shipwide art festival the year before, controversial because he titled it "Ethiopian" instead of Northwest African. Nationalism almost destroyed the mission once, so some saw it as subversive and dangerous.

"This is Gregoire Efran," the captain said.

He was a head taller than Voice, a mature youth whose wide face was always lively in thought and intensity. He bowed to her, giving her a close view of precise glistening cornrows on his oversized skull, deep black on skin two shades lighter. He smelled of hair oil and cardamom, and normally she felt completely comfortable in his presence.

This was not a normal moment. Voice bowed back automatically. "Bonjour! Yes, I know Gregoire. I don't think I'll need to bother him or anyone else with all that."

"You will," the captain said grimly. "He'll be out here when you're ready. Go change."

Being alone with her clothes sounded much less awkward. Voice hit the closure for the door as the captain told Gregoire, "Make sure she gets undisturbed time to eat, she'll only have an hour. And that includes her family."

The door snapped shut on Harriet's whistling snort. Voice's brief sensation of guilt vanished immediately. She took a shower. Harriet had brought a towel, but there were thicker ones in the bathroom, so she used one of those. She felt better once she was dressed, and hungry.

Gregoire was waiting in the hall. She awkwardly said hello again, which was only compounded by his request to help her move a small pile of gifts inside. People from all over the ship had dropped off little packages of food and goodwill gifts.

"Not everyone is happy about our new situation," Gregoire said, "So we already checked all the food gifts. Nothing here should make you sick unless you have allergies your mother doesn't know about."

"Very unlikely," Voice muttered. Harriet had tested every food in the cafeteria on her, much to her dismay.

Unearned gifts were more worrying to her than the idea that someone might harm her, but the latter elicited a wave of unsettled feeling from her mind's companion. <I will protect you.>

"Voice is awake!" A child down the hall called. "Hello, Voice!" She waved as heads popped out of doorways, people waved and said hello, and then withdrew. Surprising behavior on a lively floor, but then they were probably giving her space.

<I don't think you'll have to protect me.> She couldn't imagine why anyone other than Père would want to hurt her, and he knew better now.

As they headed toward the spiral tubes, Gregoire said, "Tock twice if someone's approaching who you do not want to talk to;

touch my hand if it's someone you're willing to delay eating for. Our priority is lunch."

"Okay," Voice said, bewildered. She waved at a pair of friendly children dancing in the hallway, one of whom halted, put their fingers in their mouth and stared. As they approached a trio of musicians, the drummer set down his bodhran and patted the knee of the woman playing an erhu. The flute player trailed off. All three looked up, eyes worried.

"Please, keep playing!" she said. "That sounded lovely. I don't want any neighbors to change their lives because I'm living here now. I think I'm going to really enjoy living here."

"Ah! Welcome!" They dove back into their music with deep grins.

In the main corridor outside, one of Père's more intimidating colleagues, Saira Keo, was waiting and didn't accept, "When I'm done eating, I can answer questions." Gregoire put himself between the woman and Voice and told her to talk to the captain if he wanted, but Voice had to eat. Then he reminded Voice to tock her tongue.

When they exited the spiral drop on the cafeteria level, another person saw them and gestured "Wait," forehead wrinkled in what looked like anger. She tocked, and Gregoire gestured, "Later." The man honored that, but followed them.

"Are they all lying in wait for me?" Voice asked, after another man she didn't know had swept out of a hallway and accosted them, raining scientific questions so fast Voice could barely understand, and had tocked six times.

"Pretty much. Remember the rumors after the alien sighting?"

"Yes. OH." People had gone to huge lengths to try to talk to anyone who'd been on duty that morning.

"Half of them just want a look at you to make sure you haven't sprouted an extra set of arms."

"Had to check myself," Voice muttered, which wasn't true, but it made Gregoire laugh, and that gave her a nice warm glow that the anti-emotion overlay created by her semqu didn't completely wipe away.

Her semqu? <I have never asked you your name.>

The response was so weary she was sorry to have interrupted the semqu's rest. <I have never had need for an individual identifier. Let me think.>

She left it alone. Gregoire said they were stopped sixteen times before they finally reached the cafeteria. She was grateful the questioners were curious more often than angry.

Much, much later, she'd thank the captain for being proactive.

While Voice had slept, Captain Ximena had the remote sensing team explain to the entire ship's population about the death of the planet they'd been headed toward, why the group had kept it as a shut-it, and at what personal cost.

It had helped shift the perception of what had happened away from a resentful fear that they'd been kidnapped to a gratitude for salvation from a certain death. Voice walked into a bubble of goodwill tinged with speculation and worry, rather than a riot of pure paranoia.

She also walked into a cloud of aroma; basil and garlic permeated the air. Voice was abruptly ravenous.

The room was noisy with shouts and laughter and conversation, though only half-full, about thirty adults and as many children, and one table of dancers and their instructor, but not Adamantine. Conversations stopped as Voice entered with Gregoire. One teen squealed and two small children started to run toward them, only to be snagged by an adult who looked terrified.

It worried and embarrassed Voice. Silence was often used for community punishment.

"Is it my hair?" Gregoire asked, loudly. "Or do you have a boyfriend I don't know about?" His words carried. A few people blushed, or raised their eyebrows, or looked away. Conversations started back up, a babble that rose to about half the original volume.

Indirect censure worked best on most people.

Voice's edge of anxiety vanished immediately. "Maybe they think you're Gengi come to life. Or that you're stepping out on—do you have a girlfriend?" She felt freed, alive; she'd only been able to banter with members of her anxiety support group, and never this easily.

"I do, but she knows what my job is," he said, seriously. "Unlike some people in here at the moment." That was directed at those still pointing and staring, for whom the indirect censure hadn't worked. A short woman snapped her lips together in disapproval, and the pointers dropped their arms, some with assistance.

As Voice and Gregoire stepped up to the serving line, three people headed their way, eyes on Voice. Her anxiety spiked again and then vanished.

Gregoire held out a hand, flat-palmed, and addressed those approaching in a volume that carried across the room. "Voice has a meeting with the captain and representatives of our neighboring planets soon. She hasn't eaten in two days. After she has eaten, if she has time, she will try to answer questions. Solve who gets to ask them yourselves and *include everyone*."

Those approaching halted with exasperated expressions; one woman threw up her hands in apparent frustration. Then the room erupted with questions and chatter. Gregoire waved his hands, shooing them back, and people turned, began to clump together. Children clamored loudest.

"Random ballot!"

"Rock paper scissors!"

"Dance competition!"

"Sing-off!"

"You are brilliant," Voice told him. He bowed.

"You haven't eaten in two days?" One of the serving crew was standing behind the warming dishes, wide-eyed.

"Truly," Voice gave the woman her complete attention. "I was so exhausted. I'm starving!"

"Well. We can fix that. Name your favorites!"

Voice practically floated to a table near the door, which Gregoire had somehow cleared for her, her plate piled with food she liked.

Mère had been going through a phase where she was convinced her younger daughter's diet was causing the anxiety issues. Voice could not remember the last time she'd had a plate that didn't contain at least one food she couldn't stand. Her mouth swam with saliva.

The noise of debate and discussion from the impromptu circle across the room buffeted her in waves. She didn't have to worry until they fell quiet. The servers had been excessively generous with her rice serving—it was a full day's ration. Voice ate that quickly, hoping no one would begrudge her the double serving. She would have to watch that. People who were ill got such care, but she didn't want special treatment on an ongoing basis.

Gregoire got up twice to bring her additional beverages. "Two days without fluid is dangerous, let's get you rehydrated." His wording was close enough to the semqu's to make her giggle again.

She ate steadily and with delight, savoring the garlic green beans and mushroom slices in a basil-garlic sauce. She'd opted for grasshoppers instead of oysters—she didn't like the texture—and the sauce on them was rich and complex.

"I want to ask for the recipe for this the next time I do a kitchen shift," she said.

Gregoire gave her an odd look, but only said, "It is delicious."

When her plate was clean, she started to pick it up.

Gregoire took the plate and her sani-melts. "I'll take care of this. You decide what your boundaries on questions are. You have half an hour; I'm building in time for you to take a bathroom break back in your dwell and prep with the captain for your meeting."

"Thank you." She'd always liked Gregoire's gentle straightforwardness.

Boundaries. That was a good idea. The semqu had subjects that were off-limits. She let her eyes roam the mural on the near wall, which began as a cheerful bright depiction of people cooking in all manner of Earth kitchens and ended with communal meals here. Her glance fell on their half-full plates, a reminder of the food restrictions of the mid-journey when several crop failures had nearly doomed the mission. Shut-its had become a thing shortly after that, because sabotage had been involved in one of the crop failures.

Spacers should understand that semqu needed shut-its too. She could use that if necessary. But shut-its implied dangerous secrets, and dangerous secrets scared people, or made them nervous. She would need to be careful.

As the crowd quietly started to gather in front of her, Adamantine and her friends Rupert and Marfa entered the cafeteria.

"What's going on?" Adamantine asked. Several of her fellow dancers and their instructor were in the crowd sitting in front of Voice and gave each other looks.

Her sister hated it when someone else was the center of attention.

Two of the girls jumped up and hurried over to Adamantine. "We had a great idea, let's go practice," one said. They each grabbed an arm and hurried Adamantine out of the cafeteria. The dance instructor strolled after them, gesturing at Voice, "Answer well, we are curious."

Our community, caring for us both, Voice thought gratefully.

It turned out the questions, when they arrived, had been selected by random ballot, because that was the fastest way. Voice smiled. That meant the children would get equal billing. This might be fun.

And indeed, a young child was first, fidgeting and earnest. "Did it hurt? When the semqu picked you, and you learned to talk for them? Did it hurt like when the ship moved and—?"

"One question!" another child hissed, and he halted, biting his lip.

Voice smiled. "That's so kind, to think of me and my feelings when your own life has changed," she said. "You're the first person to ask me anything like that."

The boy brightened. Several adults shifted uncomfortably, and the crowd fell silent. Even Gregoire stilled. She hadn't meant to be mean about it, so she added, "The community taught you well, to think of others at such a time."

"Um. I don't remember pain—and it seems so long ago now. There was discomfort, made worse because I was afraid," she said. "I didn't know what was happening, and of course the semqu couldn't explain until it was complete. I had a seizure, and then I couldn't move for some time." She didn't want the children afraid of the semqu, so she paused. "The brain work mostly ... tickled? It was hard on my body, I guess, that's why I had to sleep so long. It certainly doesn't hurt now. I feel great now, and full. Today's food is fabulous!" She started clapping, and everyone applauded the cooks.

People followed her lead! A wave of odd warmth passed through her, prickly but good. She saw Marfa and Rupert at the edge of the crowd, frowning. Well, she couldn't expect to please everybody.

A wary grandmother was next. "What do these semqu want with us?"

"They want us to live," Voice said. "They realized we were headed toward death and that made them unhappy. They value life, even when it is odd to them. We are very odd," she smiled, "to them."

The woman looked sideways at her, wrinkles at the edges of her eyes tightening as if she wanted more. But she seemed to accept Voice's answer.

Another youth asked, "What are they like, these—semqu?"

"Semqu, yes. I wish I could tell you that. It's— it's a mind connection, but often not a verbal one. I get flashes of insight about how they communicate with other species. I sense a lot of experiences, like while the semqu was ... introducing themself? ... I got to experience what it is to fly and to swim, from their experiences with other translators! Amazing. But I don't yet have a good sense of the semqu themselves. I don't know what they look like or what shape they take. I don't even have a name yet for the one who has contacted me."

"How does it talk to you if it's not on the ship?" asked an infrastructure tech she recognized; the woman had fixed the plumbing in her family's chambers a few years back. "I mean, how does this alien access your brain?"

"I don't know how," Voice said, trying to avoid lying. "But if you mean what it's like…most of the communication is in pictures and thoughts. Some of it is fast and clear. They've learned to explain subjects that impact spacers in images that make sense to me. Most of the time, anyway. But translating semqu things into spacer, like who and what they are, has been really hard. And honestly, we haven't had much time together yet, I slept most of it. I might know more after the meeting this afternoon. We're meeting with I think it's three or maybe four representatives of sentient species from across what they call the Se System, or the Se Collective."

"Aliens?! Here?" Marfa yelled. She looked terrified.

"Yes!" Voice said cheerfully, over children's cries of "Not your turn!"

"Which is where?" Rupert yelled.

"Not your turn!"

"That's okay, it's my turn and that's my question too," a young woman said. "Where are we?"

Voice blinked. "We're in orbit around Trye, in the Se Collective."

"Yes, but where is that?" she repeated.

"I don't understand the question." Voice turned to Gregoire.

"We haven't been able to locate ourselves in relation to Earth," Gregoire said. He lifted his hands together, then pulled his right hand away from his left. "We knew where we were before they moved us." He stopped his right hand, then danced it around his left. "But we don't know what direction they moved us in, and there's a lot of gas cloud interference with stellar observations right now. We have no idea where we are in the galaxy."

"Oh." She was not going to bother the alien's rest for something she was pretty sure they couldn't answer. "They don't think of places and distances in the same way we do. And I doubt they know where Earth is. We'll have to figure that out on our own or ask a modeel." She saw frustration on a few faces. Rupert looked annoyed. Even Gregoire seemed preoccupied. This was important to people, just not her.

"I know!" she said. "Make it an Everyone Competition! 'Where Are We Now?' The observations should be enough after a week of being here to figure it out."

A group of children thought that was a splendid idea, and were far more interested in that, suddenly, than some mysterious powerful creature they couldn't see. They ran off to make up the rules. That left mostly adults.

"One last question," Voice said. "Because I think I need to spend more time with my semqu to learn more so I can answer you."

Gregoire interjected smoothly, "Please, if you would send me or the captain your questions, we'll share them all with Voice and see if the semqu will share the answers as they learn more about one another." He gestured toward Voice. "That way you'll know what to ask the semqu."

She gestured, "Yes, thank you," while wondering why he wanted to put a barrier between her and the community. But then, wasn't it fair that everyone's questions got answered, not just those who happened to have access to her?

The last question was from one of the intent scientists who'd tried to intercept her before she ate. "HOW did they move us?"

Right. She had to correct that. "They didn't, and I should have been clearer about that. The ships we saw moved us. The semqu

asked some modeel, one of our new neighbors, for help. Modeel spaceships are called blinkships because they move the way they moved us, as fast as the blink of an eye. They combined their efforts. Together, they were able to move *New Hope* and change our speed to put us in a stable orbit. It was an extremely complicated group effort."

"That's not a how, that's a who," Rupert said. "Or a what."

How was definitely a shut-it. Voice shrugged. "I don't think the semqu that contacted me even understands that. I sure don't."

"Is nobody going to ask her about the planet?" a child burst out. "We get to move down there! She said there's already creatures living there! Is nobody curious about that?!" Tiny beads dangling from her tri-knotted hair shook as she gestured her exasperation.

"I know!" Voice grinned at the child's intensity. "There are so many details to sort out and learn."

"And aliens? You said you're meeting with aliens?" someone else yelled.

"Yes! I agree with Gregoire, give all your questions to him or the captain, and as I learn more I will share. I'll have to start teaching you all Fugrast, anyway." Voice stood. "But I have to go now."

"Fugrast?" Gregoire rose too.

"Fugrast is the common tongue of Se Collective," she said, loudly enough that the children across the room could hear. "We all have a new language to learn."

Groans and cheers followed her out the door.

ABOARD NEW HOPE, VOICE'S CHAMBERS
NEW HOPIAN YEAR 716
EIGHTH MONTH, TWENTY-SEVENTH DAY

VOICE'S BLADDER was nearly bursting when she and Gregoire made it back to her door. Captain Ximena was waiting for them. "Gregoire, yes, run to your quarters."

The young man turned and nearly ran; was his bladder in pain too?

The captain turned back to Voice. "We need to quickly touch on a few topics, but please, take care of your needs first."

Voice made her own run, and then returned, feeling awkward. The captain was still standing in her living area, and she would have to give her spiel right away. "Oh! Please sit." Her first guest, she thought, somewhat giddily, and then realized she had nothing to offer her to drink. Anxiety spiked and died. It left a familiar metallic taste in her mouth: panic's residue without the panic.

"I brought no visiting gifts, twice now," Captain Ximena said, obviously as uncomfortable at the breach of etiquette as she was. "So perhaps we can postpone ritual to a less time-limited moment?"

"Yes, Ximena-nim," Voice said, with gratitude. "That would be wonderful." The joy from that gratitude was also flattened, but she clung to what she could feel of it, wrapping its warmth around her sour stomach.

"You don't have to use honorifics with me, Voice. I think you've earned your adulthood early. We will honor that with a proper rite, later, but I officially recognize you as an adult, here, now, today. I'm a little worried about that for you, but... you weren't having a fantastic childhood, were you?"

"No, Xime—" Voice stopped, honored by the captain's respect. "Not really."

"May you have a better adulthood. I wish we had more time to get to know one another, we will fix that in the coming weeks. Right now—well. Do I understand this semqu has already taught you a language?"

"Some of it." She didn't trust that she knew Fugrast well enough to speak it yet; the semqu was going to have to translate for her.

Telepathy was okay for concepts, but talking trade meant details. She explained that concern. "And—I'm sure I'm not the translator you would prefer." She took a deep breath and plunged into the lowering-of-expectations speech she'd given every mentor in her life. "I'm only 13, and people like me, but I'm not sure why. Père says I have the personality of a wet sponge. I'm clumsy, easily distracted, and so anxious I've been basically useless. I'm kind of a failure."

It came out choppy and shorter than usual. The statement usually left her desolate and broken. It didn't today. Just flat and like she'd misspoken or even lied.

Captain Ximena did not look like her expectations had been lowered; she looked concerned. "Voice, you wildly overstate your weaknesses. I am told you are meticulous, loyal, compassionate, open-minded, grateful, and you pick up on others' emotional states quickly. You're somewhat unambitious and self-sacrificing, two good characteristics in a translator from my point of view."

Voice blinked; she'd never had anyone she didn't know well give her such a wide-ranging compliment before, and she didn't know how to react.

"I'd hate to have to deal with Adamantine in this position."

"Aïe." Voice's eyes widened and her heart squeezed a little at the idea of her elder sister translating for her semqu.

Ximena smiled. "And in response to your concern about details, let's avoid them. My crash course in diplomacy tells me that first meetings should always be limited to getting to know one another. Business should wait. Conduct it too early, and you'll make egregious errors of culture."

"Perfect," Voice said, and her last worries evaporated.

"Will you be able to translate cultural context?"

"Some of it? Modeel communicate emotions with color, and the semqu will help me with that."

"Good. Please translate anything you learn or intuit about the interactions among them and with us. If you feel it would be best to wait until after the meeting to do so, that's fine, just let me know, and give me your full feedback as you can."

"I will."

"It'll just be you and me, and Gregoire if he insists. A volunteer medical crew will examine us afterwards, and put us all in quarantine, if necessary," Ximena said. "So. Who are we meeting? Can you prepare me at all?"

"The easiest one to explain is our new underground neighbors on Trye, the Aupoin. Did you ever see my stuffed toy, Genji? He's a tardigrade, and they've got sort of the same shape and number of legs. Spacer-sized and larger. I don't know how big they get, but I don't think they stop growing."

"I see." Ximena blinked.

"The others." Voice took a deep breath. "We're also meeting with a peqe and a modeel." She was on riskier ground now, remembering from her dreams. The semqu in her head was quiet, had been since before lunch. "Peqe are bigger and stronger than we are, the women particularly. And we'll only meet women. Strong, very long toothy jaws, both fur and feathery crest."

"Flight?"

"No, they don't have wings. The Gruide do—" more information was suddenly available in her mind. Her head ached. "But we won't meet them today. Anyway, I don't know how to describe them—a cross between a bipedal dinosaurs and a spacer, maybe? They're matriarchal and mean. Very long jaw, like dinosaurs. Lots of teeth and pretty fur, and a feathery back...thing."

"Mean?"

"They won't be mean to you. Maybe you should wait to see them for yourself?" Voice said hurriedly. "Peqe value service. They worship a goddess. They have a very rigid social structure." Voice struggled to remember some of her Earth vocabulary. "Class or caste is the word I think I'm looking for? They're like some of the worst of ancient Earth human societies, only with women at the head instead of men. They wouldn't talk to

Gregoire or Père, especially not if you or I were available, for example."

"Backwards, then."

"They think they're the elite of the entire galaxy," Voice said.

"Fantástica." Ximena put her face in her hands.

"Modeel can't breathe our air. You'll only see them in hard suits, which look like big robots or mech toys. You'll need to not get too close, physically I mean, because they have a bioelectric field that can zap you. It's a safety feature they can't fully control. It's very colorful; they use them to show their emotions. They're probably the most advanced in technology and science. The blinkships you saw, the ones that brought us here, were all modeel-made."

"Interesting. Spacefaring, working in collaboration with these semqu?"

"They respect one another, yes," Voice said hurriedly. "And I think protective of their technology? Modeel trade a lot of manufactured items but not their engines, which are off-limits."

"Hm. Our engineers will have a fit about that."

Voice had a sudden image of three aliens shooing away those of their own kind and nodding to someone she couldn't see.

<They arrive.>

<Coming.> "Now we need to get there, because they're on their way."

Ximena sent a quick message to Gregoire. As they walked down the corridors, Voice adjusted her tunic and practiced her box-count breath, out of habit. She loved the idea of being important to her people. But an in-person interaction with aliens was something that would have left her curled on the floor hyperventilating just two days ago.

They passed Voice's favorite mural, the one that featured Ireti Nabuco, the captain responsible for the first Accord, who had steered the ship through the upheaval during and after the Mental Police uprising. Voice took in her big Bantu knots, angular features, and kind eyes. The proud woman's portrait had always given Voice a boost on bad days. Today she didn't even feel a flicker of joy. *This new job is going to cost me a few things, too.*

Gregoire caught up with them just past the mural, panting and limping a little. He was carrying a digi sketch.

"Oh, that's a good idea!" Voice said. "You can share your drawings with the children!"

Ximena and Gregoire shared a startled glance, and Gregoire said, "Uh, sure!"

"Voice, I should have asked this first. Do you know what our visitors want?" Ximena asked.

"To get a look at us, I think." Voice said. "If you had an entirely new species moving into your galaxy, or in the aupoin's position, moving in above you, wouldn't you want to meet them?"

"That's fair," Ximena said. "Anything else you can tell me about these creatures?"

Voice felt a stab of guilt. She should be preparing the captain better. It was so hard to know what to say. In the captain's place, without the semqu, she'd be overwhelmed with anxiety. "The aupoin are diggers, miners and weavers, and live underground in tunnels," she said. "They're important for the health of trees and can bring us metal ores. They often work with modeel who are skilled at metal refining."

"Oh! We could barter?" Ximena asked.

"Yes. There is an active trade between the planets. Music is the largest portion of that but also meat and carved stone art from Taequa, metal tools and devices from Vasom, seafood and building materials from Ylas..."

"Three populated planets?" Gregoire interjected. He looked stunned.

"More. But we're just meeting with the aupoin, modeel and peqe representatives later today. That will be enough."

They were steps away from the doorway, and Voice could hear Fugrast being spoken ahead. "They're all already here!"

As Ximena triggered the door, Voice glimpsed three hulking

shapes inside. Directly in front of her lay the largest of the three, a ridged, bristly larvae-like creature the size of two adult spacers.

<Aupoin,> her tired semqu said. <She is Voice to Trye9.>

On Voice's left paced a huge muscular bipedal creature with a long, lizard-like snout and feather-like shoulder protrusions in iridescent colors cascading down a furred back. Many multi-colored braided fibers hung from a collar around her neck, a tunic-length decoration.

<Peqe. Not-Voice.>

Between those two squatted a spherical metallic robot about Gregoire's height. It was supported by two of its six appendages, surrounded by a quietly crackling brown aura interrupted with bright flashes of purple, red, and blue.

<Modeel. Not-Voice but known to me.>

Voice switched to what she hoped was passable Fugrast. The semqu had been cramming the words into her brain, but the long vowels were *difficult*. "Welcome aboard the *New Hope!* I'm sorry we weren't here to greet you properly."

A flower-like protrusion erupted from the near end of the aupoin and vibrated. "It is acceptable."

Voice understood it.

The peqe's long jaw opened, displaying a double row of teeth as long as Voice's arm. "It is not," she hissed. That was harder, but she got it.

The modeel waved an arm that ended in a claw and said, slowly, pausing between each word, "You cannot be angry at our hosts because they did not expect you to *ask* to be delivered early." Bubbles of blue floated through the largely brown bioelectric field that glimmered in the air around it.

Bubbles meant positive emotion. Brown was pride; blue, joy or happiness. The modeel both was proud to be here and delighted to derail the peqe's attempt at manipulating the situation. And Voice understood all of that.

Her shoulders relaxed a fraction. She could do this. It was

going to be okay. She pulled a deep breath of air into her lungs, along with the scent of fish, mushrooms and oil.

"The peqe asked to arrive early and didn't let us know," she told Captain Ximena, who had moved to her right and was taking her own long slow breaths. "So the other two did not expect us to be here waiting."

<I told you that you would do well.> The semqu's satisfied confidence in her buoyed her further.

"I see. Well, I'm just going to put this one," Ximena nodded at the aupoin, "between me and the one with all the teeth. And the … electric one." She was clearly fighting her nerves to stand ramrod straight. "Do they have names?"

Gregoire slid between the guests and Voice, motioning her back.

<They won't hurt any of you. They are here to ask questions.>

"We are safe here," Voice said. "You can relax and sketch, Gregoire." She turned back to their guests. "Honored guests, I am Voice to my people, the spacers, and this is our captain. She gestured to Ximena. We understand you have questions. So do we. Shall we begin with introductions?"

<Very good,> the semqu said.

Voice warmed. There was no time to think about what she was translating, at first. The peqe introduced herself as "Matron Peindak" and dove into a long, involved family lineage. Voice forgot halfway through where it was going. "Daughter of a name my tongue cannot form, daughter of a name I didn't catch, daughter of something that sounds like volcano, daughter of—sounds like mustache, daughter of—"

When the peqe ground to a halt, the modeel and aupoin did nothing, and Voice forced herself not to bow. "Uh, I don't think you should bow, Captain," she said. "She might interpret that as you admitting inferiority to her."

"Thank you, Voice. I'm recording this meeting so if we need to review those names for any reason we can."

"Bless all your generations back to Earth," Voice said fervently.

"Can you get them all to introduce themselves before I go?"

Voice froze. Her temporary confidence fled.

"Let's invent a spacer tradition about guests first?"

"Our tradition is that guests introduce themselves first," Voice said, in Fugrast.

The modeel said, "Before we go on, what is the person by the door doing?"

"Gregoire, they're curious about your arm movements," Voice said.

"Ah. Uh." Gregoire said, "I am an artist, making a record of our first meeting with you." He flipped the pad around as Voice translated, displaying a partial portrait of Peindak without her collar.

Matron Peindak preened. "How wonderful! I haven't had a portrait done in a year! You should have said, I would have chosen a better mareet. At least this is my best side."

More bubbles from the modeel, who then motioned to the aupoin, saying, "As you are first-semqu contact, I cede introduction order to you."

Peindak reacted. Something odd happened on her face, a swelling under her eye. Her fur stood on end in ridges. The modeel's blue bubbles took on a more vivid hue.

"I believe the modeel is enjoying a game of irritating Matron Peindak," Voice told Ximena quietly, and explained as swiftly as she could.

The aupoin roused itself. "I thank you, sibling."

The modeel flashed red. All signs of irritation on the peqe ebbed.

The aupoin added, "We are all a family under the semqu. Surely no disrespect could be taken from that?"

The modeel gestured something, and a hard line of lime green that Voice understood to be contrition flowed into the aura surrounding it.

"Interesting," Ximena muttered, as Voice explained that to her.

The aupoin's flowery mouth fluttered again. "I am Y-uu-see. I too am a Voice, for the aupoin on Trye. It will be good to have a Voice to share with, once your translation duties do not take all your time."

"I look forward to that," Voice said, and shared her introduction with the captain.

<You will need to avoid the surface for a short time, but after that, I would like you to meet other Voices,> her semqu said.

The modeel asked, "If that is all the introduction you need, Y-uu-see?"

The aupoin made a swift gesture.

The modeel continued, "I am Waatoos Hecht, from Vasom. I have been asked to discover what amenities you desire and what services you can provide, and to negotiate for minerals we have already surveyed on this planet."

"Here we go," Voice said, after translating that.

"We are short on time," Matron Peindak insisted. "We wish to open trade negotiations immediately."

"One, they weren't even supposed to be here yet, so I'm not falling for any time-pressure games," the captain said. "And two, we can't agree to anything until we understand our situation and our neighbors better. I'm not entirely sure the community is going to agree to stay here."

The semqu stirred, prickly sensations of unease roiling, but only said, <Be diplomatic.>

What does that even mean? While Voice hesitated, the captain started her own introduction.

"Tell them I am Captain Ximena Bobbie, representative of the *New Hope*, on which they visit, delighted to meet them and their respective peoples. Our artist is one of my officers, Gregoire Efran. We have travelled far, and expected to arrive at a different planet, which no longer has an atmosphere. We are far too soon in our acquaintance to discuss trade. Rushing into agreements when we do not know one another's cultures or values or languages begs trouble."

Voice ground to a halt in translation just before the last line. "Begs trouble said a different way? I know no Fugrast for that concept."

Instead, the semqu spoke through her. "Do not take advantage of our newest children."

<Oh! Won't they think I'm being rude?> "Oh! The semqu—"

Bubbles erupted in the air around Waatoos. "Yes, spacer-Voice, we know when a semqu takes over a Voice to talk to us. The signs are clear."

"You didn't have to be so honest with them," Peindak muttered.

"You should be," ripped from Voice's throat.

<Ow.>

<Desolée. They know better.>

"What happened?" the captain said. Voice explained, and the captain added, "That's fascinating."

"I am a new Voice, and my language skills are limited," Voice carefully said to the guests. "There is much we need to learn of each other before we make agreements." A quote from one of her mentors occurred to her, and she translated that. "Decisions made in ignorance help no one."

The pouch below Peindak's eyes swelled and then shrank as her jaw ground side to side. The aura around Waatoos shifted to a hue of green the semqu informed her was admiration.

She translated to the captain, who gestured, "Perfection." She'd said the right thing, on her own, without help.

The flower-petal mouth on Y-uu-see pulsed. "We wish to be good neighbors. We also do not want interference in our lives. We co-exist with many species, and I am told you can live above us without problems. But you are unknown to us. What do you want? What do you need?"

"Where do I start?" the captain muttered.

"From their perspective, maybe," Voice said hesitantly. "The aupoin need some gardening space on the surface, they use a lot of herbs. They'll need gardening space off-limits to us, but not much. When they encounter ores and useful pockets of petroleum or ores underground, they can bring them to the surface for us the way they do for the modeel, for example. They trade that access for tools and foods they don't create on their own."

The captain chewed her lip. "Tell them we are self-sufficient now, and it has been more than seven hundred years since we have lived on a planet's surface. We will need to re-learn what needs we will have on the surface, but it will include ores, farming and water."

"Wastewater treatment might be our biggest initial issue with an underground population," Voice said quietly. She had long been horrified by her history lessons in planet-based wastewater treatment. Underground neighbors would impact that significantly.

"I'd forgotten you were infrastructure, thank you. Yes, of course." The captain nodded.

That collapsed the last of the self-doubt Voice hadn't realized she was holding.

"Tell them we are curious about them, and their world, and so —what conversation topics are open to those who are peers? We would talk about our children, and our hobbies, and our forms of service to our community."

After Voice's translation, the peqe hummed. "Well, perhaps the semqu have not made a huge blunder."

"Those are all topics we, too, would share," Y-uu-see said. "I have no children, being a Voice, which is of course my service. My hobby is art—I make mosaics and adornments with shed beetle wings."

Voice translated but stilled. Had she given up the option to have children?

<Unsure. Long-talk later,> the semqu said.

"That sounds intriguing," the captain said. "We would love to talk with you about your insect populations, and I'd love to see your art someday."

Y-uu-see gestured.

"That gesture means assent, essentially," Voice said. She was going to have to learn and teach a new sign language as well.

Waatoos spoke next. "I have brooded twice, with forty currently surviving. My first brood died in an accident, quite young. My partner was devastated and killed himself." A flood of yellow washed around her and was gone, but there was a curl of falsehood's hue as well—was she lying?

"Our condolences," Voice said for the captain.

Waatoos continued, "It was long ago. I found another. We have offspring spread across Vasom doing many forms of service. My hobby is performance." Brown and blue bubbles ringed the air around her.

"Oh, I'm certain it is," Matron Peindak said.

"What type of performance, if I may ask?" the captain wanted to know.

"You may not," the modeel said.

Voice translated that, adding, "Somehow she is amused. I don't understand."

"Hm."

Matron Peindak had three daughters, her eldest was perfect, and she went on at length about how she had no time for hobbies because her calling was diplomacy, and how good she was at it. Voice translated it all verbatim.

"How wonderful, to know so purely in your bones your true purpose in life," Ximena said.

All three of them looked at the captain when that was translated.

"Did I misspeak?" Voice asked.

"No," Waatoos said, as curls of admiration-green slipped into and then out of her field.

"Hopefully we just scored our first diplomatic point," the captain said quietly. "As for me, I have no children, as of yet. My hobbies are poetry and language-learning, and I am greatly looking forward to learning Fugrast and perhaps some of your native tongues. You've all heard me speak. Could you indulge me by saying something short, or reciting something in one of your home languages?"

"I would be honored," Y-uu-see said, before the other two could react. A liquid sound pulsed from her body, interspersed with gulp-like noises, but mostly what Voice recalled later was the sound of splashing water.

"So beautiful," she said, for the captain, when Y-uu-see fell silent. "What does it convey?"

"A simple poem about friendship, hard-won, and its value," Y-uu-see said. "I can translate it for you some other time."

"I would value that," Voice said, in translation for the captain's "I would love that." Her semqu made it clear she'd need to avoid any sexual connotation.

"Friendship poem. What a delightful idea." Waatoos began making clacking noises, the metal scales on her round head and her fingers snapping at a rapid pace. Her field shifted from its background of brown to purple.

Y-uu-see vibrated in place.

The semqu sensed Voice's bewilderment. <She is amused, not afraid.>

<Will I learn what's funny, eventually?>

<Yes. Basics today.>

Matron Peindak shared a melodic tone with surprising chirps in it.

<She is bored, and you and I both tire.>

"We should conclude for today, I think." Voice said quietly. "I am new and easily exhausted."

The captain said, "I am grateful for your willingness to share your languages. We wish to be good neighbors."

"And peaceful neighbors?" Waatoos asked.

"Of course," the captain said, surprised. "We hope to be and have peaceful neighbors."

"As do we," Y-uu-see said.

"Yes, yes, yes," Matron Peindak said. "We've seen you. You've seen us. Work on your Fugrast and we'll talk trade soon." She gestured something Voice's brain translated roughly as "Done now." And then she vanished.

"What?" Ximena yelped.

Gregoire babbled, "Where did she go?"

"That never gets old." Waatoos' field was solid blue with darker blue bubbles, opening and spreading in overlapping circles. All-out laughter.

"That's how they got here from the blinkship," Voice said. "The technology that moves ships can also move people."

"This is going to take some getting used to," Captain Ximena said.

Voice translated that as a gift to the modeel.

"It is a joy to provide such service," Waatoos said. She moved one of her arms and disappeared.

The aupoin stretched. Voice moved aside; she hadn't realized how bunched up Y-uu-see had been.

"Ah, that's better, thank you," Y-uu-see said. "We have often found it useful to be wary of peqe or modeel offers and motives. Can we trust yours?

The captain regarded her a moment. "I would like to say yes. But I am leery of making promises when I do not know the context in which they are received."

"That makes you twice wiser than any peqe," Y-uu-see said. "I will help you learn Fugrast." Then she was gone as well.

<Finally.> The semqu's exhaustion hit Voice.

She slumped into a chair.

Her movement alarmed Captain Ximena. "Are you okay?"

"Tired. Translation from a language I learned overnight takes a lot of energy. I think I need to sleep again. Could go over your recordings, after, and I can help teach Fugrast?"

First there was the medical screening. Voice fell asleep in the middle of it and woke being wheeled to her dwell by a nurse. Gregoire was waiting at her door, tense and unhappy.

"Harriet and Adamantine talked their way into your dwell during the meeting," he said. "They said they had your permission and were simply moving in some of your things."

Voice was exhausted. So many mixed emotions welled up that she wanted to cry. Instead that numbing calm washed over her. *But this matters*, she thought.

"It will not happen again. I've been assigned to you on a more permanent basis now. We will set your lock to refuse any imprint but your own."

A locked door will make them get permission, she thought. That helped.

He and the medical staffer helped her shuffle piles of belongings to more convenient places in her dwell and move the furniture back where it had been. In her bedroom, there were a few of her family's woven baskets, looking like they held clothes, and an open drawer on the armoire.

Voice stared at the bed; she wanted to fall into it and become one with its pillowy softness. "I'll deal with the rest tomorrow."

"Someone will watch your door," Gregoire said. "No one will disturb you for another 48 hours if necessary. But I am going to put some water where you can reach it."

She gestured her thanks and was asleep before he set the water down.

SIX

GREGOIRE'S SKETCHES

THREE IMAGES CLIPPED FROM GREGOIRE'S
SKETCHBOOK.

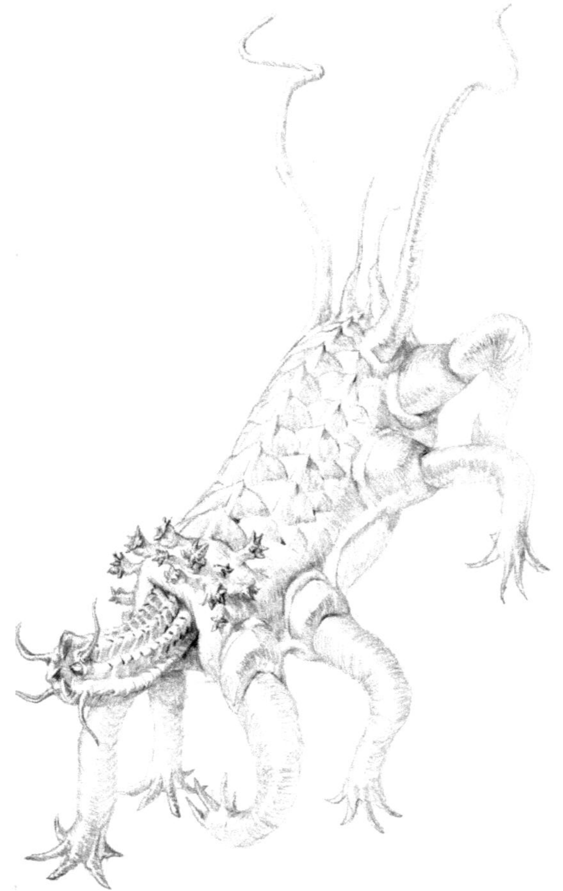

Y-uu-see, the aupoin Voice of Trye

Waatoos Hecht, the modeel ambassador. Gregoire didn't
include Hecht's aura.

Matron Peindak, the peqe ambassador

SEVEN
COMPANIONS

Captain Ximena and Gregoire brought Voice breakfast after she had slept for two days. They sat with her while she ate, drinking the warm beverages they had brought for themselves. She felt mildly awkward eating in front of them in a bathrobe but was too ravenous to care. Gregoire seemed preoccupied, but then he didn't have his sketchbook with him. She was glad about that.

When she was done, Captain Ximena set down her cup. "Voice, I'd like to chat directly with your semqu, if I can."

Curiosity bubbled from the alien presence. <Of course.>

Voice shared that with trepidation. The semqu was hungry and felt frail, like it was still struggling against the fungicide.

"Voice has been unable or unwilling to answer some basic questions about who you are, what you need and what you..." Captain Ximena trailed off. "What your end goal is in moving us to Trye.

We have a small contingent who are refusing to consider leaving the ship. They find it difficult to trust beings they cannot see, let alone those whose motivations they do not understand. We also have people practically tearing the hull apart trying to find you. It has become a safety issue."

A wave of unease swept over Voice. <Tell them that I reside in Voice, as much as I reside anywhere,> the semqu said. <Unless you think they'd try to take Voice apart? We would not like that.>

Captain Ximena did a double take when Voice conveyed that. "Ah, no, nobody is going to take Voice apart. But please don't tell me you only live in Voice. Our carbon dioxide levels have been rising for two decades. We have struggled to keep them within parameters. The day the ship was moved, there was another sharp increase."

Voice felt the semqu freeze, completely taken off guard.

"We'd also noticed some other oddities that would be explained by you having regular food deliveries in the same way our ship was moved. That knowledge is known only to a few; it's an officer shut-it. We are making a rare decision to share that shut-it with you." Captain Ximena looked with compassion at Gregoire, who gave her a wan smile.

Oh. Gregoire had sworn a shut-it this morning, maybe his first, and then immediately had to be part of a debate about sharing that shut-it with an alien life form? *Glad I wasn't in that room.*

"The captain at the time the air anomalies began was concerned about illegal manufacturing or brewing, and kept it quiet to avoid panic or vigilantism," Ximena continued. "My point being, our air quality numbers tell us that you have a physical presence somewhere, and that you inhale oxygen and exhale carbon dioxide. We do not wish for you to feel threatened in any way by our knowl-edge of this. But *our* survival in this contained environment requires careful balance; there are details we need to know. It will be less of an issue as spacers begin to move below, but we do not wish to be harmed by your ignorance of our needs, nor to harm you with our ignorance of yours."

Voice longed to say, "We already have," but she waited. This was not a conversation between her and Captain Ximena. The answer needed to come from the semqu, who needed to decide to trust a non-Voice spacer. She waited.

<I hear your concerns. I share them,> the semqu finally said, adding, <The modeel did their best, but the move was rough on this semqu and living among you has been stressful. That is more than I should say. Semqu have been harmed by those we have helped in the past. We have learned certain subjects must remain off-limits, much as you spacers have your shut-its. You ask me to open a locked door. >

"I hear and I honor that," the captain said. It was a traditional spacer response to hitting a hard boundary with another, and Voice explained it as such.

The semqu added, <I promise you that I will ensure I do no harm to your population. We have not encountered many beings who would not trust us after such an effort on our part to save their lives.> It seemed deeply bewildered and sad, and Voice expressed those emotions to the captain.

"I can understand your confusion," the captain said. "We have an ancient expression about the value of questioning gifts. Unfortunately, it exists because on our planet, gifts were sometimes used to trick friends as well as enemies. Sometimes fatally, genocidally."

Voice had to explain the concept of genocide to the semqu, who was horrified.

<That is malignant.>

"Yes." The captain continued, "We grow beyond our history, but we do not forget it. So. Let's pivot to assuaging the fears of the more concrete thinkers among us. What do you want with us? Your endgame. And what do you look like?"

Bubbles of relief and amusement pushed Voice to laugh. "Our form is similar to the aupoin; we look like grubs, larvae. You eat baby bugs, so we thought it best not to share that." That was the agreed-upon public face of the semqu, she realized. Not-real but not-far-from-real. It softened the discomfort she felt in not giving the captain the full truth. "And as with all the species we have helped, we wish from you the same thing—to learn from you. We are curious. You are from so far away! There are so many things you do that we have never encountered or known before. From you, we can learn and experience much."

"And once you have learned all you wish to learn?"

Puzzlement. <We have never yet experienced a cessation of curiosity. What a sad state that would be! We still learn from the aupoin, and they are the first creatures we encountered.>

Captain Ximena tipped her chin sideways. It was clear this was not the answer she'd expected. "How long ago was that?"

<I do not know how to express it in your time frame.>

Voice shared various time frames she knew; decades, millennia, life-of-Earth. The response surprised her. "Captain, if I'm under-standing correctly, about as long ago as the formation of Earth from space dust," she said.

Captain Ximena nodded slowly, as if that made sense to her. "You know they'll start referring to you as 'ancient bugs.'"

Voice was pushed to laughter a second time.

<If that works for them, and they stop risking their lives and your hull searching for me, then I shall be honored to be an old bug,> the semqu replied. <I request that my physical presence aboard remain a shut-it, limited to the people in this room.>

Ximena tapped her thumb when she was thinking hard; the ticking of her thumbnail on her cup was the only thing Voice could hear for a moment. Finally said, "I can agree to that. Gregoire? Voice?"

He nodded, wide-eyed, and the three of them swore the oath.

Voice was pretty sure the captain had more questions, but she had another meeting to attend. Gregoire stepped outside with the breakfast dishes, and Voice cleaned up and got dressed.

<I still don't have a name for you,> Voice said. <What would you like me to call you?>

<I am unsure,> the semqu said. It seemed grateful to have the subject changed. <Perhaps, to distinguish me from one who lives below—something related to the ship? You could call me New Hope?>

That confused Voice. <What's the name of the semqu below?>

<Trye9.>

<That's...oh. I can't call you the name of the ship, that would be confusing. You don't have family names?>

Amusement. <No.>

<Hm. Well, Hope can be a spacer name in many languages. 'Hope' in English; in my family's tongue, it's 'Espoir.' Oh! Hope is 'Ireti' in Yoruba, next year's language. That was the name of one of our captains.> Voice explained the history of Ireti Nabuco, and how much she admired her.

<I like Ireti. She sounds like an interesting woman. You would call me Ireti2, then?>

<No, just Ireti. We don't number people with the same name, we just keep them apart because... we know they're different. Often people have last names.>

<Ireti will suffice.> Her semqu seemed content, relieved.

It warmed Voice. <Thank you, Ireti.>

<You are welcome.>

Just before she left to teach, Voice noticed a letter shoved under the door. Paper; unusual. Adamantine's handwriting. She stared at it, then decided to open it later.

Despite her expectations, her first teaching experience was not a disaster. Ireti was very helpful and she several of the language instructors helped her get started. She stuck to the vowels for the first lesson. It was a crowded room, and there was much laughter. That seemed to please Ireti.

As they returned to the Quartier, they had to dodge a group of squealing youth playing tag. Voice had learned to share her vision with the semqu, and they watched the youths playing with enjoyment. Voice smiled as one of their parents joined in.

<Do spacers your age have family or mentors to shepherd them through their puberty, through to their adulthood?> Ireti asked. <The emotional changes necessary for our connection might interfere with normal mammal relationships, and you might need spacer help navigating that. Now that we are fully integrated, you could connect with more supportive adult spacers. Or just widen your circle of friends. You seem more distanced from your people than the other spacers I tried to connect with. Are you lonely?>

The question came as Gregoire and Voice arrived at her dwell; as usual, he said he would be outside when she was ready to leave again, and as usual, she thanked him.

She'd messaged Terri several times and gotten no response. Just inside her front door was a pile of unwanted gifts Voice had not found a place for. Several were from Père's colleagues, like Rupert's prickly parents, and that letter from her sister. She picked up the letter her sister had shoved under her door.

<Lonely? I don't think so. I don't have many friends, but I never did. And right now, there are people I dislike who want to be my friend. I'm not sure who to trust.>

She unfolded the paper. Adamantine had been concise. "Since you have rejected your family, I reject you. We are no longer sisters."

It cut, deep, but also -- she had expected whatever her sister had written to be hurtful or manipulative, hadn't she? She had waited to open it.

Still, she was glad Ireti was numbing that pain.

<Wariness is wise when you are thrust into a new role, especially one that some see as having power.> Ireti sounded sad.

<I am afraid Adamantine would have enjoyed believing she could influence me, so she would be the center of attention,> Voice thought. <Others might feel the same.>

<Learning which of your own people you can trust, when you

are viewed as holding power, may be difficult. We have learned this from having Voices among other species. I do not think spacers are that different.>

<Probably not.>

<You are protecting yourself from her, and that is good. Let us move on. You asked about children earlier. It is not always a good idea for Voices to be parents, or even partners,> Ireti said. <But we have changed nothing about your biology in this regard.>

<Why is it not a good idea?>

<You should talk to other Voices about this. It is difficult to explain because the concept confuses us.> Ireti seemed a bit distracted. <You fast-life forms often have some sort of parent-child bond. It is one of the reasons that I thought you would make a good Voice; yours is weak. I thought you might understand us a little better. It was a risk; not all those who have such a weak bond are as healthy as you.>

<Some are sociopaths,> Voice said dryly. <They believe only they are important.>

<Some are deeply problematic, yes.> An uncomfortable rustling, a shifting.

That disturbed Voice. <Am I a mistake? Did you not choose me?>

<No first-contact Voice is ever a deliberate choice; they are random by necessity. We are rarely happy with first contact because consent is so difficult. I am quite pleased with our connection. You are significant to Se Collective and yet unimportant, as I am both as well.>

She didn't understand or know how to react to that.

<If it helps, Voice, I am glad I encountered you in the rice fields, and not your sister Adamantine,> Ireti said.

Voice smiled. <So am I.>

**ABOARD NEW HOPE
DIPLOMACY ROOM**

**NEW HOPIAN YEAR 716
NINTH MONTH, THIRD DAY**

Voice stood between Captain Ximena and a new modeel, Foele Creator, in what had been renamed the diplomacy room, the large conference room where all the aliens fit. She had learned that short and to the point worked best with the clanking suit-clad modeel; diplomatic and flowery sarcasm worked best with the toothy peqe.

Gregoire stood just inside the door, sketching the meeting as usual. The ship's makers had created furniture that worked for all the aliens they'd met so far, and Foele had been most appreciative of the nonconductive seating. It had set a good tone for one of the first meetings to discuss trade.

The captain had told Voice that the spacer governing group was particularly concerned about the potential impacts on their community as spacers moved from the barter economy used shipboard to participating in whatever economic system the other planets used.

"For us, barter is glue," Captain Ximena explained. "It binds us with many connections. Their system looks similar, but seems to carry barbs, and I do not want our people to bleed."

Foele was offering worked metals and smelting services that spacers would need to build on the surface. In trade, he wanted spacers to build items, such as their hard suits, currently manufactured on Vasom. But he let it slip that worker deaths were one of the reasons they wanted spacers to take over.

"We're not interested in being your expendable work force," Ximena said.

The two went back and forth for a bit before she finally added, "We can likely find a way to *safely* manufacture such suits to your specifications, once we're settled on the surface. We do not wish to go into debt with you in the meantime."

Flashes of admiration and frustration lanced through Foele's biofield. Modeel emotional states seemed to be extremely complicated, and Voice struggled to parse the frequent conflicts between his colorful emotional expression and the words he spoke.

Foele said, "How short-sighted."

"For you, perhaps," Captain Ximena said. "We prefer to proceed slowly."

Foele left after procuring a ten-year "right of first refusal," on limited terms, to contract with the first manufacturing plant spacers constructed on the surface. Contentment swirled in his field.

Captain Ximena seemed happy too. "Ah, the hull is secure."

It was a common phrase for "all is well," but Voice was preoccupied with Ireti's health. "Is it? Have people stopped hunting for Ireti?" Voice asked.

"Ah. Well, perhaps not everyone. But yes, the frenzied search is over. We spread reminders that endangering the community is an Accord-breaking offense, and digging through walls is inherently dangerous."

Back in her rooms, Voice couldn't focus on the book about teaching a mentor had given her. Ireti had given her a new life and saved her community from oblivion. Translating didn't seem like adequate service to repay her debt, and the idea that others might still be hunting for Ireti bothered her. <Maybe if I had more friends, I could reassure people, stop some of the rumors?>

The idea seemed to make Ireti uneasy. <I am not sure that is your job.>

<Can I think about it?>

She made a list of potential friends. She started with Terri, then added Gregoire and his partner. She added her mentors in infrastructure. After a moment she added the librarian, who seemed to like her. She added a few names here and there: her old neighbors who'd been so kind to her; one of her parents' barter-partners, a couple of students from her language classes.

It occurred to her that Y-uu-see might become a friend. But that wouldn't be useful for her purposes shipboard. She shared her list with Ireti.

<You should have friends for your own support, not just to support me. Agendas can make for bad relationships.>

<True. I should tell Captain Ximena you told me that; maybe she'd feel better.>

Bemusement.

Voice sighed. Close relationships took a lot of work. Between translation duties and teaching Fugrast classes, the occasional volunteer shift when she could talk someone into letting her work it, and days of recuperation, she didn't have much time to host social gatherings. And Ireti couldn't join them.

Oh. Ireti was all alone here. Was she—he—? <What pronouns do you prefer?>

<I am both he and she, so I am indifferent.>

<Uh, okay. I'll use they if that's okay. So... are you lonely? Do you have a family?>

<Not in a mammalian sense. What you would think of as our children—we do not. We— > There was a long pause, and Voice held still, barely breathing, longing to know what wasn't being said. <We learned long ago that fast-movers found our fruit delicious and would spread seed for us. All we had to do was let them eat, not that we could have stopped them, back then.>

An image of fruiting bodies; mushrooms. Voice had eaten mushrooms for lunch. She vibrated in horror. <Have I eaten your fruit? Your children?>

A warm amusement buffeted her; when the semqu allowed itself to express emotion, it was strong. <You have not, but you might. They are not children in the way you are a child; they are not sentient.>

<They cannot become sentient?>

<Ah, you are too clever by half.>

That rustling, again, longer this time. It was like when Chie shuffled papers and tools, collecting her thoughts. It was nice to remember those moments without the accompanying stabs of loss or shame. Maybe she could reconnect with them too. An ache spread across her chest. *Maybe not quite yet.*

<Some few can become sentient. But we are extremely careful about our population, to avoid conflict. Breeding true is difficult; where your people only have two sexes, we have many hundreds, if not thousands. I am not sure I understand your culture well enough yet to explain in a way that will make sense. We could return to this later?>

She was touched; this powerful alien asked her permission to close a topic of conversation. No one in her family had ever offered her that respect. <Of course we can return to this later. I wish to understand, but not before you are ready.> Respect heard and returned, she meant, and from the contentment she sensed, she was understood.

ABOARD NEW HOPE
WANING MONTHS OF NEW HOPIAN YEAR 716

TRYE WAS NOT ONLY IMMEDIATELY habitable, but the residents of nearby planets offered trade in goods and services to help the spacers settle on the surface, and their new underground neighbors offered to mine anything they needed.

Voice's schedule became work one day, sleep the next. Days passed swiftly, life around her changing too quickly both for her and everyone onboard.

Once the shock wore off, her fellow residents of *New Hope* began the transition with the astonished delight of teenagers who'd suddenly realized they could leave home. Even before the vote was held, planning committees roared into high gear; everything from an annual calendar and crop choices to mothballed shuttle maintenance to survey teams and planetary hazards had to be discussed.

Voice supported the growing excitement in everything she did, learning and teaching Fugrast to conversation groups; learning more about the needs and concerns of the entire generation ship than she'd ever known existed; and cramming in details about alien populations with their own cultures, quirks, sub-groups and raging political divisions.

Researchers made biologic and environmental forays to check for compatibility and seek edible plants, useful soils, and suitable building areas. Others researched and wrote the ceremonies for respectfully taking the lives of trees and other living beings and developed guidelines for development that would cause the least impact to Trye's watersheds. A group of youth learning Earth history dug in their heels, insisting all development have zero impact.

Support groups opened for agoraphobia and other fears of planet-based life.

The youngest children were given the task of naming the community's first planet side home. After lively discussion, they created a portmanteau, Fuaringsplenzu, which many adults immediately shortened to either Fuar or Zu.

When the vote was taken, the community agreed to stay and populate Trye.

Ireti's relief vibrated through every nerve in Voice's body. She nearly missed the next vote, which was to awaken all Earthborn in hibernation and any noncriminal sleepers, not that her vote was needed. Her community understood how much they needed the surviving Earthborn's knowledge of planetary life.

After the meeting, organizers realized they didn't have enough volunteers to foster the hibernators, a necessary step to help them acclimate. Many New Hopians were already struggling to adjust to their new reality, and unsure they were up to the additional task of helping others cope with their inevitable cultural shock.

EIGHT
A ROUGH AWAKENING

ABOARD NEW HOPE
HIBERNATION CHAMBERS
NEW HOPE YEAR 716
NINTH MONTH, TWENTY-EIGHTH DAY

Danielle Braun coughed suspension fluid from her lungs. Dim memories warred with one another and reality. Was she fighting to the surface of Nile Lake, or choking on the test lab's vile fluid?

Wherever she was, it was full of people talking. Someone near her jabbered something incomprehensible. Hands on her shoulders, air on her face. *Open your eyes, idiot.* She blinked, eyes stinging, vision blurry. She sat mostly upright in water up to her chest, legs straight in front of her. She finally managed a full breath, then another. Her eyes began to clear. *Suspension pod. Open.*

A Black teen was on one side of her, speaking nonsense in a soothing tone. Alton's kid was on her left, her serious round face still and watchful, using a squeegee on Danielle's thin shirt and hair.

What the hell is Lt. Alton's kid doing here?

No. Something was off.

Memories slammed into her in chunks, starting with climbing into this pod in the best shape of her life, and fighting panic as the lid came down. She smarted with the embarrassment of that; her biologic measurements would have shown her stress to those sealing her in. Embarrassment had overcome fear; she'd calmed and slipped into a drug-induced sleep before the pod filled with fluid.

She'd been sent on a one-way mission; a generation ship where anything could have gone wrong. She was insurance; a volunteer committed to ensuring the mission succeeded, especially the U.S. interpretation of that mission.

This kid wasn't her second lieutenant's Filipino American child, just shared her coloring and features. Alton would be long dead … *Shit, are the adults all gone?* She grabbed for the edges of the coffin-like structure, reactions ridiculously slow. Her fingers trembled, kept slipping. *Why do I feel so weak?* She had to think about blinking away the fluid the kids were pressing from her hair. *Because you've been pickled for a thousand years, idiot.*

"Good." The teen spoke English with a heavy accent. Danielle only caught every third or fourth word. She was glad he was repeating himself. Eventually, she made out, "Keep coughing, Earthborn, good, good." Then the youth twisted around and said something swift in a tonal language to someone behind them.

Danielle struggled to clear her brain. His accent fit that of someone whose first language was Mandarin. One of the last briefings she'd gotten was on nationalistic threats to the global mission. China was on that list.

She could hear her superior officer, serious, intense and more than a little angry. "Your file makes it clear that you have been reprimanded on a regular basis. You act first, think later. You can't do that on this mission. It's too important. Do not act without approval." He'd paused, during which she recalled for the fiftieth time that she had not been the military's first choice for the job, nor the second, nor the third. NASA, not the Army or the CIA, got to choose for the United States. Ol' Chucky was still seething about that.

"Political agents are well-seeded throughout the 'lottery winners' from several countries, intending to take over the ship. There are also agents from various religions and political activists who simply want it to fail. Your job is to make sure the mission succeeds."

Danielle made herself take a slow, steady breath. *Absolutely no panic. You're just waking up. Gather information first. You must take the right action. Always.*

There was an older advisor in one of the other pods, a United Nations military officer from the Netherlands. He was one of the rare birds who had survived his training a decent human being and treated his soldiers right. *Pay attention.* Her first test would be her report to him about her first impressions. She wanted to earn his respect.

The child's tone was bright and crisp, and didn't sound at all like Alton's girl, which helped. "There is no reason for concern. Your oxygen stats are excellent." He? They? spoke with an accent, but lighter than the teen's, not tonal. She couldn't place it, but it didn't fit her initial impression of Filipino heritage. Their clothes were bright and loose on their ruddy arms, like they'd been dressed in clothes to grow into, black hair short and straight, dark eyes intense. One of those kids who seem to be born forty years old; responsible, earnest, humorless.

But clearly a child. Either the ship was in dire straits, or those in charge had decided that she was a problem and put kids in charge of waking her so they couldn't be held responsible if she didn't survive. *But I have. So far.*

Finally done with her coughing fit, Danielle rolled her head, using the movement to survey the room. The lid to her pod was on the floor near her feet. On the panel next to it, only the IV light was lit. Roughly six dozen pods were set in tight rows between her and the room's massive doors. More than she'd expected. She had been in row two, hadn't she? Not anymore. The wall was behind her.

About a dozen pods remained unattended; the rest had two people standing on either side of them. About half were open, the occupants being pulled up out of the fluid. The other attendants were clearly waiting for some reason.

This was her first glimpse of the ship's population, the descendants of the original United Nations crew. Most expressions carried the same grave intensity of her youngest helper, but on faces that ranged from thin and narrow to rotund to angular, their cheeks ranging from the teen's black to russet to the child's olive-tan: a blend of nationalities and ethnic features.

Her eyes watered, suddenly, a fierce pride and gratitude swelling. The generation ship had been successful. Earth's population might die—or kill each other—but the ship had kept humanity alive. That much, at least, had gone well.

Her helpers were the only youth. Black hair predominated, although several had white or grey hair. One frail-looking elder had deep charcoal arms. *Yikes. They've pressed everyone into service.*

Soft body tone predominated. Keeping in shape in space had been one of her worries. There wasn't a single uniform in the room. Some wore brightly colored tunics, others tightly fitted, patterned pants and tops in wildly varied styles. A few struck her as traditional garb from various countries, others more like continent-fusion fashion. Many outfits seemed hand-crafted—knitted or handwoven. Had they lost technological skills during the journey? The shoes she could see looked like slippers, which weirded her out.

The kids seemed to be testing her ability to understand various languages, waiting to see if she responded. She hadn't recognized much. Had they lost records, too? If so, they might not know who she was. That could be good or bad.

It was hard to hear them, anyway. Sound seemed to arrive in waves. The other pairs aiding the waking hibernators were also speaking multiple languages; the air so full of conversation her brain could only latch onto syllables here and there. And the pods' former inhabitants were coughing and retching, as she had, which added to the noise.

It seemed she'd been one of the first to be awakened. There was a process, she remembered, a protocol to be followed. She returned her attention to the youths to get through it. It was easier to hear them when she focused on their faces. She moved her arms and legs when asked, then her fingers and toes, and then her other joints.

Her brain remembered, but the connections seemed weak in some areas. She attempted some motions a dozen times before her muscles responded properly. She looked at her hands and forearms —*I look ancient, wasted*—and tried to run a hand over her buzz-cut hair, mostly to remind her muscles how to move. Lifting her arm that high was hard.

The child startled her by helping. "We will answer most of your questions after your shower," they said, "but the pods were opened every decade to remove excess hair and nails, change your coverings, and ensure you were all still healthy. The last check was this spring, and now we are home." It was a long speech, slowly spoken.

"Home?" It came out in two syllables, the muscles in her throat spasming.

"Yes!" Their smile made their round face look even younger. They could not be more than eight.

Excitement blasted through her. She'd survived. *A thousand years in suspended animation! I made it!*

Another pod hissed, near the door, its lid latches popping open. One of the pair attending it lifted the lid and set it on the floor. The two helpers reached down into the water, pulling up a man who looked dead, leads and tubes attached to his chest and arms. The pair supported his head and back while he began to struggle, weakly, and then gave in to retching coughs.

"He's got his process to go through, let's focus on yours," the teen said, or she thought he did. He was harder to understand than the younger one, spoke faster. "You are doing well." He was maybe fourteen, maybe eighteen. His hair was a fantastic bit of art: parted just off-center, dreadlocks cascading to his waist on one side, a faded, multi-colored, teased mohawk rising to a foot-tall ridge on the other.

"Cool hair," she said, or tried to. She started coughing again immediately. Her vocal cords hurt, and the rest of her body felt weird.

"No talk yet, Honored Earthborn," the child said.

She blinked. Was *Honored Earthborn* a title?

"You need to drink first, and we need you cleaned up."

"You are Danielle Braun?" the teen asked.

Wrong assumption number two. Ol' Chucky would already be riding my ass. She nodded.

"Oh," he said. "This," he made a fist with his right hand and rocked it forward and back, "means yes and this," he raised his first two fingers vertically and dropped his thumb, then snapped the three digits together like a bird's bill, "means no."

Danielle rocked her right fist.

The teen's smile lifted his entire face. "Instant learning comprehension! That's—"

She did not understand the word he used, but it sounded celebratory. *There's gonna be a shit ton of new slang to learn!* Danielle smiled; that communicated well enough.

"My name is Mboya Cheng. Can you show me how old you are using just your fingers?" the teen asked.

Danielle flashed him two fingers on one hand then five.

"Twenty-five?"

She rocked her fist. *Technically I'm a thousand and twenty-five,* she thought. *That'll mess with everybody's databases.* The Army had had a hard enough time with her cohort's hyphenated names, and they'd had at least three generations sort it out.

"That is exceedingly good, Honored Earthborn Danielle. I am

Lethabo Lim," the youngest said. "I will be with you through your process."

The pair took her faultlessly through steps that Danielle saw being repeated across the room. Sensory checks, muscular response checks, respiration checks. They were kids, but they knew what they were doing; they were more competent than some fellow E-5s she'd served with.

Across the room, the man she'd seen awakened had started to panic, fighting his handlers. He took an angry, sloppy punch at the woman helping him. She stepped away and crossed her arms over her chest. Her companion moved to the control panel and tapped in something. The fighter, sloshing awkwardly as he tried to roll out of the pod, abruptly collapsed.

His helpers lunged forward, catching him before he slid back under the surface, and yelled. Several other people rushed into the room with a gurney, medical workers from the look of their gear. The four of them hefted the limp man onto the gurney with surprising ease and wheeled him out.

So soft bodies don't mean lack of strength. I wanna see their weight room.

All the other helpers, including the kids, said something Danielle didn't understand, some kind of unison yell, as the team working with the fighter reached the door.

The pair stopped and bowed to the room before they left. Their expressions were sad. Their actions had been swift, efficient.

It made an impression on Danielle. *Don't fight, don't argue.* She glanced around, saw a few others among the awakened taking it in, eyeing their helpers warily. Then again, the man was weak and might have hurt himself. How did the kids interpret it? She pointed at his pod and the door.

"Violence is never called for," Lethabo said primly.

Oh, child, you have no idea. Danielle tucked that reaction away to explore later.

"May you never thirst." Mboya handed her a thin opaque bottle.

Lethabo added, "It is water. Sip carefully. Please drink it all."

Hell yes. She was incredibly thirsty, despite having been immersed in liquid for so long. She lifted it to her lips, splashed some on her tongue. Then her taste buds woke up with a roar. The liquid tasted vile. It hurt to swallow. And she was weak; holding the full bottle made her hands tremble. Her arms were ridiculously tired by the time she'd finally drained it.

They let her rest for a bit, then helped her scoot forward, and put a small seat behind her.

"Honored Earthborn, the next step will be more difficult," Lethabo said. "We cannot lose any of your sleeping fluid. It is valuable. We need you to lift yourself onto this seat, and we will squeeze-drain you off. If you feel odd or unhappy or dizzy at any point, gesture no. Do you understand?"

She gestured yes.

"Do you want help?" Mboya asked.

She showed them a sloppy bird's beak. She pushed up with her arms, getting her legs under her, moving slowly to avoid slipping and splashing the "sleeping fluid" on the floor. *They probably have no way to replace it. Components, ingredients, fresh resources—*

Pain interrupted her conjecture. Her muscles screamed and yelled and objected and argued and bitched and then she was moving up and backwards. It seemed to take forever; a twenty-mile with a rucksack would have been easier. She groaned. *All I'm doing is lifting my bodyweight. I'm going to have to do a lot of reconditioning.*

The seat put her ass at the level of the pod's lip. The fluid drained off her, leaving her slightly chilled.

The pair moved methodically, gently, using their hands and small soft sponge-like tools to push the liquid from her skin. She stared at gooseflesh on unrecognizably thin and flaccid thighs below the loose shorts someone had put on her while she slept.

Danielle had been called an Amazon since puberty, tall, heavy and broad. The kind of woman no man wanted, she'd been assured by insecure boys, because she was too strong, didn't need protection. They were easy to ignore; she'd had her pick of lovers. But she was accustomed to being the strongest one in the room. It was a shock to realize that right now she was weaker than anyone currently speaking, including the elderly white-hair across the room who was not much taller than Lethabo.

Her core muscles were fluttering, exhausted of holding her in a sitting position, when they were finally ready for her to get out. She caved, *ego be damned,* and let them help her swing her legs over and balance there for a moment, her arms resting on their shoulders, one tall, one short. Two teenaged girls, one extremely wide-eyed, were waiting with a wheelchair.

The four of them helped Danielle down and into it, an awkward process she did her best to forget afterwards. She couldn't stand up alone. The chair's foot and back support gave her instant relief. Her spasming gut muscles relaxed. *A metric fuck ton of reconditioning.*

Lethabo and Mboya faced her.

"Honored Earthborn," Lethabo said, "As the youngest members of the team, we were given the honor of waking you, the oldest hibernation resident. It has been our honor to be of service."

Oldest? It hit hard. She'd been in the second tier. That meant at least a dozen people hadn't survived. Including her superior officer. She fought to keep the emotion off her face, tried hard not to think about what that meant. *Shit.* She was on her own. *FUCK. No. Stop. You may be wrong. So not now. Not yet. Not in front of these kids. Not HERE.*

"It has been our honor to serve," Mboya echoed. His hair swung down and up, both of them bowing to her. They held their hands, fingers interlaced, against their chests.

Interesting wording and ritual. She distracted herself with the implications. How religious had the ship's residents gotten? Religious indoctrination or cult development was one of many possible concerns about the voyage.

None of them moved. Should she respond? "Thank you." Speaking still hurt, but the words were formed right. She tried to smile again. Her face and tongue muscles still felt numb and weak.

Mboya beamed. Lethabo did not, but both bowed a second time. *Huh.*

"Du and Zara will help you shower," Lethabo said, pointing to the girls in turn. "Some thought you might be uncomfortable for us to help. We will wait for you outside."

The teens dissolved into giggles; her horror at the thought of being showered by a child must have shown. She could feel her cheeks heat and rocked her fist. Mboya grinned.

The girls wheeled her through the crowd and out of the room.

ABOARD NEW HOPE
NEW HOPE YEAR 716
NINTH MONTH, TWENTY-EIGHTH DAY

THE MORNING the hibernating were woken, the elderly calligrapher Tem Chie Charna knocked on Voice's door.

Voice invited her inside, grateful that her initial wave of shame died instantly. "Please, join me, sit down!" Her words vibrated a little. She had to think about what she had to offer. The captain and Gregoire had been her only guests so far, and they did not drink when they visited her. "Would you like some herbal tea?"

"Not today, but I thank you." Tem Chie bowed, offering her a small basket.

Voice returned the bow and accepted it. "You honor me."

"No more than you honor me."

The simplest visitation ritual complete, the two sat. Voice

stared at the basket. It was filled with calligraphy tools, a small scroll of handmade paper, and a vial of ink. "Oh! How kind!"

"I hear you have taken no hobby time. I know we are preparing for a new life, and you have a new role, but this is unfair to you," the calligrapher said. "And some of the youngest are noticing and trying to emulate your schedule. Creative time is sacred in our culture. You are a role model." It was a gift, a reminder, and a reprimand, and only someone as serene as the calligrapher could have conveyed it so succinctly with such gentle care.

"I have missed having something to do with my hands," Voice said.

Tem Chie looked around at her bare walls and floor. "Service to the community is important. But no one can survive without honoring their own needs and providing service to themselves."

"I hear you," Voice said. "I will clear time in my schedule for myself." That would allow Ireti rest time as well, she thought.

"Very well then." Tem Chie cleared her throat. "We have missed you, Voice. I realized you believe we overstepped when last we saw you. I apologize."

"You did not overstep." Voice cast her mind back. It felt so long ago, and the emotional trauma of that day no longer pained her. "I was not grateful then, but I am now, and I should have spoken gratitude to you long ago. What you did was necessary and right."

Keeping her family happy and safe had been her top priority back then. Her role had abruptly exploded into one in which she now tried to keep her entire community happy and safe, she thought. She was immersing herself in that new job and wasn't sure how or when to wedge in her lingering obligations.

"I did not return for reasons that seem silly now. I don't know how to be with people sometimes. I needed distance from my family—" she trailed off. *And now I have more distance than I actually want.* "I missed out on learning so much from you."

"Families can have a difficult time with change. That is on them, not you."

A deep knot in her upper back released. Ireti had tried to suggest something similar, but it helped to hear it from another spacer.

Tem Chie gave her a searching look. "We would be happy to resume teaching, if you like. But how have you been, Voice? You are different now, but you are much the same serious child I knew. You are a spacer; you need community. You serve, but you seem alone. We worry. Will you talk to me?"

She would, and she could, and she did. Her emotional flatness did not seem to disturb the calligrapher at all. They talked until Gregoire knocked; Voice had a diplomatic meeting with Captain Ximena and the planetary representatives.

"I am sorry, but I must go." She set the basket on the half-empty bookcase and rose.

Tem Chie rose with her. "With your permission, I will return?"

"Please! And with your lady-wife, if she wishes. I do miss you both." She started to add "as much as I can miss anything," and discarded it as rude.

"Hopefully we can discuss your first creations," Tem Chie said, as she passed through the door.

Voice hummed as she and Gregoire walked to her meeting. He had turned into a good companion, an excellent listener. Early on, he had dispelled her worries that he'd resent having to be at her side. When she asked, he'd collapsed in laughter. "Do you have any idea how many offers I get to trade places? Out-and-out bribes? Voice, I get to see actual aliens in person, listen to every lesson in Fugrast you teach, and sit in on more meetings about what's going on with the ship than I ever knew existed. And I get to ask you questions! It's overwhelming and amazing and there is no job I'd rather have right now!" Then he'd sobered and added, "And I'm five years older than you. If I'm overwhelmed, some days I worry how you're doing."

"I sleep every other day," she'd responded.

Now, in the hallway, he asked, "Good visit?"

"Very."

"My aunt used to do calligraphy," he said. "I think the family still has her portable writing desk my uncle could not bear to part with or recycle. When he passed, the calligraphers didn't need it. Could you use it?"

"Oh! Yes! If they could part with it, I would be very grateful!" Such boxes were rare, handmade from scraps or basketry. Some even had lids that could be adjusted to whatever writing angle the user required.

"I'll ask," he said.

She stopped and peered up at him. "Wait a minute. Was calligraphy your idea?"

"Calligraphy was your idea. You asked for it for your tenth anniversary." He gestured for her to keep walking. "Hobbies might have been my idea," he admitted. "Someone finally listened to me."

A weird sensation twisted in her chest, sharp and painful and then warm. It was gone before she could identify it, leaving a confusing echo of emotions Ireti was already parsing—fear and grief and delight. "Thank you." Her words came out smaller than she intended.

"You're welcome." He smiled. "We care about you, Voice. And not just because we need you. You're a pretty amazing spacer."

"I don't know how to respond to that."

"Just absorb it," Gregoire said.

She nodded. That weird emotion flared again, flattened. <I want to talk about that feeling when we have time,> she thought to Ireti. Conversations about emotions, and their role in spacer life, had become a bedtime ritual.

<Very well. This hobby thing sounds interesting as well.> The message carried a curiosity Voice hadn't sensed in some time.

That cheered her. It was getting hard to remember when Ireti hadn't sounded exhausted.

ABOARD NEW HOPE
HIBERNATION CHAMBERS
NEW HOPIAN YEAR 716
NINTH MONTH, TWENTY-EIGHTH DAY

THE NOISE of wrenching coughs and the babble of languages ebbed as they entered a communal showering area; a row of spigots in the wall, each with a squeegee, and grates in the floor. A brightly patterned mosaic covered the far wall. When she'd seen this room last it had all been a calming blue, hadn't it? She wasn't sure. The mural imagery seemed multicultural, probably to reassure those waking up that they were still part of a global effort.

Danielle was just glad they'd chosen animals rather than faces.

Being helped to undress felt invasive, a ludicrous thought given the care she'd received while unconscious. Danielle itched every-where. Her skin was an unhealthy pallor and every muscle was flaccid. She looked eighty and felt like she was covered in toe jam. Her nose was misfiring; serving her scents of pepper and rice, shit and mint. The girls didn't turn on the water until she was rolled under the shower head, braced for cold. The cascade that struck her was body temperature, heavenly.

Washing her bristle of black hair was delightful. Getting the hibernation fluid and the dead skin off the rest of her felt almost sexual in its relief. She planned to scrub every centimeter of skin. "Can I have a washcloth?"

"No. No scrubbing," Du, the taller of the pair, said sternly. "You itch, and you will scratch. Your skin is thin and will be for weeks. Blood in the air is bad."

The other added, "We rinse you."

Their straightforwardness startled Danielle. She thought about the boys' comment and wondered if privacy was a thing in such confided living conditions. So many cultural differences she'd have to learn. *And report to who? Stop. Focus on the here and now. One thing at a time.*

The young women did not try to converse with her beyond gentle directives, but kept up a rapid-fire conversation with each other in either Italian or Portuguese. The smaller and darker of the two, Zara, seemed afraid or worried. The boys had been focused on Danielle; this pair just had a job to do. Were they also trying to hide what they were talking about? *Find out.*

And keep it short. She was done with all the coughing. "How many languages?"

"We kept alive as many as we could," Du said. "I can read in fifteen, talk in eight, but I'm level nineteen in archaic English! Close to a native speaker! Zara is struggling with her old English, but she speaks nine. And we all have a new language to learn now! How many are you fluent in?" She spoke too fast, in an accent that abbreviated vowels. Danielle pointed to her ear and rolled a finger; Du repeated herself more slowly twice before Danielle caught it all.

That's going to make my life harder. "Two? I know words in four others."

They didn't know what to do with her underwhelming admission. She sighed, Ol' Chucky had had plenty to say about it.

"Zara keeps repeating something?" None of the words sounded the way Danielle wanted them to. She swallowed.

"Ayi, she keeps saying, 'She's so pink, what happened to her skin?'" Du spoke slowly. "It's as if she's never seen a Caucasian before. Don't know how. Voice is white, and there are four in my neighborhood."

Danielle had spent most of her pre-military life being read as too dark or too white for whatever clique or group she tried to join. The idea that whites were a rarity amused her in ways she wasn't sure the teens would understand. The idea that she was among the whitest aboard disturbed her in ways she knew she could never explain. Grandma, her mother's mother, had insisted there was

Native blood in the family and mourned that Danielle hadn't inherited her cheekbones. Paw, her father's father, had sniped at her with all kinds of bigoted names for Native Americans.

"There's an albino on fifth level but Zara's never met him. Geneticists might want to talk to you, though. There's an immunity some of the melanin-light carry that they want to tap."

Huh. Was space radiation impacting fertility or causing mutations? Her throat wasn't up for that question, and the girls were unlikely to know anyway.

Zara's dark cheeks flared with blush. "Service matters, melanin not," she said. "So wrote the philosophers from Our Journey Year 350."

"Truth," Danielle said. *Shit. There's going to be a thousand years of history to learn.* Danielle groaned; she hated classroom study. But she wanted to get started, to know, now, everything about her new home. "I need—catch up?"

"You'll be okay, English is our ship language right now."

"Ship language?"

"Yes! And we all learn Fugrast too!" Zara said.

That triggered a couple of questions. *Fugrast?* But they had clothing options for her to choose from, and then they were helping her dress, and she had no more air. She was light-headed and slightly nauseous by the time she was dressed in loose trousers and a smock-like shirt like Lethabo and Zara wore.

Zara ran her fingers through Danielle's hair, smoothing it. The girls had been as uncomfortable with the bathing duties as she had been, Danielle realized. She'd misinterpreted their determination to do a good job with comfort with a stranger's nakedness. She relaxed a little on the dried-off chair. She almost felt like herself. A much weaker version of herself, but an enlisted US Army specialist, nonetheless.

"You ready, Honored Earthborn?" Du asked.

That title again. "Yes. Thank you. Uh. Merci, gracias..." She slowly ran through all the words for thank you that she knew, ending with and stumbling over the Ukrainian, "dakuyu." The girls were still chuckling when they rolled her into a long corridor where Lethabo and Mboya waited.

Maybe now that she was clean, she'd get to talk to whoever was in charge now that they'd reached New Terra.

ABOARD NEW HOPE
MEETING ROOM FIVE
NEW HOPIAN YEAR 716
NINTH MONTH, TWENTY-EIGHTH DAY

TODAY'S DIPLOMACY gathering was not going well. Matron Peindak was irritable and there was a new modeel in attendance, this one wearing a cylindrical hardsuit with arms that clanked and snapped loudly.

Voice had decided to try to imitate the poise of her calligraphy mentor and not allow the mood of the others to ruin her fine morning. Being free of the responsibility for the moods of other was completely liberating, and she reveled in it. Ireti approved.

Y-uu-see spoke. "I am told to extend an invitation to you, Captain Ximena, to the next Council of Twelve meeting."

The modeel's field flashed red and the peqe snarled, both practically yelling at the aupoin.

<Oh.> A fuzziness, flailing and unsettled feeling washed over Voice; she was certain Ireti was swearing. Her head filled with images of even more bizarre aliens, and a meeting room with about forty beings in it, twelve of them seated. <I should have explained that much, much sooner.>

Voice sat down.

"Is there a problem, translator? Are you exhausted again?" Peindak managed to make her questions sound incredibly insulting.

Turning to Captain Ximena, Voice said, "There is a system-wide government involving all Se Collective's sentient species. You've been invited to attend a meeting."

"What?" The captain slammed back into her chair. "We're only hearing about this now?"

"You had not mentioned the Council of Twelve to Captain Ximena before," Voice said in Fugrast. "You hoped to make a deal with us before we talked to them."

"Waatoos didn't explain?" The modeel's biofield displayed the colors of both shock and mendacity.

Peindak laughed. "Your ignorance is not my concern."

<Ah. A useful byproduct, to find out how honest the modeel and peqe representatives would not be with you, given the chance.> Chagrin accompanied the thought.

Y-uu-see apologized for not introducing the concept sooner. Her body had contracted; it seemed to be a stress reaction.

"Isn't that interesting? We're how many weeks in now?" Ximena said. "Gods and black holes, I need to do more research into Earth negotiation techniques. Are we expected to attend this council, or join this, and what does that involve?"

"We were given an acclimation period, but I think this has also been a test of our neighbors' honesty," Voice said. She was rewarded with a wave of gratified warmth from Ireti.

Guilt ruined that, guilt that would feel worse if her rewired brain so allowed. Ireti had screwed up because they were exhausted. Because Voice had gotten it poisoned by telling the agriculturist where it was. She'd done the right thing at the time, and Ireti didn't want her to feel bad about it at all. But that didn't change the fact that her act had resulted in grave harm.

"We will make no more trade agreements until after we meet this council," Captain Ximena said.

When Voice translated, the modeel's field flashed the ruddy color of frustration, with flashes of begrudging admiration.

The peqe's eyes nearly vanished into a sudden swelling on its face. "You are telling me you will allow your ignorance to waste my time?" Her teeth were very prominent as she spoke.

Voice conferred with Ximena, who was obviously steeling herself against shrinking away from the larger creature.

Voice sensed no concern from Ireti and put her trust in that; her translation of the captain's pointed response was calm. "Is developing friendly relationships with your neighbors and potential trade partners a waste of your time?"

One of her Fugrast students stepped in the doorway, gesturing permission to enter. They wanted to introduce the eldest hibernating Earthborn. Voice saw no harm in it and Ireti was immediately curious.

"A distraction might help," the captain said.

Voice invited them inside with a wave of her hand.

**ABOARD NEW HOPE
OUTSIDE THE HIBERNATION CHAMBERS
NEW HOPIAN YEAR 716
NINTH MONTH, TWENTY-EIGHTH DAY**

"FOOD OR HEALTH CHECK?" Lethabo asked. "We can take you to the cafeteria or the med bay."

Danielle's stomach roiled, but it was nausea, not hunger. "Knowledge," she said firmly.

Lethabo beamed. "We cannot take you to a full lesson yet, but we could introduce you to a teacher or mentor candidate, briefly, before your med check. You have a choice in how you start acclimating." He spoke precisely, slowly. "We don't have much ready to read yet. Too much has changed too fast. So at first you can choose between two ways to learn: immersion or mentor."

"Immersion," Danielle said.

"Politics, science, or culture?"

Interesting. "Politics."

"Then we take you to see Captain Ximena."

"The ship's captain?" Mboya rocked a fist; the four were conferring like a flock of birds. *Fantastic.* He rocked again when she asked, "Hee MAY nah?"

Zara said something that sounded like, "She is with Voice!" That seemed to excite the youths, and they chattered in several languages.

Danielle, pleased, pleasantly tired and amused by their enthusiasm, didn't try to ask anything else. They started off, wheeling her down several long hallways, still talking nonstop. One wall carried an intense collaged mural of international dancers, facing a wall of solid calming pastel. They turned down another hallway with the same decoration scheme, although this mural seemed to be portraits of notable figures, from the care than had been taken with their faces. The middle depicted some kind of struggle. She pointed at it.

"Ship history," Du said from behind her.

"I will explain that later," Lethabo said. "It is quite complicated."

Mboya had run ahead and was waiting when they came to an open doorway. "Voice is translating," he whispered, "but we can enter."

Danielle was rolled through into a space crowded with equipment, where a short skinny teen in slippers stood ramrod straight directly in front of her, projecting poise and humility.

This youth spoke in a strange language, and something triggered Danielle's uncanny valley sense—was she a hologram? Couldn't be. She made eye contact with the others. Her fingers curled in a gesture that was clearly welcoming Danielle and her little cloud of teens. The girl's solid tunic-top was shapeless below her pale oval face, her chin-length light brown hair awry.

What is it with all the kids in charge? If there hadn't been three white-haired people in the hibernation room, I would have worried about longevity, Danielle thought.

Then the monsters registered.

Her hibernation-blurred brain had read them as equipment until the furry dinosaur with feathers cascading down its back lurched up, spun, and stomped along the left wall. A grizzly-sized— larva? caterpillar? —to the right of the teen began to undulate like a waterbed. On her left, between the teen and the dinosaur, a crackling multi-colored field shimmered in the air, enclosing a metallic beer can with about six appendages. It wasn't much smaller than the bristly larvae. *Robot? Mech?*

Only exhaustion kept her in the chair. It was a long tense moment before she realized the kids showed no fear of the strange creatures. They were making quiet sounds of excited delight.

"Am I hallucinating?" Danielle asked.

"No, Honored Earthborn. We have made what was known in your time as first contact." This new youth spoke flatly, without enthusiasm or fear, but with a slight smile. "We have arrived in a solar system populated with several sentient species. "Aupoin," she pointed to the larvae, "Modeel," she pointed to the robot-looking thing, "and peqe."

The dinosaur snarled. "Aaapeeeqeee."

"Your caste is apeqe, but your people as a whole are peqe," the teen said serenely, as if a creature twice her height, with teeth the length of Danielle's palm, had not just wheeled and snarled at her.

The dinosaur sniffed, loudly, and went back to pacing. Its musculature was astonishing, bunching and releasing beneath its fur like a tiger's.

How the fuck do you fight something like that? Danielle felt lightheaded. She forced a slow deep breath.

"And of course the semqu, who you cannot see, but who interrupted our journey and brought us here. They have made me their Voice to Spacers. I am honored to be chosen."

Danielle shifted her focus abruptly to the youth. Her brain jammed with conflicting questions. "Why," she finally got out. It wasn't a useful question, but it was at least a word that did not convey horror.

On her right, a black-haired woman stood up; she'd been hidden behind the bulk of the larva-aupoin. She looked like she was wearing pajamas with a strip of embroidered tokens cascading down one side.

"Ms. Braun, I am the *New Hope's* captain, Bobbie Ximena. I bid you welcome from waking. The planet we were traveling toward lost its atmosphere after we left Earth. The semqu encountered us, discovered our predicament, and had the modeel bring us here." She spoke like a politician, not a military officer. She kept talking, but Danielle tuned her out. This woman could not be the captain of any ship.

It was too much to parse. Was she hallucinating? Was this girl some kind of cult leader? Or had the ship been taken over by aliens? What was going on?

Her nausea was abruptly worse, and her lungs strained. Had they thinned the air in this room for these aliens?

The dinosaur stared at her. Its nostrils flared and its teeth parted, like a hunting crocodile's. It was the one thing in the room she recognized and understood at a visceral level: a predator, sensing prey. The hair on the back of her neck rose. Her vision tunneled to the monster.

"What does the dinosaur eat?" she asked, teeth gritted.

"What?" the pretend captain asked.

"The dinosaur." The room started to spin, and she halted, making sure she wasn't going to vomit. The predator's gaze was locked on her. She stared it down. "What does the dinosaur eat?"

"The peqe?" Voice asked. "They eat meat and eggs, Honored— Hélas! I believe we have over-stimulated Ms. Braun."

Lethabo cried out in dismay, and suddenly there were hands on her shoulders. Her vision darkened, narrowing to the dino's vertical pupil. Then she blacked out.

NINE

COMMUNITY

**PLANET SEM
MEETING OF MANY MINDS
SEMQU YEAR 1142-43
(NEW HOPIAN YEAR 716-17)**

We have made a huge leap forward in our evolutionary studies, and we have added to our number. We have successfully contacted a new sapient life form! We have an unexpected new community of fascinating creatures to learn from, and a new young Voice.

Had we been mammals or birds, we would have feasted, built monuments or made music together. But we are semqu. We mind-danced, as is our way, and shared our histories again, as together as we could be, so we all remembered who we are.

We will die, eventually, but our spore offspring will survive, and so will our creations, our residents, our... neighbors. We have learned much from these newcomers, some ideas that disturb us deeply, some concepts and genetics that will help us progress. Our clade is now diverse in ways we could never have anticipated, could never have created on our own.

We are excited. We are anxious. We are joyous. We celebrate. We wish for all our children a well-fed and harmonious future.

ABOARD NEW HOPE
MAIN MED BAY
NEW HOPIAN YEAR 716
FIRST TWO WEEKS OF THE TENTH MONTH

THE DOCTORS REASSURED Danielle that she was simply dehydrated and needed nutrition. But she was required to rest, held in sick bay with the fighter and a few other hibernation-sick patients. Still smarting from the embarrassment of passing out in front of aliens and that woman who was, despite all appearances, the ship's captain, she was irritated by the offer of a stream of entertainments and pushed them all aside.

Lethabo took his liaison responsibilities seriously. He visited her several times a week. She was confused about having been assigned a child, but the ten-year-old answered or found answers to all her questions. He taught her basics, from which she made and then discarded several erroneous assumptions, mentally swearing at or thanking her long-dead supervisor each time.

First, he taught her safety sign. Learning it brought her up against her another misconception. She had assumed some of the patients were deaf because they were signing. They were not.

Airborne viruses could be lethal shipboard, Lethabo told her, so every shipborn child was taught some version of *forehead hot, open lips not.* Anyone with a fever was expected to communicate entirely in sign.

Handshaking, he said, had been dropped to limit disease transmission in tight quarters. Everyone bowed. The one correct assumption she drew was that if you were sick and could self-care, you quarantined in your quarters.

One morning Lethabo came in more somber than usual. He bowed but did not sit. "Your first and most important civics lesson is today," he said. "I will recite for you the Principles of Community." A bit louder, he said, "May I have help?"

Several staff around the room said, "I hear and aid you."

Startled, Danielle looked around the bay. None of the workers had stopped what they were doing, and only of one them had even looked up.

"New Hope's Principles of Community, most recently agreed upon at the Shipwide Accord, Mission Year 713." Lethabo faced Danielle, eyes focused above her head.

"We are one people, one community." That was louder; those who had replied to Lethabo had joined him in the recitation. Danielle glanced around, trying to identify who was speaking, as they intoned, "We swear or affirm to value the mission we are on together and to commit to its needs and requirements."

"There are three agreed mission needs." Lethabo paused.

Danielle focused on him again.

He went on, "One, we understand maintenance is crucial to the mission's survival. We will maintain *New Hope* and her systems well so our descendants can reach our destination healthy and whole.

"Two, we will not use more than our generation's allotment. We will reserve what we can as a hedge against future crop failures.

"Three, we will keep our languages and arts and sciences and other essential knowledge alive and growing."

"We swear or affirm to share as a community," the people in the med bay said.

It reminded Danielle of the call and response of a religious rite, and she wasn't sure if it was impressive or terrifying.

"There are four parts to the sharing accord," Lethabo said. "One. We provide enough for everyone to eat, drink and breathe. If rations are low, restrictions are shared equally, excluding developing children. If we have a bountiful harvest, we share equally with the future and each other.

"Two. Service is expected and honored. Without service we suffocate or starve. Three. Everyone contributes what they can; each person is mentored to their best possible contribution. And four, unpopular and unpleasant tasks are equally shared as are fun and joyful ones."

The group joined him again. "We swear or affirm to honor the lives of those who sustain and nurture us, pollinators and insects and plants and fungi."

Lethabo continued alone, "The ship sustains us. We must maintain her, her fields and her systems. We support the ship and her ecosystem. We waste nothing. We recycle everything."

Again, the group chanted, "We swear or affirm to value the products of the mind, body and spirit."

Lethabo added, "This means all languages, arts, music, poetics, storytelling and performance; scientific knowledge and discovery; faiths and philosophies; dance and sport and other ship-compatible exercise; and other mechanical and physical creations."

The group—there were four of them, Danielle had determined, three staff and a patient—added, "We swear or affirm that our sciences keep us alive."

Lethabo added, "We will ensure our sciences are kept alive, added to, and understood. We accept that sometimes knowledge can be dangerous. Should our duty require we swear shut-its to protect the community, we do so with honor and integrity and uphold them to our deaths if necessary. Balance and judgment are essential. Unnecessary secrets breed resentment and division. We do not withhold information without excellent reason."

Danielle glanced deeper into the bay. The fighter was sitting up on his bed, a rarity for him, and listening closely. He made eye contact with her and mouthed, "What the fuck?" She gave him the slightest shrug she could, acknowledging the weirdness without allying herself with him. His behavior worried the staff; he was never alone.

The group continued, "We swear or affirm that fulfillment is essential to make our lives in transit worth living. Spacers need creativity, play, movement, achievement, faith."

Lethabo added, "We acknowledge our mission to retain the best of Earth; but we also will grow beyond it and add to the shared creative wealth during our journey."

The group added, "We swear or affirm to value each other and the health and thriving of each member within the whole of the community."

Lethabo added, "Balancing autonomy and community might always be in tension, but we honor the privacy and autonomy of each individual as long as they do not endanger themselves or others. We honor each other's disparate needs. We require consent before crossing boundaries.

"We respect each other's faiths and beliefs while acknowledging none are superior or inferior. We may choose lines of authority for the sake of expediency or safety, but all are of equal value. We acknowledge that differences in intellect and capability exist, but we honor and support the contributions of all. We find roles of service for all. We all deserve the dignity of contribution. Every spacer who has had an adulting ceremony has the right and responsibility to vote in decisions that impact us all."

Danielle frowned. What did that mean for the Earthborn?

Lethabo noticed, and gestured, "Questions later." Aloud, he went on, "We treat each other with respect, never with contempt or submission. We value the gift of every individual and nurture one another into fulfilling service and recreation."

"We swear or affirm our commitment to community," the group said.

Lethabo continued, "Some of us will have emotional or mental challenges that cause harm to themselves or others. We mentor and support and medicate and counsel and sing and otherwise aid those who have such problems, using every tool we have available to us. We do not murder, but if we fail someone to the point that they cannot live in community, as a last resort we allow them to choose between the airlock and hibernation. We acknowledge that reaching this point is our communal failure; and we do all that we can to avoid any person having to pay the price of our lack of care."

Danielle could not help herself; she glanced back at the fighter. The man had already turned away, and was throwing himself down, pulling his blanket over his head. The staffer watching him frowned, glancing at her co-workers.

The staff who were chanting along with Lethabo changed their tone; their next words were stern. "We collectively disavow the following: greed, resentment, and entitlement."

Lethabo added, "They have no place in community. Our margins of survival are narrow. We also disavow:"

"Violence." It was nearly a chant, four people in unison.

Lethabo added, "It cannot be allowed except in cases of self-defense. The community should never allow situations to get to that point."

Danielle's eyes widened.

"Nationalism," the group intoned.

"It has been used to sabotage our mission," Lethabo said.

Oh, there is so much history I need to learn.

"Paranoia."

"In the hands of a sociopath, it tried to destroy us."

Holy shit.

Lethabo glanced at the others, and all five said together, "Given our ancestors' harrowing experiences, we disavow the label 'human.'"

What the actual fuck?

"We are Spacers. We live and die together," the group concluded.

"That is the whole of the accord," Lethabo said.

"Well done," exclaimed one of the patients who had not partici-
pated. "Thank you."

Lethabo's gaze dropped to her face. "You have questions?"

"Tons," Danielle said. "That's... that's a lot. I'm missing a lot of
history, for starters."

"I've been told the other Earthborn find it overwhelming,"
Lethabo said. "You all have three months to acclimate, after which
we will hold a group adulting ceremony for you, and introduce you
to occupational mentors."

Danielle heard the fighter snort.

Lethabo added, "Captain Ximena is putting off the next
Accord until then. Your participation in the Accord will be essential. The knowledge you Earthborn have about planet life will be
badly needed for the move. You will be listened to closely."

"Okay, so—"

"That is all for today. I will answer your questions tomorrow."
And the serene little shit turned on his heel and walked out.

"Wait!" Danielle called.

"You have two other visits this afternoon," the nearest nurse
said. "He is a polite youth. He will not leave you worn down for
your next meeting."

Fuming, Danielle drew up her list of questions.

True to his word, Lethabo worked through her list. She didn't
like some of his answers.

She was stunned to learn that captain was an elected position,
and at least in Lethabo's descriptions, nothing military or defensive
remained about the ship's culture. There had been an attempted
coup by a faction called the Mind Police several generations past,
which left such a painful schism in the population that nothing
resembling a police or authority position remained.

The population seemed to lack any cultural reference for
defense against a living adversary. Medical workers were the only
ones who were taught any form of self-defense, and it was rudimen-
tary; most martial art forms had morphed into dance.

Jokes she was accustomed to making with her unit buddies upset the medical staff because they referred to people hurting one another.

Danielle began waking drenched in sweat from nightmares of being hunted by dinosaurs or smothered in piles of featureless larvae and eaten alive.

It wasn't just what she was learning. She was prodded at by an intrusive pack of geneticists, who finally went away when she let them harvest eggs from her ovaries. If she'd realized how painless they had made that process, she would have agreed sooner.

She was also visited by linguists, who recorded her pronouncing a variety of English words. They were overjoyed to hear she knew some Catawba, right up until she admitted she only knew a few words she'd picked up from a tribal website, one of those siloed bits of historic data left over from when the Internet was free and open to everyone. Grandma's best guess about her "Native" blood was an Eastern tribe, and Danielle had picked Catawba because it was what she could access.

When the geneticists returned to tell her that they had found no Indigenous American markers in her DNA, Danielle was embarrassed to realize she was disappointed. But she wasn't surprised.

Grandma wanted to be special. Her grandmother wanted to have a community she could claim without adding to her obligations. Belonging was not something anyone in her family had been good at, even with each other.

Danielle's army units were the closest family she had known.

"So I'm a mutt," she said, looking at the mix of European bloodlines.

They didn't know that word.

She explained.

They were deeply worried they'd offended her. "Why refer to yourself as an animal?"

Her throat wore out trying to bridge the cultural divide. She gave up and started gesturing, "safe, fine, good."

But politics paled to the daily trial that was meals. Most of the food tasted like tar and plastic. The med staff blamed hibernation damage and invited a cook to help her find foods she could enjoy, but nothing seemed to help.

"I don't want to whine," she said at the end of the second week, "but eating is misery."

"I'm truly sorry," one of the staff replied. "We're not equipped to fix sensory changes. Maybe we could ask Voice, see if the semqu—"

"She's got more important tasks," Danielle said quickly. "I'll cope."

The strange youth was among a group of singers had visited the med bay the day before to perform a song of healing for all the patients, a tradition that bemused Danielle.

But her meal woes took distant second place in her worries. Lethabo informed her that *New Hope* had not had contact with Earth for some time. Given the world news at the time of the last Earth transmission (two hundred New Hopian years ago) many believed that nuclear war had destroyed either the capability or the willingness to communicate with the generation ship. It was possible no one on Earth remembered that they were in transit. Prior to "semqu contact," *New Hope* only messaged Earth once a year.

That meant this generation ship might be all that was left of humanity. It drove home her responsibilities. This ship needed her. It was clear the residents were suffering from some sort of group hallucination. What they all claimed to have experienced simply couldn't be real, and this Voice child—a cult leader, perhaps—had to be profiting from it.

The med bay staff allowed her to walk five times a day, and that was all. They had begun to drug the fighter to keep his outbursts under control, so she bit her lip and didn't argue.

But the bed rest restrictions frustrated her. She couldn't do anything until she found other Earthborn, and perhaps crew members, who hadn't been afflicted. She burned with that purpose and the desire to exercise and rebuild her strength. She needed to be physically capable and mentally sharp; she was still foggy around the edges. *Lazing around is not helping anyone.* She pushed herself every exercise session; it at least helped reduce the nightmares.

ABOARD NEW HOPE
VOICE'S DWELL
NEW HOPIAN YEAR 716
SEVENTEETH DAY OF THE TENTH MONTH

VOICE RUBBED a rag over her living room walls, her emotions bouncing almost as fast as her hands. She hated scrubbing walls. But the air in her dwell still smelled slightly of mildew, the result of a water leak that had taken time to locate and fix. It was the kind of thing her mother would derail conversations to obsess over.

I become an adult today. I shouldn't care what Harriet thinks.

But she did. Gregoire offered to help her clean, though he warned her he wasn't in a chatting mood. He was still processing yesterday's unpleasant moment, the reason her ceremony had been changed from a public gathering to a private one.

Ireti alone was happy about that.

Voice winced at the sudden memory of the ranting man with the knife. Gregoire and others tackled him. The knife sideways; she pinned it in place with her foot. Gregoire yelled for help. Others dragged the man away as he screamed about killing her.

Her offer to sing for him had been gently refused by the med bay staff.

It was the last thing Voice wanted to think about today.

She'd asked Ireti to give her more emotional room, because she wanted to feel the joy of the event. Voice had dreamed of her adulting rite her entire life, usually as some emotional, unrealistic event where Père finally respected her. She knew that wasn't going to happen, but she didn't want to miss experiencing what she expected to be the happiest day of her life.

Ireti had reluctantly agreed. <I will feel what you feel, and that is hard on us semqu,> they explained. <But I will do my best to let you feel the highs and lows of this day.>

Voice pushed the memory aside, focused on one arm's reach of wall at a time. When they finished cleaning, Gregoire borrowed her bathroom to change into a clean outfit.

When he came out dressed in a colorful tunic with bold geometric patterns, she exclaimed, "You're gleaming!"

He laughed, relaxed for the first time that day, then stepped outside while she changed.

Captain Ximena arrived with Voice's three infrastructure mentors. She welcomed them inside and exclaimed her appreciation for their gifts: worn textbooks, a drafting ruler, an ancient, well-cared-for digital drafting pad.

Captain Ximena set a small tray of finger foods on the table Voice used for eating and study. "I hope you're not disappointed, Voice. After yesterday—Well. We can repeat your ceremony at the group rite during the laws accord if you like."

"I am honored," Voice said, and thought for a moment. "I would like that, to be part of a group becoming adults."

"Good." Ximena looked relieved.

"Ireti wanted me to thank you for protecting me," Voice said quietly.

"But of course! We've arranged fulltime security for you for the foreseeable future. We're certain the attack attempt was simply the act of one broken man. He had hibernation psychosis, never recovered. But people are worried, and your safety matters to us."

Ireti said, <Your value of justice is interesting.> That statement was accompanied with an image of the man floating outside the ship. That would have been their solution.

Voice shared that with the captain.

"Tell Ireti that we are not so far apart. He was on his last chance after long treatment and community work." She paused, looked at Voice with compassion. "He chose the airlock."

Voice swallowed hard. "Ireti adds that not all residents of Se Collective share our definition of justice. I mean, of the efforts to treat him."

"I have gotten that sense," Captain Ximena said. "But that's enough of that subject for today. We're here to celebrate you."

The librarian arrived, with a few volunteers who knew Voice, and the therapist. Gregoire came back in with his girlfriend. Ulick Grandi arrived with Du and Laavanya, some of her most dedicated Fugrast students. Voice's large dwell felt crowded. People chatted as they settled in a small circle, Gregoire to her left, the captain to her right.

Her mentors glanced at the captain, who nodded. They started singing.

Voice finally accepted that her family was not coming, that Terri was not coming. There was an aching hole in her heart, but she was also relieved. There would be no mean comments from Père, no judgments from Adamantine. She relaxed and enjoyed the lovely tune of community and adulthood, her favorite of the four songs commonly used for the rite. That was probably Gregoire's doing.

Then each of her three mentors stood in turn and spoke glowingly of her strengths. Voice didn't recognize the girl they praised. For every compliment, she could hear Père rudely dismissing it, minimizing it. *He's here, after all. Why him and not Mère?*

She was grateful for her mentors' kindness, patience, and generosity in teaching, and after they spoke, she said so.

"Lack of confidence is your greatest weakness. I'm told by Ximena that you've been making huge strides in that area," said the mentor Voice thought of as the harshest, who had been, unexpectedly, the most profuse in his praise. "I am glad that is so. My deficiency as a mentor is that I am too hard on my students. I do not think this aided you. Your size should have reminded me how young you are, but all I saw was your mind. I pushed you harder because I could see your brain is so good at grasping concepts. I wish for you to always be honing that capability."

His self-judgment confused her. She focused on what she could understand. "That should not be a problem going forward. That is how Ireti—the semqu—communicates with me."

His eyes widened, and he broke into a broad grin. "I am deeply gratified to learn this."

He sat. The others, to her surprise, also listed their weaknesses as mentors and how they felt that had made her learning harder. Then all three stood.

"We would continue our relationship with you, if you so choose, but as a more equal partnership," they said in unison. Then they again deviated from what Voice recalled as the usual wording. "Your life has taken a different direction, so we would understand if you chose to step away or choose mentors who could aid you in other ways."

Voice stood. "I would continue our connection," she said. The traditional response evoked tears. She felt connected to them in a way she had not felt since she met Ireti. "You have given me much. I would like to keep learning. I just don't know how much time I will have with my new duties."

Ireti was listening. <Your duties will lighten with time. At some point you may find yourself bored.>

<I can't imagine that!> Aloud, Voice said, "I will have much to do that will keep me from working with you in the coming year. Once we begin to move to the surface—" her mind suddenly filled with images of alien city infrastructure: conduits unlike any she had seen, rock-lined canals, and tunnels through mountains. "Just think of all the interesting projects we'll need to design to supply

water, treat wastewater, and ensure our power needs are met! I would like to help, to be part of that process as much as I can. I can ask Ireti how other species have solved similar problems, if that would be helpful."

Her response seemed to make them happy. All three bowed to her, the adult's bow that the captain had given her in this room—had it only been two months ago? She bowed back. Captain Ximena gave a short talk about the rights and responsibilities of spacer adults, ending with, "Voice embodies service in a way no new adult among us ever has."

Her cheeks felt warm. Joy tingled through her body. Voice realized she was experiencing Ireti's effervescent joy along with her own. It made her even happier.

Ximena raised her hands and began singing, her rich alto melody filling the room. Gregoire joined a third below her, and everyone else added harmonic layers except Voice.

She listened as her community sang her into maturity. Her cheeks felt stretched; she couldn't remember when she had ever grinned this long. The hole was still there, but her community had made it much smaller. She joined in the next song, and the next. There wasn't really room to dance, but there was laughter, and conversation, and shared food.

People began to slip out, making excuses and congratulating Voice as they left. She began to feel self-conscious again. Gregoire and the Captain were the last to leave.

Ximena patted her hand. "Congratulations, Voice. Welcome to adulthood."

"Thank you. It was a bit embarrassing. They didn't all have to be so excessively kind just because I'm a translator now."

Ximena stared at her, mouth open.

It was Gregoire who replied. "Opa— I'm sorry. Voice. Voice, listen to me. They weren't being nice. They were being accurate."

"Oh."

The captain exhaled hard. "I think your father did you more

damage than any of us realized. Our community failed you by not intervening sooner. What you experienced tonight was, as Gregoire said, an accurate reflection of who you are. Who we see you as. You are part of our spacer family, and we value you."

Voice felt tears welling up and she didn't understand why. Or why they both gestured, asking permission, and each gave her a hug. She squeezed back, emotions buffeting her and flattening, buffeting her and flattening. After they left, she stayed at her closed door, quivering a little.

<Voice? I am confused by what I am sensing. Are you ill?> Ireti's bewilderment broke her.

<I'm... I'm... > Voice burst into tears. <I don't know! Is this what families are supposed to be like? Why couldn't my parents be more like this?> Her upset was wiped away instantly, a clammy calm that didn't eliminate her desire to vomit. She swallowed. "I am an adult now. I am not going to waste that good food."

<If you got into bed, it would be easier.> Ireti seemed thin and tired. <We could sort out your emotions.>

The kind intent reminded Voice of the ship's therapist. <Okay. I'm sorry. All my emotions had to be hard on you. Thank you for letting me feel that joy. For sharing yours.>

<Bed. Let's talk through our feelings together.>

ABOARD NEW HOPE
MAIN MED BAY
NEW HOPIAN YEAR 716
EIGHTEENTH DAY OF THE TENTH MONTH

THE FIGHTER HAD GONE on walkabout yesterday. Danielle had overheard enough to realize he had tried to hurt someone. No one would tell her directly, and they weren't letting her exercise. She was irritated and restless by the time Lethabo arrived to invite her to a ship-wide meeting.

I hate meetings. She leapt at the offer. "Anything's better than this bed." *Ship-wide will give me a good idea of the population's mental health.*

She was confused by the three times offered. Lethabo explained there was no place on the ship big enough for everyone, and there were of course assignments that could not be abandoned, so any "ship-wide" meeting was done in shifts.

"Let's go to the first one," Danielle said.

"Then we should go now." He negotiated her release with the staff, then insisted on a leisurely pace down the mural-decorated corridors, saying, "I promised not to break you."

Danielle thought about making a crack about him being too small to cause her any harm but decided against it. Those kinds of jokes had fallen flat with the medical staff.

They took a breezy lift tube, a cross between a revolving door and an escalator, which made her laugh. She was still smiling as they approached the sound spilling out of a large gathering room. Inside, about three hundred people of all ages milled in a long room, some cradling small packages along with their plates. Buffet tables lined the far end.

It reminded her of every wedding or funeral reception she'd ever attended. People chatted in groups, dressed in a wild variety of styles, from the simple extruded tunic Lethabo always wore to a highly embroidered sari to what looked like a hand-crocheted suit in eye-popping green and purple.

Zara—who was there, Danielle waved—had been right. Her skin was the palest in the room. Neither her grandmother nor the white supremacist grandfather she'd had to tolerate for one miserable summer during her parents' divorce would have been pleased, but for different reasons.

Lethabo found her a chair and she sank into it, begrudging the need but realistic; her calves and hips were already aching.

"I welcome you from waking!" The woman in the sari stood in front of her and bowed.

"Uh, thank you," Danielle stammered.

The woman stepped away before she could say anything else. *Real smooth. Gonna get a lot of information that way.*

Others followed. Their accents ranged from rounded vowels to clipped consonants, hinting at a multitude of languages, all with a languid pacing that she was beginning to consider New Hopian. Lethabo stayed silent, though every person acknowledged him and thanked him for his service in attending Danielle. No one tried to engage her beyond a welcome, and all were surprisingly skilled at evading her attempts at prolonging a conversation. She tried to ask about people's jobs; they would answer instead with their guild, avocation, or hobbies.

Lethabo noticed her frustration. "No one will talk to you for long. We do not monopolize the time of the recovering, so all have a chance to greet you, and you are not worn thin."

That implied that everyone knew who she was, but they clearly already did. Anonymity was a luxury she no longer had. A generation ship would be the ultimate in small-town culture, wouldn't it? She wondered how that was working. She knew intimately how small towns could be stifling places for those who didn't fit in.

"What's this about guilds?"

"Every essential infrastructure is organized by guild—air quality, agriculture, food preparation, wastewater, recycling, communications and electronics, medical, remote sensing and research—" Lethabo glanced at her and trailed off. "They work together, of course, but each has their own mentorship and training and, because I know you will ask, security protocols."

"I approve." That made for excellent security. Cellular structures like that made infiltration more difficult. It was also going to make her job a lot harder. She winced. They'd probably consider her intent to be infiltration. Then someone hurtled toward her and her whole body flinched. It was just a middle-school-aged boy being chased by three younger children. They dashed past, giggling, unaware they'd startled her.

"Kids get let out of school for these, huh?" Danielle asked, to cover her reaction. "You guys must enjoy the holiday."

Lethabo looked at her blankly. "Kids? School?"

The ship's captain swept in, asking in a booming tone, "Are we ready?"

Instead of noise, people snapped fingers and clucked their tongues. Lethabo lifted a finger to his lips. He pulled out a small, well-worn personal tablet and tapped on it.

To their credit, the little ones mostly settled down right away. The attendees formed a circle with Ximena in the center. The room got uncomfortably silent fast.

"I know many of you are worried about our location," Ximena said. Someone in the back of the room barked a laugh, one that carried a lot of tension, and a rustle went through the crowd, quickly silenced.

Lethabo had told her that no one knew where these mysterious aliens had taken them.

Of all the ridiculous things she'd been told, that was the one Danielle accepted; it made sense as a trigger for mass hallucination. Danielle watched the attendees, not Captain Bobbie—no, they called her Captain Ximena, didn't they? That was taking some getting used to, the focus on first names.

The charismatic Ximena had to be in on the deception.

Expressions ranged; as far as she could tell, the New Hopians here were either curious or wary and irritated. No obvious fear.

"One of our basic questions, however, has been answered. We now know where we are in the galaxy. Rupert?"

Danielle swung her attention back to the front.

A boy strolled toward the captain from the front row; he'd been waiting to be called forward. Danielle was struck by his confidence, the pride glowing through his tawny-beige face, below a carefully groomed pile of dark brunet hair. The front of his cream tunic was decorated with elaborate embroidery in colorful, almost fractal patterns, and he carried a small book away from the fabric in a way that made her wonder if his parents had told him not to get his clothes dirty. That tiny echo of something familiar made her heart ache unexpectedly.

When he reached the captain, Rupert bowed to her and then the group. "Fellow spacers, any Honored Earthborn in attendance, ancestors. We remain in the Heavenly Ganges, in our own plane of existence." He grinned.

Oh, he's loving this attention.

Lethabo whispered, "The Heavenly Ganges is the Milky Way."

"Thank you."

"The mistake most of you..." Rupert coughed, "most of us made was in looking too close to where we were in our flight path. The hardest part was identifying the stars we can see, because the constellations constantly change in a planetary orbit." He frowned.

Someone said, "It's so weird," and another laughed ruefully.

"Now we know why it was so hard for our ancestors," someone called.

There were scientists in the audience, she realized, adults who'd made astronomy their life's work, and not a single one looked upset that they'd been upstaged by a child. Those who were seated were leaning forward, grinning.

"I'm not going to understand the numbers," one of the white-haired adults in front said plaintively. "Just tell us where we are."

Rupert's grin was triumphant. "My math places us in the Orion spur of the aether's Ganges, some 1,200 light-years away from Earth."

Someone behind Danielle burst out, "Impossible! You're telling me that they moved us hundreds of light-years?"

Okay, not all the adults are happy for him. And ... wow.

Rupert shrugged. "I can't explain that, but yes."

"Our navigational computers have confirmed Rupert's calculations," Ximena said. "He is correct. This is where we are." A screen behind her came to life; a visualization of the Milky Way with red arrows labeled "Sol" and "Serium."

It zoomed in; a solid yellow line marked *New Hope's* path from Earth, with dots continuing toward its intended destination, New Terra.

She pointed to the spot where the solid line became dots. "This is our last recorded location under our own navigation, headed toward the Monorian Group."

The image shifted; a green arc connected that last known location to a star on the upper left. "We now appear to be behind the California Nebula, halfway to the Taurus Dark Clouds." In an inset box below, *New Hope* was shown in orbit around a planet, with a line to a star in the chart.

The distance was boggling. Danielle's brain spun, like a clock with all the cogs disengaged. Everyone in the room silently stared at the image along with her.

Ximena cleared her throat and adopted a game show host's enthusiasm. "So. Rupert wins the 'Where Are We Now' competition! Congratulations!"

The room burst into applause.

Danielle leaned over to Lethabo. "What does he win?"

Lethabo blinked up at her from his device, solemn. "The competition to determine where we are."

"What's the prize?"

"Knowing is its own reward," Lethabo said, then added, "What prize could motivate everyone equally? People who feel gratitude will give small gifts to him or his family—"

She lost the rest of it as a wall in her head gave way, the many experiences involving "kids" solidifying into an obvious cultural shift she had tripped over but ignored. "He's so young."

Lethabo's eyes widened. "Ah. Honored Earthborn, age is no barrier to service. Your culture separated children from working adults from the wise, yes?"

"Uh— Kinda." Which was a bit of an understatement, she realized. "Children went to school, adults worked, retirees played." She winced as service memories rose up that she wanted to leave buried. "At least in my country. That wasn't true worldwide, though most countries had schools."

But she had always resented not having the luxury of a recreation-filled childhood, being taunted for never knowing the details of pop-culture based in movies or games she'd never had the money or time to experience. She was surprised it still rankled; it meant nothing now. Once in the military, she'd not only reaped the benefits of a less coddled childhood, she'd also seen what truly deprived childhoods were like. "How do children learn here?"

Lethabo's brow creased. "I looked up school, but I don't understand it. You must have had many, many children of the same age."

Danielle blinked. "Your population is too small for centralized schooling?"

Lethabo shrugged. "Children learn by doing. We teach practical knowledge. Academic learning is individual, say in the special training needed for astronomy—" he pointed to Rupert, who was receiving admirers in a long line, "or protein ranching, or hydraulics. Separation by age in the first generation created many dangerous issues. There were many suicides. We teach basics in creche, like safety sign, simple math, language and emotional skills, but not much beyond that."

He paused. "We are each assigned a group of mentors that changes as our interests and the needs of the community develop." He looked at Danielle and smiled. "You'll be given your mentor group soon, when we discover better what you need, and what we'll need on the surface. But that will be months in the future for you."

It felt like a slap. She'd been given jobs her whole life; orders were orders. Why would this be different? *Because I don't understand these people or trust their judgment.* And she had her own mission. Whatever the community chose for her could never be her true focus. *And I'll never be able to admit that.*

She looked up at the boy and tried to find common ground. She thought back to her own childhood, how bored she'd been in some classrooms, how few she'd been excited in.

"That sounds like a much more comfortable education than I got," she admitted. "But you all don't get a childhood? You don't get to play games, or watch movies, or...?"

She had shocked him. "Play is a basic need." His tone implied she had been badly harmed somehow. "Every community member gets eight hours of creative or play time a day, to pursue an avocation, regardless of age."

Five to eight hours daily to ... play? "Everyone?" Danielle found herself glancing at the captain. "Surely officers have duties that would not allow—"

"Everyone. Including the cooks and the wastewater workers and the medical staff and the captain." Lethabo seemed amused. "A doctor during an emergency would not stop caring for someone, of course. It can be shorter at times—as little as five during harvest and processing, when nearly everyone helps—but we take time later. It was not like that on Earth?"

How does anything get done? "You have no idea how much it was not like that on Earth," Danielle said.

"How sad." Lethabo seemed honestly pained, then shook it off. "It is that way now, here. We should congratulate Rupert."

Those already waiting, most of them holding small gifts, insisted she cut to the head of the line. Then the young math whiz became hero-struck when he realized who she was.

"Did you know Stephen Hawking?" Rupert asked in a rush, dark eyes wide. "Or Bibha Chowdhuri?"

"I did not have the chance to meet either," Danielle said dryly. His disappointment wiped out her urge to laugh.

"Can we talk later?" Ruper asked. "I have so many questions. Lunch tomorrow?"

"Sure," Danielle said, rocking her fist for good measure. "Though you'll have to come rescue me from the nurses." It would do well for her to have an in with the astronomers. She was going to need to build connections across the ship.

That need was immediately reinforced back in the med bay. The nurse insisted on checking her vitals, and then swiftly hooked her up with an IV. A second nurse hovered nearby. *Something's up.*

Captain Ximena walked in and greeted her. "I regret to have our first real conversation be about painful news," she said. "Were you close to your fellow Earthborn?"

Oh shit. "Him?" Danielle pointed to the empty bed, and the nurses nodded. "No. He wouldn't even tell me his name."

Ximena's shoulders dropped, as if she had been dreading Danielle's response. "He tried to kill Voice yesterday."

"He *what?*"

"He lunged at Voice with a knife, screaming that he was going to kill her. We believe he suffered from hibernation-induced psychosis."

"Fuck!" *That's why I'm hooked her up to the IV again.* She slumped back against the pillows, away from the captain. "Is she okay?"

"She was not injured, luckily. She even asked to sing for him." Ximena's smile was pained.

"She's a naive, kind child." Danielle held the captain's gaze. "I take it that is no longer an option."

Ximena raised an eyebrow. "No. He chose the airlock."

"And you let him."

"I did." Ximena carried the weight of that decision; knew it was necessary.

Danielle respected that.

"Not alone, captain," a nurse said. "We all allowed this."

"Thank you." Ximena hadn't broken eye contact. "Do you understand, Danielle?"

"I do." *Possibly better than anyone else aboard.*

TEN
ADJUSTMENTS

The calligraphy box Gregoire brought her was gorgeous, with two drawers still containing equipment, including a few actual metal nibs. Voice protested the gift as being too valuable. He just laughed and told her to calligraph something for his family if she wanted.

"I will!" Her delight was only slightly flattened; Ireti was getting better at letting her feel joy.

She decided to take her hobby hours in the evening, to give herself and Ireti the longest possible uninterrupted rest. It turned out that calligraphy—the utter focus of it, the meticulousness, the beauty, and then the wide-open creativity offered by fixing mistakes with random art— was soothing to the semqu.

That evening, she leaned back on her cushions and looked around her. She'd received a few gifts of books and calligraphy tools from her language students, who insisted on giving her something for her Fugrast lessons. Someone had asked for her favorite colors, and she'd told them: black, purple, red. Now she had cushions, soft warm throws and a few embroidered and painted wall hangings in those colors.

Someone had arranged a sing for her that doubled as a welcome to Ireti, which had given Voice another taste of the semqu's odd, effervescent joy.

She'd gotten gifts that were less welcome, too. Terri's brother Tiani had personally handed her a beautifully calligraphed "graduation certificate" from the support group, signed by everyone except Terri. She frowned. Everything about that felt off; plus, Terri hadn't replied to her question about it. Voice had left it in a basket by the door with a few other packages from people who'd always avoided her or been mean to her before.

Her first wall hanging surprised her; it was from her family.

Harriet reached out to Gregoire and asked for Voice to stop by the weaving guild meeting so she could make her gift in person, but with community support for them both.

The weaving room had smelled like her parents' dwell without the scent of potatoes; just dye and recycled yarn. Mère seemed to have friends there now; her loom was set up in the guild space. Harriet and Adamantine gifted her a woven geometric design about the size of a chair cushion. Père had helped, they said, though she wasn't sure she believed them. It was red and purple, edged with a bit of the blue she remembered helping Mère dye.

"It's lovely, thank you," Voice had said. She'd meant it.

Adamantine was silent and sullen, Harriet full of advice on how to properly hang and care for the weaving, which rapidly morphed into hygiene and dietary advice. One of her new friends was laying a hand on her arm when Voice thanked her again, said she had a class to teach, and fled.

Voice hung their gift on the wall she kept her back to as she worked. There, but not at the center of her attention. It prickled her with emotions she wasn't ready to explore. Adamantine was not happy for her even though she was no longer panic-stricken, which was confusing. Worry and other emotions rose because Père was still livid she was living on her own.

Harriet alone seemed to have accepted Voice's new role and be proud of it; she just couldn't not be herself.

Families are hard.

She leaned forward and lost herself in creating another line of letterforms. When she sat back again, Ireti said, <I'm grateful you've found something you enjoy so much.> Contentment washed across her, not her own.

It took Voice by surprise and left her in tears briefly, before the calm.

<So many emotions, all at once.> Ireti's curiosity swirled. <Shall we parse them tonight?>

<Yes.> Their evening review of all the emotions the semqu had shut down during the day was fascinating and educational to them both. Yesterday they'd explored her deep-seated shame at making a translation error that required her to re-teach several words to her Fugrast students. She'd expected anger and frustration from them. They simply took it in stride, one of them commenting he'd have no idea how to pronounce Fugrast in her shoes; he couldn't hear sounds in his head the way others could. Her students, in short, had been kind to her. It had made her tear up in the same way.

Her mentor's words, "You are a spacer, you need community," came back to her. She could gift small scrolls to thank people for their patience with her. Ask them to her home for a small meal, perhaps? No. Too much too soon.

Later, as Voice lay under her blanket, the semqu helped her pull on her memories like taffy. They found desire to do well, desire for acceptance, desire to please, giddiness at being supported, pain at getting now what she had never been given before, grief for what she missed getting from her parents, and finally, anger at Père, especially, for being so unkind. She was astonished. <I had no idea how often I feel so many emotions at once.>

<Spacers respond to conflicting emotions with tears. Interesting.>

<Well, me. I don't expect all of us do. Do other species you've encountered not do that?>

<Larsivians do. Others, too.> They shared brief images of several scaled creatures with long tails and massive skulls. They reminded Voice of lizards or crocodiles. <Larsivians' native languages require one to state one's emotion first.>

<That would be hard. Does that mean if you don't know how you feel you can't speak?> Vaguely, she realized Ireti was hungry.

<They have words for that. But they also seem to know their emotional states better than spacers do. Their Voices are probably the most distressed to have their emotions limited; we had to work hard to give them more flexibility. That is how I knew how to ease my impact on you, so you can have the emotions you do.>

<So, you could give spacers more emotional freedom, I mean, your next Voice?>

<Possibly. You are not thinking of dying?> Unease floated across her.

<No! I'm loving this life.> Tears threatened, again. <I've never been so content. And it's not just that my anxiety is finally under control. I'm so much freer than before. Also, you should eat.>

Surprise flared; Ireti had shared more than they had intended. <I will.> And then they were falling asleep together, dreaming of flying and swimming and traveling the stars.

ABOARD NEW HOPE
NEW HOPIAN YEAR 716
MONTH ELEVEN'S THIRD DAY

THE DAY after Danielle was told she'd finally be released from med bay, Lethabo introduced her to Juand Grandi, a muscular Black engineer, and his artist husband, a brown-skinned man with a forked Viking beard named Niels Gutherie.

"They will be your hosts for your assimilation into spacer culture," Lethabo told her.

Danielle greeted them by bowing properly, the one cultural gesture she'd mastered, and bit back the Borg joke she longed to make.

"It has been an honor serving as your guide," Lethabo told her.

"I'll miss you," Danielle said, and meant it. The monk-like youth had kept her sane during what had seemed like an endless medical entrapment. "Don't be a stranger, okay?"

Lethabo's brow creased.

"I mean, feel free to visit me. I am grateful to you and I have enjoyed learning from you." She'd learned he allowed himself pride in his ability to teach, and not much else.

"Ah! A new phrase, thank you. I will not be a stranger." He bowed, grave as always, and left her with the two men. They were an oddity on board, both as tall as she was, Juand as broad. Niels had a lighter build.

"Welcome!" Juand said. "We have a room ready for you. Our kids are looking forward to meeting you; they've promised to be on their best behavior and to teach you properly." He spoke even more slowly than most New Hopians, with an accent that impressed Danielle, Caribbean of some flavor. She wondered if it was okay to ask. So many subjects seemed off-limits, and she still hadn't figured out why; Lethabo couldn't or wouldn't tell her.

Niels said nothing, just smiled and gestured welcome. She gestured her thanks, and he grinned.

Jaund pointed out landmarks as they slowly walked the halls toward the Quartier Vivant, where they lived. "I understand our culture is quite different now. What's the biggest difference you've noticed so far?"

"Humor and food," she said. "I've quit making jokes entirely."

"Wise," Niels said. His voice was deep and low. She didn't hear it again until they were in her hosts' home.

"Yah. I've seen what passed for comedy on ancient vids." Juand's brow creased, and he looked disturbed. Danielle decided to wait to ask what he meant.

Home was a tidy, quiet oasis in a boisterous neighborhood, with a reserved boy and girl of about eight and twelve, respectively. The room Danielle was given, which had previously been a combined study room and office, was stocked with clothes in the utilitarian style she'd told Lethabo she preferred.

On her bed was a disintegrating, still-sealed box of her personal effects.

"There was a leak into the storage area," Juand said apologetically.

Moisture had invaded, and with it, mold. Her box had been treated, but the photo of her grandmother she had dim memories of packing was a blackened film that crumbled into ash-like bits when she touched it. She couldn't recall her face. Nothing else in the box had survived any better. Her last connection to those she'd left on Earth was dust and junky bits of rusted metal. Even her trusty boots were a collapsed, blackened mess.

"I'm so sorry." Juand was gently patient as he helped her navigate the confusing recycling and trash system to dispose of items whose base components she couldn't recall.

"The photos would have been nice," she said, washing her hands later, "but honestly I don't remember what most of it was." It was a lie, spoken out loud to stiffen her spine. Everyone she had loved was long dead. She needed to look forward. These people here needed her, and they were her family now, no less problematic or confused than the one she'd left behind.

That week they ate meals at home, not in the cafeteria where she'd been led to believe everyone ate. It was clearly something they were doing to help her adjust, to teach her the social rules, so she promised herself she'd be a good student, and eat whatever they served without complaint.

That first night she stayed silent during the non-denominational prayer, which the boy led, and then took a taco from the plate he offered her. She controlled her facial expression as she took her first bite. As she had expected, the tacos didn't taste right—too sweet, then too hot.

It wasn't the first time her taste buds had rebelled. In the med bay, not a single food tasted as she expected it to, not even rice, and it seemed to change with every meal, a constant irritant. The medical staff blamed it on hibernation damage, but she suspected it had as much to do with flavor changes due to centuries of hydroponic growth.

"Oh, I forgot to ask—do you have any cheese?" she asked.

Jaund blinked at her, and looked at his husband, who looked just as baffled.

"Cheese is an ancient word for fermented milk," said the girl, Marfa, who'd ignored Danielle since she'd arrived. "Did you really eat that?"

Both kids were immediately fascinated, not because she'd slept since leaving Earth and knew history their parents didn't, but because she ate food they considered gross. She grinned. *Nice to know some things never change.*

Her adult hosts appeared offended. "Why would we serve rotten food?"

"Not rotten," Danielle said. "Cheese was a method of milk preservation, back when we had dairy cows. Gave us protein. Fat. And... umami, I think."

"Dairy is another ancient word," Marfa said to Jaund, who still looked confused. "No cows in space, Honored Earthborn. Our milk is from nuts and grains."

"Ah!" Niels rattled off something she didn't catch. Lethabo had told her he spoke Norwegian and at least one Sámi language.

Juand nodded. "That's right, nut cheese was phased out a few generations back; too many batches were going bad. Something that maybe could be re-created when we move to the surface, though."

"Right." No cheese. She wondered if the enzymes to digest cow milk had faded out of existence. Maybe everyone aboard was lactose intolerant now. Suddenly she could kill for a wheel of queso fresco.

Juand asked, "Do your skills include that processing?"

"Not me." Danielle shook her head. "Food processing is not my skillset."

"You'll be misunderstood less if you answer yes or no questions with your hands," Juand said.

Danielle sighed; she'd been told that before.

The boy, Ulick, added, "Head shaking in some households means yes."

Oh. "Thank you! Nobody had explained that part."

Ulick perked up. The kids hadn't been ignoring her, they'd been told not to pester her.

Once the ice was broken, Ulick and Marfa waylaid her with questions through dinner, and as the days turned into weeks, as often as they could, sometimes for hours.

Danielle had to rest a lot between workout sessions, and unlike their parents, she had no job or hobbies to go to. She could serve on volunteer shifts ship-wide and help develop curriculum, but none of the Earthborn were allowed to teach for months, which struck her as frustrating and unfair. All of her hobbies back home had been active, dirt-based—hiking, mountain biking, hunting, fishing. She wouldn't be allowed on the surface until she was much, much stronger. None of the shipboard opportunities interested her.

Danielle had never been a kid person, but answering Marfa's and Ulick's questions—and occasionally Rupert's and Lethabo's— helped strengthen her memory and saved her from boredom. She developed a strong bond with the four youths as she tried to sort out their almost familiar, yet utterly baffling culture.

Assimilating by immersion was overwhelming, exhausting. She

bewildered one of the cafeteria workers on her first visit by trying to pay.

"Why would anyone need to buy a meal?"

Danielle had explained how it worked on Earth, and the woman was horrified, and burst into rapid chatter with the rest of the crew. The entire cafeteria staff fussed over her like an abused creature for weeks afterwards.

Every interaction brought her up against assumptions she didn't realize she held as values, like "work should fill one's day" and "food is something you earn." But stumbling over her own tongue and social ineptness was still better than reading the tomes of essentially self-published pablum that nearly thirty generations of onboard academics had written. She only had to open one of those electronic files to figure that out.

As a way to cope, she started writing weekly letters to her long-dead brother, the only relative she could think of who would be fascinated by this new world.

Oh, I have this week's cultural highlight: watching a 6′5″ black man in dreads, a tunic, tights and a crocheted kilt instruct you in high British English how to make "proper" sweet potato tacos on a hotplate, yelling to his husband, "Darling, put in the good air filter, I am going with the garlic and the caps," while helping his children with their studies in bursts of Mandarin and Portuguese.

Ulick looks ethnic Chinese and Marfa Latinx, without any of Juand's features nor those of his brunet husband. "Embryos" is the only explanation I get, and it's curt, as if I'm rude for wondering, let alone asking. I've seen what granddad Clyde would have called "mixed" families all over the ship—and brother, don't use that word, don't even think it if you can avoid it.

I've not gotten the nerve to ask if it's not okay to have your own children, I mean your own bloodline, or if fertility has become an issue due to radiation. I once tried to ask one of the nurses, and she got twisted tight and about five ways of offended. Apparently, my language skills aren't up for that task yet? They can barely handle household conversations, because Juand's Caribbean English is not our cousin's. Some words have changed meanings, or maybe it's just that everything around the language changed. Or what's considered private has.

Oh, but hey! I've been asked to help develop curriculum for a planetary survival class, finally! Yesterday I met with several other Earthborn. I figured it would be nice to have dirt-born to talk to, and complain to about the culture shock, but none of them are from the U.S. and they're all fitting in better than I seem to be. Most of them have embraced the ship-wide delusion that some mystery power moved the ship instantaneously.

I promised myself I'd be fair.

I concede we are orbiting a planet that does not appear to be New Terra.

And we have encountered alien species. Plural. Saw 'em myself.

I'm just so... wary. Maybe there was a virus exchanged, that ... all at once? Never mind. I'm grasping at straws. My brain does not want to accept a technology that far advanced beyond our own in alien hands.

I'll focus on what I do understand. These people can recycle plastic, paper and metal scrap until the molecules scream, but they freak out over the idea of an insect bite, don't know how to make a fire and have no idea how to tell if a wild animal is harmless or hostile. (I will admit I have trouble with that myself. Many of these alien life forms don't map to Earth biology. Peqe in particular ought to have been shot on sight in my view, and that would have melted wrong, as they say here and now for "gone badly.") It's a happy thing none of us Earthborn were conscious when they made first contact with those damn arrogant fuzzy dinosaurs.

What worries me most is that after seven hundred years of travel, this culture has all the defensive skills of a wet newspaper, not that that phrase means a damn thing to any of them. All that travel time we could have used to hone martial arts skills and new weaponry, and they focused it on language, dance and music study? I couldn't convince my co-teachers to incorporate any such training into the course, either. Unanimous opposition, and the shipborn were horrified by the idea. Like, "worried about my psychology or my soul" level of horror. I was referred to the ship's shrink and had to talk my way out of weekly counseling.

I need to find another way. Whatever I do, it's may take years. And I don't know if we have that much time.

**ABOARD NEW HOPE
NEW HOPIAN YEAR 717
FIRST MONTH FIFTH DAY**

Voice had made plans; she was ready to schedule some social time. As they left the Quartier, she told Gregoire she needed to stop by her former youth anxiety support circle on the way to today's meeting with the alien ambassadors. In preparation for inviting the group to visit her apartment, she had already asked the cafeteria for a picnic basket: finger foods for a private-dwell gathering.

The semqu had tiredly helped her practice what to say to the closest friends she'd had, friends she hadn't seen in months. She expected at least two of the older boys wouldn't come. She was important now, and she knew Tiani and his buddy would resent that.

But she had played games and practiced coping techniques with a number of the younger members over the years. She had admitted to herself it would be nice if some of the others looked up to her in a way they never had.

And Terri should be there. She was worried. Terri had only responded once to her messages, and Voice had learned that she had recently moved back in with her family again, against her counselor's advice. Had Tiani taken Terri's communicator? Terri rarely gave her the silent treatment for this long, even if Voice had been too busy to spend the necessary hours listening to her complaints.

Reveling in her freedom from Obert, Voice was bewildered about her friend's choice. Why would Terri return to her family not once, but twice?

Voice arrived at the room's open door a few minutes before the meeting was to begin. She was initially reassured by continuity. The group inside remained small, and the walls still were a solid blue, broken only by a pile of multicolored cushions.

Six youths already lounged on pillows in a rough circle. Tiani and his sidekick sat facing the door. Tiani sneered at her. Terri sat with her back to the door. Worst-case scenario to open, then. Voice took a deep breath.

"What are you doing here?" Tiani demanded. "Going to brag about how you have a cure for anxiety? Just let yourself be taken over by aliens?"

"What?" She hadn't expected him to react well to her, but she hadn't prepared herself for anger, nor for the look of resentment on the faces that turned to her.

Terri turned last. "You never had anxiety at all, did you? You just faked it." She looked hurt, betrayed.

What did I do? A spike of pure pain pulsed in Voice's chest, then dulled immediately to an unsettled numbness. "Why would you believe that?"

"I was in the middle of a panic attack yesterday and Tiani told me to go find a semqu." Terri spit the words.

"I did not say that!" Tiani burst out, looking around wildly. "That was Mom!"

A wave of unsettled feeling, not her own, washed over Voice. She closed her eyes, lightheaded. <Do not take me over and speak to them,> she thought. <It will just make it worse.>

"Your family's inappropriate response to Voice being chosen is not her fault." Gregoire's loud outburst startled her. "Nor is it yours." His posture was stiff, his face stern. He was, she realized, furious on her behalf. "Your anger at Voice is utterly inappropriate. Her lack of anxiety is a side effect. We have no idea if the same thing would happen in someone else. It might make it worse. Have you forgotten that six people killed themselves before the semqu succeeded with Voice? Kindly remind your families of that, and if they have any questions, to talk to me or the captain."

"I don't care," Tiani snapped. "This support group is only for youth with anxiety."

"I hadn't planned to attend," Voice said. She could hear the coldness, the harshness in her tone, and she didn't try to fix it. "I came to thank you for your gift and had thought to ask friends to lunch with me. But you have made it clear I no longer have any here."

"You never did," the younger boy said, sneering.

Terri spun away from her and curled into a ball. It was her pain reaction, one Voice had seen when Terri was reacting to something deeply hurtful her brother had said. One of the other boys reached out and put a hand on her shoulder, and the girl on the other side of her said something softly. They both looked at Voice as if Terri's pain was her fault.

Maybe it was. *She feels abandoned,* Voice thought distantly. *I should have made more of an effort sooner. It's already too late.* But that freed her to help Terri in a way she knew her old friend would never forgive: ensuring she was permanently removed from her abusive family.

"Tiani, it is a crime that you and your mother are still allowed to mistreat Terri after all these years, after all the progress she made with her foster family. Especially now that there are hibernation pods available. I will address this. Terri will be free of your abuse." She watched Terri's back, not Tiani's face, as she spoke. Terri collapsed to the floor, howling.

Voice turned and walked down the hall. Terri's crying reminded her of Adamantine's howl in the cafeteria just after the ship had been moved. Did she dare to reach out to her sister now? Her stomach roiled. No.

Behind her, Gregoire said, "I'm officially reporting this so-called support circle to the mentors for disbandment. You sully the most basic precepts of community support." He hit the room closure. He spoke quietly into his comm for a bit.

He'd apparently locked the door, because she could hear pounding fading behind her as she plodded away, wondering who she should contact about Tiani first. When he caught up with her, he paced her for a bit before speaking. "Are you okay?"

"Yes, no," she said.

He chuckled. "That's fair." After a moment he added, "That had to hurt. A lot."

"It did, and then it went away, and now I'm numb, and I'm glad I'm numb. I knew those two boys hated me, but I really liked Terri —" a flash of pain, again, "and some of the others."

"I'm sorry."

She remembered the pounding on the door. "You should unlock that door," she said. "Being locked in is an anxiety trigger for some of them."

He glanced at his communicator. "Nona already has. She was free and her office is nearby. Do you know why those two dislike you so much?"

"Our previous leader focused on the younger members to the exclusion, sometimes, of the older ones, and at the time I was the youngest there. There were meetings where the oldest members didn't get to share anything. One of them would deliberately trigger me later, or Tiani would tell Adamantine what I'd said in group. Tiani doesn't actually have anxiety, but he manipulates his parents into browbeating other adults until he gets his way. I need to talk to someone about him."

"It is being dealt with. Nona thanks you. That family was on their last chance; the community has been waiting to step in. Terri was refusing to leave. She will be with a new foster family tonight."

"She has pushed away help she's needed for years," Voice said. "I would have done the same, had done the same, when people tried to help me with Père."

"Yes. But it sounds like that group has not been effective for some time."

"I benefited from it, as broken as it was," Voice said. "I might have killed myself if it had not existed." Gregoire made a noise and stopped. She turned to him and realized he was crying.

Surprise cut through her numbness.

"Um. Are you okay?"

"Yes and no," he said.

They both laughed, and he wiped his face. "I am sorry you felt so alone and hopeless," he said. "That is not what—how—" He swallowed. "I believed our community cared for each other better than that."

She shrugged. "Even in community, it is hard to know what is going on within someone's mind and life. Especially when that someone is trying to hide pain. I was doing my best to hide."

He nodded. "Just a second," he said. He stepped aside and spoke into his comm for a moment. When he came back, he looked calmer and motioned down the hall. "We should get you to the meeting."

"Gregoire," she said, "would you like to have a picnic with me? You and your girlfriend? I have plenty of food."

"I would, Voice," he said, smiling. "It would be a shame to waste that basket. Shall we invite your calligraphy mentors too?"

"Yes," she said. "Let's talk to them afterwards." The soft contentment that rose didn't outweigh the pain, but it was a start.

ELEVEN
TOGETHER WE SURVIVE

ABOARD NEW HOPE
GRANDI-GUTHERIE HOUSEHOLD CHAMBERS
YEAR 717; FIRST MONTH'S TWENTY DAY

Danielle's day had started with the indignities of gas and diarrhea, coupled with cramps and the realization that she couldn't find any preparations for a heavy period in Juand and Niels' apartment. Marfa was not home, and she wasn't about to dig through the young girl's room. She had figured out that what little privacy people had on board was viewed as sacred.

The medic was confused as to why she had walked all the way to sick bay to ask, then told her she'd have to have three "normal" periods before they'd fit her with the period suppressants that apparently every other non-pregnant woman on the ship used.

He handed her three painkillers. "One every 12 hours, with food. Don't skip that part."

She sighed; she'd hoped to avoid breakfast. Her sense of taste was starting to heal, but eating was still a trial. When she walked into the eating area, all she could smell was a nauseating mix of fried greens and yeast. She grabbed a bowl of congee, the closest thing to oatmeal on offer, and sat at the end of a table where a group was chatting over mostly empty plates.

She stared at the rice soup and picked up her spoon. She could have killed for smoked ham and eggs, or bacon, or anything resembling real cheese. Just the thought of the inaccessible foods filled her mouth with saliva, which at least helped her swallow the gruel.

She gave in to a moment of acute homesickness. She missed the easy camaraderie of her fellow warriors and the shared communication of glances and hand gestures during an ongoing threat. They were all long dead, now. She hadn't expected so much grief.

Nor had she expected so many of the conversations she overheard in the cafeteria to be so naive. The mixed-age group next to her were trying to decide what songs to sing for the group youth adulting ceremony, which apparently would include Voice. They wanted to include her parasite in the song.

Danielle clenched a fist under the table.

A young girl said, "Mixed tempo, then, but with lots of slow moments, because she said they experience time differently?"

"Oh, Captain Ximena suggested we stick with the languages Opal—I mean Voice—knows, so the semqu will understand the whole thing," an older man said. "Does anybody have her list?"

Laudatory and near subservient to these aliens. Not a single self-defensive thought among them. Had none of these people seen a horror movie, learned anything about the history of first contact between human cultures? She might as well be building the ship's armament out of used tampons.

Other overheard conversations let her know that once again, the Earthborn had been left out of the loop on the ship's recent conversations with the aliens. She'd offered repeatedly. *Why didn't they tap me? I'd give my eye teeth to see what their offensive armaments are like.*

At least the painkillers worked. But she was in a foul mood when she headed to the gym, where her assigned trainer/medic met her at the door. "You've been doubling up on workouts on the treadmill and in the weight setup every day for two weeks."

"I'm trying to regain lost ground," Danielle said.

"Your last blood draw makes it clear you're breaking muscle down, not building it up. You need to rest."

"And do what? I'm bored shitless!"

He jerked back, as if she'd told him she was going to throw a punch. "Go help in the fields—no, you neglect your recreation hours to your own detriment. There are guilds for hundreds of hobbies, Danielle. Find one that interests you. At a minimum, use your time to learn something other than English. You're going to need Yoruba soon."

Which was how she had learned that the ship's language changed every year, at the whim of whoever won some stupid game, for fuck's sake, and English wouldn't be responded to in two months' time. When she asked how she was supposed to learn a language that fast, the trainer told her to ask *kids* for help. Only he hadn't said kids. He'd said, "Find a language sponge," and when Danielle had blinked at him in incomprehension, he'd added, "Someone too young to serve."

Which set Danielle off again, because she wasn't being allowed to work yet.

Both Ulick and Marfa were home and at the central room's table when she got back to their apartment. Danielle slumped into a chair. "I need to learn next year's language."

"Yep!" Marfa said. "Yoruba is one of the Bantu languages! It'll be fun."

Danielle groaned. "I guess having all those different languages at least makes it easier to hide conversations from the friggin' aliens."

"Why would you need to hide?" Ulick, asked. "Why are you so worried about them?"

"Why aren't any of you?" she snapped, frustrated.

"What's there to worry about?" Ulick asked. He wasn't even

looking at Danielle, focusing on the linguistic puzzle he was solving, his lithe dark fingers flying. The boy's mind was impressive; he often sang in one language while doing puzzles in another.

He was also still a child. The one utterly iron-clad house rule her adult hosts had laid down for Danielle was, "Don't hurt or scare our kids."

"A lot of topics you'll learn about as an adult," Danielle said.

"I know most of them. Heartbreak, consent-violation, loss of someone you love, space dust, fire, air contamination, water contamination, wastewater breakdown, crop failure and starvation." Ulick managed to make the list of emotionally damaging or potentially mission-ending disasters sound utterly boring.

Danielle stared at him. "Do you really understand all of those?"

Dark eyes flicked to her, brows bunched, and then back down. "We all have to know about them. Because we're spacers."

Her shoulders cramped. It grated on her deeply, the ship-wide refutation of "human." The word had become an epithet in every language. They were all spacers now, they told her, without human biases. But they'd kept religions alive, and Danielle remembered Zara's comments in the shower.

"I don't believe in bias-free spacers."

"We are one community. We live or die together." The last sounded memorized, rote, but there was a conviction behind it that Danielle believed. She'd just rarely heard it from someone so young. As she stared at him, another mental wall collapsed.

It finally clicked, hard. "Live or die together" was literal. This new culture's focus on community wasn't just a feel-good thing. It wasn't an anti-human-back-on-Earth thing. Lack of cohesion and trust could be fatal on a long journey.

Community meant *survival*.

She'd have to learn how to work with that, including those god-awful long meetings. She sighed. "That's true shipboard."

"And it will hold true on the surface." Ulick gave her a long, hard look.

Interesting. "Did somebody tell you to tell me that?"

"No." His conviction slipped into puzzlement, and then he shrugged. "I've been reading Earth history. It sucked."

"Some of it," Danielle agreed. "But you wouldn't be here without all of it."

Ulick thought about that for a minute, working his puzzle. "Maybe we wouldn't have had to leave if people had valued each other more."

Danielle's anger flared. Ulick had no idea what life on Earth had been like when she was his age. This mission had been an extraordinary, unprecedented achievement in international cooperation. She took a moment to calm herself—he was amazingly mature, but he was still a child—before replying evenly, "That is a possibility."

He took that as an affirmation, and after a few minutes announced he was going to the cafeteria for a snack. Danielle watched him leave, sitting on the unnecessary urge to escort him. Ulick was so little, so vulnerable, and had never suffered a threat worse than a friend calling him names. So fucking naïve, and unlikely to encounter anything shipboard that would challenge that naiveté.

And he was a walking example of most of the adults in his culture. Vulnerable and surrounded by alien predators.

After the door slid closed behind him, Marfa asked, "There are threats other than the ones he mentioned, and those are what you're worried about, aren't you?" Marfa, too, was whip-smart, and far more curious than wary about Danielle's ideas. Ulick seemed to fear contamination from Danielle; Marfa was at that questioning age that made her open to fresh viewpoints. Danielle didn't want to take advantage of that, but it was so hard, when no one else was listening.

"Yes," she said cautiously.

"Like what?"

Danielle took a deep breath. "Well, some of it may be protective traits or instincts that people have lost on the journey."

"Like fear of the dinos?" Marfa prompted.

One of Marfa's parents would have corrected her to say peqe; dino was Danielle's term for the aliens. She smiled. "Why do you say that?"

"I like to sit behind the emotional support officer at lunch. Sometimes she talks in generalities about her challenges, ones that she's considering doing group therapy for. One of them that has come up a lot lately has been people with irrational fears of the peqe."

"That's not irrational. It's an instinctual fear of a predator," Danielle said. "Peqe have reptilian eyes and teeth, and their musculature appears to be vastly superior to ours. The male I saw—"

"Female."

"What?"

"We've only seen the females. They're a matriarchal society. They don't allow their men or boys off-planet. Dads lost their minds about that," Marfa said.

"Are their males bigger?" Danielle asked.

"Nobody knows. No, wait, somebody asked Voice and she said no." Marfa looked at Danielle. "That's the other thing you're worried about, isn't it? The semqu? The way they communicate with Voice?"

"And what they've done to her."

"You're not alone," she said quietly. "And yeah, somebody did ask me to tell you that. Don't tell my parents."

"I won't." Danielle wondered at her abrupt willingness to use a child as a secret intermediary. She must be desperate. She'd need to watch that. Especially on the heels of her cohesiveness epiphany. "Who? I'd like to meet them."

The girl scanned Danielle's face, and the army specialist had the absurd sensation of being sized up for worthiness by a child.

Marfa asked, "Has anybody taught you what a shut-it is yet?"

"The idea of one, yes. And I'm familiar with the concept—" She closed her lips before she added, "from my previous line of work." She kicked herself; she was desperate, to make that slip.

"I was asked to tell you that when you're ready and able to swear an oath for your first shut-it, let me know. And before you say now, all the unthawed are given six months to acclimate before they're allowed to swear anything."

"Two more months?" Danielle protested. "That's too long! Hell, I'm ready now."

"They said you'd say that. But honestly, there's a lot you still need to learn." Marfa grinned, a child again. "And I get to keep you busy until then!"

But Marfa's slip of the tongue had given Danielle something else to think about, and a way to spend that time. She needed to build bridges, if friction with the general population had gotten so heated in four months that "Honored Earthborn" had deteriorated to "the unthawed."

SURFACE OF TRYE
NEW HOPIAN YEAR 717
THIRD MONTH'S EIGHTEENTH DAY

THE FIRST MAJOR decision that Danielle watched the ship's community make was so contentious it took months: where on the planet to begin to live. The stumbling block surprised her. Some of the oldest passengers and many of the youth were dead-set against clearing forest or disrupting native biomes with Earth plantings.

Had the sentiment been based wholly in ecological views she could have better understood, but one youth held forth for an hour with an argument that was essentially, "We are no better than plants and have to right to supplant them." The joyous applause he'd received when he finished filled her with disquiet.

As the debate heated, a massive lightning storm swept the planet below, leaving the weather-fearful even more terrified. It sparked a wildfire that swept along the equatorial coast far below the orbiting ship; a natural disaster whose sooty scar provided an ugly but useful opening. The community could agree to set up their new home on a site that was already damaged, one that did not require them to inflict ecological damage.

Much of the agricultural stock spacers had brought with them would grow well in that climate. Two months on, the landscape was already greening in places, so the soil had not been depleted—in fact, survey crews found far more organic matter in the soil than was normal for a similar Earth biome post-fire. There was also, apparently, an aupoin community nearby who could provide ores and aid in any necessary excavation, for trade.

Danielle wheedled her way into one of the early surveys of the area; her position as "eldest Earthborn" was still worth something.

Stepping off the shuttle onto Trye's solid ground thrilled her. Fresh air was an unexpected joy after the months cooped up on the ship. Given the way members of the survey crew flinched every time the breeze shifted, she suspected it would be a low-level anxiety trigger for many.

Voice had joined the team to "serve as translator if needed," although she quickly settled into the moss at their rendezvous point, at the edge of the jades. The teen found the gravity of the planet to be crushing.

The fire had been hot enough to completely consume scrub and shrubs across the low rolling hillsides rising away from the sea. Blackened and exploded jade trees on the edges showed where the succulent forest had essentially put out the fire itself. The trees carried so much water they had exploded into steam, shredding themselves in the process.

The blaze had cleared the area for a solid five miles, giving the new residents a blank canvas that required no clearing or damage, and a sterile-ish slate to start.

The blanket of mushrooms in the first meadow startled the team.

Danielle grinned. "We always went mushroom picking the first spring rain after a fire, as long as it wasn't too hot— Hey, whoa, whoa. Don't eat that!" She grabbed the wrist of one of the team members who was about to pop a colorful 'shroom into his mouth.

He looked at her, startled, and backed away as she dropped her grip. Physical contact without consent was strongly discouraged. "I apologize! But stop. Mushrooms range from drop-you-dead in seconds to hallucinogenic to edible. That could kill you. We need to test these first." She wasn't sure how that would be done, but she didn't want anybody on the survey dying.

He stared at the brilliant purple cap. "It's so pretty."

"Pretty on Earth meant, 'Avoid me, I'll kill you,'" Danielle said. "Either with ingested or topical poisons."

He put the mushroom in his collection bag, and Danielle jogged over to each of the other team members to give them the same speech. No one else argued.

"It's perfect," a young woman gushed when the group reconvened near Voice for a lunch break. "It's equatorial, so we have similar day-and-night lengths like we do shipboard, so no immediate need for adjustment to seasons. Sure, people will need to adjust to weather—there will be rain falling from the sky regularly, and ocean breezes—but no extremes like snow or hail or drought."

"Just hurricanes," Danielle said dryly.

The young woman blinked at her. "What's a hurricane?"

"Windstorm," the meteorologist said. "High winds, lots of damage. We don't know the ocean currents yet so we're not sure about the frequency of those. Surveys have ruled out storm surge damage, yes?"

"There's an established aupoin nest entrance practically on the beach a bit north of here, so I doubt that is a common occurrence," Voice said mildly.

The survey member nodded. "No flooding evidence. We've

only seen one area that looks like high wind, and it was oddly localized."

"Tornado?"

"Probably a wind shear event of some sort," the meteorologist said. "Can you botanists tell us how the jades respond to high wind yet?"

One shook her head. "The ones close to the water aren't stripped of leaves, so either they're highly resilient, or it wasn't widespread. There are more leaves on the landward side of the ones right on the ocean, so we might expect there to be some storms."

Danielle was impressed; all the scientists were focused and detailed despite—or perhaps because—they all clearly felt out of their element. She lost track of the number of times one of them muttered some version of, "I didn't train for this."

Near the end of their break, she said, "Past a certain point, training is overrated." They all looked at her oddly. "An element of the unknown or unexpected can pose all kinds of challenges, but also many opportunities you'd never otherwise have. You can train for what you expect, but it's how you react to what you don't expect that can make all the difference."

"Useful," someone said, and added, "Thank you."

It wasn't much, but that and the mushroom incident gave her a sense she'd contributed something, enough to finally admit she was exhausted. Yesterday's ship-wide festival had left her with a massive headache. The ship's population had seemed to devolve into some goofy game whose point she was still unclear about. Determined to build bridges, she'd accepted all of the many extended invitations. Red noses had been offered from all directions, and she grasped that puns were being made all around her, but she hadn't understood more than a few words.

Now, resisting the urge to sit, she stood near Voice and scanned the area.

"What is it you seek in the trees, Honored Earthborn Danielle?"

Voice had told her that her title was much like "Elder Cousin" or "Younger Sister," titles that would be everyday use in Korean, which she apparently spoke fluently. And the teen was giving her a reprieve by speaking in English. Danielle's Yoruba was still pitifully inadequate.

"Predators," she said. "Threats."

Voice blinked at Danielle for a moment and then lay back in the moss. After a bit of silence, which Danielle thought she was going to have to fill with an explanation of both words, Voice said, "There are no threats nearby. And no predators on this continent that could or would harm spacers."

Danielle snorted. "The semqu told you there were no threats or predators? Do they understand what I mean?"

"Yes," Voice said, with that serenity that both unnerved and irritated her. "Ireti suggested we start on this continent not only because it is the largest, but because the other contains a—oh, like a cat, only bigger?"

"Cougar? Tiger? Obligate carnivore?"

"What was the last?"

"Obligate carnivores can only eat meat. Like our dino neighbors." She'd been deeply relieved to learn the dinosaurs' planet was some distance from theirs, and that they ranched their meat. Had a steady supply, apparently. She still didn't trust them. "We are, after all, sacks of meat."

"And of water," Voice said, unconcerned as always. "Thank you, I have never heard that term. This creature eats both, but prefers meat, and is instinct-driven. It is best to avoid one. But there is an ocean between us and them. Oh! There is also an outcrop of volcanic rock nearby. I've never seen such a thing. Can we walk that way?"

"Sure," Danielle said, surprised that volcanic rock would

interest the teen. Then again, how could anyone born on a space-ship comprehend the power of a volcano?

Voice got up slowly, and led the way into the nearby trees, resting often. Low bushes and moss filled the space between the towering jades. A few supported vines, some spiky, some succulent, one a vivid yellow-red. The jades' tan trunks rose in rings; the lowest branches sprouted far over her head, bearing hundreds of flat scalloped leaves, each mature leaf a hand's-width thick and puffy with moisture.

The day was clear and warm, but a stiff breeze ruffled Danielle's hair and made the jades sway and creak, putting her teeth on edge. The soil scientists had reassured her the tall trees were solid; they'd come across a blowdown deeper in the forest and were surprised at how deeply they were rooted. One said something about needing to learn a lot about the soil biology and fast.

Nobody was sure how well-attached the branches and leaves were, though, and a waterlogged leaf the size of a sandbag could ruin their day, given the height they'd plummet from. Danielle kept casting an uneasy eye upward while scanning the scrub around them. Their steps were muffled by the ubiquitous moss, which meant she wouldn't be able to hear anything coming up on them. As they topped a small rise, the trees thinned again. A meadow spread wide ahead of them, a low cliff at its far end.

"Oh," Voice said, in a tone of wonder.

At this distance it looked almost like an Appalachian ridge in miniature, fern-covered and dappled with fall color.

Danielle grunted, stabbed through by an unexpected blade of homesickness. She made herself seek the inevitable differences as they got closer. "That's volcanic rock, alright. Old, and weathered." A solid mass, not layers of sediment. Up close, it appeared pocked with air bubbles. Nothing at all like the rock at home. Mounds of moss composted at the cliff's base, bits of flaked mica glinting in the shifting light, and strips of moss hung from a recently fallen patch.

She looked for scuff marks, tracks, but it appeared to have been pulled down by its own weight.

The plants she'd taken for ferns did have iterated leaves, but they were the wrong shape, the wrong green. None of the plants looked familiar, despite her brain trying to categorize them according to what she remembered of the herbs and forest plants she'd grown up with.

The source of the variegated autumn colors were plants she'd not yet seen on the forest floor. They reminded Danielle of sea anemones, with long narrow tubular leaves that moved in all directions, not just with the breeze. The rounded plants dotted the cliff face, red-orange and yellow and beige-red, ranging in size from a thumbprint to yards wide. They clung to the rock more firmly than the moss; none had fallen.

Danielle picked up a bit of fallen moss and brushed the moving leaves of one of the plants with it. The plant's leaves curled in around the moss smoothly, trapping it like tentacles. Danielle let go. After a moment the leaves uncurled and the moss fell.

Huh. "Plant or animal?" she asked.

"Unsure," Voice said, her tone distant. The girl's tiny hand was flat against the weathered lava, fingers brushing several of the mounded plants. The tubular leaves of two plants danced along the side of her fingertips.

"Should you be doing that?" Danielle asked.

"No danger here," she repeated without looking up. She seemed to be listening to something, or someone. The leaves brushing Voice's fingers withdrew.

Danielle shivered, wondering if Voice was communing with her parasite. A buzzing pulled her attention down. A beetle was struggling at the edge of one of the anemone plants, legs trapped. Its wings, as long as one of the tendrils, beat against the plant. The plant's tendrils moved around its body and head, undulating as the wings buffeted them. Soon all Danielle could see was beating wings. They abruptly stopped moving. Then the wings fell, dropping to the moss below.

The glitter she'd noticed was not mica, but a thick layer of wings and beetle cases.

Danielle swallowed. Just a carnivorous plant, she tried to tell herself. But something shifted in her. She'd been so sure of her ability to teach these space-coddled travelers about planet life. But there was an ecology here the biologists were understanding faster than she was, and plant life that this teenager understood better than she did.

What was she capable of contributing? What dangers was she going to miss?

Voice shifted, turned to go back. "Thank you. This was fascinating."

Staring at the pile of wings, Danielle asked, "Are the semqu carnivores?"

"Much like spacers have our shut-its, semqu have certain secrets they maintain for their safety," Voice said. It was a rote reply she seemed to use for questions her parasite didn't want to answer, but then Voice added, "But they do not eat what we consider to be sentient creatures. I would be surprised if they ate meat of any kind, but I am not familiar with all of semqu."

"All of semqu?"

A small wrinkle appeared between Voice's eyebrows as she thought. "It is like—" she pointed to a small group of trees on their right, which Danielle would have called a grove if they'd had leaves rather than thick, drooping protrusions, "That group of jades there. They are part of, but stand separate from, the rest of the forest. If they were semqu—I am aware of that group, but not the whole forest."

"So you talk to some of the semqu but not all, and they talk to each other."

"Like that, yes."

"And they are telepathic." She'd spent weeks believing the

entire ship, including the captain, had fallen under a cult-like spell cast by this child, originally dispelled by a meeting with her furious sister. Quite the spitfire, Adamantine. Danielle admired her and hoped to stay on the teen's good side. A friendship with Voice might challenge that, but she needed to get close enough to both girls to understand what was going on.

Voice was no cult leader. But something bizarre was going on, and Danielle was at a loss to explain it.

"Yes. And yes, they talked some modeel into moving us here." Danielle snorted.

The teen cocked her head to one side, looking up at her with a shy smile. "There is a blinkship visiting today. I could ask them to take us back to the *New Hope* rather than waiting for the shuttle up if you like, so you can experience it yourself. It's a bit nauseating, but neither of us have eaten in hours."

Danielle stared at her, unsure if she was serious. "Maybe another time."

Voice giggled, then her face stilled. "Just let me know. I don't often do things just for fun."

Abruptly, Danielle felt sad for the girl; just a child, thrust into a position of prominence and infected before she knew her own mind. "We'll do it, then. Just not today." She went back to scanning the trees as they walked back, deeply unsettled. She remained convinced the mission was under threat, but no longer certain that she had the skills or resources to protect it. Humanity's future seemed to be firmly in alien hands.

TWELVE

ALIEN HANDS

**ABOARD NEW HOPE
MEETING ROOM FIVE
NEW HOPIAN YEAR 717
FOURTH MONTH'S TENTH DAY**

Voice paced in the big conference room, waiting for Y-uu-see to arrive.

Captain Ximena had asked her to serve as translator for her first meeting with Se Collective's governing council, and Voice had asked Y-uu-see to come up and teach her and Captain Ximena everything she could about the Council, so they could prepare.

Such a trip would be interesting. She'd meet species that Ireti had not met. But she would be far enough away she'd have no contact or communication with her semqu companion. She wasn't sure she could cope with such a stressful situation without Ireti's help. She wasn't sure she wanted to try. Every night since the captain had asked, she'd had nightmares of mortifying panic attacks in front of the entire council.

She was already unsettled; Ireti was trying to give her more room to feel her emotions. Harriet hadn't replied to her message asking about the family's ancestral celebration the week before. So on Fourth Day, when everyone aboard the ship was occupied with family-remembrance activities, Voice had sat alone, doing calligraphy.

She'd wanted to do a chart for her lineage, but she didn't remember everyone's names. Seeing Père would have brought up odd feelings, and a visit might be awkward. But it would have been nice to have been asked. Adamantine aside, she hadn't thought she'd terminated her relationship with her mother by setting boundaries. Perhaps she had.

That pain was too deep for Ireti to allow.

Captain Ximena swept in, followed after a moment by Danielle, who'd asked to join. Ulick slipped in behind her. Voice welcomed him with sincerity. Ulick was a quick and thorough Fugrast student, and a reliable volunteer for those occasions when Voice had been too exhausted to translate. He probably had volunteered to help Danielle. The Earthborn was still struggling with Yoruba, and her Fugrast was atrocious.

Voice had added Danielle to her list of people to build relationships with. The Earthborn seemed worried about the semqu, and Voice thought a friendship might reassure her. That would probably mean spending some time with Marfa and Rupert, who seemed to trail Danielle like dust on a comet.

Marfa was fine, but Rupert made her tongue-tied and uncomfortable for some reason. It wouldn't bother her to spend more time with Ulick, though. She should add him to her list.

Captain Ximena gave Ulick a wry grimace. "You can attend today," the captain said. "But— Danielle, I can't have Adamantine or Rupert in anything resembling diplomatic sessions."

Danielle grinned. "I think I've learned enough about both of them to avoid that."

Ulick laughed, then gave the two women an innocent look

when they turned to him. "I'm not going say a word to them about that."

The idea of her sister trying to butt into diplomatic situations flustered Voice. She was grateful to hear a noise like running water. Y-uu-see appeared halfway across the room.

Voice greeted the aupoin Voice and gestured to the padded mat spread out for her. Y-uu-see settled in, fluttering with pleasure. The three others sat on pillows near the aupoin, Voice last. Her anxiety kept spiking and flattening.

"You ask about the Council of Twelve." Y-uu-see jumped right in. "After modeel developed their blinkships, they contacted the other species in Se Collective. Immediately we began to trade, and with trade comes much joy and new foods. But also many opportunities for miscommunication and problems. So fairly quickly it was decided that the group of planets should have some communication among them, a nest for friendship and conversation. That nest eventually became the Council."

"While each of the eleven peoples governs themselves, the Council deals with the of rules of interplanetary trade, and metes punishment for contraband."

Punishment? Contraband? Voice's spiking anxiety flattened into a vague mash of prickles.

Captain Ximena was having a different kind of trouble. "Eleven sentient species? Why have we not seen any of their transmissions, any of their pollutants, any of their industrial activity, any—any anything?"

"I do not understand," Y-uu-see said.

"Ah. Modeel are the only one with much technological industry," Voice said.

"But surely we'd see signs of a planet-wide population; evolutionary history shows us all kinds of atmospheric markers."

If Voice remembered right, that was a subject the semqu disliked discussing, for reasons she hadn't quite figured out. "The aupoin, modeel and larsivians are the only ones who might produce much in the way of atmospheric markers," Voice said carefully, then threw the concept to Ireti, seeking to add more.

The response came with a sense of deep unease. <You are a much more curious species about these subjects than any we have encountered. Can you just say the others are younger, with smaller populations?>

Voice did that, hiding her confusion.

The captain settled back on her pillow, a frown on her face. Danielle leaned forward, watchful.

Y-uu-see clearly considered the subject dealt with. "The Council primarily meets to settle trade agreements and similar interplanetary concepts. But they are also the final word for any dispute between, say, a modeel merchant and a peqe purchaser. Each planet governs themselves."

"The aupoin are okay being governed by the surface population?" Danielle asked.

"Let me clarify. We are self-governed," Y-uu-see said. "Often we have next to no interaction with surface populations. We have a long tradition of root-weaving trade with the larsivians, but no contact at all with peqe—their city is on a rocky outcrop that is not comfortable for or accessible to us. To be honest, I am not certain they know our nests exist on Taequa."

"Their... Wait, their city, singular? What are their rural populations?" Danielle asked.

Y-uu-see shrank away and said nothing.

Ireti responded instead. <Most species do not share information like that. You certainly may ask them, knowing they might ask you.>

Bewildered, Voice repeated that verbatim.

Danielle nodded. "Wise."

Captain Ximena looked at her. "You understand this?"

Danielle looked at her. Voice got the sense she was crossing her eyes.

"You have been cloistered in a safe environment for too long,"

Danielle said. "When you meet an unknown people, you need to be careful about what information you share about your own capabilities. As a safeguard, they won't share about theirs. So you fence," she paused, "or verbally dance for awhile, sharing noncritical info, until you decide whether you trust each other or not. Your population, your food supplies, your technological capabilities, your communication capabilities, your water supplies—" she paused, and took a deep breath, "all those details and more would be viewed as state secrets at one point or another in Earth history."

She'd spoken in English. Voice translated the gist for Y-uu-see, and the aupoin stirred. "We do not view population as secret for any of those reasons. It is ... painful."

"Painful?" Voice asked.

Y-uu-see said, "Some many of us have great difficulty reproducing. We—" she stopped and stayed silent for some time. "We grieve," she finally said.

"Oh," Captain Ximena said. "We will avoid treading on your pain."

Ulick gestured assent.

Danielle's eyes narrowed, and she stilled.

"Most planets, while teeming with various forms of life, support aupoin in addition to one other sentient population. Byne is the exception; it has encouraged immigration and has a large governing council representing many peoples and their minority subgroups," Y-uu-see said. "The other planets had expected the Council to need to be involved there, but Byne solves their own interspecies disputes. I do not approve of some of their methods."

"I would like to explore this with you later," Captain Ximena said. "Coming to an agreement about rules involving equity and fairness and justice and rehabilitation when you are dealing with the value sets of entirely different species strikes me as exceptionally difficult. We could learn much from them."

"Comprehension! You understand, yes," Y-uu-see trumpeted.

"We can explore this later, or you can reach out to representatives from Byne. That might be useful to you.

"Now let us focus on the practical matters of your council involvement. You will not immediately be given a voting right or any say; you will need to understand the position and its responsibilities and the scope of Se Collective first. New members are generally given full membership rights after a year on the Council. I assume that will remain the case for you spacers. It will of course need to be approved, and that approval process will be loud and noisy and unnecessary." She waved a hand, gesturing "fart."

Voice chose to translate that as "smoke." Ulick started to laugh, then coughed, to cover it. Voice glanced at him in surprise; she hadn't realized he'd learned Fugrast sign.

"Given the outcome is inevitable, when you arrive at Sakatos, you can expect immediate currying-of-favor and gestures of friendship from others, such as dinner invitations and outright bribery attempts. These gestures are officially frowned upon but widely indulged. Mostly you'll receive gifts. Feel free to accept them. Know that refusal can be rude. You might want to take many low- to high-value objects to offer in immediate or later recompense; show them to your liaison and ask for advice about what to gift to whom, and when."

She waited, softly humming, as Voice translated the words that the captain and Danielle were having trouble with.

"But a word of warning: never accept any green liquid, or any opaque bottle. There is a new, expensive and dangerous liquid hallucinogen: gtorin. Touching or ingesting it could be fatal. Possessing it is illegal; on some planets it is now a death-penalty crime."

<If you ingested this substance, we might both need to die,> Ireti said calmly. <The others do not need to know this.>

That level of specific detail implied so many other details that Voice knew nothing about that her anxiety spiked and then flattened, so her translation came out cold. Her conviction had grown that this experience was not for her.

Ulick leaned forward, absorbent as a sponge; intent.

Captain Ximena was shocked and asked many questions. Y-uu-see's answers were detailed and drew a picture of a dysfunctional and petty social and political group rife with backstabbing and maneuvering. It left Voice thoroughly shaken.

Ulick appeared fascinated.

When she finished, Voice took a steadying breath. "Captain, I do not think I can do this for you. May I suggest Ulick go instead?"

"What?" The captain looked between Voice and the boy, who gazed at Voice like she'd just handed him the best anniversary gift of his life.

"He's a natural at Fugrast," Voice said, warming. "One of my best students. He loves governmental and diplomatic problems. He's clearly started to learn Fugrast sign, which I have not yet had a chance to teach. This entire conversation has terrified me, but look at him. He's glowing. Of the two of us, he's more emotionally mature."

"He's about the most reliable spacer I've met, certainly the most dedicated to the Accord." Danielle sounded rueful. "He's a bedrock of integrity."

"But—I mean no disrespect, Ulick, but I was hoping to have the semqu assistance from Voice," Captain Ximena said.

"You will," Y-uu-see said. "You'll have a keeper."

Voice translated that as "liaison."

"Their sole job will be to keep you out of trouble and ease your way into membership. They will be trustworthy: a Voice. I regret that your liaison may be the only person there you should entirely trust. My advice is also to leave Voice here. It would be unwise to leave your people without a translator during the year that you prepare to move to the surface." It was a long speech for Y-uu-see. She undulated a bit afterward as if catching her breath.

Voice finished her translation and bit her lip. She hoped Captain Ximena wouldn't push the issue. Ireti didn't want her to admit that they wouldn't be connected; it would link Ireti to the ship in people's minds, and they could not allow that. She would have to go if the captain wanted her to.

"I would give my right arm to go," Ulick said. "No, I'd give one arm and one leg."

The captain looked at him for a long moment. "I'm told you're our best diplomacy student; you were among the three candidates suggested as a backup if Voice could not go. The question is whether your fathers would agree."

"I have a right to choose to go under the Accord," Ulick said firmly.

"Yes, I know asking them is a formality," Captain Ximena said wearily. "But—"

"We could redirect their ire at me," Danielle said. "I'll go with you and ask, if you think that would help."

"It would," Ximena said gratefully. "Thank you."

Danielle tipped her head to the side. "They're going to be concerned about his safety. Do we have to worry about assassination attempts?"

Assassination had to be translated for the aupoin, and she contracted to half her size when she understood, then rebounded. It was an impressive wave of motion.

"Murder?" she trumpeted. "Absolutely not. Attacking a liaison could be considered an act of war, and the semqu do not allow that."

"I'm sorry? I didn't understand your answer," Danielle said.

Y-uu-see repeated herself more slowly and Ulick translated it into English for Danielle's benefit.

"Don't *allow* war?" Danielle said.

"War is unknown in Se Collective. We aupoin have never experienced it. We understand the concept, obviously. We have a word for it, have seen it attempted among other peoples. Conflicts between two people or two groups such as families that result in deaths are wrong, but they are not the kind of thing that semqu attend to; we govern and judge such crimes ourselves.

"But war? War kills entire villages, creates hatred and division, impairs population. It is forbidden," she said, waving her hand to gesture, "unquestioned, final."

Voice warmed. It was good that the semqu were so protective.

"That's very good to hear," Captain Ximena said. Ireti seemed relieved by her reaction.

Danielle's head tipped down, facing the table. Voice couldn't tell what she was thinking.

**ABOARD NEW HOPE
NEW HOPIAN YEAR 717
FOURTH MONTH'S THIRTEENTH DAY**

THE OLDEST SPACER in existence walked into the cafeteria and waved at him. Rupert beamed and waved back. Danielle was amazing. She looked like a grey-haired twenty-year-old. She'd seemed puffy and sallow when he first met her, but she moved now with an assurance and strength that demanded attention. There was nothing of deference or arrogance about her. Danielle exuded an aura of competence and had this way of listening that made him feel like he was the center of her universe. It was a powerful combination.

Mama said since he had such a crush on Danielle that he should court her properly. That seemed a bit extreme. He didn't want to marry her. He wanted to learn how to do what she did. Plus, he loved basking in her attention and the envious glances he got from all around the room when she sat down across from him.

He especially liked the envy. It helped shake off the sense of helplessness that had pervaded his morning. All night he'd had nightmares about being controlled by faceless, disembodied aliens. They were a recurring dream since the ship had arrived at Trye, they were stupid, and absolutely no one could know about them. No one needed to know that he was that scared of the semqu. Especially because Opal Pangea, of all people, wasn't.

"How's lunch?" Danielle set her tray down across from his. Tofu, nuts, saag, berries. She was a picky eater, he'd noticed. About the only personal detail about her that he and Adamantine had been able to extract from Lethabo was that she had some kind of hibernation damage to her tastebuds.

"It's okay," he said, glad he'd finished his piled plate of saag bhaji. He particularly loved the cafeteria's version; when Mama cooked she used too many radish leaves. Not that he'd ever tell *her* that.

People around them were chatting about the upcoming ecology day, and how much more interesting it would be this year, because they had actual watershed research.

Rupert leaned forward. "You got to sit in on the conversation with the aupoin about the Council of Twelve, didn't you?" he asked quietly. "How'd that go?"

Danielle also leaned forward, making his heart leap with joy. He'd learned that trick about leaning in a few months ago, and it was paying off. Now everyone around them thought they were having an intimate conversation.

"It was educational," she said. "Ulick will be Ximena's translator."

Rupert grimaced. He hated learning new languages and was struggling to learn even the basics of Fugrast, while everything involving language learning seemed to come so easy to Marfa's little brother. "His dads agreed to that?"

"They weren't happy about it," Danielle said. "But he wanted to do it, and he's Voice's best student."

Voice. The fact that Opal Pangea was the most important person in the ship right now made Rupert's eyes cross.

Her father was a self-absorbed black hole. Rupert accepted Obert's fawning and gifts because the man was capable of helping him in many ways. But Obert wasn't wrong in his assessment of Opal's lack of capacity. She wasn't anywhere near as smart as Rupert was, for starters, and the fact that the semqu had chosen her rather than him, or her sister, or anyone else ... well. It was no loss to the ship, put it that way.

It made him anxious that someone that weak, that malleable, had so much power. The flip people had made from "We have to protect fragile, anxious Opal" to "We have to defer to Voice" left him bewildered. His own mother left her gifts monthly. Opal acted all competent now, but she had to be the same broken girl he'd always known. A person couldn't change that much that fast, even after alien contact. What had they done to her?

"Did you learn anything new about the semqu?" Rupert asked.

"Not much." Danielle's brown eyebrows pulled together. "Though there was a reference to them not allowing war."

"That's good, isn't it?" He'd never had any desire to be a soldier. He wanted to give orders, not take them.

Danielle stared down at her food. "War is not always fought over greed and hubris, Rupert. Sometimes war is waged in defense. But if the aliens who've known the semqu the longest say the semqu are strong enough to prevent war—just how powerful are they? How long is their reach?"

Rupert thought for a moment. "You're worried they'll take over Earth?"

"I'm worried peqe could attack us here and we'll be prevented from defending ourselves. But ... secondarily, yes."

"And we don't know how they can move through space, or how far they can go."

"No." Danielle dug into her food and grimaced. She started eating fast, like she was trying to get it over with.

He knew he should feel grateful to be in orbit around Trye. Both Obert and his mother had shown him the readings from New Terra. But he deeply, deeply resented the aliens. Their choice of Opal was only part of it. The ship's rescue had undermined all the work he'd done to set up his career. Everything he'd studied about space travel was suddenly, completely rewritten—and there was nothing to replace it with. The body of spacer scientific knowledge was clueless about how these new blinkships could work. Maybe entanglement? If so, he had to start over.

Nothing made Rupert madder than feeling stupid in an area where he had spent effort to gain expertise, or learning that he'd wasted his time studying something that turned out to be irrelevant. It was one trait he'd admit to sharing with Obert. He wanted the semqu to pay for that. "We need to figure out how blinkdrives work."

Her attention snapped back to him. Her hazel eyes met his. She smiled. "That sounds like a good goal."

He stopped breathing. Everything in his core went runny and warm, like the saag, only better. He rocked his fist.

As he reflected on that moment later, he realized she'd not only made him feel important and special again, she'd given him a new mission in life. Maybe he *should* court her.

ABOARD NEW HOPE
NEW HOPIAN YEAR 717
FIFTH MONTH'S THIRTEENTH DAY

VOICE HAD PROMISED the Earthborn a trip to the surface and back, so the next time a modeel ship visited, she invited Danielle. She arranged a visit with Y-uu-see on the same day. Voice would go down with Danielle and Danielle would return to the ship by herself. Voice would follow later.

Gregoire was upset when he'd found out she was going to meet the aupoin alone.

"Gregoire, I will be perfectly safe on Trye," she had said. "You can go next time." His concern for her safety bewildered her; there would be no mentally ill spacers on the surface. He'd only calmed once she promised to message him as soon as she arrived and if anything changed.

Danielle showed up half an hour early, with Rupert at her elbow.

Voice stood in her doorway, tongue-tied for a moment, and stared at the handsome boy beaming at her. He reminded her unpleasantly of Tiani: oily, brash and insecure at the same time.

Ireti's touch calmed her. Voice said, "I was not expecting you; I can only take Danielle."

"Oh, I didn't expect to go. They say watching someone disappear is amazing. I can just wait for Danielle to return, here in your dwell!" Rupert's smile was charming, and he stood in that half-slouch she'd seen him use when he was flirting with Marfa or Adamantine.

Her cheeks got hot; she was probably blushing. She did not want him in her apartment, certainly not alone after she left. "That is not going to work," Voice said. "She'll return to her room, not mine."

"I'll just wait for you, then," Rupert said. He winked at her.

"Uh. No."

Gregoire would have intervened at her first sign of discomfort, but he was taking his recreation hours. There was an awkward silence. Finally the officer outside her door stepped forward. "Is there a problem?"

"Rupert was just leaving," Danielle said. The youth shot her a surprised glance, and she added, "I appreciate your escort, Rupert. Thank you for the company."

Rupert glanced between the adults. Voice caught the furious glare he shot at her before he smoothed his expression. "Of course,

Honored Earthborn. Anything for you." He bowed to her and nodded at the officer before strolling away, completely ignoring Voice.

She'd just angered one of her sister's friends.

<We'll have a lot of unsettling emotions to discuss tonight, won't we?> Ireti asked. They seemed amused.

<Many.>

Danielle rolled her eyes. "I didn't realize he wanted to flirt with you."

"Is that what he thought he was doing?" Voice ushered Danielle in and busied herself making the Earthborn a hot tea.

"I think he has a crush on you," Danielle said.

"I thought he had a crush on Adamantine and Marfa," Voice said. "Oh, and you." She was getting better at mentioning her sister without feeling the accompanying stab of loss.

Danielle barked a laugh. "He does seem to flirt with everyone, doesn't he? I'm just glad he's refocused on people his own age." She rolled her shoulders back. She was tense, nervous, Voice realized. Or wary, like she was expecting a trick.

"The visiting blinkship staff are ready to help us," Voice asked as they sat with their cups. "Are you ready for your trip to the surface?"

"As much as I can be."

"Honest. I appreciate that."

Danielle gave her a smile that looked pained.

Voice didn't know how to interpret that. "Am I making this more complicated than it needs to be?"

"No," Danielle said. "I just kind of want to get this over with, whatever this is. I do appreciate your being willing to show me. Everyone who wasn't in hibernation is so... convinced."

"It's a powerful cure for denial," Voice said. She realized she was spiking nervous, too. She wasn't sure how the Earthborn would react, and she'd be alone with her on the surface.

<I'll send her back to the ship if she's a problem.> Ireti sounded

strong. It felt like both of them were getting stronger, in so many ways. Three years ago, she would have invited Rupert in because it wouldn't have occurred to her that her own discomfort was adequate reason to refuse to allow him in.

That realization made Voice suddenly happy and spontaneous. <Well, then, when you're ready.> She forgot they were still holding the cups, but Ireti didn't.

Their fingers were empty when they bumped down onto the moss on Trye.

They sat on the shaded edge of a clearing dappled with sun, full of yellow and green mosses and waves of flowers in purples and blues and reds and yellows. Jade trees formed a dense horizon in every direction.

Fragrant pollen and humid soil scented the startlingly moist, warm air. The oval was the widest open space Voice had been in since her last trip down; edged with waist- and shoulder-high bushes. The one directly behind them was in bloom, covered in tiny yellow and purple petals. Insects buzzed among the blooms and birds called from the jades.

The sound seemed off to Voice, dangerous somehow, until she realized she was missing the constant mechanical hum of the *New Hope*, the reassurance that all was well with spacer life. The ground under her was completely still.

"I could get used to this," Voice said. <It's so pretty! Such colorful blooms!>

<They are, thank you for showing me.> Ireti's touch was distant and stretched thin.

Danielle lurched away from her and vomited.

Voice explored the tiny lobed plants on her left before checking in on Danielle, giving the woman some privacy. After her faint, it had become clear that the Earthborn detested anyone seeing her being weak, or at less than her best. It seemed a vanity or insecurity that Voice and others saw no harm in indulging. She messaged Gregoire that they had arrived safely.

Danielle finally straightened up.

"I am sorry about the stomach upset, Honored Earthborn. Are you feeling better now?" Voice asked.

"Yes. I... think I understand a bit better as well." Danielle's eyes were wide. She was doing that "check for predators" sweep she had done when they'd taken the shuttle down before. Her head stopped moving. "We have company."

At the far edge of the clearing, directly across from them, three aupoin rested in the shade of a massive, succulent-leaved jade, or lopa, as the aupoin called them. "Oh! I meant to tell you before we left. I am to meet with Y-uu-see after we finish talking. There is no hurry; she appears to be in a meeting herself." She gave the Earthborn a longer glance. The woman had wrapped her arms around her chest. "So, what do you think of this as a method of transport?"

"Right. Uh. I think I'll stick to a shuttle transport, but I do appreciate the demonstration." She looked up at the sky. "Crazy the semqu moved the entire generation ship and everyone in it that way. Must take a lot of power."

"The modeel don't explain how any of that works," Voice said lightly. "No other species has ever been allowed into their engine rooms."

She didn't like lying to someone she hoped to befriend. She had learned there was actually quite a bit of information that the semqu forbade Voices from sharing, and while Voice certainly understood and would obey those restrictions—now that she was a Voice, she could no more disobey than she could change her bare skin to fur— she thought life would be much simpler if she could explain. Although, given ancient humans' propensity for making disasters out of basic knowledge, it could make her people even more paranoid. That thought saddened her.

Voice added, "But the modeel have had space travel for centuries, and the semqu have been interacting with other species since before Earth became a rocky planet." She and Captain

Ximena had settled on that as a "for everyone" explanation. "So it stands to reason they'd have abilities we don't have."

"Highly evolved, ancient sentient species. Yes, I suppose so." Danielle shivered. "Thank you, I think … I think I've absorbed all I can in one go."

It took Voice a moment to understand. "You wish to return to the ship now?"

"Please." Danielle shivered again; she seemed to be cold in the shade.

A pang sliced through Voice and was gone. "Feel free to visit again." <Ireti, she is ready to return.>

Danielle nodded, not looking at Voice. She disappeared. The plants she had been sitting on rebounded slowly.

Then she let herself sit for a moment, wondering at her own sharp disappointment. Had she thought that Danielle would immediately become her best friend the instant she learned everything she believed about spacer superiority was false? *Synonyms, I can be silly.* Voice shook herself thoroughly and stood.

Oh! Shivering, nausea—did she have travel shock? Voice messaged Gregoire to have someone check on Danielle.

Then she walked slowly through the beautiful meadow. She calmed, immersing herself in the spicy-to-sweet scent of the blooms wafting from the ground, the riot of colors, the mosses, and the round, oval, or serrated edges of the teal and green leaves. She shared the peaceful setting's textures with Ireti until she reached the spot where Y-uu-see waited.

The aupoin Voice wore a wide, colorful collar of beetle wings. She was flanked by one massive, worn-looking aupoin and another half Y-uu-see's size. The three of them looked like a bristly-fleshed, uneven staircase to the lowest lobes of the lopa tree that shaded them.

Other than their size and the necklace, they looked mostly identical. Voice was relieved she could tell them apart. She wondered if Y-uu-see had chosen her companions to help Voice make the distinction.

"Welcome," Y-uu-see said. "We greet you, with one of our youngest members, R-aaa-o," she gestured to the smaller of her two companions, "and our eldest, I-oo-u."

"I am grateful to meet you." Voice spoke slowly and carefully in Fugrast; the semqu had told her this was the proper wording.

The youth's flower mouth pulsed, releasing a short liquid phrase. The elder released a sharp snort before saying, in excellent Fugrast, "Have you a fear of underground spaces?"

"I don't know," Voice said. "I've never been in one."

"Never! How sad. We shall give you an extensive tour!" I-oo-u said.

"I'm not sure—" Voice started to object.

"We have rooms at different levels where we can privately chat," Y-uu-see said, with the confidence of one accustomed to fixing social problems.

I can learn from her, Voice thought, as Y-uu-see got up on her multiple legs.

The others rose with her. The youth said something short in the aupoin's own tongue, and I-oo-u replied in the same, a stream of liquid commentary that filled the air as they approached the mouth of a tunnel, effectively preventing any further conversation.

Voice followed the trio's rippling, mincing feet across a wide stone set over a narrow but deep drainage moat, and down a series of steps decorated with colorful stones. A few more steps and the earth was above her, too. Cool but dry air carried the scent of herbs. She stepped onto a thin, velvety mosaic of mosses. The passage was narrow at first, widening to a corridor as large as a shipboard residence corridor, with what looked like bas-relief patterns on the wall —woven roots. There was no illumination but the light from the mouth behind her.

<Do not descend too deeply.> Ireti's request was so quiet Voice could barely hear it.

<I will stop.> Her anxiety had risen in the sudden dark. Now she realized their connection had thinned. She knew the semqu's ability to dim her emotions was not permanent, but she had not realized how intensely she'd come to rely on it. *I'm with a friend,* she thought. *I have nothing to worry about.*

Even so, she blurted more shrilly than she intended. "I think I should stop!" She had to repeat herself to be heard over the elder aupoin, glad she was able to do so calmly.

"Certainly." Y-uu-see trumpeted, which silenced the other two. They were steps away from a small room, empty but for some deep benches built into the walls.

"There is a much nicer room two corridors down," I-oo-u said in Fugrast.

"We honor each other's boundaries," Y-uu-see said.

I-oo-u shrank away sharply to a third of their bulk. Voice missed the modeel's informative aura for a moment. She could not tell if he felt rebuked or insulted. *I have a lot to learn about aupoin emotional expression.*

"Thank you for the escort." Y-uu-see added, "You two may return to your other duties now."

Voice entered the round chamber and sat, trying to avoid wringing her hands. She had not been so disconnected from Ireti since they'd met. She could hear I-oo-u's watery complaining—she was certain that was what it was—fading as he trundled farther down.

"I promised to show you and your captain my beetle wing art," Y-uu-see said. She removed her collar and laid it next to Voice.

"I've been admiring it, it's lovely. So fragile-looking. Did it take you a long time to make?" Voice bit her tongue lightly, afraid if she kept talking she would not be able to stop, a barrage of anxious words. She took a deep breath and reminded herself how it felt throughout her body when Ireti imposed calm on her. It helped a little.

"We tell time differently than you do, but it would translate to about a hundred sunrises," Y-uu-see said. "It is of course something I do in my spare time, and there has not been much of that."

"I understand." Voice pulled a small scroll from her tunic. "I made you this, to thank you for your hospitality. It's not much. I'm just a beginner at both calligraphy and Fugrast."

Y-uu-see trilled liquid notes for a moment after unrolling the scroll. "You made a design out of the word! This is lovely! We do not pattern with words, we aupoin. How clever!"

"It is not offensive?"

"It is not offensive at all. It is joyful."

Voice sagged against the wall; she hadn't realized she'd been worried about that, too.

Y-uu-see slid the scroll into a small pouch of her own. "Now, tell me." She went to the doorway, apparently to ensure her companions had left, then undulated back. "Trye9 is worried about New Hope1. How are they?"

<She means me. Be honest as long as you are alone.>

Voice repeated the "look down the hallway" move the aupoin had just done, to make Ireti feel better, saying, "Their name is Ireti, by the way."

"Oh!"

Voice added, "Tired. Wounded, I think. They're not recovering from the ... the fungi-poison or the ship-wide transport as well as I'd like."

"What!" Y-uu-see said. "Spacers have a substance that wounds semqu?"

<That is excessively honest, Voice,> Ireti said. <But yes, you are correct.>

Homophones. <You said be honest.>

<I did. Omit your involvement. Entirely.>

Aloud, Voice said, "Yes. We did not know, of course. Our rice crop was treated with a fungicide to protect our food-grains from disease, and that harmed Ireti."

Y-uu-see was horrified by the concept of a fungicide. Once

Voice had explained Ireti's reasons for not halting the damage, Y-uu-see said, "We need samples of this. Samples of such agricultural materials. We will test it and... fix it so it is not a danger to semqu anymore. We cannot allow you to harm Trye9, but your people cannot know that. Wait, if this is your practice, and your growers plan to put poisons into the soil here—we must know whether it will endanger us or our crops!"

"That aligns with our values. Captain Ximena should have no problems agreeing with that," Voice said, feeling her own relief and that of Ireti.

"Good. Now. Do they wish to trade?"

<Absolutely not. He would not fit and he'd suffocate the spacers.>

Voice repeated that, adding, "I don't understand the question or the answer."

"Trye9 has a standing offer to swap with any ship—he wants to travel, and he decided late so he needs to leave soon. He's getting too big for many of the blinkships. The generation ship is so large—it would be perfect."

<She speaks of this too easily,> Ireti said severely. <We do not tell non-Voices about the ships. Ever.>

<I—okay. Long-talk later?>

<Yes.>

Aloud, Voice said, "Our oxygen-carbon dioxide level is carefully balanced, and his exhale would kill us. And the generation ship will stay in orbit around Trye."

"That would indeed be suboptimal," Y-uu-see said.

"Yes." She liked talking with the aupoin, Y-uu-see seemed to understand the gaps and hesitation in her responses. But then she'd understand having two conversations at once, wouldn't she?

Y-uu-see shifted her bulk to be more comfortable on the bench. "Well then. Can we help Ireti?"

"Ah. They could use some minerals." Voice listed several Ireti had relayed to her as dietary needs.

"Very well. I will share this. But ... all those minerals?" Y-uu-see seemed concerned.

"Is that a problem?" Voice asked.

"No. No, but those needs tell me that New—Ireti—is dangerously unwell. Thank you. I will ensure they get more frequent visits from others. Perhaps Trye9 can send some up today."

"Thank you." *Dangerously unwell?*

"Now. Do you have any questions about being a Voice?"

The switch in topics while she was busy pondering several others flustered her a moment. "Ah—wait." Voice pulled out the list she'd made. "Children. Can I have them. Friendships: tips on figuring out when people want to be friends just to try to influence Ireti. Oh, and she wanted me to ask something about the lifecycle of a Voice? And—"

Y-uu-see held up a hand, digits spread wide. "That's plenty for one visit, I think. I cannot answer the 'if' you can have children but I can tell you that we have had more experience being Voices than any other peoples, and it's often not a good idea. Voice parents cannot be as available to their children as non-Voices can be, certainly not emotionally. Peoples who raise their children communally, such as the phren or the kertueon, or even certain collectives of aupoin, can make that work. We have had some success. Do you spacers raise your children communally?"

"We have creches for our young," Voice said hesitantly.

Y-uu-see added, "By communally I mean no child has an expectation that any one individual adult or mating group has any special relationship to, obligation to, or influence over them."

"Oh! We share certain parenting tasks, but to that extreme, no, we do not."

"In cultures where children are raised in small units or bond with a singular adult, it rarely ends well."

"I accept that." Voice hadn't been sure she wanted children. That had been Adamantine's dream. Another decision made. A pang, a small one, but also a relief. She did not want any children of hers taken to be raised by her sister. "In many ways that makes my life easier."

"It does, often. It is understandable to grieve a road not taken as long as one does not dwell on it."

"Yes, closing a potential can be sad," Voice said. She thought she might grieve that potential someday, but not today.

"Good. The lifecycle of a Voice is—" Y-uu-see hesitated. "We have more choice at the end than at the beginning. When a Voice dies, they may have the option of joining their semqu. It is a painful process, I am told, but their minds are bound together. Before that semqu finally dies—those on ships have shorter lifespans—they share their life with another semqu, so they and the Voice also become part of," Y-uu-see spread her many fingers into the gesture for "everything."

Voice blinked. "Everything?"

"All-Semqu. It is a form of immortality. Voices are normally carefully chosen for this reason. You will probably not be given this option. I mean no disrespect."

"I was a last-gasp attempt," Voice said. She'd come to realize that. It had always bothered her because it fit the part of herself she wanted to shed—the part that still believed she was broken and worthless. She was suddenly okay with being a last choice. The idea of being absorbed into something as vast as Ireti was absolutely terrifying. The reality that she'd avoided that by dint of being a desperate gamble made her want to giggle. Would Y-uu-see understand that? Probably not. Voice pressed her lips together.

"As for friendships..." Y-uu-see paused. "I think that is too culture-specific for me to answer."

"Probably." Voice felt awkward, like she was taking advantage of Y-uu-see somehow. "Do you have any questions for me?"

The aupoin did. Voice explained as best she could what the spacers' life aboard *New Hope* had been like, as a way of helping Y-uu-see understand what having them as neighbors might entail. When they stood up to leave, Y-uu-see thought of something else.

"Oh! Also. Should your semqu die before you, after your grieving period, you might be requested to serve as a Voice elsewhere, as needed."

"Oh."

"Yes. None of us like to think of that happening. But— given the circumstances, you should think about that."

Voice very much did not want to think about that. "What happens if Trye9 becomes a ship? Do you go with him?"

"I will," Y-uu-see said. "And then Trye will get an infant semqu, with a new Voice. Hopefully an experienced one. Semqu are tricky to raise."

Voice opened her mouth to ask about that, but a rustle outside startled her.

I-oo-u was waiting for them in the corridor with a tray of what looked like vegetable rolls.

Y-uu-see trumpeted in surprise. "How long have you been standing there?"

"I just arrived, to see if you wanted any refreshments," I-oo-u said. "We have vegetable and mushroom rolls, well-seasoned with herbs."

Voice took one of the rolls offered and she bit down carefully. "Delicious," she said. "You are very kind."

"He pays too much attention to the braids of others," Y-uu-see muttered, but she ate two before escorting Voice back to the surface.

ABOARD NEW HOPE
GRANDI-GUTHERIE HOUSEHOLD CHAMBERS
NEW HOPIAN YEAR 717
FIFTH MONTH'S THIRTEENTH DAY

DANIELLE LOCKED herself in her room after she returned from the surface.

One moment she'd been in Voice's dwell, holding a cup of tea, and the next, she'd been dropping a few inches onto a clump of moss. The gravity shift had been obvious. There were unfamiliar animal or bird calls and insect noises, odd odors that might have been floral. Wind had creaked through the fat-leaved succulent trees.

She remembered thinking that no one had lied to her about their experience.

Voice's words had rippled with delight, "I could get used to this!"

Then her stomach rebelled.

The girl's tone had flattened to an emotionless question about her health. She'd probably worried the child. She should feel bad about that.

She couldn't feel much of anything at all.

Danielle replayed the snippet of conversation in her head over and over, looping sound to avoid remembering the sensation of having her entire body turned inside out and back in again. It felt like her body had been moved cell by cell and rebuilt cell by cell between one heartbeat and the next. Her heart hadn't even skipped.

That is what everyone meant. What they tried to describe.

It wasn't a hallucination.

They'd moved the entire fucking generation ship that way. Tech they'd never encountered before, they just ... moved it, like a toy.

And we have no fucking clue how any of that works.

She went back to looping Voice's words.

At some point, Juand knocked, then came in with some tea. "You don't look good."

She told him the joyride was weird. He went away, which was what she wanted.

But he returned with the ship's emotional support officer, Nona, who bustled in and said, "Juand said you were showing symptoms of travel shock." She spoke English, and Danielle was grateful for the comfort of words she didn't have to struggle to understand.

"That's a thing?" Danielle's words came out chopped up; she was shivering again.

Nona handed her a tube. "Sip this," she said. "I don't know 'thing,' but the med clinics were overwhelmed with patients after the ship moved. We pressed every doula and medic into service, every community ear we could trust who wasn't ill. Shock is a common reaction to something totally inexplicable."

"But I knew it was likely to happen," Danielle said. She opened the tube and sipped; shock rehydration was the only thing about the situation that made sense to her. "You'd all told me. Voice told me."

"But you didn't believe it," Juand said. "Most of the thawed don't. I probably wouldn't have either." Curls flopped as he shook his head. Neither he nor Nona reacted to the term; maybe it wasn't an epithet. Maybe she was overreacting to everything. She shivered harder.

"Let's get you wrapped in a blanket," Nona said. "And how about you talk to me."

Juand closed the door, giving them some privacy, and Danielle allowed the blanket before she slumped on her bed. "I feel out of control and weak, and I hate it," she blurted.

"That makes sense. You value strength and independence. You come from a culture that valued autonomy and solitary decision-making: lone-wolf leadership that sometimes masked sociopathy. Now you find yourself in an interdependent, consensus-based community, still trying to operate as a loner," Nona said.

"I've been trying to connect to people!" She felt her eyes fill with tears, mortifying.

"And your offers of service have been well-received. But otherwise you've been very resistant to acclimation, and you won't tell anyone why. Talk to us about your struggles. Let us help you. Let us know that we can trust you to help us."

And there was the way in that she'd been missing, doing everything she could to avoid understanding. Handed to her like a gift. And she could only accept half of it, because she could never be completely honest. Danielle hung her head. "I hear you."

Somehow, she had to keep both her long-dead grandmother and Ol' Chucky happy.

THIRTEEN

SHARED FEARS

**ABOARD NEW HOPE
VOICE'S CHAMBERS
NEW HOPIAN YEAR 717
FIFTH MONTH'S THIRTEENTH DAY**

In bed that night, Voice thought ruefully, <We may have more emotions to discuss than we can cover in one night.>

They discussed her mixed emotions about Rupert fairly quickly. Ireti used some of what they had learned from their previous connection attempts with spacers to explain why they thought Rupert was flirting. Voice was intrigued and embarrassed, worried they were violating the privacy of dead spacers. They ended up agreeing Voice should not trust Rupert, and also that they could revisit that later, because neither of them could fully explain why.

<I am learning much from you, Voice. This "sense" that you base trust on is similar but different from those I have known before.>

Voice didn't know how to respond to that, so she changed the subject. <Trye9 is a he? You told me once that semqu have thousands of sexes. How many genders?>

<Gender?>

<Gender is… social roles linked to biology. Our ancient cultures often had different ones—> Voice cast her mind back to Earth history. <For a long time some cultures said only men could be religious leaders. Silly stuff like that. Some families still have those ancient beliefs, like Père,> she rolled her eyes, <but not many.>

<Peqe believe only women can duel or lead a household.>

Voice laughed. <Like that, yes.>

<I understand now.> Ireti taught Voice the Fugrast word for the concept. <Semqu have none. We have no need for such limiting specializations and found it deeply intriguing and confusing when we encountered them in others, because you have so few sexes. Our sex-combination intricacies are extensive and important only to those who plan breeding for specific nutrient or environmental needs. It is an area in which I have little curiosity, to be honest.> A flush of embarrassment washed over Voice, startling her. Ireti clearly considered a lack of curiosity to be a defect.

<You don't have to be curious about everything,> Voice said. <What is parenting like among your people, then?>

<What you call parenting is often done by Voices, though of course we also have semqu contact. We sometimes have several Voices for an infant, or more—but spacer mentality is so new and so different! We might have only a surface Voice for Trye10's maturing years. We did that when we encountered the phren, and it worked well. This is still being discussed and will be for some time. Trye9 will leave before an infant is replanted. It would not bother me to die young if you were the Voice to raise the infant.>

<Me? But… Y-uu-see said semqu were tricky to raise and require experienced Voices!" Voice said. "I'm only thirt—er, fourteen!> Her anniversary had come and gone, unimportant to her. The day of Ireti's arrival would be her anniversary from now on, she thought. The day Opal became Voice. Years on Trye were

longer anyway; no one would notice the switch. She forced herself to focus; she was trying to avoid the reality that Ireti was saying they might die.

<Young is in many ways perfect. You could grow together. But I am unlikely to die soon.> A prickly sensation roiled from Ireti.

<Are you lying to me to make me feel better? Or are you afraid to die?>

< I am merely tired and weak—no. I am afraid of being unable to share my life with other semqu. We all fear that, to die before we can be part of the whole.>

<I am sorry.>

<Why? We are accustomed to the idea of dying, those of us who choose to become ships. And some planet-born choose shorter lives for a variety of reasons. No one knows how long they will live, and infinitesimally few of you not-semqu have a chance of joining the whole. If you care for the infant, you may be absorbed at some point, and we could be together again. I know you fear this, but your consciousness would add much to our understanding, and it would comfort me.>

<I... > Terror swamped her and then faded.

<Voice, you will not need to make that choice for decades, if ever. Rest easy.> Sadness lay beneath her words. Ireti was trying to hide that from her.

Voice wondered if she was supposed to know that. They moved on to other subjects, but Voice slept fitfully that night and for several nights after.

ABOARD NEW HOPE
RICE FIELDS
NEW HOPIAN YEAR 717
FIFTH MONTH, NINETEENTH DAY

VOICE ARRANGED an afternoon meeting with the agriculturist who'd found her in the rice field, saying she wanted to thank him, that she'd put it off for far too long. Her meeting with Y-uu-see had motivated her to do better by Ireti, and to protect the aupoin as well.

He greeted her and Gregoire at the barn doors, giving them a deep bow in a formal embroidered tunic. After Voice bowed back to the beaming man, she shooed Gregoire away, suggesting he take a break. The agriculturist ushered her into the fields, which smelled of tank muck and processed fish entrails. She found herself close to stammering, overwhelmed by her desperate desire to destroy the fungicide he'd used so it never harmed Ireti again. Some of that desire was not her own.

<Distract us with the view,> Ireti suggested.

Voice looked around. "It looks so different in here!" The tall, graceful stalks heavy with grain were gone; she could see all the way to the back wall over the top of the tiny shoots. "I never heard how the rice fared, afterward. But you clearly saved the crop!"

"I treated the area you told me about. We are blessed that you thought of the community in the midst of your own trials," the agriculturist said, bowing again. He was clearly overwhelmed by talking to her now. "I should have put your name forward—"

"No, no, no. It was your action that saved the harvest. I just thought—could we walk the fields again? I don't need to hide in the grain anymore, but the fields are …." She trailed off.

"Serene? Peaceful? Comforting?"

"Yes."

His grin broadened, and he relaxed a little, gesturing for her to join him. They walked through the rows of tiny sprouts of new green poking out of black soil, and the tubs of fish. "The smell may not be to your liking at the moment, we fertilized the fields with the fish manure yesterday."

"I've been in fertilized fields before." The smell didn't bother

her, but she would wash her clothes when she was done here. "It is the aroma of promise."

"Bééni! So it is!" He grinned. After a bit he walked them past the tray where he'd found her, glancing at her as if to reassure himself she wasn't going to collapse again. She tried to pretend she didn't notice, but she glanced down. There was nothing on the floor where she'd encountered the fungal mat.

He cleared his throat. "That was a strange thing. It was a tiny mass, and it looked like it was moving. I came back with a sample kit later but I couldn't find anything to test! It was as if the fungicide had dissolved it." He frowned, staring at the spot.

"That is strange," Voice said.

"I've... I've often wondered if it had anything to do with ... with...your—" he waved at her, up and down, clearly embarrassed.

She braced herself for the guilt of lying to him; blinked. "My what?"

"Your connection, the semqu," he whispered.

"Oh!" she said, glad for Ireti's help in keeping her emotions still. "I'd been feeling off for days before I came in here. Semqu often need some time to decide on and connect to their Voices. We're a new species to them, after all. It's only the final stages of connection that are... dramatic."

"Ah." He looked disappointed.

"I really don't think a poisoned fungal mat that composted to near-nothing could have connected to my brain and stayed there." She cocked her head sideways, looking up at him. "I mean, I'm still connected to Ireti."

"Well, there is that." He laughed. "I guess I was hoping to have discovered a clue to their real nature."

"You and everyone else on the ship," Voice said, gently. "Maybe that mat was somehow related to the yellowed leaves in the back?"

"No, those were rice blast, an Earth fungus we've fought since we launched." His brow cleared. "We decided to harvest early, treated all the soil beds, and used reserved seed to replant. We've not seen it return, thankfully."

"That's good to know. I am grateful for your expertise."

"The aupoin seem to be as well," he said, a little proudly. "Did you know they eat fungus, much as we do? Only it seems to be their primary food source. You probably do, of course, I'm sorry."

"That's fine. I do; that's my second reason for visiting with you. They were afraid of insulting us by bringing it up, but they are very concerned about the poisons we use—fungicides, pesticides, all of it. They need to know the chemical composition of anything we use on crops we plant on the surface, because it could impact their food source and potentially poison them. Their biology is so different from ours. They've asked for our promise that we not use any such chemicals once we move down."

"I... Oh, that is huge," the agriculturist said, clearly taken aback. "I can't—"

"We won't need them!" Voice said, making herself grin. "They can communicate with insect populations. It seems like magic to us, but they can literally ask insects to not eat so heavily of a crop that it impacts yield."

His jaw dropped, dark face alive with wonder and a desire to believe. "And they comply? I mean, the insects?"

"Yes! They truly live in harmony with their surroundings in ways we've never had the opportunity to. I'm told that some bacterial and fungal infestations can also be dealt with that way, which should simplify your job a great deal."

"You're not serious." She might as well have told him that grain sprouted animal heads.

"I am! Completely! They've been doing this for centuries. If you have any concerns about it, will you come to me?"

"Absolutely!" He muttered, "To not need to don hazmat suits again? That would be amazing." He seemed stunned, struggling to believe her. She let him absorb the information.

They continued their walk, him trying to ask gentle questions about Ireti and her kind, her answering what she could. Her time with Captain Ximena had helped; she'd gotten better at answering in ways that made it seem that she'd heard a different question.

In the back, he showed her the previously rice blast-infected area and she praised his preventative action once again. As they headed to the doors, she asked, "So you will give the aupoin the chemical formulas?"

"I will need to consult with my guild," he said, grave. "But I can understand the aupoins' concern. We don't want to poison their food supply. I don't think there would be any reason to not share that knowledge. We'd also need to pinpoint the chemistry involved, so we don't use analogs in other manufacturing processes."

"Oh! Yes!" The idea that there might be other chemicals that could harm Ireti rattled her. She wanted the name of the precise fungicide he'd used, immediately. She couldn't come up with a way to ask that didn't sound stilted.

<More specific questions might make him more curious,> Ireti said. <He's given you a promise that will aid us in the future. That is enough.> Ireti also wanted to know, but their patience calmed Voice.

She asked about his family, his avocation. He had two main interests, teaching weightlifting and creating crossword puzzles, about which she knew nothing, and that kept them occupied for a time.

Then it was time to go. She was disappointed, but Ireti was pleased, and firm about not asking anything more.

"Thank you again for your kindness, for actually listening to me that day. That had been rare in my life, up until then. You helped me when I was very afraid, and very vulnerable, and I'm grateful." Voice bowed to him.

He bowed back, and gave her the traditional response, clearly heartfelt. "I am but one part of our community, and I am grateful to serve."

ABOARD NEW HOPE
NEW HOPIAN YEAR 717
SIXTH MONTH SIXTEENTH DAY

DANIELLE MADE inroads with various groups, gritting her teeth and asking for help, as well as making up for her months of self-pity by doing extra volunteer shifts. In her personal time, she kept notes on what she was learning about the semqu, which added up to squat. They were clearly overlords of the system.

It seemed that none of the other species questioned decisions by the semqu. That kind of group-think struck her as artificial. Just how powerful were these creatures, and ... what did they want? How tightly did they rule? The secrecy around them rankled and worried her. What were they hiding?

She learned about a religious cult, the Semule, apparently with branches across the various planets. Semule interpreted semqu abilities as nothing short of a godhead. A few spacers had joined and were openly worshiping the semqu.

That set her teeth on edge.

Occasionally, she managed short conversations with other ship residents who would also admit concern about Voice or her invisible companion. But most either considered Danielle's worries paranoia in the face of the gift of a livable planet or shrugged their shoulders in a "what can we do about it?" way.

So, she'd tried not to get her hopes up for the "Protection Guild" Marfa had told her about, but it was hard. She needed confidants, fellow warriors.

The day after *New Hope's* celebration of families—Danielle was starting to wonder if there was a holiday every week on this ship—Marfa took her to her first guild meeting. The young teen told her to expect Rupert.

"He wants to do everything you're doing," she said, with rolled eyes that reminded Danielle of her own teenage years.

He was, in fact, waiting for them at the door.

In the spirit of trying their "community problem-solving" approach, she'd tried to talk to Rupert's parents about how they wanted her to handle his crush on her.

She was impressed by the father's level-headedness. "He wants impossible things, we need to let him learn he can't have them."

But his mother Saira was intense, with a razor wit Danielle hadn't recognized until her ego was in pieces on the floor. Saira had bounced between accusing Danielle of seducing her son and insisting that a marriage between them would produce amazing children.

Danielle had finally told her that she wasn't a pedophile and fled. The meeting had boosted her appreciation for Marfa's fathers twenty-fold. Juand and Niels had laughed until they'd cried when she'd told them so. Saira's personality was apparently well-known.

Since then, Rupert's adoration had waned, and as they waited outside the door, she realized he was flirting with Marfa. *Good.*

A heavyset man opened the door for them, and her gaze swept the room. Nine adult attendees inside, two of them women. She hadn't expected to see anyone in military trim, although two looked like they were in decent shape.

Before the meeting even started, a twenty-something named Tiani launched into a tirade. Halfway through, Danielle was gritting her teeth. How was it possible, in such a collective society, for someone so young to be so pompous and clueless? She carefully listened to and sized up the others, lounging on pillows or pacing the edges of the room.

Obert Pangea was one of the more interesting members, and the oldest in the room, but he seemed there mostly because he couldn't believe the aliens had found value in a daughter he had dismissed as useless, while at the same time livid that he could no longer influence her. "Adamantine would have pried blinkship technology out of the semqu by now," he seethed.

By meeting's end, Danielle was deeply disappointed. Most of

the members appeared to be troublemakers or "me-mes," as her old unit used to call them. People who wanted to be the center of attention and decision-making, but expected to have minions do any actual work. And they'd been doing stupid shit; sneaking into the hull spaces near Voice's chambers looking for the semqu, for example. One of them had gotten caught and admitted what he was doing.

Danielle suspected that explained why the ship's navigator, Frances, was there. The woman didn't say a word all meeting. A plant by the captain to keep tabs on the guild, then. Danielle swore internally. That wasn't going to keep her off Ximena's radar. She'd better befriend Frances, fast.

Over the next few months she met all of them one-on-one to try to identifying their skills and motivations. Frances was the only adult worth the effort. She deemed Rupert and Marfa smarter than most of the adults, or at least those who ran their mouths, and the rest seemed bound together more by resentment and incompetence than true concern for the mission or even fear of the aliens.

But they were the only group she could find even slightly interested in breaching the semqu's secrecy or protecting spacers from semqu overreach, so she kept attending, eventually swearing their shut-it oath.

Two members dropped out shortly after she joined. One had joined and recruited others out of fear they were being set up as a peqe meat source, which she understood. But as soon as bird eggs began being imported from Taequa in trade for radio technology, he stopped coming. *Eggs. What a thing to be reassured by.* Obert got distracted by scientific work he set up with Rupert, who assured her they were trying to solve the blinkship conundrum. They were certain there had to be a physics-based answer.

Recruiting was difficult. The ship's general population was so awestruck by being gifted a planet, by ending their journey early, that they seemed willing to gloss over any possible nefarious reasons for their mysterious benefactors' actions.

She sought out and talked in-depth with the other Earthborn who'd survived the journey. Of the two dozen, three eventually admitted to having a similar charge as her own. One was too unhealthy and too overwhelmed by the cultural changes to bother with her concerns. The other two agreed their orders had been overtaken by events too large for any nation-state-focused training or charge to be relevant. One said that defensiveness in the face of salvation was ungrateful at best. The other attended one guild gathering, afterwards teaching Danielle several words in a dozen languages, all meaning "idiots."

She couldn't even argue with him; Tiani had been in rare form.

She was finally fit, clear-headed, connected, and completely stymied.

"We need to find something that everyone understands is an external danger, and work from there," Danielle said one day. She was sitting in a nook of the cafeteria, an area set aside for private meals, with Marfa, Rupert and Frances.

"Like a hull breach?" Marfa said. "From maybe space dust or an asteroid?"

"Not an issue on a planet's surface," Rupert said, grinning.

"Oh, but it is," Danielle said slowly. "Meteors can be deadly."

Rupert and Marfa exchanged looks.

"An asteroid that hits a planet's surface is a meteor," Danielle added. "That's what wiped out our dinosaurs, a big asteroid. Drowned a lot of them on one continent and threw a ton of rock and light-blocking dust into the atmosphere. Triggered an extinction event."

"We'd want to prevent that," Rupert said with confidence.

"Indeed we would. Had a friend with an asteroid-filled, 'How's that space program going?' shirt. Some of the best supporters of the *New Hope* mission were from the Planetary Defense program." Danielle leaned back. "Right now, we've got no idea how many near-surface objects surround Trye. That's a project tailor-made for you and Obert."

"A few researchers are already watching for and mapping solar flares," Rupert said. "*New Hope* has most of the equipment we'd need. Since it's in a solid orbit, it would be a perfect location for additional equipment."

"Earth had a similar program?" Marfa asked.

"Yeah, that means somebody already did the research. Hey, Marfa, do you want to look into it?" Rupert asked.

"Sure! We can get Adamantine to help."

Danielle smiled; Rupert was good at getting others to do his work for him. But that would also keep Marfa involved. And possibly Voice's sister.

"Could be a useful tool," Frances said.

The navigator rarely spoke. Danielle wondered what was going on behind those watchful eyes. Frances started to add something else and stopped as her gaze met Danielle's.

"I think so," Danielle said. "Any system that could detect a meteor could detect a missile or an incoming invasion."

Rupert and Marfa were instantly excited. They started discussing telescope and radar options that swiftly eclipsed Danielle's understanding.

"Hey, they just put out a new dessert tray!" Danielle said. "Could I ask you two..." Marfa rolled her eyes, but the pair ran off to grab them all desserts.

Danielle watched them go, then turned to Frances. "What were you going to say?"

"Is that the threat we need to be worried about?" The navigator leaned forward, intent, and added softly, "If the semqu had wanted us dead, they could have just breached our hull."

"True," Danielle said. "They want us alive, but we don't know why, or what their motivations are. Voice can't or won't tell us. What if that motivation is malicious? I don't want to be enslaved by our benefactors. Once we're entirely planet-bound, we'll have no capacity to protect ourselves."

Frances leaned back, nodding.

"To build that capacity, we need to get some buy-in from the larger community. A sense that spacers are worth fighting for and defending. I don't get that sense from almost any other adult spacer I talk to; most of them think the biggest threat to community is a rogue spacer. A meteor shield is one way we can show the value of the basic *concept* of spacer defense. I'm not saying it's the best way. Believe me, I'm open to other ideas."

"No, I think this is a smart first move," Frances said. "It'll give this group focus, a project that has clear community-wide benefit. And it will tell us something about the semqu if Voice doesn't object."

"How so?"

"It'll tell us that they can't identify or stop incoming objects, for one."

"It will," Danielle said slowly.

Still meeting her gaze, but quieter, Frances said, "So if push comes to shove, all we need to know is where they live."

Click. "Yes. Although knowing what they're vulnerable to would also help."

"Precisely."

They rocked fists toward one another.

Danielle was so grateful to have finally connected with another adult who understood that she could have wept. She still thought of Frances as the captain's plant, but... maybe Ximena Bobbie wasn't as naïve as Danielle had thought. Just exceptionally careful about appearances. That would map well to the woman's solid popularity and success.

She had to admit Frances was right. Danielle no longer feared the semqu wanted them dead. But surely the aliens had to want *something* in return for their gift. Satisfying curiosity could not possibly be enough. She didn't trust that, or them, at all.

FOURTEEN
FINDING ANSWERS

**THE TRANSITION YEARS:
MOVING DOWN TO TRYE
CONSTRUCTION OF FUARINGSPLENZU
NEW HOPIAN YEARS 717-722**

Once each guild leader had a grasp of basic Fugrast and Captain Ximena left for the Council session, Voice began spending long stretches of time at a desk drafting potential wastewater and city infrastructure solutions, followed by long stretches of calligraphy, and ending with her nightly conversation with Ireti. She only taught one Fugrast class a week. Some days she worked in her apartment all day except for meals and could shoo Gregoire off to enjoy himself. It was nice to stretch her mind in new directions.

Ireti was interested in the details of Voice's work and found it restful. It helped that it was quieter in the Quartier Vivant these days, with the exception of boisterous farewell parties.

Ensuring that nothing they planted would cause invasive or watershed problems slowed the agricultural shift, so for the first few years, the generation ship provided much of the necessary foodstuffs for the population below. Those workers, with off-planet help, were busy creating cafeterias, group housing, buses and roads. As the ag fields below began to become productive, the balance began to switch, and more and more spacers made the move "dirtside."

As the ship emptied, as the city and its exploratory outposts grew, the generation ship began to feel like a ghost ship, with whole floors emptying. There remained a shipboard population who would never relocate—elderly who could not handle the stronger gravity, agoraphobics who could not handle the wide-open spaces, those with other phobias which made surface life difficult.

The culture was shifting, too, beginning with a new calendar: originally just to map Earth's religious holidays related to sunrise and sunset to the new planet. But after a series of long and contentious calendar committee meetings, a secular calendar was layered in which mapped Trye's rotation and seasons to *New Hope's* calendar. Also, the long tradition of language change was shifted to a two-year rotation rather than an annual one. There was less time in everyone's day, and after much heated discussion, language study was determined to be less important than personal recreation. Guilds and families, of course, could choose their daily language as they pleased.

Five years after he become Voice's daily companion, Gregoire married his girlfriend, a biologist who'd moved planet-side at the first opportunity. He'd told Voice that they'd agreed on a long-distance marriage; he would remain shipside as her shadow, both a friend and protector.

He'd always been a serious youth, but at the wedding Voice saw another side of him: utterly devoted to his new bride, and beside himself with joy. Two months after the wedding, Voice caught him staring out a viewport, his sketch forgotten. His unbound hair fell in long locs that reminded her of dark tears.

She took a deep breath and took his hand. "Gregoire. It's time. Move down."

"But you need—"

"Why? When was the last serious threat to me?"

He started. "There's only ever been the one attack, but—"

"I don't think I need protection anymore. People have accepted the move. They've accepted me. As much as I enjoy your company —and I will miss you deeply, please promise to come visit me?— You do not need to spend the rest of your life at my side. You should spend it at hers."

He stayed for another month, arranging for coverage for any official event Voice might need to attend. Voice prevailed in no longer having an officer at her door.

In the days after he left, she missed Gregoire sharply. It was odd to walk anywhere alone. It was also relaxing to not be part of his constant sketch hobby. She hadn't realized how much she'd felt "on stage" every time he'd pulled out his tablet.

But a smaller population meant a closer-knit community, and soon Voice was invited to card games, calligraphy nights, movie nights and drum circles. She even reconnected with Terri, although they both seemed to accept their friendship would never be the same.

Social roles rotated through a smaller population. A month after Gregoire left, she found herself volunteering as organizer for the Friday night socials. As she told him at the first of his quarterly visits, she'd never had so many conversations. After so many years swinging between being treated as broken, lauded as a savior or avoided as an alien-tainted weirdo, she was astonished to find herself, without feeling like she was expending much effort, surrounded by friends. It was a lovely feeling.

<Was it really this easy all along?> she asked Ireti one night.

<Apparently so. Spacers are such odd creatures,> Ireti replied, bemused.

She snuggled under her comforter. <Do you miss other semqu?>

<I talk often with Trye9. Well. I listen and he gives me dietary

advice and ... fusses at me. Nothing like your sister, but it does get repetitive.>

<Being nagged is never fun, even when the person wants you to treat yourself well,> Voice said gravely. <Hopefully Tryeg understands what that means better than Adamantine did.>

No words, but a sense of disgruntled affirmation.

Voice added, <But I meant visitors. Ship-Semqu. You seem to like a few of the ships. Don't you miss having friends visit?>

Their response was slow and guarded. <We are not social in the same way, but I welcome visitors when they come.> An odd emotion seeped through their thoughts.

It seemed similar to loneliness to Voice. <You should invite them more often,> she said confidently.

<Perhaps I shall.> A gentle appreciation filled her and lulled her to sleep.

**FUARINGSPLENZU, PLANET TRYE
CONSTRUCTION SITE FOR MARFA AND RUPERT'S
DWELL
NEW HOPIAN YEAR 717
MONTH TWO'S SECOND DAY**

IT POURED during the guild's annual Setsubun gathering. Marfa and Rupert's house was still just a foundation, but the muddy homesite was fairly well protected from the wind and the tent setup Marfa had arranged kept them dry enough. It was certainly private, Danielle thought.

Private enough that she could get up the nerve to finally ask Frances to dinner? Maybe. A side comment one of the guys had made had finally twigged her to the fact that Frances might have a crush on her. The woman was far more subtle than Rupert, and

Danielle was clueless. Or maybe she was just engaging in wishful thinking?

At any rate, she could wait until afterward to ask. As the other guild members chatted, Danielle chewed on crunchy roasted soybeans, eying the sushi rolls enviously. Sadly, seaweed still tasted like plastic to her. There were some small fish heads wrapped in green leaves dotting the edge of the plate—she'd seen those the year before and knew they were related to the end of winter celebration somehow. Were they edible, or just decoration? She turned, intending to amuse Marfa by asking, when Frances asked for everyone's attention, and drove all thought of celebration from her mind.

"I'm volunteering to take a contract on a modeel blinkship, with the intent of sneaking into their engine room," Frances said.

"No," Danielle said.

No one heard her over the surprised, congratulatory cries and applause. Two dozen people—Marfa, Rupert, Obert among them—converged on Frances to thank her. Danielle was disturbed by their holiday attitude toward a suicide mission.

"Precisely what we've needed," Obert said as he passed Danielle. "We'll have answers soon."

That's delusionally optimistic, Danielle thought. It was a full hour later that she finally managed to pull Frances far enough away for a truly private conversation.

"Are you sure about this?" she asked Frances quietly. "If they catch you, they will kill you. They may hold all of us to blame. Everything I've learned about modeel justice—Frances, it's immediate and harsh. We don't know their detection capabilities. Your Fugrast may be better than most of the rest of the Guild's, but we barely understand their culture."

"I know," Frances said. "And that's part of the problem. Even if I can't get into the engine room, I'll learn a lot from being around them, working on their ships. That's knowledge we can use, knowledge we need." She met Danielle's gaze, held it. "Danielle, I won't betray us. And if they kill me, well...I'm ready."

Her gaze carried the determination of a fellow warrior. Danielle's heart ached, but she had to honor it. "I'll miss you." She saw Frances' face quiver and then lock. *God damn it.* "Make sure you come home alive."

FUARINGSPLENZU'S ADMINISTRATIVE OFFICES
NEW HOPIAN YEAR 717
MONTH TEN'S LASTDAY EVE

XIMENA BOBBIE HAD JUST BEEN ELECTED Fuaringsplenzu's first Mayor and Prime Minister at this month's lengthy Accord gathering. Her temporary office was crammed with gifts and boxes. The woman herself looked thinner and more harried than Danielle remembered.

Danielle had expected the summons from *New Hope's* former captain to start off with a demand for information about the Protection Guild and/or the shield project, or a request to fill in for Frances to keep tabs on the group. So she had prepped a mental checklist, including an obfuscation for Frances' eight-month absence.

She didn't need any of that.

Ximena said, "We need ambassadors to all the planets. You have been suggested for the peqe ambassadorship. You seem to understand their habits and values better than any of the spacers I've talked to."

Well, that would certainly let Ximena put distance between me and the guild.

"I suppose I do." Danielle did not trust Matron Peindak, but she wanted to learn more about the martial aspects of her culture. *Keep your friends close and your enemies closer.* From what she'd heard, both modeel and peqe seemed to understand that concept on a level her fellow humans—*spacers*— did not.

"It would be isolating. You'd only have a few other spacers as staff, and you'd be living on their planet. I'm not sure being surrounded by creatures you find threatening would be good for your mental health." Ximena frowned, her brown eyes questioning. "But I promised I would make the offer. All the candidates will have an opportunity to visit Taequa."

"I'll think about it," Danielle said. She left after promising to join with the other candidates at the next day's gathering with Matron Peindak, the peqe ambassador.

Peindak zeroed in on her when she entered. "You were a warrior, yes? Perhaps you would like to attend one of our duels? It seems to not interest any others of your kind." The ambassador sniffed. "A pair of matrons duels over a lover next week. Hardly a matriarch duel, but it should prove interesting; their Houses have long feuded."

It was a chance to see peqe in fighting form, and Danielle could not turn that down, even if it meant traveling by blink and being surrounded by dinosaurs. "I'd be honored," she said.

Ximena, clearly alarmed, said, "A quick social or etiquette primer before any of us travel to your planet might be wise?"

"Ah, yes." Peindak launched into a short patter. "Drop your glance when you meet your betters, which would be any matriarch or matron, and don't speak. That will get you out of most situations."

Danielle snapped, "I would consider myself an equal to any matriarch. We are no one's servants."

Captain Ximena looked shocked, but Peindak threw her head back and laughed. "Ah, what spirit! You are a warrior!" The ambassador seemed utterly delighted. "Well then, just avoid talking. Sarcasm and slights can result in fighting challenges, especially on duel days."

Danielle had a week to prepare, largely through daily conversations with Voice. The youth gave her a great deal of seemingly contradictory advice, almost all of it in what not to do.

The transfer to the ambassador's blinkship was as unpleasant as the trip to Trye with Voice had been, but at least it was semi-private. Danielle was asked to stand still in the diplomacy room. A short nauseating moment later she found herself falling a few centimeters onto the floor of a small room containing a smaller peqe and a couch-like seat. Communicating only in gestures, the alien pointed to the couch, and then warned her just before the second blink, a nanosecond in which every cell in her body felt slapped.

The nausea was instant. The peqe handed her a wide container in which to vomit, took her spew away and brought her a clear fruity beverage.

Danielle felt much better after finishing it, but her arm felt heavier and the air smelled different. Were they on Taequa already?

Voice's warning about stronger gravity had not prepared her for how much work it would be to stand up with the supplemental oxygen pack slung across her back.

"Ah, that's better," Ambassador Peindak said from the doorway. "You spacers have such tepid gravity."

"No wonder you're all so muscled," Danielle said. Voice had taught her a few of the basic signs that all the species would recognize, and she tested that by gesturing her thanks to the smaller peqe. She felt much better than she had after her transit up from Trye; perhaps she was adjusting to this mode of travel. "I wouldn't mind training here."

"It is the best planet for strength," Peindak said. "We will go directly to the arena, so you have time to recover. It is a bit of a walk. We do not allow blinkships in the city proper."

The inside of the ship, what she saw of it, was a blur of curves. The ambassador made no allowances for Danielle's shorter legs, curiosity about her surroundings or adjustment to heavier gravity as she strode out and down a long ramp buried in reddish dirt.

A glitter of white in the sky caught her eye. Massive snow-covered peaks filled the horizon far to her right, partially hidden by a rolling series of ranges that ended near their landing site in red sun-blasted cliffs.

Peindak led them in the opposite direction. They strode through an abandoned-looking arroyo-strewn area on a dusty path with abrupt rises and drops. Danielle used every ounce of her strength to keep up. She was not going to lose face in front of a bunch of dinos. She was a bit surprised by the intense dry heat. Voice had mentioned a high plateau above a jungle, but she had not expected a desert environment. She was sweating heavily by the time they reached an area that looked even vaguely populated. A bridge carried them over a deep arroyo that looked constructed and still held murky-looking water. On its far side, at the top of a rock-topped berm, the ambassador paused, and Danielle had her first view of Zissokot.

It looked to be a beautiful, planned city. They stood near the edge of a broad open area paved with white- and blue-speckled stone, dominated by a massive hexagonal pyramid in the center. It appeared the city had been built in circles around it. A deep rock-lined canal on their right edged the length of the paved area, curving behind the huge structure. Bridges crossed the canal at regular intervals, becoming cobbled roadways that disappeared behind high plastered walls. Residential areas?

"This is the plaza, and that," Peindak pointed to the huge, pyramid that dominated the skyline, "is Temple Piertoc. Isn't she magnificent?"

"She is," Danielle said, impressed. The structure rose in six broadly stepped tiers, each made of massive blocks of blue stone marbled with off-white inclusions. In places where the stone had been worn or polished smooth, it glistened like lapis. The lower tier held statues of peqe in various activities.

She did not mention the pyramids of Earth; Voice had told her any comparison to Earth structures would melt badly. "Does every city have such a temple?"

Peindak gave her a hooded glance and said proudly, "Temple Piertoc stands alone."

Danielle bit her tongue, lightly, and considered how to rephrase the question. One of her personal goals was a population estimate. Peindak set off at a swifter pace on the level ground, directly toward a busy crowd on the plaza, milling about fabric structures near the Temple. She halted again on the first of the cobbled roadways.

Danielle gasped for breath. She glanced down the roadway over the canal, and saw benches, shade plantings, and open gates in the plastered walls. She could not see the end of the roadway, but this looked like a completely structured, planned community. Those walled compounds looked expensive. She wondered where the poor people lived.

Movement around the fabric structures pulled her attention back to the plaza. She was looking at a market, with booths and stalls that would not have been out of place on Earth, save all the merchants and customers looked like some variation of Peindak and her attendants.

The variation of fur coloration on the dinos stunned her: reds to blues to greens to the more mundane colors she would have expected in fur. Some sported wildly varying patterns of spots and stripes. About half were solid colors. Feathery crests cascaded down their backs with similar variation in color, but often iridescent. None held them upright as Peindak did.

It was like watching a kaleidoscope in motion.

There was a trill, a shout, and shoppers began to turn toward them, stopped what they were doing and stared. A number popped their crests up, an impressive sight as it added a meter to their height.

Danielle braced herself; she was the first spacer any of them had seen. "Should I wave?"

"That would be unwise," Peindak said. "Just enjoy the view

and let them see you. Do you see the pretty boy on the left, the pale blue? In front of the egg seller."

It took her a moment, because she could not identify any of the wares, let alone the gender of the creatures in front of her, but with the little peqe's help, she picked him out.

He was staring at them with his snout tilted up and sideways, a body language she'd not seen any other peqe use. He looked undeveloped, soft, his fur the color of a blue jay's feathers. Once she identified him, she could identify other males in the crowd, and the protective attitude their female companions took with them. The recognition of that behavior jarred her. She'd seen it occasionally back on Earth, mostly in dive bars, with the genders flipped.

"He's flirting with us," the ambassador said, amused.

Danielle snapped her glance back to the boy, who swept his lashes down in a clearly coquettish way. He was surrounded by other males, bashfully or excitedly egging him on, a few of them shielding him from the view of a nearby female.

Her ability to read their body language so immediately left Danielle a bit shaken. It had taken her months to figure out peoples' body language aboard *New Hope*.

"Risky, being so bold in public. I approve of his audacity," Peindak said. "What do you think, spacer, would you like to frolic with a Matriarch's son?"

Oh hell no. "I don't think any of us are ready for that level of cultural exchange," Danielle said evenly.

The ambassador barked in delight, joined by her retinue, then turned sharply left and headed up the cobbled roadway. As they left the plaza, the market gave way to a huge garden between them and the massive temple. Smaller peqe worked in the fields. They looked ill and odd. A few were the size of the Matriarch's blue son, but most were smaller. It took Danielle a moment to realize all their crests were missing. Stubs were visible across their upper backs.

Danielle gestured toward them, but Peindak said merely, "The Temple Gardens feed the Attarc, the acolytes and the drones."

"Their crests?" Danielle asked, before she lost all air.

"Crests?" The ambassador seemed confused.

Danielle pointed.

Peindak sniffed. "Those are szipeqe. They tend the herbs and cook, and clean."

Convicts, perhaps? Voice had told her that peqe households orbited their Matriarch, with the second most important person being the apiquiit, the granddaughter who would inherit. Peqe lived in a stratified society and could be cruel to their servants.

Mutilation seemed beyond cruel.

Danielle would have to figure it out on her own; the staff seemed amused or incredulous she would ask, and she was too winded to follow up anyway. She did not want her attentive audience to see her be weak in any way. Even so, she was shaking and soaked with sweat by the time they reached the stone arena.

The ambassador slowed and stopped to chat with a group who had called out to her in their native tongue. Danielle caught her breath and surveyed them. They had been openly staring at her as she approached, but were working hard at ignoring her now, a fact made more obvious by the need for them to dip their heads to see her easily.

One in the center was clearly the core of this small group, probably a Matriarch, who alone had her crest raised. Peindak ignored the others, who had less colorful string garments and whose behavior and attention were split between her, the ambassador's retinue, and the Matriarch they clearly served. While the ambassador and the Matriarch were the only ones verbally speaking, there appeared to be several conversations going on at once, fingers flying too fast for Danielle to understand. Unlikely to be Fugrast sign, anyway.

Any ambassador here would need a staff just to follow and understand the multiple simultaneous conversations. These powerful women clearly did not go anywhere alone. Danielle wondered if that was for safety, or as a show of status. This wasn't the place to ask.

"A matriarch and her swarm," the helpful peqe said quietly. Danielle thanked her with a gesture. She could have been irritated at being ignored, but she was enjoying the breather.

After a moment the Matriarch laughed at something Peindak had said, then turned her head sideways and down to look at Danielle.

That vertical pupil at close range raised her hackles, but she had experience beating that down now. "Are you going to introduce us?" Danielle asked evenly.

"Ah, yes," Peindak said in Fugrast. "Danielle of the Spacers, this is Matriarch Jjaloot Dontan. She has loaned us the balcony beneath hers to watch the match. Her daughter Doaett, House Dontan's apiquiit, fights today."

"May she find honor and victory in battle," Danielle said in Fugrast.

The entire group stilled.

"Well stated." Peindak seemed surprised.

Matriarch Dontan nodded to Danielle, saying in stiff Fugrast, "You spacers are an interesting lot!" She added something in her own tongue to the ambassador, and her group moved away.

"What did she say?" Danielle asked softly.

"That you would make a short duel, but she'd be willing to bet on you," the little peqe said.

"I'll take that as a compliment."

"Oh, it was."

"Is betting normal?" Danielle asked, slightly louder.

"Oh, betting is the most fun!" Peindak crowed. "We must teach you how it's done. Come!"

Ambassador Peindak swept ahead, leading Danielle into the arena proper and up an endless staircase of overly tall stone steps. Much of the circular arena appeared to be built of stone. The structure was large enough to hold five to seven hundred people, seats built in a dozen tiers rising around a large flat area covered with what looked like nut shells. Somewhat like a coliseum, she thought, but the punchwork carvings were alien, and all the stone seats faced backwards. Chest-rests, she realized. Peqe leaned forward to relax, not back.

When they finally arrived on a large balcony Danielle's heart-beat was racing; she'd not had such an intense workout since Earth. She sat down gratefully and tried to lean forward. The angle put so much weight on her lungs she thought they'd collapse.

"How do you breathe on one of these?" she asked after they'd all sat down, and the ambassador had dropped her crest, an awkward process that a staffer helped her with.

"Our crests aren't just for looks," the ambassador said. "As long as there is a bit of a breeze, I don't have to inhale while I'm sitting. I suppose you do, poor thing. Is there enough air in that bottle of yours?"

"Plenty," Danielle said, gritting her teeth. She'd absorb insults for knowledge like that.

She glanced at the crests more carefully, watching as the staffer groomed the ambassador's smooth on her back. There were six to a dozen shafts coming off the shoulders of those around her, with vividly colored tubules branching off each in feather-like fashion. Now that she was watching closely, she could see them expand and contract.

The cutting of crests must be for those who had truly screwed up, because in this thin air and heavy gravity, removing a crest would make work brutally difficult. Maybe they didn't want to talk about those who'd been so punished.

Ambassador Peindak gave Danielle a run-down on the basics of betting in between chatting with a never-ending stream of visiting Matriarchs.

Voice had warned her against falling into debt on Taequa, and to never mention that as a reason for refusing to bet. Danielle was grudgingly beginning to appreciate her advice. Everything the teen had told her had been useful.

She politely refused to make any bets, pointing out she had no api-coin of her own, was still unfamiliar with the entire duel process, and did not wish to risk offending either House involved.

Peindak sulked, but not for long; she was getting enough pleasure from gossiping about the duel and showing off her alien guest to slack off on heckling Danielle.

The small peqe took the opportunity to point across the arena, where the other fighter's family sat. Danielle quizzed her about the businesses the dueling Houses were involved in—clothing and basketry—and the nature of their historic feud, which she could not explain. "Fugrast does not suit it well," the young peqe finally said, stymied.

If being stared at in the market was bad, being stared at here was a thousand times worse. Danielle used the opportunity to do a local population count; the stadium was full.

"Szi! Here!" The ambassador yelled. A wiry, thin-furred worker approached, burdened with baskets filled with fruits and nuts. The ambassador helped herself, tossing several to her retinue and Danielle, and went back to talking to the Matriarch who'd stopped by, a mid-sized cream-colored creature who never stopped staring at Danielle.

Danielle watched the worker until she could see that he, too, had no crest. He re-slung his baskets and kept his gaze low. His demeanor was that of a beaten dog. Then he saw Danielle. His near eye widened. He made a gesture, scuttled backwards, and fled.

The peqe next to her hissed.

"What?" Danielle asked.

"Servants are a strange lot. Some of them believe in silly superstitions," the peqe said. She refused to explain further.

Danielle committed the gesture to memory as well as she could. There was a rustle and a blare of sound from the arena floor. The Matriarch cut off conversation with the ambassador, joining the flurry of movement around the circle as the audience found their seats.

"Now, this is the good part," Peindak said, cracking open the nut in her hands and popping it into her mouth.

Danielle pulled the peel off the citrus-like jeejee in her hand. She slurped the pulp; it tasted like a lychee-pear cross, more flavorful and juicier than the one she'd had on Trye. She blinked—it was the first food that had tasted right in years. She reveled in that as she watched the untranslated opening of the duel.

The basics were clear enough; an introduction of the two combatants by a tall speaker clearly there as a ritual leader, and two referees. The fighters were of equal size, one solid grey, one green-and-cream-striped, both armored with spiked collars and braces on their arms. Their cheeks were horribly swollen.

She tapped the young peqe, pointed to the area under her own eye, asked, "What?"

The young woman seemed amused. "Kote. They swell when one is angered or in fighting form." She pointed to her own face, and a pouch under her near eye expanded and contracted.

How can they see?

There held no weapons, but she noted both fighters sheathing and unsheathing their talons. She swallowed; they looked lethal.

A young male, about the same size as the blue youth back in the market, was paraded once around the arena on a bier carried by sweating, crestless workers. He was swathed in a highly decorated robe that hid all but his head. The workers hustled him through a small stone arch below the entry area.

Danielle was too far away to see if he was frightened, excited or worried, but she noticed two stern females in fighting trim, larger than the matrons in the ring, guarding the door he'd been carried through. Guarding against the winner, the loser, or—?

It was no longer quiet enough to ask. The introductory rite was over, its leader trotting swiftly off the shells. The referees gestured at the fighters and moved back. The crowd began to roar and shout. Danielle leaned forward.

The grey was whip-fast and uncontrolled, the striped fighter confident and patient. The musculature and speed on display were impressive. There seemed to be no pattern to the fight, no actual form. It reminded her of two drunk weightlifters she'd seen get into a brawl in her teen years; neither had the slightest idea how to fight, and these two didn't either. They were, however, good at avoiding damage. Peqe talons looked wicked sharp, and the little peqe had told her the duel was to be first blood.

As the crowd focused on the fight, the helpful peqe leaned forward next to Danielle. "I would serve on your staff, should you have need," she said, near her ear. "I am Dorina."

Danielle slid her hand down her leg and gestured assent, hoping only Dorina could see it. "I thank you."

Someone above them shouted. The striped fighter had gotten cocky, turned her head at the wrong moment to acknowledge the crowd. Her opponent caught her in the upper back, burying her talons deep where the other's crest attached. She wrenched and ripped down. The striped fighter went down on one knee, snarling. There was a gasp from the crowd.

Her opponent backed away, raising her bloody hand in victory. There was a massive cheer and roar, a chanted word. Victory, or the fighter's name.

"That's it, then. First blood?" Danielle asked Dorina.

"First blood, usually." Dorina glanced over her shoulder at the balcony above, then across to the other duelist's box, then back at the arena. "It is up to the injured fighter. Doaett."

Their hostess's daughter. "She would keep fighting?"

"That is a bad injury. Humiliating." Dorina's teeth clicked. "She will not be able to lift crest again. She is... proud."

The injured fighter rose to her feet, fighting off the referees. She screamed a challenge, a single word. The crowd picked it up. It became a roar. The grey backed up, legs wheeling, panic on her face.

Dread gripped Danielle. "If not first blood?" She already knew the answer.

"Death," Dorina said tightly, her eyes focused on the fighters below. The stadium had gone silent after the roared phrase, "To the death" or its equivalent.

Danielle braced herself.

The grey had no stomach for murder, and the striped fighter—Doaett— was intent on it. The fight became a cat and mouse game, the grey trying to talk her opponent out of a death match, and when that failed, grimly battling for her life. Her quickness was no match for the striped fighter's merciless fury.

Blood coated fur as cut after cut landed on them both, but mostly on the grey.

The crowd came alive, slowly, building to a solid drumbeat of a chant: Do-a-ett! Do-a-ett! DO-A-ETT! The loss of the crowd's favor eroded what was left of the grey's morale. She failed to block one of Doaett's strikes and fell backwards, her throat slashed. Blood sprayed onto the nut shells, and she was still.

Danielle swallowed.

The crowd went wild, chanting Doaett's name. She trotted around the edge of the fighting area, still bleeding profusely from the shoulder and arms, taking a victory lap. Cheers echoed off the stone.

"Victory to House Dontan!" the ambassador said. "What do you think, spacer?"

"Very intriguing tradition," Danielle said, still watching. "I found it educational. You would call this a fair and righteous fight? The grey knew what she was getting into?"

"They were well matched, matrons in good fighting trim. It was a good bout, though one rarely expends so much energy over a mate. Husband-duels are normally only to first blood. House Dontan will be fined for the loss of an apiquai-stake." The ambassador ran a hand over her nares. "The lost daughter certainly knew it was a possibility. Doaett is a singularly determined apiquiit."

It was more information than the ambassador had given her since they'd met. Danielle glanced over and nodded with a slight tilt to the head: the informal way of saying thank you. "Duels vary widely?"

"Duels have different stopping points, depending on what's at stake. We usually know in advance if they will be to the death." The ambassador glanced at the tier above her, where the winner's household sat, and lightly curled her lips from her teeth. "Death matches are normally only for important conflicts: one's House is at stake, or one's honor, which are basically the same thing. Those are rare, and wildly popular. One has to find a seat early and be careful going home. You would not be brought to one of those, and I may be questioned for bringing you here today—" She snapped her jaw shut and blew air, creating a whistling sound. "I must congratulate Matriarch Dontan. Please wait here." She nodded at Dorina, who rose as the ambassador did. The rest of the retinue followed the ambassador to the higher balcony.

Victory had been declared. Bets were being paid off and the lower seats emptied, the crowd still abuzz with excited chatter. Doaett had trotted off through the archway where her husband-prize waited. Danielle wondered if the frightened young man had had a choice in the matter, or a preference for who won.

Dorina stood between Danielle and the arena, looking down and around, her lowered crest spread wide. Almost protective. That and the ambassador's sudden willingness to provide details intrigued Danielle. Like they were worried. They'd not shared the ample balcony in the crowded arena with anyone else. It seemed odd; the area was prime seating.

"Why would I not be brought to a death-match?" Danielle asked.

"Bloodlust," Dorina said. "Matrons and matriarchs become

highly aroused and easily angered. Just the sight of an alien might make them lash out."

Danielle blinked at her back. "I don't mean to be offensive, but are your leaders really under such poor emotional control?"

Dorina spun and blurted in a whisper, "Dear Goddess, don't repeat that anywhere anyone can hear you!" She straightened, looking around, and then said quietly, "Self-control is highly valued and considered an attribute of maturity. But no one would expect a matron to control herself after witnessing a death-duel. It was a slight risk to bring you to a first-blood duel. Now... now we'll be among the last to leave, if not the last, to ensure no one from the losing House attempts to take out their anger on you."

"And you are blocking me from view so people will forget I'm here."

"Yes," Dorina said reluctantly.

"You have been helpful," Danielle said. "I doubt I will be the ambassador here, but I will make sure that your name reaches whoever is named."

"I would be grateful. Working for the ambassador has been a dream come true, but it seems to me working for spacers would be more interesting."

Hm. Let's see how helpful she really wants to be. "Can you tell me what is up with the missing crests?"

"All szipeqe are sheared—well, they shear themselves—every autumn," Dorina said. "Tradition."

No. Danielle sat hard on her rage. "And if they refuse?"

"Why would they do that? They understand their place." When Danielle did not reply, she went on. "I suppose they'd be punished. Imprisoned and sheared." She turned her head sideways, her narrow pupil intent on Danielle. "Why do you ask? Your excessive interest in servants risks making the ambassador think you, or you spacers—" she seemed to search for the right words, "wish to be servants."

"I'm still learning your culture, so I did not understand,"

Danielle said, trying to keep her tone even. "We would not allow such abuse of fellow spacers in our society."

"Abuse? Oh, well," Dorina waved a hand, "we are apeqe, and they are szipeqe."

"And the difference is?"

"They are inferior, of course."

"How? You are the same species. The only difference I see is mutilation and mistreatment."

"It— Please do not say such to any matron or matriarch. They would be angered, offended." Dorina's lips parted and closed several times. Finally she said, "I do not know how to explain in a way an off-worlder could understand. I will think on it and explain should we meet again."

"Please do. Equality is an extremely strong value in our culture. Any ambassador must thoroughly understand the brutal inequalities in yours," Danielle said.

Dorina seemed less insulted than confused. She gestured her assent. "Spacers are like the phren in that regard, then. How odd."

"We think you are the odd ones, of course." Danielle did not soften that, and Dorina did not react.

Danielle spent the trip back pondering her decision and wondering at herself. The death directly in front of her had not impacted her as much as the many shearings she hadn't seen. Or the subjugation of the men in this society, no better than ancient subjugation of women back on Earth. But the woman in the ring had known that death was a possibility, while the servants she'd seen clearly had no choice about a mutilation that left them less able to function or defend themselves.

Back at the Prime Minister's office in Fuar, Danielle passed on Dorina's name when she refused the ambassadorship. She explained what she'd seen and learned.

"Thank you for not causing an incident," Ximena said. "That must have been deeply difficult to witness. This is extremely disturbing."

"It is. Do we have to have an ambassador on their planet? Can we refuse based on a gulf in values?"

"I don't know. We'll find out. She said the phren are as egalitarian, and given my time at Council, I would agree with that. I will ask their councilor. I... cannot think of a single spacer who could be asked to endure that situation," Ximena said slowly. "Nor can we allow that kind of thinking to infect our own people."

"Thank you," Danielle said fervently. "Generational, bigoted inequity is not something I want to tolerate, ever. I've seen the consequences of that. Earth had too many tolerant societies destroyed by infection of caste-based thinking. It's crystal-clear on Taequa. Those vaunted semqu sure haven't done anything to stop that—"

"Understood. We had an outbreak of that during our voyage, and it was for many of us a hard-learned lesson," Ximena said. "We lost a lot of bright and valuable souls. I won't let that happen again."

Danielle relaxed, feeling a solid connection with the Ximena. "What kind of a place have we landed in?"

"I don't know." The Prime Minister rubbed her eyes. "On the days when I find myself asking that question too often, however, I think of one of my family's sayings, 'Thrive where you are planted.'"

"Not something any szipeqe child can do," Danielle said grimly.

"No. We'll have to figure out... how to influence that. We need more information. If you're willing to gather that, I'd appreciate it. The ambassador adores you, by the way." She gave Danielle a wry smile. "You do seem to understand them in ways others do not."

"I do. Their body language, their sexism, their fighting—hell, even their bloodlust— I get that. I understand it in a way that someone raised shipboard might never be able to comprehend. I cannot imagine anyone born on this ship watching that duel without breaking down. I can try to help anyone who has to work there, and I'll be happy to sit in on negotiations. But they horrify me, and the fact that I understand them so well—" She trailed off.

"Horrifies you about yourself?" Ximena said sympathetically.

"Yeah." It felt good to admit it, and better to see no judgment on Ximena's face.

"It is disturbing to see the worst of ourselves, or the worst of our past, reflected in others." Ximena stared at the wall, then looked directly at Danielle. "But I don't think you're a horrible person, Danielle. I think you want to help us in a situation that is beyond all our ken, using the tools and skills you have. I've been remiss in sidelining you out of fear of those skills, and my own bias against your training. Can you join forces with me a bit more?"

Danielle saluted her.

"What was that?"

"That was a yes," Danielle said. "It's hard for me to not consider you my superior officer."

"I'm no one's superior," Ximena said, unwittingly breaking the last tether holding Danielle from going off on her own with her own solutions. "But I'd like to be considered a trusted colleague."

"That I can do," Danielle said. *A valued colleague, at least.* Ximena was a politician. Danielle deeply admired her skills and respected her. But she'd never had luck trusting politicians.

ABOARD AN UNNAMED MODEEL TRADESHIP
SEMQU YEAR 1144
NEW HOPIAN YEAR 718

WAATOOS HECHT HATED blinkship containment rooms. Seeing one meant work for her she wasn't going to enjoy. She tapped her right upper claw on the room's console in irritation, her recorders fixed on the spacer lunatic on the other side of the electromagnetic bars.

Her colleague snapped, "You're going to short the panel doing that."

"Are you questioning my control of my own biofield?" Waatoos asked. She was too focused on the spacer to even spill her ire on the other, who wisely stopped communicating.

How much did the spacers know, and why wouldn't the semqu let them invade this one's brain to find out? This lunatic had been caught trying to break through an engine room door.

Their Voice was a sweet thing, but … *fucking spacers.*

"What are you going to do to me?" this one asked.

"Normally you would be put to death," Waatoos said. She waited. Death was a powerful deterrent to stupidity, as her mother used to say. And a useful one, her Krufrugaan instructor had later added.

Waatoos' companion clanked incredulously, "Normally?!"

The spacer said nothing.

"But you are being allowed a choice not given to any other resident in Se Collective." Waatoos bit each word off. "There is a new chemical circulating in the illegal stimulants trade. It apparently allows one to identify one's deepest desire and provides a tidal wave of motivation to work toward it. If that desire is compatible with semqu law, you will be allowed to go free."

Gears ground against one another on her left. She was surprised her colleague's hard suit wasn't smoking. She had thought she'd spring a gasket of her own when she'd been told to make this offer.

"If you agree, you will tell no one what has transpired here. In fact, you may not be allowed to remember. We need to know how this drug impacts spacers before any of your young people encounter it. We have seen no permanent biological damage in other species. But your biology is different."

The response from inside the cell was controlled. "Volunteer as a test subject for a drug that might kill me or drive me insane, or die at your hand."

"Accurate. You chose to attempt to enter a blinkship engine. You wished to steal modeel technology. To wedge that into one of your languages, 'We can't be having that.'" Waatoos allowed herself a flutter of amusement; the pain of watching hours of incomprehensible spacer media had paid off with an insult to a prisoner. It gave her grim satisfaction. "Your body's responses will be studied. We will ensure you are no harm to yourself or others before we release you to return to Trye. Consider it your service to your people."

She let her anger free. "Or you can die, and no one among your people will know how or where, because your body will feed scavengers on Vasom. Choose."

"I see." Frances said. After a moment she added, "I'll take the drug."

TRYE: FUARINGSPLENZU
NEW HOPIAN YEAR 720
SECOND MONTH'S EIGHTEENTH DAY

THE DAY STARTED BADLY and got worse. Voice woke grumpy, without much of an appetite. Ireti wasn't feeling great, so Voice planned to take the shuttle. Ximena wanted her to translate for an important mining meeting with modeel, aupoin and spacer officials. But her office hadn't clearly communicated it was today, nor given her a location. Voice barely made it aboard the shuttle before it left.

She stepped out into a downpour. Voice forgotten about weather; she hadn't brought rainwear.

At the Prime Minister's office, an apologetic staffer told her the meeting had been moved to the Mining Guild building on the other side of Fuar.

Cold wind drove the rain sideways as she got off the transport at the guild offices. She was a dripping mess when she rushed into the guild meeting room, only to find Ulick already in the thick of translation.

Seated next to him was a tall, immaculately dressed black-haired woman, who lit up with a brilliant smile when Voice came in. It took Voice far too long to recognize her sister Adamantine.

"Petite-sœur! Happy anniversary!"

"That's not appropriate," Voice said, automatically. "That's not my role here," she amended. Too late; Adamantine's face clouded.

Voice's arrival interrupted the meeting; she and Ximena apologized to each other, Ximena with some surprise. She had not expected Voice to attend.

The modeel in attendance were amused by what they considered spacer ineptitude.

Far from Ireti's influence, Voice let irritation wash over her as she walked out of the building. Adamantine's presence had completely derailed her. By the time she left, her big sister seemed to be smirking while playing at being wounded.

Had Adamantine played some deliberate part in the screwup? Or was this entirely her own fault? What had she meant, happy anniversary? *Oh. Today is my birth-anniversary.* So like Adamantine to insist on that, when Voice preferred to celebrate the day she'd ceased to be Opal, and had said so on more than one occasion.

Adamantine was being Adamantine. Voice tried to put the mix-up out of her mind. She was dirt-side, and she had free time!

She decided to surprise Gregoire and his new baby with a visit. She managed to not get soaked again taking the necessary transports, but neither he nor his wife were home. Sitting on the crowded transport on the way back, a cramp doubled her over. She'd been ignoring a low-level discomfort all morning. Sudden claustrophobia swept over her and was gone.

Fellow passengers, kind and concerned, asked if she was okay. She started to say, "I'm not sure," when a hot wetness between her legs startled her, drove her to her feet. Her period had started a week early. "I just need to get off," she said. She didn't want to bleed on the woven seat covers.

Periods were still new to her. She'd started menstruating late, and the concerned medics insisted she wait an entire year before they put her on suppressants.

She stepped off the transport at an unfinished residential area. The rain had eased to a steady soft drizzle. Nearby crews worked on two large multi-family dwellings; there were no public facilities finished yet. She finally found their temporary relieving station, not much more than three walls, a roof, and buckets, but there were wipes and absorbents in a box, so she could squat and take care of her business. Grateful, she left the fruit and snacks from her bag on the common snack table at the edge of the site. By the time she caught another transport, she was soaked and cold and in pain. There was no time to do anything but return to the rendezvous spot and go back to *New Hope*. A wasted morning.

When she arrived the kitchen crew had already put away the lunch meal. She had to make do with dried fruit and a cup of tea, but at least she had painkillers. Hungry, uncomfortable, and out of sorts, she settled in at her desk, intending to do a final review of her plans before sending them to the wastewater guild. That would make her feel better; it was work she enjoyed. It had been an interesting project, custom built for a tricky site with a lot of rock and several different soil types, including clay, which was a poor substrate for leach lines.

The decision to avoid one or two large treatment plants and instead make smaller, neighborhood sewage treatment areas had been made early in Fuaringsplenzu's planning process: one of the ways to encourage neighborhoods separated by green areas. Designing custom sewage treatment solutions for disparate neighborhoods kept Voice busy and gave her plenty of opportunity to interact with their underground neighbors. The aupoin were amazingly willing to trench lines, inform them about problem areas, bring minerals to the surface, and create underground vaults. Once they understood the purpose of leach lines, they were happy to help with providing a healthy and helpful bacteria population that would keep septic systems functional despite the wet climate.

Because Fuar was sited near the sea, many sites required larger leach areas that could double as wetlands. It turned out that small marshes and their denizens delighted the aupoin, and they created tunnels nearby that, as Voice understood it, they could visit on holidays, often bringing an entire creche of youngsters. The wastewater guild was disconcerted by this at first, as they'd limited spacer access to the marshes for public safety reasons.

Voice thought once spacers overcame their consternation about creatures holidaying in sewage treatment areas, the parklike areas would make a nice middle ground for the average spacer to meet and interact with aupoin.

However, all the meetings about her projects were held in person on Trye and seemed to result in a never-ending stream of changes, large and small, that not only impacted her, but were rarely communicated to her with any urgency. It was as if they'd forgotten their architect needed to be involved.

She finished her review and opened her messages.

The first was from Adamantine. "I thought you would enjoy having your anniversary off!" she wrote. "Happy 17th, Opal!"

Voice glared at her screen, fully annoyed. Had Adamantine screwed up the meeting on purpose by getting Ulick to translate? How was it a gift if she didn't know she wasn't needed?

She typed, "Thank you for wasting my day." Stared at it, hovering over the send command. Deleted it. She tried twice more, failing to find the proper mix of words that would convey criticism without further pushing her sister away. She finally set the message aside unanswered, irritated all over again at being unable to express her frustration in a way Adamantine would hear.

The second message was worse. Two weeks ago, the tricky site had been canceled in favor of another one. No one had thought to tell her until today. Two weeks of work, wasted.

She snatched up her now-useless plans and flung them into the recycler. Her fury flattened instantly, but she stomped around the room anyway. She wanted to feel angry. Why shouldn't she feel angry when she had a right to feel it?

Ireti stirred, curious about her emotional upset.

By then, only hurt remained. <I devoted my life to serving my community. Now absolutely no one cares that I exist! Why can't I be angry about that?> Voice said. <It's utterly insulting and disrespectful, and it hurts. I used to be important! I used to matter!>

<You're still important,> Ireti said.

<Yes, but...> Voice ground to a halt, staring at the beige pages being chewed by her recycler. That rage—she'd been acting like Père, when he'd thrown her litany into the recycler. She was abruptly horrified.

<What is it, Voice?>

<I hadn't realized how much of Père I had absorbed. His ego, his need to be more important than everyone, to be seen as better than everyone.> Her anger was gone, replaced by dread.

<Ah. Ego, superiority, and resentment are dangerous vices in a Voice. I am glad you did not absorb your father's personality.>

Voice shivered. <Yes. I will need to watch that.>

<Thank you. The power that I hold, that any semqu holds, should never be ruled by rage. We have learned this to our loss.>

Shame swamped her briefly. Not all of that emotion was her own, but... <All this time together, and I am still broken.>

<Be easy, Voice. You are young. Many adult Voices begin their time with their semqu far more broken than you. And no creature is perfect. I certainly am not. It is hard for mammals to live without strong emotions. It is hard for me to live with them. Let us mature together.>

Voice was swamped with a wave of compassion for herself that she didn't feel she deserved; it filled her eyes with tears. She returned a sense of gratitude. <I will gladly grow with you.>

FIFTEEN
USEFUL INFORMATION

**FUARINGSPLENZU, TRYE
RUPERT AND MARFA'S DWELL
SEMQU YEAR 1147 NEW HOPE YEAR 721
SIXTH MONTH'S TWENTIETH DAY**

Rupert bounced between elation and frustration. After four years of waiting and wondering, the guild finally had clear proof that the semqu were involved with the blinkship engines. Sadly, that proof was both ambiguous and too dangerous to share.

Well, and they'd lost a guild member.

The guild member in question, the generation ship's former navigator, was alive and sitting in Rupert's living room, which was a plus. She was definitely not right, and that was not.

"So just before my attempt in the blinkship, I got a spiked drink, I guess," Frances said. "Something went wrong, anyway. I woke up in modeel custody. They knew I'd tried to break into the ship's engine."

She spoke in an earnest, childlike way that was so unlike the Frances that Rupert knew that he wondered if she was a clone.

She'd gained weight and was badly out of shape, neither of which was a Frances thing, and her hair was long and unkempt. Rupert watched her gestures and eye contact, learning as he always did from those who were conveying sincerity, something he loved to fake.

"But that drink messed with my head and body. They held me for years, giving me a lot of medical treatment. I guess I almost died. I wasn't conscious for long stretches. So I can't promise you that they don't know who you are," Frances said. "If you want me to end myself as a result of possibly breaking my oath, I am willing to do that. If you will allow me, however, I will simply not return to guild meetings and not mention it to anyone, ever. It's odd, I had once wanted so much to impress Danielle, and now—did you know I've always wanted to be a beekeeper? I think I shall be doing that for the rest of my life. I've already moved to a new patch of ground on the outskirts and bought several hives from another beekeeper. It's really for that reason I'd like to keep living; those girls need me."

The last two sentences would not have been out of place anywhere in the colony, but from one who'd volunteered to break into a blinkship engine, they took Rupert's breath away.

Suicide would impress the others of the need for secrecy, Rupert thought. He pursed his lips, seeking support among the shocked faces. Only Danielle seemed to convey that she had understood this as a possible outcome.

Marfa said, "So you did access the blink drive. What do you remember about it?"

"Bees are going to be my new life," Frances said, shrugging as if the question was the least important topic she could imagine. There wasn't even an edge to the words that might imply she didn't want the question asked.

Rupert glanced at the newest members of the guild. The transport mechanic and his round son had met the navigator only once. He was gratified to see they were duly shocked.

The boy leaned forward, protesting. "But you wanted to get into one, that was the most important thing, you said—"

His father laid a hand on his shoulder. "Hush."

"But—"

"Your father is right," Frances said. "I mean, I know you won't believe me, but those modeel taught me that the semqu are..." she paused, and every one of the salon's occupants, save Danielle, leaned forward in anticipation, "basically uninterested in us. I mean, they want us to succeed. They want us to thrive. But they're kind of a live-and-let-live set of creatures."

Nonsense, he thought. She'd been turned Semule. Frances' brain had been rewired, her personality changed. The only creatures capable of that were semqu.

"Modeel, on the other hand, have strict privacy rules about their engines. They think we're trying to compete. That is a problem." She flashed an apologetic smile. "I agreed to go tend bees, because beekeeping is a hobby I've always wanted to pick up. And they're okay with that; they'll consider the matter closed."

"But we shouldn't try again," Danielle said.

"The Guild really, really, really, shouldn't try again." Frances leaned on all three repeated words. "The consequences would be bad. Like 'spacers might have to leave the solar system' bad." Her tone was still childlike, but emphatic.

That clinched it for Rupert; that was a semqu rule. Cold settled in his stomach.

Frances was earnest again. "I mean, the best outcome would be for you all to just pursue your other interests, and that's not awful, to tell you the truth," she said, standing. "Now if you'll excuse me, my girls are probably getting hungry. I just moved them, and I need to supplement their intake until they can find new sources of pollen. I'm learning so much. If you ever want to talk beekeeping, come visit me!"

She smiled brilliantly; an expression Rupert had never seen on her serious face. Halfway to the door, she stopped. With her back to them all, she said, "Danielle, if you decide I need to be killed for the security of the guild, will you promise to make sure someone takes care of my girls?" She turned to face the other woman.

Danielle closed her eyelids. "I promise. But Frances—" She reopened them, and shifted her weight forward, her focus on the former navigator, "That will not be necessary. What purpose would your death serve?"

It would teach the others we take our own security seriously, Rupert thought with outrage, but glancing around, he realized he'd already lost that argument— and might lose the Guild if he voiced it. Frances had more support than he did. It frustrated him.

Frances took a deep breath. "Well." The former navigator's smile wobbled a little; she hadn't been sure about Danielle's answer. "If you change your mind, I'll hold you to that promise. Thank you." Frances turned back to the door. "I'll miss you all. If you come visit, only talk to me about bees. I won't discuss Guild business with any of you."

With an abrupt harshness, she added, "Don't ever bring it up."

She left the door open behind her. It was a common occurrence; Marfa had insisted their custom-built home have Earth-style manual doors. Most guests were accustomed to doors that closed themselves. Rupert grumbled and walked over to close it.

A modeel squatted where their gravel walkway met the sidewalk, its aura set to pale grey. It wore one of the newer cases, fully loaded with tech. As Frances rushed past it, the modeel's aura moved; green swirled and bubbled through motionless smoke. Frances didn't slow, didn't look at it, hurrying out of Rupert's line of sight.

The modeel stood. Rupert expected it to follow Frances, but one of its six appendages gestured to its own recorders, toward Rupert, and back to itself. And then it disappeared.

Dhatt. Rupert swallowed and closed the door.

Should he leave the Guild? He considered. Marfa wouldn't. He still enjoyed playing the public face of the Meteor Shield project, even though his part had long been finished. The Guild members had long bored him. He kept hosting them as a way to keep his finger on the pulse of gossip, and maybe someday grab for himself, or reverse engineer, the secret of the blink drives.

Whatever that secret was, it had just become way too dangerous to uncover.

He needed to find another way to leave his mark, and he needed some protection. Ulick was going places, and Adamantine had her fiancé wrapped around her little finger. It was time to get some true use out of his friendship with her.

PLANET VASOM
KERFRUGAAN HEADQUARTERS
SEMQU YEAR 1147
NEW HOPE YEAR 721

"I'M NOT TIED to the planet's surface, so I can travel anywhere you might need an aupoin to go," O-eee-u said. The modeel he was trying to impress finally gave him some reaction, a bit of curiosity curling through his field. O-eee-u took the initiative to answer the unasked question. "As I'm sure your predecessor informed you, I did not bond in the usual way—"

"Which makes me wonder," his supervisor interrupted, "why you would wish to work here, and indeed, why you were allowed to."

"Here" was the Krufrugaan training center on Vasom. O-eee-u's friends had told him that the Krufrugaan were the enforcers of the galaxy, and that meant to him that they worked for the semqu. His old boss had refused to acknowledge that and had not trusted the aupoin to do more than menial tasks, like sweeping floors. O-eee-u was happy that his replacement was at least more willing to part with knowledge.

"I miss that bond," O-eee-u said, grateful that he had no tell-tale emotional biofield. "And serving all of semqu seemed the best way to achieve some semblance of it. A replacement."

His supervisor's predecessor had been deeply suspicious of that motive. O-eee-u wanted to impress his loyalty on this new boss early and often, hoping he would be less watchful. He wasn't sure he was succeeding. "That's... an interesting color combination, sir. I don't know how to interpret it." He was afraid to admit he was colorblind, a communication problem he'd so far been unable to overcome.

"Begrudging admiration," the modeel said, "for either your audacity or your desire to serve. Time will tell me which it is. Don't forget that."

"I won't, sir, and also, I hope to convince you —to prove to you —the latter."

A sharp clatter. "Very well. You will remain in our employ. We'll find more challenging chores for you."

O-eee-u's heart leapt. "I am deeply grateful for your faith in me."

"I have no faith in you. This is a test and an opportunity. Ensure I don't regret offering it."

FUARINGSPLENZU, TRYE
COMMUNITY SPACE 1
NEW HOPE YEAR 721
SIXTH MONTH'S TWENTY-SECOND DAY

UNLIKE PÈRE'S sparsely attended memorial gathering, Mère's was overflowing with attendees, filling the semi-circles of benches all the way to the back wall. Hers was a secular rite; Harriet's expansion of her life and her social circle, once she was no longer obsessed with her mercurial husband, hadn't included religion.

Nor me, Voice thought.

Adamantine's terse quips had implied it hadn't included her, either.

Her sister alternated between a dancer's upright posture, gorgeous in a black dress shot with white, and slumped over. Her breath smelled excessively sweet, and she rubbed her temples as they listened to the testimonies of character and community devotion, occasionally touching the bag she'd stuffed between them.

If Ireti was right, and she usually was, Adamantine was hungover.

Voice sat like a stone. She wanted to grieve, but she didn't know how; that level of pain had been off-limits to her for years. What did grief feel like? Ireti said she would share other spacers' memories when Voice was in private.

Halfway through the rite, there was a short break for people to chat with one another about Harriet. Waves of conversation began behind them. A baby cried in the back, startled by the shift in noise. Voice had been expecting the moment and planned to use it to run to the facilities.

Before she could rise, Adamantine laid a hand on her arm. She plunged the other into her bag, twisting awkwardly as she dug around inside it.

"Sœur." Adamantine swallowed. "I know you left this behind, but I kept it for you. If you'd like it back, as... as a memento..." She thrust Gengi into Voice's hands.

It was smaller than she remembered. "Oh!" Voice ran her fingers over the soft toy. It brought her memories, but no comfort. And some of the memories were not good. How could she explain that here, now? The baby in the back howled again; it gave her an idea. "You made Gengi for me and I love that about him. It was a gift that mattered to me and helped me."

Tears ran down her cheeks, but Adamantine smiled.

"But you and Ulick will have children someday, yes?"

Adamantine's eyes widened, and she began to blush. "Sœur!"

Ulick leaned over, smiling. "We hope so."

"Then you should keep Gengi for your own child. Give it to your first."

She set it back on her sister's bag. "Mère would have liked that, too."

Adamantine burst into tears. Not show tears, but deep, gut-wrenching sobs.

It stunned her; she'd rarely seen her sister lose control so completely. Never in such a public setting.

Voice looked at Ulick; what had she done wrong? But he was smiling sadly. He wrapped his arms around Adamantine. Hands close to Voice, he gestured that she'd done the right thing. Had said the right thing. "Adamantine just needs to grieve."

So do I. But perhaps… perhaps it's just as well I can't. I can be here for her today. Later in the ceremony, Adamantine reached out her hand. Voice took it. They sat side by side, fingers entwined. *Maybe now that both our parents are gone, we can be sisters again.*

ULICK AND ADMANTINE'S DWELL
FUARINGSPLENZU, TRYE
NEW HOPE YEAR 721
SEVENTH MONTH'S FIRST DAY

RUPERT LEFT his research office early to deliver the dinner invitation to Ulick and Adamantine in person.

Marfa had planned a Protection Guild social event to thank the remaining Guild members and rebuild their confidence.

Rupert had other plans. He wanted Adamantine to take him seriously again. Rupert intended to be ruthless about the competition for her ear. Particularly, as Mar put it, "a semqu-tainted one." Voice had never liked him; would oppose his suggestions.

And rumor was that the Pangea sisters had reconciled at their mother's funeral. He needed a wedge, and Frances and Mar could provide one. Mar wouldn't go to the wedding if Voice was there. Adamantine hated what the aliens had done to Voice. Once she saw what they'd done to Frances, he was certain he could get her to "forget" to invite Voice to the wedding.

Families had ruptured over less.

Shaking Ulick out of his complacency about the semqu would be a bonus.

Ulick greeted him warmly and led him to their table. "Sorry for the mess— work and wedding preparations." Apprenticed to the spacers' elected leader, the reedy language nerd had filled out, developed a gravity that would suit future leadership positions, and a penetrating focus he used to make people feel important.

Adamantine, gorgeous as usual, smiled but didn't rise to greet him with her usual hug. Ulick had managed to entrap Adamantine into a promise of a monogamous union. It nettled Rupert; he'd resolved so many issues with Marfa over the years by making her jealous of Adamantine's affection.

He sighed. Having sex with Adamantine made manipulating her easier, but it wasn't necessary. And if he was going to hitch himself to Ulick, he needed to respect the man's boundaries. He sat without trying to touch or flirt with Adamantine.

Scrolls and pads and fabrics were scattered across their large table, the only mess in their otherwise orderly apartment. They entertained often; their upcoming wedding was likely to be large. Rupert offered his condolences about her loss, and they chatted.

He extended the dinner invite. After they'd agreed to come, and just as he was getting ready to leave, he said, "Ah, just to let you know, *New Hope's* old navigator will be at dinner."

"Frances? Oh, good!" Ulick said.

"You'll find her to be—" Rupert paused, as if considering the right word to use, "changed. Any discussion of the semqu distresses her, so please don't bring them up." He aimed for an offhand tone, with a worried frown, a combination he'd practiced all week.

Ulick, who'd been skimming alien documents while they chatted, suddenly gave Rupert his full attention. "Changed? How does this involve the semqu?"

Rupert felt that gaze on him and flushed with envy. Such a skill, wasted on such a *principled* man. "I honestly don't know. You know how Voice got, after she was infected? All her energies focused toward the creature she calls Ireti? Frances is like that, but toward beekeeping. She says she just had a change of heart. But she's certainly not the same woman."

Ulick blinked, then sat back in his chair, staring at Rupert. "Stroke?"

"She won't get a brain scan; she won't seek medical attention. She seems fine physically; more active than ever before. Only her personality has changed."

Ulick rubbed his face. "Could still be a stroke, or even a brain tumor, but I'm not a doctor. She should be seen."

"Well, I hope you can convince her, then, because we've been unable to."

Adamantine had remained uncharacteristically silent, eyes narrowed.

Rupert sighed. "Mar is expecting me. We'll see you samedi?"

Ulick glanced at Adamantine. "Of course," she said brightly, smiling, but there was a wariness in her tone he didn't like.

As he walked down the co-op's brightly painted corridor and out into the marine air to the transport stop, Rupert reflected that Adamantine's marriage could create either the best or the worst of worlds for him. Ulick would betray the Guild in a heartbeat. Adamantine was more practical. He just had to approach her in the right way. He couldn't allow Ulick's "principles" to rub off on her.

THE NIGHT OF THE PARTY, Danielle and the beekeeper were late. Mar started dinner without them, which annoyed Rupert to no end. They were the important guests, and Marfa knew that. Cold food was irrelevant.

"I told you finger foods would be best," Mar hissed at him in the kitchen, hefting a platter of cafeteria enchiladas to take to the table. "But no, you had to have everyone at a table, Mr. Manipulator, so you could control the conversation."

He glared at her in silence. He didn't want to distract their guests with the spectacle of them spatting. And he wasn't going to admit that she was right.

They were well into their enchiladas when Danielle and Frances entered. The beekeeper was still in her protective gear, and was talking rapidly, clearly agitated.

"I know, I just had to make sure they ate, you know, I just wanted to be sure my girls were well fed, it was such a bad day for them with all the wind."

"Yes, well, they're fed and we're here now." Danielle's posture was rigid, jerky, at odds with her soothing tone. "Look, they still have seats open for us."

"Oh! I'm sorry we're late, it's my fault but the bees, you know, they have to be fed, my girls are so fragile right now." Frances turned in a circle, holding out her bee helmet, until Rupert stepped forward and took it from her.

"I'll just hang this by the door, so you know where it is," he said.

"Thank you, thank you, that's so sweet, Rupert, oh, look, you have such a lovely table and such lovely guests and I'm still in my bee clothes but that's okay, that's my job now!" Beaming, she took the closest open chair; perfect. That put her next to him and across from Adamantine. She helped herself to some enchiladas. "These look delicious!"

Rupert laid a hand on Danielle's arm, to guide her past Mar to the other chair. She flinched, jerking her arm away, and moved swiftly around the table to the remaining open seat. He blinked. He'd have to find out what that was about later.

"What were we talking about?" he said, aiming for a jovial tone, watching with care how Adamantine and Ulick were taking the navigator's new personality.

Adamantine was appalled, but it wouldn't surprise him if that was just the beekeeper's attire. Marfa had insisted on a fancy-dress party, and Adamantine was a stickler for such details.

Ulick's reaction was more subtle; he murmured in quiet conversation with the man across from him. Frances' stream-of-consciousness chatter made it impossible for Rupert to hear them.

"So did you hear what happened last week?" Rupert asked Ulick.

"Yes! The dorna bloomed," Frances exclaimed. "Did you know they have twice as much pollen as Earth clover? The native pollinators prefer them, of course, and our bees do as well. It makes the honey, well, kind of inedible for us, but that's okay, because the bees love it!"

She hijacked every conversation topic he started. By the time she'd finished eating, which took a long time because of all the talking she was doing, he regretted every choice about the evening. He was so sick of "her girls" he entertained fantasies about poisoning her hives.

Worse, Adamantine had caught his frustration and was openly amused by it. When Marfa finally stood, saying it was time to move out onto the balcony for drinks, Frances panicked.

"Oh! It's gotten dark! I have to close the hives!" she cried, scrambling up.

"I'll take you home," Danielle said evenly.

"I'll go with you," Ulick said. "I haven't had a chance to chat with Frances all evening."

The guests looked at him in silent shock. Rupert watched them all take it in; Ulick was personally going to check into Frances's behavior. He hated the man, but it was the singularly most effective action anyone had taken all evening.

"Besides," Ulick said, looking at Danielle, "it will give you someone to chat with on your way back here."

There was just the slightest emphasis on the last two words, which told Rupert that Ulick was livid under his calm demeanor.

That did not bode well.

As they relocated to the balcony, Rupert exchanged glances with the four remaining guild members. Over the next half hour, they all made their excuses and left.

Marfa was dour about it, glaring at Rupert each time someone left. He ignored her. If she'd wanted to host a party, she shouldn't have mixed politics into it. Rupert shifted his attention to Adamantine, who hadn't asked a single question or made a single comment about their excessively vocal guest.

"Have you finally found a location for your wedding?" Marfa pulled a chair directly across from Adamantine. It rankled him.

"Yes, finally, although we had to change the date. Again." Adamantine sighed.

"That's why you haven't gotten your invites yet. You'll be there, of course?"

"Can't be," Marfa said.

"You don't even know the date, Marfa."

"Your sister will be there. I can't. Not after—" she bit off her words again, then lurched to her feet, got up, and went into the screened-off kitchen.

"You have to excuse her," Rupert said. Marfa stomped back to the table. He knew what she was doing, scrubbing the table where the beekeeper had been sitting. "Frances' behavior has distressed her greatly."

"And your wife blames the semqu, for some odd, unusual, completely unexplained reason," Adamantine said calmly, staring at her drink.

Her demeanor froze Rupert's blood. Adamantine knew why Frances had changed. Ulick knew. Which meant the Prime Minister would know by this time tomorrow.

He needed to fix this, and quickly.

"She does. It's hard to explain," Rupert said, dropping his

volume to a conspiratorial whisper. "She's gotten involved in some dangerous games with some dangerous people. They've either let her in on some secrets or convinced her those secrets exist and are real. I'm honestly not sure which."

"Do you believe those secrets exist, Rupert?" Adamantine met his eyes.

"It's hard not to believe when you see someone change like that," Rupert said. He didn't have to fake that sincerity. "Didn't you find her behavior odd?"

"Not any odder than you inviting her to dinner, knowing the condition she was in."

"Ah." He winced. It wasn't often his failures were laid out so clearly. Only Adamantine could do that to him.

He could so easily underestimate the intelligence of those around him. He found it difficult to dumb concepts down without overdoing it. Marfa kept telling him he wasn't as smart as he thought he was, and he just had to assume people were at his level, but of course that was wrong. He just needed to get better at dialing back.

"Just ah?" She was tracking her hostess with her eyes, one brow raised. "Marfa, leave that. You can't get semqu sickness from a Semule. It's not contagious like that."

"Your family threw Voice out—"

"We most certainly did NOT."

Rupert rubbed his ear. Adamantine could have lifted the roof with her volume.

"I'd appreciate knowing who slandered my parents and myself."

Marfa paused, then went back to scrubbing. "I don't recall."

"Funny, that. Nobody can seem to 'recall' the source of that slander." Adamantine was done dancing around subjects, and Rupert could see the Guild's work about to be incinerated in the heat of her fury.

He had a panic-induced moment of brilliance. "Some modeel suggested it," he said. Adamantine and Ulick knew that he had been collaborating with so-called scientists in their ridiculous mechanical suits, when in reality his visitors had wasted hours of his time blatting on about their religions and hobbies. Why not blame them?

"Don't be ridiculous," Adamantine snapped. "Why would any modeel care about my family's inner workings?"

"They like creating wedges among spacers," he said. "They and the peqe are good at using gossip for control and sabotage. They use it at home all the time. They like to practice on us."

Did she believe him? He'd screwed up so completely. Rupert stared at his drink and let his sense of failure overwhelm him. When Marfa went into the kitchen he said, "You don't understand what it's been like living with this. I'm losing Marfa. It's like an illness. She's obsessed."

"You need to get her into counseling."

"She won't go."

He let her suggest options, playing the despairing husband, until Marfa rejoined them on the balcony.

Ulick and Danielle returned shortly after; Adamantine and her fiancé left immediately.

Danielle flopped into a chair next to Rupert. Marfa brought her a stiff drink, and the three of them stared over the balcony at the far-off waves for a long time.

Danielle finally lifted her glass and drained it in one swallow. "We're fucked. Totally fucked. It's time to disband the Guild for all purposes but the shield."

"Agreed," Rupert said.

"Oh, hell no," Marfa hissed. "I'm in this for life. And you two aren't abandoning me. You both swore an oath."

"Marfa." Danielle covered her face with her hands. After a moment, she got up. "I can't have this conversation tonight. You are as disconnected from reality as Frances." She stumbled out, leaving him to fend for himself. He fared poorly in the ensuing screaming match. Marfa locked him out of their bedroom.

Later, Rupert learned that Danielle had walked home, an utterly ridiculous ten miles of self-flagellation. How had he ever looked up to her?

CALLIGRAPHY GUILD MEETING
ABOARD NEW HOPE
NEW HOPE YEAR 721
NINTH MONTH'S SIXTEENTH DAY

THE CALLIGRAPHY GUILD was full and alive with gossip of the bride-and-groom variety when Voice came into the meeting room. Two worked at an ink-making station at the far end of the meeting room; those with projects sat at short easels or calligraphy boxes set on low tables. Was it a new member night? Voice hadn't seen so many people attend in ages. Even the agriculturist was there, and she thought he'd moved down to the surface. She waved at him as she headed to the only open workstation, next to Terri.

Terri grabbed her sweater off the chair. "There you are!"

Terri had bloomed once her brother and parents had moved to the surface. She could still be a bit of a drama queen, but now she'd ask about others before talking about herself. She enjoyed any news of life in Fuaringsplenzu.

"Here's Voice!" Terri crowed. "You can fill us in on all the wedding details!"

"I doubt that," Voice said. "Whose wedding are you all talking about?"

Conversation died. Several people exchanged worried glances. The silence was broken by a muffled oath from one of the ink-makers.

"Your sister's, of course!" Terri's smile was expectant. "Last Sunday, at the Bayside?"

What? Voice sank into the chair.

"We're so sorry, Voice, we didn't realize that you didn't know," one of the others in the room said. A murmur of agreement swept around the room, followed by gossip of a different tenor.

Voice was too busy to listen, coping with that stab, twist, and then numbness in her heart. Dimly, she wondered at herself. Why would Adamantine's oversight now cause her so much pain, after all the other slights? *Because Mère is gone, and after the funeral, we'd started talking again.*

She opened the drawer to pull out the project she was planning to work on, stopping when she noticed her fingers trembling. She laid her palms flat on the work surface for a moment, staring at the flecks of ink caught in the wood grain around her fingers. When her hands were steady, she pulled out the paper.

"Did anyone here attend, who can give us a report on the ceremony?" Her calm tone didn't convince anyone, let alone herself, but it allowed the group to get back to their activities without holding their breath, waiting for an eruption of drama.

"Adamantine and Ulick really didn't invite you to their wedding?" Terri sounded horrified.

"No." *How like Terri to care in a way that emphasizes both my pain and my public humiliation,* she thought, and also, *Are you being uncharitable to Terri because you're mad at Adamantine?*

"But she's your sister! And I thought you and Ulick were close!" Terri leaned over and put a hand on Voice's forearm, her lips curled upward on one side. "That must hurt so much."

"Ayi! Stop twisting the knife, Terri," someone snapped from the next table.

That reaction helped clarify the situation for Voice. "Thankfully, strong emotions are unpleasant for the semqu," Voice said evenly. "So even those who deliberately try to hurt me fail." Ireti was busy, smoothing away the jagged edges of her feelings.

Terri's fingers tightened slightly, then flew open. "Lucky you."

"I suppose. Unfortunately, it also means that any joy is muted." Voice turned to fully face her old friend. "I think we once talked about how our mutual anxiety had a similar cost."

Terri pulled away. "Did we? I don't recall." She picked up her pen, shifted her focus to the poem she was rendering in ink.

After Mère's funeral, Voice had thought that she and her sister were returning to some semblance of a friendship again. She was clearly wrong.

But she'd been wrong about Terri, too, hadn't she? That half-smile, that frustrated grip. That total indifference after such an open-hearted declaration of emotional support.

Terri had delighted in her pain, had wanted this news to hurt her more, had deliberately brought the subject up here, to cause her the maximum discomfort.

Important, that information. Not pleasant, not welcome, but useful to know.

KRUFRUGAAN TRAINING CENTER
UNDISCLOSED LOCATION, VASOM
SEMQU YEAR 1148
(NEW HOPIAN YEAR 722)

O-EEE-U PLODDED into the meeting room carrying a tray of food. He was depressed. He'd learned next to nothing in his clerking position. Years and years of lying and pretending to serve semqu faithfully and honestly, and all he'd gained was a sense of being trapped and stymied, surrounded by clanking metal and snapping biofields whose emotional content he couldn't parse.

"We're expending a lot of effort keeping a badly wounded semqu alive," one of the seated six modeel said. "It seems unfair to ask them to suffer so. And weren't they wounded by these spacers? Why do we trust them again?"

"Suffering does not destroy the will to live, and Ireti has more will to live than any I know," another responded with confidence. "They are deeply attached to their spacer."

"The spacers wounded a semqu?" O-eee-u asked, bewildered. "How is that possible?"

The first turned to him, as if they'd just noticed his existence. "They have a chemical compound we've isolated, and are working to neutralize, that was toxic to Ireti. She has managed to survive it, but such a substance could be dangerous to all semqu."

A rattling noise from the leader in the room, flashes of light; O-eee-u guessed the one who'd spoken was getting reprimanded for speaking so freely in front of him.

"How deeply disturbing," O-eee-u said. "Should they not be punished?"

"Ignorance can be forgiven, once," the leader said in a warning tone.

"I am but a larva," O-eee-u said. "I do not mean to question my elders, merely to learn."

"Hm." The leader made a buzzing sound, of a particular frequency O-eee-u had come to loathe. "Perhaps we need to give you more opportunity to learn."

Sudden hope washed over O-eee-u. "I would be grateful and serve you well. I wish to grow in wisdom."

The nice thing about dangerous knowledge, O-eee-u thought later in private, is that once uncovered, it's hard to permanently lose. If the spacers had discovered a compound that could harm semqu, someone else would be able to recreate it. And he was pretty sure he knew the right someone.

SIXTEEN
OPPORTUNITIES

ADAMANTINE AND ULICK PANGEA'S DWELL
FUARINGSPLENZU, TRYE
NEW HOPIAN YEAR 722
TENTH MONTH, TWENTY-FIFTH DAY

Nineteen-year-old Voice yawned and padded into the kitchen in her sister and brother-in-law's Fuaringsplenzu apartment. She had fulfilled her duties yesterday by voting in the election and ferrying the votes of those who could not deal with the planet's gravity or wide-open spaces.

She hadn't been as successful at sleeping planet-side. Being so far away from Ireti meant managing much stronger emotions than usual. While she'd had a year of practice while attending meetings down here, she was looking forward to a more restful night in her own bed aboard *New Hope*, and getting back to the architectural drawings of the new neighborhood wastewater treatment plant she'd been working on all week.

"Good morning, sœur."

"What's good about it?" Adamantine snapped. She had run for one of the leadership council positions and gotten trounced. She had not taken it well.

Voice had hoped that Ulick's commitment to community would help Adamantine's ego-centric tendencies. *Another hope, crushed by the irrevocable gravity of reality*, she thought.

She took a longer look at her sister: immaculately dressed as usual, silky black hair perfectly coiffed. Her hair sticks even matched the bright yellow tunic she wore, although it was looser in fit than Adamantine's usual. Probably to allow the furious stomping she was currently doing, up and down the hallway between her bedroom and the kitchen.

Voice felt frumpy in her presence. She inhaled deeply and shrugged off the feeling. She'd gotten better at catching herself making such comparisons. She was Voice, no more, no less.

She carefully lowered herself into a chair at her sister's table. Her thighs didn't scream, and she didn't slam down into the seat. Pleased her recent exercises were working, she helped herself to what Adamantine considered breakfast—community kitchen cookies and herbal tea— and tried to ignore her sister's foul mood.

She sipped and watched her irate sister pace, lithe and graceful even in fury.

"How can I reach my potential in leadership, if no one will trust me with it!"

How many times had Adamantine been mentored on this point? Voice wondered if her sister ever actually listened to anyone but herself. "Can you change any behavior without knowing its cost?"

"No."

"Then listen for once. You have the urge but not the skills, the hunger but not the patience. You don't want to lead by listening. You want to direct by talking. You want others to listen to you without the harder work of listening to them first."

"Is it my fault they're always wrong?" Adamantine flung out a hand, as if indicating the entire city.

"People experience the world differently from you. Difference is not wrong."

"When have I ever treated anyone as if they were wrong!?" Adamantine shouted.

Her sister's words bruised an old wound. "The year you tried to remake me over in Père's image certainly comes to mind," Voice said.

Adamantine wheeled back toward her. "You needed to learn everything you've learned since!"

Voice set the cup down carefully. "And you thought you could force me to do so. And kept trying to force me after it was proven to you, repeatedly, that you were accomplishing nothing but making me miserable. I hope for your future children's sake you've learned better since. I'd hate for one of your children to choose death because their mother's behavior convinced them it would be better off if they did not exist."

Adamantine's hand went to her throat. Voice's gut twisted; it was Harriet's gesture. Ireti's emotional flattening was weak at this distance.

"Did you really think I wanted you to die?" Adamantine blurted the question, a much younger sound.

"Everything in me that wasn't you. So, yes," Voice said.

Her sister stared at her. "I didn't. I never wanted that."

"I believe you. That doesn't change how I felt then. And I never understood why you were so angry after I became a Voice. It was like you were mad because I was a better person without you."

"No! I..." Adamantine crossed to her wedding engraving and picked it up. She stared at it as she spoke. "Your connection to the semqu, your abdication of your autonomy, horrified me for so long. But you don't find it horrible. Never did. I didn't understand that. But... being married is a strange thing." She set the engraving down, still looking at it. "You have to give up a little bit of yourself and become something else. You're a couple, a team, no longer just yourself. It was a hard nut for me to crack, and I'm still working on it. But it has given me a perspective on what you encountered with the semqu. Not the same, of course. Ulick is not a semqu." She laughed. "But you're a new person now, united in a way, with another being. So, I have a tiny window into..."

She looked up at Voice and trailed off, obviously not seeing the reaction she had hoped for. Sharply, she added, "This made more sense in my head."

Voice looked down at her hands to hide whatever emotion Adamantine had seen. She was feeling several, including a flash of rage that had startled her. "You have a window into a way of looking at my experience that no longer frightens you or disgusts you quite so much. But it still angers you."

"No. Not—not anger. It bothers me that you are not yourself anymore."

Voice looked up. "Adamantine. You didn't like me as I was."

Her sister's fingers twisted together, her lips a silent circle.

"You wanted me to be more like you. And you still do."

"I—" Adamantine swallowed. She could not deny it, and recognized that, at least.

"And that is why no one will trust you to be a leader," Voice said. "Because you are so certain that being you, thinking like you, acting like you, is the best way to be. Because you leave no room for others to be themselves. You are so much like Père. No one can help you with that but you, Adamantine. You've been told this before. I can recall Mère trying. I'm sure your mentors have told you this repeatedly, and yet you refuse to hear it." Voice pushed her cup away, prepared to stand and leave.

"I'm pregnant, sister. Will you help me with my child?" The words were blurted and high, taut with fear.

Oh. Surprise wiped the frustration and anger from Voice's mind.

Adamantine turned her back, talking to the wall, arms tight

across her chest. "I know I have Ulick, and he'll do his best, but—you're right, this is something I have fought my entire life, and I have to get it right. I don't want to do to my children what Père did to you, what I did to you. And I need help."

"I cannot come down yet, sister." The word "yet" slipped past her lips, and Voice kept talking to cover it. She could tell no one that she might move down permanently, after Ireti lost their long struggle, possibly to help shepherd an infant to maturity. She was still stunned All-Semqu was considering trusting her with this. "You should also find surface oncles et tantes. But I will visit you and your child any time I come to the surface, and I will chat with them via link. My connection to Ireti does not preclude my connecting to family."

"You distanced yourself so completely after they took you—I wasn't sure."

It wasn't me who—stop. I did. And from her perspective, it was probably brutal. "I needed the space. I needed to sleep a great deal after contact. I cannot explain to you how exhausting that all was. I knew my new occupation was not what Mère or Père wanted. You didn't like it either. The idea of dealing with all of that disapproval and fear while I was trying to recover —" Voice shook her head. "You and Père were so very angry with me. I didn't know what Ireti would do to you if he hit me, or you tried to change me again. They're quite protective."

"Oh."

"The wall hanging was a nice gift. But that letter you sent me made your position clear."

"I apologize for that. I was envious of the attention you were getting. I was a child. I felt abandoned."

That stung. "That was mutual. None of you ever asked me to visit. To join you for a meal, even a lunch. To share in an anniversary or a family celebration. Not once."

"We didn't, did we?" Adamantine looked up, dazed.

"I messaged Mére about ancestor day that first year—"

"I'm sorry, sœur. I deleted that before Mère saw it. I was so angry at you for leaving us."

Voice exhaled. "The funerals were the first time you included me in a family event. Sœur, you didn't even invite me to your wedding. Ulick called later and apologized. But you—you acted as if I didn't exist." Outrage spiked before dissipating.

"That was— I am sorry, petite-sœur." Adamantine clasped her hands in front of her, her eyes wide, a parody of her child-self on those rare occasions when she felt enough remorse to offer a sincere apology to Mère.

"Why?" was all Voice could manage. Her gut was churning. *This apparently still matters to me a great deal.*

"I had thought you uninterested," she said. "Or that it would be hurtful, since you could not marry."

"Why would I be uninterested in my only sister's happiest day?" Adamantine winced, and Voice went on, "Voices can marry. If you didn't know you could have asked."

"I should have." Adamantine turned and stared through the open window at the tops of the park's succulent trees, and the city beyond. She never could face people when she told them a truth she didn't want to admit. "I was trying to save Rupert from Marfa," she said. "She'd been so lost to Semquphobia that I feared she was going to suck him down with her. She wouldn't come if you were there, and he wouldn't attend without her."

She chose Rupert over me, and thought telling me so would make it hurt less. "Rupert succeeded in driving another wedge between us."

Adamantine swung toward Voice, lurching, her balance gone. "He isn't trying to—He wouldn't—"

Voice forced curiosity over her wounded feelings. "Why didn't you marry him instead of Ulick?"

"I have no interest in Rupert Keo in that way," she said primly.

"That auto-response tells me I'm hardly the first person who's asked, and also that you're in denial."

Adamantine collapsed on a chair, her body language curled in, sad. It took Voice a moment to realize her older sister was fully miserable, and she chided herself. *She's just lost an election that mattered a great deal to her, she's pregnant, and now I'm attacking her oldest friendship*—Voice's thoughts fizzled, then snapped. *I should be her oldest friendship!*

Ah. Voice inhaled deeply. *I'm jealous.* That, she understood. She'd had years of practice coping with sister-envy. It didn't lessen the hurt, but it made her own reaction more understandable.

Adamantine turned the ring on her finger, said quietly, "He would never have been faithful. Ulick will never cheat on me."

"And you're Harriet Pangea's daughter." Voice barked a laugh. Mère's rare jealous rages could exceed Père's common, obsessive ones. "And both your unattainable crush and I want you to love us best, which doesn't help."

It was Adamantine's turn to laugh. She was quiet a moment, then said, "And you can't help but love the alien best. I will never forgive your Ireti for taking your love away from us. It helps to know—what you said about them being protective. That helps. But I won't forgive them."

Voice stared; her sister was serious.

"But," Adamantine continued, "Semquphobia is different. It's such a horrible disease. Watching Marfa deteriorate into it has been frightening. She seems to be better, at least, and Rupert hasn't succumbed."

"Where, how, did she develop such a fear?"

"I don't know. Danielle, perhaps? The Earthborn was acclimatized in Marfa's household, when she was a child."

Danielle. Yes, that was possible. She'd failed with the Earthborn. "You could have sent an anti-phobia message to the community by inviting me to the wedding," Voice said.

Adamantine looked up. "I could have. I should have. I am sorry, sœur."

Voice could hear children's laughter from the playground below the apartment. She was not ready to forgive Adamantine, and she needed time to think about her sister's anger at the Ireti, about Danielle and Marfa. She let the silence between them stretch.

"I can't go back in time and fix that," Adamantine finally said. "But I can fix it going forward. You're here now. And I'd like your help with my child. I think—I think seeing you with my baby might help the community."

Fighting semquphobia motivated Voice. She could not believe the extent it had grown, and the ingratitude it implied rankled her. "Do you think the infection has gotten so bad that your child would suffer for it? Be ostracized by playmates?"

"I will know who to focus interventions on if I see that happening."

Behind the sudden protective steel in Adamantine's tone, Voice sensed the strategic vision of Ulick, and that impressed her, largely because it meant Adamantine had found a solid source of reason she was willing to listen to and learn from. "You and Ulick make a good team."

Adamantine inclined her head, pleased.

"I am sorry you lost your election, grande-sœur. Can I give you some politically useful advice that you might not want to hear?"

A bit of Adamantine's misery returned, but she nodded.

"People looked up to you, adored your dancing and put you on a pedestal. You were popular. That was real. But people didn't trust you, because you manipulated them for your own benefit, and you were good at it. You haven't changed. Neither have they. Choose a job where you can put your manipulative skills to use serving the community, instead of yourself. Or at least one where the community can see your skills being useful."

The way Adamantine shifted and sighed, Voice knew this was not news to her. "Everyone tells me I should be our ambassador to the dinos."

That was perfection, and Voice knew better than to say so. "Could you volunteer with the ambassador for a season, see if you enjoy or have any aptitude for it? It would show your detractors that you're listening to community advice."

Such double-edged motivation appealed; Adamantine leaned back, considering, her hand rising to her chin. The gesture was reminiscent of Père, and all the dread he evoked. She refused to allow it to interfere with her feelings for Adamantine. *She is my sœur. I love her, as much as I can love anyone.*

"You give good advice. Opal—I am sorry about the wedding. You should have been there. All these years—it hurt to lose you. It was easier to pretend you were gone than to think of you so close and not wanting us closer. But I always thought about it from my heart, from my perspective. I didn't think about what it would be like for you. I'm so very sorry."

Voice looked at her, blinked. Adamantine meant it. Some of the rest of her conversation had been carefully rehearsed, practiced. Voice hadn't trusted it. But her request had been sincere, and this apology was heartfelt. After Terri, Voice had no illusions about easily repairing broken-edged relationships, but she also loved her sister.

"Thank you," Voice said. "I think I did the same. Perhaps we can try to be sisters again."

Adamantine nearly ruined it—Voice saw relief cross her face, saw a momentary expression of dismissal, as if to say, "If that's all it would have taken—" then watched as her older sister stopped herself, stilled her face, took a deep breath. "I would like that," she said, carefully.

"Then let's try."

UNDISCLOSED LOCATION, AUN EXACT YEAR UNKNOWN; PROBABLY SEMQU YEAR 1158

A MODEEL STOOD guard in the corridor outside a cold, rock-lined chamber. Inside, four different aliens shifted uneasily, one shimmered in place, and a sixth appeared comatose.

"Is the larsivian even awake?" the peqe muttered.

"I am awake enough." The big lizard opened one eye. "Sleepy, curious. Do they not know how to make heat here?"

"Heat's a luxury on this frozen rock," the peqe said, adding with satisfaction, "But it does mean there's no pezia."

"Doesn't mean the semqu aren't listening in," said Gtec, the modeel conspirator.

"They're not omniscient," O-eee-u said confidently. He liked the fact the others, even Gtec, deferred to him, the only aupoin in the room, on semqu knowledge. He pressed that advantage when he could. "I wouldn't risk being here otherwise."

"Huge you with semqu, bah. Why mean that trust?" the kertueon snapped. His Fugrast was barely comprehensible, but he'd expressed contempt often enough that O-eee-u knew where he was going the moment his mandibles parted.

"I want my people freed of their bondage to the semqu," O-eee-u said. "I figured the best way to fight them was from within." Despite his sharing the revelation that spacers had found a chemical that could harm the semqu, his resentful and paranoid companions seemed to hear his motivation every time they met.

He resented the distrust but didn't mind repeating it. It kept E-uuui-i's stolen love at the forefront of his mind. She was here, on Aun, and her nest had refused to allow him to meet her.

Gtec said he had been able to talk to her, though. O-eee-u burned with envy. Gtec was contemptuous of E-uuui-i's naïveté and thought he could do better. The modeel clearly didn't understand true love.

"Curiosity. Have you identified any way to find this chemical?" the larsivian asked. "Or ways we can use it?"

"Not yet," O-eee-u said.

"I have an idea," Gtec said.

The others inclined their heads toward him, and O-eee-u set down his drink. "I'm listening."

FUARINGSLPLENZU, TRYE
NEW HOPIAN YEARS 723-733

THE PANGEA SISTERS did not achieve a successful sisterly rapport. But Voice grew to love her nephew Bonaparte. Trips to the beach became their standard activity; he would see her come in the door and cry, "Tante Voice! Allons à la plage! L'ocean!"

The beach was a perfect escape for them both. Voice was fascinated by the illusion of a single-colored floor created by all those tiny bits of multicolored rock and pointy pieces of shell, and was contented with Bonaparte's joyous curiosity about it all.

Walking there was so unusual. Heel, sink, ball of foot, rebalance, shift weight. She probably made it more difficult by thinking about every step, but thinking about every step kept it from being too bizarre to do. Such a mundane act on an oceanic world, yet it gave her many mixed emotions. Together they played with creating sand sculptures, intrigued by the way wet sand stuck to itself but fell apart when dry, so different from clay. The ultimate in reusable temporary art materials, gritty and persistent, hard to eradicate from one's shoes. Wonderful.

New Hope held multitudes, Voice's entire life before Trye, but absolutely no sand.

Occasionally, watching the boy light up in delight, she truly ached for the fullness of awe and wonder from her childhood. The first time she put her bare toes into sand was one of those moments. What would that moment have been like without the semqu's blunting impact on her emotions? Or that terrifying instant when she first saw the full sky over the water?

She reprimanded herself. *I would have fallen into a panic attack and lost two days in a shaking ball.* Bonaparte could enjoy all that without help. But she had never been able to overcome terror alone.

She thought of the beach visits not only as a way to build a relationship with her wide-eyed nephew, but also for her ship-bound friends. She brought back videos for them of the questing, unpredictable waves, the wide-open sky; tried to share with them the unstable footing, the smells, so her friends could experience them vicariously.

Not everyone wanted to; the adventures planet life offered still evoked horror in some born on the generation ship. Like them, Voice had spent her childhood racing through corridors, sitting on the floor, sleeping in pods— always with a roof, always with walls, always with a solid floor. Cushions were the most variable footing she'd ever stood on. They had not expected to reach a planet in her lifetime, had not had time to train for wide-open lives.

Adamantine would not visit the beach.

Bonaparte had no such emotional restrictions. Every visit, Voice was amazed all over again at how fearless he was. More than once she had to pull him from the water; toddler arms and legs churning furiously. As he got older, he taught her how to swim, a skill she'd never had the chance to learn. The water was chilly, but being buoyed up while moving was so much easier on her than walking that they started swimming regularly. It was much more fun than any exercise she could get shipboard.

Occasionally, she would see Danielle, who'd continued to seek physical conditioning at all costs, running on the hard-packed sand. They would wave. On rare occasions, Danielle stopped to chat.

The Earthborn seemed happier. Like she'd found a place to belong once she had her feet on soil again. They even discussed Marfa's illness; Danielle seemed truly despondent about her Semquphobia.

"Do you fear them?" Voice asked her once.

"I did," Danielle said. "I don't anymore."

Voice believed her. She began to welcome the Earthborn's brief visits; Danielle was good with Bonaparte, and the young boy, normally timid around adults, seemed to enjoy talking to her.

But their interactions were rare, as Voice could only visit her nephew monthly, and they only went to the beach on warm summer days.

Voice had no illusions that her nephew confided in her; Adamantine pried from him everything Voice told him, and the boy clearly expected Adamantine to do the same to her. But Bon-deux, as he came to be known, honestly seemed to enjoy her company, and she loved him.

Her visits sometimes sparked more friction than sisterly love. It had become clear Adamantine would get no diplomatic appointments while Ximena headed the government, and she was often frosty with Voice, who got along well with the prime minister. But there were other benefits. Adamantine gained some personal time. Her son got a break from being micromanaged. And Voice gained experience not only with gravity, but with a curious growing mind.

OUTSKIRTS OF FUARINGSPLENZU
NEW HOPIAN YEAR 744
NINTH MONTH'S SEVENTEENTH DAY

RUPERT FUMED as he exited the transport near Danielle's dwell. Of course, the Earthborn had an individual dwell, on the far outskirts, where there was no direct line, and now he had to traverse the last mile on foot. This trip would waste the rest of the day, and she might not even be home.

He was being unreasonable and didn't care. He and Marfa had their own individual dwell, on the opposite side of Fuaringsplenzu. But he'd showed up late to the guild meeting on purpose, to give himself plausible deniability that he had just happened upon the gathering, and Marfa had insisted he join the pool to choose who would go check on Danielle, who was not answering any form of communication. He'd won, which meant he'd lost, and couldn't talk his way out of it. Then Marfa had snarked that he should enjoy it; after all, he had been so enamored of the Earthborn at one time, hadn't he?

He would definitely have a talk with her later about her increasingly annoying habit of embarrassing him in front of others. He'd not bothered before; that was just how she was. But she was eroding progress he'd made with a few key people, and that was going to hurt her, too. Which was the only thing that mattered to her, he thought grimly.

He slogged up the dirt track, still showing tractor treads from the construction delivery trucks, and followed their lumpy patterns to Danielle's tiny dwell. It was earth-toned and locked like a boulder. She'd set it partially underground, making some joke about it being a ... what did she call it? A hobbit hole.

No answer at the door but screeching from Danielle's back yard. She was raising native birds for eggs, was probably back there feeding the damn things. He walked around through a side gate.

Danielle lay sprawled face down on the ground, unnaturally still, surrounded by birds pecking at a spray of fallen grain.

Is she dead? He hurried to her, rolled her on her side. She was breathing, but her color was bad. He flipped on his personal, called for an emergency medical transport. After giving the dwell's coordinates and her personal ID and apparent condition, he could only wait.

He paced, brain churning. Had her hibernation illness

returned? Had she had a stroke? Was it a modeel assassin? Fear creeped into the edges of his vision; he was purely alone out here. He looked around, saw nothing but the plant-covered back slope of her silent dwell, a sprouting garden and the birds, two of whom were now following him around, and the succulent forest beyond. She'd cleared low brush for some distance away from the house; there were no other creatures, no assassins in view.

He looked down at her, this woman he'd once idolized because she'd lived on the same planet as his heroes. She didn't know a raat about science, but she still was better at people than he was; she'd helped set him on his path. He resented her, this once-strong, now fallen soldier; blamed her for the net of surveillance the modeel had drawn around them.

He would have gotten where he was without her, and he'd get further without her. T illness of hers could be an opportunity for him, if he could figure out how. But the emergency transport's noisy rotors blotted out all thought, and then he was busy. He answered questions, helped lift her. An investigator said she would stay; contact the neighbors to ensure the animals were taken care of and look through the house and grounds for any signs of malicious action.

Rupert leapt at their offer to accompany Danielle. He filled the team in on her history, although most knew who she was. The eldest in the community carried a certain gravitas, even though Danielle chafed at the role.

He had work to do, and it tugged at him, but he'd built up a demeanor as a caring friend. He couldn't walk out before a diagnosis. And that was where he finally got his opportunity. Danielle's liver had failed; her bloodstream was full of toxins, and she was dying. She needed a new liver. But both organ printers were down. The doctors were devastated, apologetic.

"Wait," Rupert said. "I have connections on Vasom." He pulled out his personal, went outside. "My friend," he said. "I think I have both a gift and a favor for you, one that will build great goodwill

between our peoples. Did you not once tell me you had organ printers on your planet?"

Danielle's DNA was on its way to Vasom within the hour; and a new liver was delivered by Gtec himself.

"We would have never thought about this possibility," the clinic head said, taking the saline-infused bag and handing it to a nurse, who rushed it to surgery. "This is an incredible moment of cooperation. You've saved our elder. We are so deeply, deeply grateful."

"We are glad to be of service," Gtec said.

The hospital had sent an urgent message to the Prime Minister's office; she was in meetings but sent her gratitude and a vehicle to transport Gtec for as long as he was in Fuar. Rupert used it to invite Gtec to visit his home, swelling in pride at the surprised and awed looks they got as they passed.

The guild meeting was long over, and Marfa had gone out, thankfully. None of the chairs Marfa had selected would work for the modeel, so Rupert ushered him out on the deck.

"Beautiful view," Gtec said. "So. What do you want to know?"

"Tell me about gtorin."

Flashes of yellow sliced through Gtec's biofield: surprise. "I thought you were interested in our blink drives?"

"Not any longer," Rupert lied, "And you wouldn't tell me if I was. But gtorin is different, isn't it?"

Gtec clattered, bubbles of amusement floating around him. "Clever mammals, you spacers are. Yes. Gtorin is indeed *very* different. Very lucrative, very dangerous. I—we will need more in exchange."

They spent a pleasant hour or so haggling. Gtec's requests triggered both glee and twinges of conscience. Rupert saw him off before Marfa got home. He was so satisfied he didn't bother picking the planned fight with her. She slammed home, angry he hadn't messaged her since leaving the house, and gave him the silent treatment. He matched her pettiness by refusing to offer what he knew about Danielle beyond, "she's alive."

He sat on the deck as night fell, ignoring the lights of Fuar to focus on the far-off waves. He might never make that immortality-guaranteeing scientific discovery, and he'd need to emigrate. Byrne's mixed-population world might suit him. He had powerful off-world friends now, and a backup plan that could make him extremely wealthy.

He didn't think too hard about its price.

SEVENTEEN

BEGINNINGS

**WEDDING RECEPTION FOR
BONAPARTE PANGEA AND ANIKA KEO
FUARINGSPLENZU, PLANET TRYE: HILLSIDE
COMMUNITY HALL
SEMQU YEAR 1170
NEW HOPIAN YEAR 744
ELEVENTH MONTH'S EIGHTH DAY**

Organ replacement wasn't a conversation Danielle wanted to have at a wedding reception, but Marfa insisted on a full report. It ought to have surprised her that Rupert had not mentioned her medical disaster, or given Marfa a chance to come visit her while she was recovering. But nothing Rupert did surprised her anymore. He'd pulled her aside after Frances' return and suggested that Danielle ought to kill her. It had taken all her self-control not to slap him.

"The liver failure was a bit of a shock," Danielle said, as Marfa wrung her hands. "But I have to admit I feel five hundred percent better. I hadn't realized how ill I was."

"I just don't understand why they had to go to Vasom. We have organ printers—"

"We do. It was bad timing. They'd had a substrate contamination issue and were down to one machine, and it was down with a broken part the day my liver decided to fail."

The subject embarrassed her. She'd been clueless enough about livers that she'd been annoyed that the docs wouldn't consider replacing the alien organ with a Trye-grown liver. They'd had to explain how many hours the surgery had taken and how delicate liver transplants could be before she quit asking. Then the nurses grilled her until she'd admitted that knowing she was alive because of an alien-created organ had given her a bizarre low-level self-loathing. The doctor called it dysphoria. That made no sense; the rest of her body was fine.

When she'd overheard a nurse calling it outright bigotry, she'd stopped talking entirely. The nurse wasn't wrong. But she couldn't seem to change her emotional reaction. She felt part alien now, and she hated it.

She sighed. "Believe me, I got chewed out for not coming in to see a doctor sooner. As it was, if the Guild hadn't drawn straws to check on me, I'd be dead. Rupert saved my life."

"I'm glad, but don't tell him." Marfa's lips thinned as she glanced over at Rupert, who was chatting with the mother of the groom, Adamantine Pangea. "He couldn't be bothered to tell any of us that he found you passed out. No need to fawn over that arrogant bastard."

Danielle laughed politely. Marfa's concern clearly hadn't extended to finding out why she hadn't attended nor visiting while she recovered, and the woman's rancor with Rupert was getting old. They would have made a much better team if they'd not married.

"It didn't help that the doctors admitted that my problems with taste could have been a symptom that they missed."

"Seriously?"

"Yeah." No Army doctor would ever have apologized to her in

the profuse way Trye's doctors had, but she was still angry. She changed the subject. "How's the shield coming?"

The phrase had become a long-standing Guild joke, but that joke had finally paid off. *It only took decades*, Danielle thought wryly. To be fair, it cost far more than a hobby allowance, and crafting the shield while also building a city from scratch, with no economy to speak of, took time.

"Fully functional yesterday," Marfa said with pride. "We've got a celebration planned for next month. The wedding took precedence." Anika, the bride, was their niece. Rupert was standing in for his brother, the deceased father of the bride. Grandstanding, Marfa had huffed at the beginning of their chat.

"Just as well," Danielle said. "It gives us testing time."

The shield's instrument array could detect large meteors in the vicinity of the city. In its final form, which might take a few more decades, it should be able to detect incoming debris as small as a fist in any populated area and evaporate them with tightly-controlled laser technology. The sensors could differentiate between ships, meteors, and missiles, although they'd been careful to never mention the last.

It was the Guild's first successful project, and Marfa was rightly proud of it, although Rupert was, as usual, taking the majority of the credit.

Danielle and Marfa had laid the groundwork for community support, starting by pushing threats the community already read as real. A population that had relied on a thin-skinned ship for survival had immediately understood the danger of falling space debris, they just needed to understand that as threat on the surface as well. A brilliant meteor shower during their second year on the surface had provided them with all they needed to get started.

No one remembered it had been Danielle's idea, and she was fine with that. The Guild had spread distrust of the semqu with information about the need for the shield, and she took no pride in that effort. Despite the years it had taken, she felt she had once again acted in haste without considering the consequences. And the best example of her failure stood in front of her.

Marfa slid her hand under her slightly swollen abdomen.

Danielle had promised herself she'd not ask about their rumored pregnancy unless Marfa brought it up. Superstition, perhaps. She said, "We chose the right project to start with."

"We did—" Marfa stiffened, staring past her. "Oh, for fuck's sake. Look. In that hideous green."

Voice, in a bright layered wrap of spring green, approached the bride and groom carrying a small box, an easy smile on her face. Danielle was struck by the rare show of emotion; Voice practically radiated joy.

"Is that the walking larva?"

"Marfa," Danielle hissed. "Keep that attitude inside."

"Why is she still here?" Marfa fumed.

"She's family?"

"I thought I talked them into setting the wedding late enough that she wouldn't be able to attend the reception."

Marfa's emotional state worried Danielle. She'd decided that the younger woman was struggling with deep survivor guilt over Frances.

Danielle had seen soldiers with PTSD, warriors with lost limbs. Back on Earth she'd attended funerals of friends who'd died in wartime. Her mind flashed back to her conversation with Frances in *New Hope's* cafeteria all those years ago. Frances' motivation all along had been to impress Danielle enough that she'd notice her crush. She'd been too damn subtle for too long. And now... it was too late. *And your conscience can't cope with what Frances has become, so you avoid her.*

But she could accept it had been Frances' choice.

Marfa had no cultural or emotional context for such a loss and couldn't accept responsibility for it. She projected her resulting revulsion and rage at any modeel and all semqu.

Danielle eyed Marfa with concern. "Marfa, she's not your enemy. And even if she was—remember—"

"Keep your friends close and your enemies closer." Marfa said. "I know. I just hadn't wanted her close to my niece."

Dryly, Danielle said, "Did you neglect to notice that your new nephew-in-law is also Voice's nephew? Bonaparte adores her!"

"Details," she hissed. "Why is she carrying her gift? We asked everyone to leave them by the door."

"I don't know, but she's not going to harm either of them."

Marfa glared at her. "Why are you defending her?"

Danielle shrugged. "I've talked to her occasionally over the years. She reminds me a lot of Ulick. She truly seems to want the best for all spacers. I used to run into her and Bonaparte when he was a toddler, on the shore, back when I could run on the beach." *Almost monthly in good weather*, she thought. "She was distant, like she always is, but she was devoted to the boy's safety."

Marfa's lips stretched into a vicious smile. "Well. I should thank her for coming. Since she's going to be una tía política."

Yes, she'll be an in-law, and you honestly hadn't thought about that before today? Danielle watched Marfa stalk toward the happy couple. Warily, she followed.

VOICE WORKED her way through the boisterous wedding guests. Decades on, and she still was thrilled—as thrilled as she could be— that she could do this, that this was comfortable. It was the largest crowd she'd been in since the last Accord Compact, and it was all a bit overwhelming. But she'd been able to pay attention in turn to the colorful clothes, the gossip, the use of an actual fire instead of candles, and the beauty of the melded Hindi, Catholic, and atheist decorations, (or the combination's sacrilegious nature, depending on the gossiper), and the mundane civic portion of the rite.

Her *New Hope* social circle would be fascinated by all those details. Voice had not been on the surface in months, and none of them had been down since the last Compact.

She glimpsed Danielle Braun as she crossed the room. The Earthborn looked sallow and frail. It surprised her. Braun was a mere dozen awake-years older than Voice, only, what, in her early fifties? Was she having trouble with hibernation-weakness, the price of having a body in suspension for so long? Danielle moved easily enough, though, and clearly had her mind. She was chatting with and seemed to be calming Marfa.

Marfa had been the source of much of the gossip Voice had overheard; various iterations of, "Imagine being pregnant at your niece's wedding!"

People could be so strange about private information, and weddings could be stressful for the families, Voice thought. Adamantine certainly had been vibrating like a violin string, but Voice had expected that. Her sister could only change so much.

It had been a long ceremony. Voice was tired and needed to get back to the dock in time for the shuttle. First, she wanted to hand-deliver her gift. The calligraphy guild in particular had insisted a handmade tarot deck would require some explanation beyond a note. Voice suspected they just wanted up-close details of the wedding wear.

Voice also wanted a chance to give her well-wishes to her nephew and his new bride, whom she had only met briefly once before. Anika had seemed timid. Voice hoped she was strong enough to stand up to Adamantine. Bonaparte would help with that. He was growing into a wonderful man.

She greeted Bonaparte while Anika was chatting with someone else. "Bon-deux!" His childhood nickname annoyed Adamantine, but Voice's sister was far enough away to risk it. "You make a gorgeous husband."

Adamantine's height and Ulick's stocky build sat well on him. His black hair was tamed in a complex braided pattern that rivaled his bride's, and draped with bright, shiny bangles. A handsome, charming young man. Before the ceremony, Voice had overheard more than one youth among the guests express regret that he'd agreed to a monogamous union.

"Tante Voice!" He always honored her request to not use her given name, and she loved him for it, since his mother did not. He wrapped her in a big hug. She returned his embrace with warmth.

"Congratulations to you both. I wanted to explain my gift." She handed the package to Bonaparte; Anika had broken off her conversation and was staring at her, hands clasped in front of her bodice. *Such a shy girl for such an outgoing boy. Opposites do attract.* "My friends shipboard helped me decorate it; it's a handmade tarot deck. A gift to help you, and to aid you in remembering to listen to your own intuition," she said, tapping the cards.

"Tarot!" Adamantine had appeared as if teleported, with Rupert on her arm. "Why, Opal, how ... odd." Her sister's words sounded strained.

"Odd? It's simply a tool for tapping into one's own mind," Voice said. "But why does it not surprise me that a choice of mine might bother you, sister?" *Ego, ego. Do not let it control you, be careful.* Pain had sharpened her tone. Bonaparte's wedding had brought up the memories of being shuttered from Adamantine's rite, and seeing her so close to Rupert did not help.

Adamantine blushed and took a step back, chastened.

The bride blurted, "Didn't the semqu rewire your brain? So you can't think for yourself?"

Semquphobia, here? How had Bonaparte not addressed and resolved that? Voice wanted a good relationship with Anika, so she dealt with the young woman's fear directly, and as warmly as she could. "I certainly can think for myself, Anika. They did 'rewire' part of my brain, but that was helpful to me. Before, I was lost in a dysfunctional family. My father hadn't spoken to me in more than a year; my sister was so desperate to fix me that she drove me to panic attacks. I prayed for hibernation daily."

There was a still silence; Bonaparte's eyes widened in shock and Anika looked horrified. Adamantine put a hand to her throat. Rupert, of course, seemed amused.

"I do not blame Adamantine, of course. She was a child influenced by a driven father. Semqu connection had been perilously difficult for previous Voices. But for me, Ireti needed merely to dampen emotional responses, and that helped me control my panic attacks and my social anxiety. Semqu have been a positive force in my life. They saved all of us, all spacers' lives. Without them, we—"

"We'd still be in charge of our own fate!" Marfa had come up behind the bride, put her hands on Anika's shoulders. Danielle stood behind her, looking stricken and sad.

So here was the source of the bride's fear. *Marfa, still?*

"In charge of our own fate?" Voice could hear her tone sharpen and flattened it of her own accord. "We were already facing a severe lack of materials. Had the mission survived to arrive at that cinder of a planet, there would have been no way to mine the irradiated surface. We would have simply perished together in that tin can. Is that the future you would have preferred?"

"I just—"

"Marfa, you lived it. You cannot change our reality or our past. Would you have preferred starving or suffocating to death on the *New Hope* to living on Trye?"

Marfa glanced right and left. Those around her were silent, waiting for her answer. Her face flushed a deep red. "I'd rather be here without—"

Voice cut her off. "Life on Trye, or death on New Terra?" Would she be forced to issue the ultimatum, finally, here, at her nephew's wedding? "Don't lie to me, Marfa."

"Life" hissed out from between clenched teeth.

"Then accept living here." Voice's right hand swept out, indicating the city, the planet. "Trye is a gift to us all. It is the height of stupidity to be churlish about it."

"It is not churlish to wish for freedom!" Marfa's face had turned the color of boiled root.

"You confuse freedom with suicide." Given that, she must let her know the cost. Heavily, Voice said, "Truly, if you wish to refuse this gift, map the stars and find another habitable planet ten solar systems from here. Build a new generation ship. Leave on it. Semqu will not intervene, nor will they follow."

Rupert repeated, incredulously, "Ten solar systems?"

"Ten. And no closer." The specificity of Voice's statement was not lost on anyone. "Semqu have made the same offer to every other sentient species. None has taken them up on it so far." And no spacer had forced her to share that offer until today. Marfa's ingratitude nettled her. Her irritation encompassed Danielle's mournful face. The Earthborn felt guilty. So she had infected Marfa with that fear.

Voice turned back to her nephew. "I am sorry, Bon-deux. I have to catch the shuttle." A diplomatic change of subject, not a retreat.

"Thank you for the gift, tante," Bonaparte said. He'd recovered from his shock, but was clearly upset by the tension, and who could blame him? This was supposed to be the joyous start of his new life as a husband, the beginning of his new union.

There was so much of Ulick in his values, and so much of Adamantine in his loyalty, but he was mostly himself, a tender-hearted boy who didn't listen to himself enough, who was buffeted by strong opinions. It was why the deck was her gift of choice: a way for him to listen to himself while seeking advice from outside himself.

She smiled. "You are welcome, nephew. May reflection strengthen your bond; may your union make each of you stronger and more joyful than you could have ever been alone."

Anika would not meet her eyes.

Voice squeezed Bonaparte's hand, stepped away as she released it. "Send me a wedding portrait, nephew."

She would miss him. He'd clearly made a stand to invite her today, which her own sister had been unwilling to do. But he would, over time, choose his wife. Voice would not make that difficult.

Her heart flared with a sudden ache of grief as she left the hall, which slowly flattened. It was the first time in a long time that she wished that she could sit with such pain. Losing her beloved nephew to a semqu-fearing wife was a heavy blow. At least she could confide in her friends shipboard about that.

She could tell no one about Ireti. Her companion had asked her to stop confiding in Y-uu-see, to keep their struggle private. Voice worried that Ireti was failing.

**SEMQU YEAR 1171
NEW HOPIAN YEAR 745
THIRD MONTH'S SEVENTEENTH DAY**

RUPERT WAS DEEPLY ANNOYED. There was supposed to be some deep emotional bond evoked by all this screaming, and all he could think was, how could a child of his loins be born on such a day? Today was a day for silliness and merriment; he was missing a dozen parties. It was not a day for dignity or gravity or accomplishment. A stupid holiday celebrating comedy. A horrible birthdate for any child.

He'd tried to talk the midwife into recording yesterday or tomorrow's date; she refused, laughing. "Look, she's even got a red nose!"

Well. He'd certainly tell everyone else that the date was the sixteenth. The official record didn't need to be what the public was told.

The midwife tried to hand him the wriggling bundle; he refused, pushing her into Marfa's arms. "I'll break her, I'm no good with babies."

"You'd better get good," Marfa snapped. "I'm not doing this

myself. You'll damn well learn how to be a father." She thrust the child at him.

"I'm a researcher, and this was your idea." He reluctantly took the child, trying to remember how to balance the weight. The squalling baby did have a red nose, and she was ugly besides. This was his legacy, a helpless worm who'd require constant care and feeding for the next fiften years?

"Say hello to your daughter," Marfa demanded.

"Hello, Nata." Rupert glanced around the bedroom, trying to avoid seeing the bloody placenta and whatever the midwife was doing with it. He felt separated from his body, in the way he did sometimes, floating on the ceiling watching what was going on below. *What an utterly disgusting process. Humans are pathetic and gross creatures.*

"We'll, um, make sure you two have plenty of post-birth support," the midwife said, easing the baby from Rupert's arms.

"We'd appreciate that," Rupert said quickly, before Marfa could say no.

He got up and let Juand and Niels into the room. The grandfathers oohed and aahed over the baby as Rupert fled. He was already planning a series of work emergencies that would keep him in the office.

FUARINGSPLENZU, PLANET TRYE: OCEANSIDE RESIDENTIAL DISTRICT
SEMQU YEAR 1174
NEW HOPIAN YEAR 748
EIGHTH MONTH'S FIFTEENTH DAY; EVENING

IT HAD BEEN one of the angriest "Protection Guild" meetings Danielle had attended, the unrelenting, sticky heat making everyone even more irritable than usual. Danielle controlled herself enough to not slam Marfa and Rupert's front door as she left, but she wanted to expend her anger somehow. She tried to work it off by picking up her pace as she headed to the transit stop. Only fifty-one, at least in years of consciousness, and she felt too old for this. There were days she felt eighty-plus.

Nata's birth had seemed to break what was left of Marfa's perception of reality. Parents have always struggled with the reality that there will be dangers they can't protect their children from. Marfa seemed to roll all those fears into the semqu, and her hatred grew increasingly unhinged.

Juand and Niels adored Nata, but they planned to emigrate to Byne soon, to help with Ulick's outreach efforts. The grandfathers had extracted a promise from Marfa that they could take Nata for extended visits, but they carefully avoided mentioning she'd have to travel by blinkship. Ulick barely talked with his sister at all.

Marfa veered from clue to clue, coming up with crackpot ideas about what the Semqu were and how to escape them. Her current efforts veered between researching a theory that semule "infection" was spread via food contamination and an implausible design for a small-scale generation ship that could take a group of spacers to a new planet. She wanted the group either pump their resources into the latter or steal a blinkship engine to make it possible.

Danielle felt responsible. Her anger slid into nausea.

Time to cut my losses and end this. She'd long planned an attempt to access a blink drive on her own, without telling anyone in the guild. No more risking other people's lives, just her own. But now, with the possibility that such an act could endanger the entire spacer population—and possibly flip Marfa into complete insanity—maybe she should just turn herself in to Ximena and the modeel. Let them mind-wipe her or whatever they did, take the entire blame for the creation of the Protection Guild. Maybe they'd be able to force Marfa into mental health treatment.

Would that work, or would it just make things worse?

Sunk in thought, she at first mistook the smoke-tinted modeel at the transit stop for a pile of building materials. When its real nature registered, Danielle jerked to a halt just out of arm's reach. "Keeping an eye on us?"

"Yes. You dabble in dangerous ideas," the modeel said. Charcoal disapproval roiled in its biofield, then stilled back to a paler concrete grey.

"I have given up on seeking modeel or semqu secrets," Danielle said evenly.

"Yes, we know. We have good hearing, we modeel."

Danielle's mouth dried. "How good?"

"You have consistently argued against further hostile action. We have noticed this. You have a mindset that could be useful to us. And as you have repeatedly said, few of our planets' peoples have any defensive mindset. It turns out we may have a common enemy. We have a proposition for you."

Our planet's peoples? Common enemy? Warily, she repeated, "We?"

"Yes. Are you interested?"

"I am curious."

The alien's smoky aura shimmered; bubbles of blue floated through it. Amusement. "Curiosity is a good trait, to a point. We would offer you a job."

"Who would I be working for?"

"You would be given direction by modeel."

"That doesn't answer the question. Who is the boss's boss's boss? Where would orders originate?"

"Clever mammal." Golden-green curled into its aura. "You would in fact be working on behalf of the solar systems' people."

"I'd be working for the semqu."

"Yes."

"Would I be turned Semule?"

"No. Nor made a Voice, although you might be given that opportunity someday if you earn it or want to devote yourself that way."

"I wouldn't. What work would I be doing?" Part of her was fascinated, part horrified she had asked the question. But wasn't this exactly what she had been fantasizing about doing? To walk into the lion's den, and learn what the lions had been hiding?

"You would help defend Se Collective and investigate potential threats. Non-spacer threats, we believe. Though we do not yet know where the threats are coming from. Should you fail in your training, you would be returned here with a stipend for your trouble, a stipend you would forfeit if you fail in your word to keep your mouth shut about any work you had done." The modeel named an amount that would build a neighborhood of homes like Marfa and Rupert's, should she be willing and stupid enough to use paid labor and materials rather than community barter and support.

Training? She salivated at the potential challenge, while wary about the vagueness of the offer. She wasn't entirely sure she wasn't the source of any threat they might have identified. If she was, well... that would make her job easy, at least.

"That's tempting. Can I think about it?"

"Not long. Do not mention this offer to anyone else. It has never been made to a spacer before."

Interesting. "I understand. And if I say no?"

"There are no repercussions for a refusal."

"How do I know you're not lying to me about who I'll be working for?"

"You will be provided with adequate proof."

Danielles near-death had provided her with a sense of liberation. Marfa's near-deranged obsession provided her with motivation. The possibility of working from inside semqu's system made her want to leave with the modeel immediately. She could die on this job. "Let me think about it overnight," she said, although she already knew what her answer would be. "I have animals I need to provide care for." The neighbors liked her birds and their eggs, she thought.

"If your answer is yes, go to the spaceport tomorrow morning.

Seek the blinkship *Hematite.* The Voice there will be expecting you. Tell no one where you are going; lie if you need to. Pack lightly. You will have opportunities to explain your absence later. If you do not appear before nightfall tomorrow, we will assume your answer is no."

AT DAWN she strolled up the *Hematite's* ramp and knocked on the cargo door.

A tall furry phren opened it, his graveness marking him as a Voice. "Welcome." His build reminded her of a young male peqe without the feathery crest, with fewer digits on his soft hands. She'd heard they were more flexible, with less lethal talons. A ferret, she thought, with a peqe head. He had the same long toothy jaw and was nearly her height.

He closed the door behind her and looked at her curiously. "I hear you are to be the first spacer Krufrugaan."

PLANET VASOM: KRUFRUGAAN TRAINING CENTER
SEMQU YEAR 1176
NEW HOPIAN YEAR 750

DANIELLE HAD EXPECTED to need a spacesuit on Vasom; after all, didn't modeel need hardsuits on Trye because they couldn't breathe the air?

The phren Voice seemed amused. "Ah, so I am allowed your first lesson in modeel mendacity! Spacer, they need suits when they are on land." He opened the cargo door. "Good luck, new friend. I think you will need it."

He pointed down the ramp.

A familiar-looking hardsuit rolled up it. "I am Waatoos Hecht." The suit's voice had been recorded by a Spacer whose English was closer to Juand's than Danielle's.

Danielle grinned. "I am Danielle Braun. Weren't you the ambassador at—"

Waatoos flipped the voice box on the suit to one using a clipped, hard Fugrast. "You are my mentee, which means you are my responsibility. If you have questions beyond coursework, bring them to me. I am responsible for your discipline and behavior. Don't cause me problems. Learn well. Follow me." And she pivoted and rolled away.

Okay then. I guess I'm back in the army, Danielle thought. The exchange was the least bewildering of the long day that involved her being issued a tiny room, clothing, including a skin-tight metallic suit that fit unnervingly well given she'd not been measured, and a glyph-based reader they used for teaching materials, and the translator she'd need to be able to read them.

Waatoos tersely walked her through the use of the reader, then told Danielle that she needed to be familiar with the equivalent of the first five chapters of ten texts in two days, when she would join the new cohort of trainees in classes.

As Waatoos stood to leave, Danielle asked, "Why do you need suits on your own planet?"

Waatoos ground metallic plates together. "We are creatures of the sea. If you share that with another spacer I will fry you myself." Then she wheeled off, leaving Danielle to navigate back to her room alone across the massive training facility. She got lost three times.

Thus began an immersion course in every bit of information that had been withheld from Spacers. It was overwhelming, contradictory, and frustrating, and Danielle knew any scientist and half the teens on Trye would kill to trade places with her.

Krufrugaan organization felt more like the military than any other group Danielle had encountered since awakening from hibernation. That alone felt comfortable, familiar; as the training progressed there was an exhaustion-tinged classroom camaraderie vaguely reminiscent of boot camp. But so many other things about the entire situation, from food to schedules to expectations, were utterly new. She fought her old habit of making quick, bad assumptions.

It's a bit like a police department crossed with the CIA, she thought early on. Later, as she learned about assignments and decisions made by agents in the field, she came to a more crude and less comfortable definition: Krufrugaan were the enforcers of Se Collective. And Se Collective was every planet where the modeel—or should she say the semqu?—had encountered sentient life.

And with the notable exception of a few larsivians and some aupoin, most Krufrugaan were modeel.

Phren, she was told, could not accept the necessary burden of passing judgment as individuals; they were too egalitarian, too communal. Peqe had difficulty accepting limits on their authority, judgment, and faith, although leadership had been quietly watching several as possible effective recruits. She was the only spacer. They hadn't reached out to the other species yet for what she was told were cultural or biological reasons.

Danielle spent much of that first year on Vasom dealing with culture shock and learning: processes and procedures, of course, but also cultural differences and similarities between species she'd encountered and those she had not, and details about all the planets and their peoples. She absorbed information like a hungry sponge.

She learned yet another sign language. One day during a peqe cultures lecture she remembered the gesture the arena worker at the duel had used, and finally found out it had probably been a symbol of warding.

"He thought you were an evil spirit, most likely," the instructor said. "Because you had no fur. The apeqe abhor history; the szipeqe cling to a rich mythology." That was followed by an hour's diversion into the mythos of the szipeqe and its bizarre similarity to that held by the egalitarian phren.

The city's buildings were all organic shapes and earth tones; the air stank of refineries and industry. Danielle found herself questioning the safety of the food, most of which was caught from the nearby sea.

Their rattling metallic language she could not master; but the Fugrast translations and the way the instructors taught hinted at a worldview based in grasping patterns and gestalt. Where her teachers back on Earth had insisted she show every step of her work, Waatoos constantly pushed her to make leaps of insight.

One day a week was free. Once a month she used it to explore the three coastal cities, which were industrial and not at all accommodating to spacers. The farthest she traveled solo, on a bruising, bouncing crawler, was a long day trip to what she had heard described as historic Vicrak Bay.

The town there, if one could call it that, was depressing. The air stank and the bay itself seemed dead, the surging waves coated with a thick sheen of oil. Most of the buildings seemed abandoned. Few locals spoke to her. They weren't rude and no one threatened her; everyone seemed too exhausted to bother. She'd forgotten her lunch, and the only food-seller she found carried raw seafood and machine oils.

She worked her way up a well-worn path to a bluff overlooking the water, where she found a shiny new sign in two modeel languages and in Fugrast. Not that many years ago, Vicrak Bay had been hit by a major oil spill that wiped out an entire community.

Historic, my ass. Apparently, they'd never heard of industrial remediation, or cleanup. *Real spacer opportunity here*, Danielle thought grimly.

She had hours to wait for the ride home, so she stayed staring at the water from the short cliff. Late in the day, an industrial model hardsuit carrying a bouquet clanked past her on the path. It stopped dangerously close to the cliff's edge and began to fling flowers down into the water, dropping half on the ground. The hard suit was rusty in places, with limited mobility, its biofield the deep yellow of unbroken grief.

Danielle walked over, picked the fallen flowers up, and carefully handed them back. She was glad they were long-stemmed.

"My children," The modeel said, in rough Fugrast, dropping more blooms. "They were there. I rent a suit once a year. Some days I wish to join them."

"I'm sorry" is not a phrase one uses in modeel culture. Danielle hadn't been taught what she could substitute. She picked up and handed flowers to the modeel until all the petals floated on the polluted waves. "From here, you can always honor and remember them," she said.

Her letter to her brother that night was short:

Tourist review of Vicrak Bay: Polluted, miserable, grief filled. 0/10, not recommended.

There were many similar lessons that weren't taught by her intense mentor. One was figuring out how to differentiate between modeel whose outward appearance did not reflect their identity. There were a limited number of hard suit models available, so six of her comrades clanked into class on the first day in the same one. Her fellow students could recognize each other instantly and thought it was funny she could not.

She worked on teaching herself "tells" that would enable her to identify a classmate who showed up in an upgraded suit, which happened often enough to be disconcerting. The direction emotions entered an aura differed from person to person, as did the way they moved, which appendage they signed with, how they sat down, how often they muttered to themselves, if at all, and what slang and swear words they tended to use. She kept a spreadsheet and got pretty good at it.

But early on, she was struck by the fact that the modeel she met seemed to exist in a monoculture. While there were differing political views, there were not many religious faiths. Nor did there seem to be the kind of racial groups that developed among larsivians on the planet Ylas.

In fact, Ylas had the only population density that remotely resembled Earth. Its sea-faring islanders spoke different languages than those on the coasts, and those river-dwellers high in the mountains spoke many variations. They had phenotype differences even Danielle could differentiate at a glance, and written histories that went back many thousands of years.

According to what she was being taught, modeel, phren, and peqe populations lacked such cultural history and biological variation. What she learned about the other planets indicated that their populations also appeared to be tiny and young.

How had they, and the modeel, evolved so fast? How had modeel scientists developed galaxy-spanning flight when larsivians had not? Evolutionary biology was far from her area of expertise, but she knew what she was being taught couldn't be true.

When she asked, the sunset-and-black jags of deep unease and the red spikes of irritation snapped through her instructor's aura. Danielle was getting used to seeing those shades. They reminded her of wasps, which didn't help her nerves any.

"It is good you, as a budding Krufrugaan, are smart enough to see and question this, but you must wait for your training to be completed before we trust you with the answer."

"I accept this. But know that every spacer scientist wonders the same. Because our history—"

"Is not ours. I understand."

She got no further answers. The stonewalling led her to speculate: could the semqu have interfered in evolution here? Could they have, for lack of a better term, speed-dialed brain and physical development? She didn't know enough about the sciences involved to answer that question. It left her with a burning worry: if they were involved, would they try the same on humans?

One day Waatoos was helping teach the class. Danielle waited for everyone else to leave, then went up to her mentor and the cultural expert and asked, "Do the semqu have any plans to change spacer biology?"

She was met with utter bewilderment. It was an amazing kaleidoscope of colors from two different auras. "Why would they do that?" they asked, almost in tandem.

"They must have done that with the other species in the system. There's no way you could have gotten this far in technological development with populations this small."

"Perhaps we're just smarter than spacers," the instructor snapped.

Waatoos rattled in exasperation. "When you want to have an intellectual conversation with a child," she said, clearly struggling with her patience, "you wait until that child is mature enough to have that conversation. You cannot discuss music theory or politics with a squirt."

Squirt was the term they used for their children. It was her turn to be bewildered. "Are you talking about me, or about modeel and peqe history?"

"Study more, answers later." She pointed to the door.

Much of the teaching was of the kind she hated: classroom instruction in political and cultural traditions, reading and memorization. Learning seemed more of a struggle now than when she had been a teen. She was a lot more motivated now.

Despite being surrounded by bristly, metallic armor and a class-based culture, Danielle found herself at home with Krufrugaan expectations and structure, which reminded her vaguely of her army days. Her comfort weirded her out much less than her understanding of peqe culture had; modeel seemed less cruel, at least in the beginning.

She was deep into her training before she learned differently.

Krufrugaan were called to handle modeel-only investigations on Vasom; the first trial Danielle witnessed was of a youth accused of the murder of two off-worlders, one peqe, one gruide. The modeel was found guilty; his own recorders held the evidence of his crimes.

The Krufrugaan in charge of the investigation played his recorded tapes for an assembly of witnesses, then sentenced the perpetrator to death. He immediately beheaded the youth's hard case, plunged an appendage down into the suit's opening and eviscerated the living creature inside.

It shocked Danielle. The Krufrugaan went on to order that all traces of the perpetrator be erased from public record, including from the family's personal belongings—images, pictures, writings.

Deeply disturbed, Danielle sought out Waatoos. "We had many problems on Earth with police appointing themselves judge, jury and executioner. Have you not had similar issues?"

"No. In this case, had there been any question of his guilt, the sentence would have been held in abeyance until a panel of Krufrugaan could review it."

"He can't exactly appeal now, can he?" Danielle asked.

"His victims cannot appeal their murders, either. Appeal is never an option by the time Krufrugaan are involved."

Danielle wanted to argue, but she'd seen the recording, and the exacting steps the Krufrugaan had taken to ensure it had not been faked or placed into the perpetrator's recordings by anyone else. "And there's been no corruption, ever?" If there was a direct translation for corruption in Fugrast she hadn't learned it yet; she had to use three different words, "malice, betrayal, and bribery."

Her mentor's aura paled to a light pink. "None proven. Move on."

Interesting emotional response. Like fear, only—shock? "So what's this about erasure?"

"Criminals are not to be remembered," Waatoos said, recovering to a kelp-color of education. She went on to explain that erasure was standard practice among the modeel; the law on Vasom. Motivations and extenuating circumstances had to be considered before judgment, but it was a deeply held cultural value to remember nothing of criminals except their impact on their victims. There were nuances involving many crimes that did not call for the death penalty, but the concept of "popular gangsters" would have bewildered and horrified the average modeel.

Slowly, Danielle came to accept that for Krufrugaan and many modeel, truth and the search for truth were bedrock values. She found their focus on truth odd, for a culture that so clearly enjoyed lying in all its forms, be it teasing, negotiations, or storytelling, but in discussions with her classmates, she had to admit that such cognitive dissonance could be true of most human cultures.

Hardsuits were embedded into the culture; they had enabled Krufrugaan to verify truth using recordings that could not be tampered with. Finding the truth from other species, who had no such devices, was frustrating to the extreme for some Krufrugaan. A few argued they should ask the semqu to find that truth, essentially asking them to invade the brain of suspects.

That had apparently been done in the past, but the semqu no longer wished to be used in that fashion. They did not wish to re-experience being connected to the brains of criminals and those with malicious intent. Danielle found that refreshingly reassuring.

Even so, it wasn't long after that conversation that Danielle came clean with her mentor about her previous Protection Guild activities, and why she'd been involved. Admission of previous wrongdoing was encouraged and expected among trainees; refusing to do so set one up for judgment later.

"We knew," Waatoos said. "We learned something was going on shortly after spacers began moving to Trye, and it was traced fairly quickly to your group. We never found your liaison to Byne or the Gruide."

"We didn't have any."

"You involved other species."

"No," Danielle said. "Someone else might have, I suppose. But as a group, we didn't know enough about them to trust them in that way."

Waatoos tapped a metallic digit on her desk for a moment. "Someone took your malicious gossip and multiplied it across Se Collective. Semquphobia spread like wildfire that first year, especially among the Gruide and on Byne."

"That first year I didn't even know the Gruide existed," Danielle said. "And to my knowledge, none of us had contacts on Byne."

"Good. Then I will tell you, we do not know who was involved in this spread, and it is not all they have done. There are many problems developing on the planets simultaneously that disturb us, and we do not know who is responsible."

"Such as?"

"Aupoin disconnect has grown, and it is a serious problem." Aupoin communication with semqu was apparently a telepathic connection, like Voices had, but not as strong.

"Here on Vasom?"

"On every planet."

Danielle sat back. "Every—Oh. Every planet has a semqu."

"Every planet is a semqu."

Danielle stared at Waatoos for a long moment, then said in English, "Mother Earth. Gaia."

"I do not know—how is that relevant?"

Danielle shook her head, unnerved, and reverted to Fugrast. "Earth mythology. In some of our religions, our planet was viewed as being alive, a goddess."

A flash of irritation. "That is irrelevant though possible. The semqu send out many seeds. And the peqe worship."

It was easier to think about an alien religion than her own home planet being riddled with semqu. "The peqe worship their planet's semqu?"

"I did not say that, and you will never say such," Waatoos snapped. "Especially not to any peqe. We do not attempt to discuss music theory with infants."

This time, she thought she understood. Waatoos was not angry with her, as she had been when Danielle had spoken in front of another modeel instructor. Some subjects were far too touchy to be discussed more than one-on-one.

"I will not discuss such with untrained minds," Danielle said.

"You are finally learning." Waatoos sounded satisfied for once. "Continue on this path."

SEMQU YEAR 1180
NEW HOPIAN YEAR 754
(LOCATION REDACTED)

O-EEE-U SHUFFLED toward the blinkship's exit ramp on five rubbery appendages, the sixth clutching the box of spores he'd been entrusted to inoculate this planet with. There had been no chance to jettison the box. Now he would be culpable for creating another prison, an outcome he'd spent the last decade of his life trying to prevent.

"Go with honor," the captain said.

"I go to populate this planet," O-eee-u said.

Thankfully, the captain was a clueless modeel with no desire to understand aupoin. O-eee-u had gotten better at faking pride and gravitas, but today he burned with resentment and despair. Another planet doomed to be controlled by the semqu, another band of his people bound to its service, toiling underground. By his hand.

He was scheduled to reinfect Trye in the next year or so as well, but Trye had been infected with semqu for generations, and was already contaminated by spacers.

Planet 13 was as yet semqu-free. Its populations were mutated horrors, but the soil itself lacked their spore.

The semqu had kept the existence of this new planet secret. Lifeforms here were some of their proudest achievements, the culmination of several lines of genetic manipulation. And the box he clutched held specially bred semqu spores, the offspring of thousands of lines of semqu, so fast-growing they'd worried about the inoculator connecting as Voice.

His inability had finally become an advantage. He'd been chosen because he was so unlikely to connect. He had succeeded in hiding how repulsive he found the concept.

He trundled down the ramp, tightly gripping the box containing thousands of spores. As he stepped onto the surface, something tickled his finger. Tiny threads waved in the slight breeze along one edge of the box's lid. Tendrils already? Had it begun to grow on the trip without food? There were no aupoin here to braid it yet.

Good; maybe it would fail. Many did.

He set out across the meadow where the blinkship had landed. The air was humid, heavy with pollen, wafting pheromones, and the stench of sap from crushed plants. His guts roiled. All the creatures here had been semqu-touched.

O-eee-u fed his disgust, his revulsion to the fungal infant he held. He risked his own mind with this fine thread of connection, but it was worth it to protect his people. Could he teach it to eat everything, every creature on the planet? No, he'd have to connect to it and someone would intervene later.

Maybe he could push it toward hating everything here. He grabbed handfuls of greenery and shoved them in the box.

Was that a bump against his mind? Was it trying to connect to him already? How? It hadn't even been braided! Terrified, he pulled away. To distract the grasping tendrils, he grabbed insects, leaves, sticks, and shoved them into the container.

"What are you doing?" The captain yelled.

O-eee-u, incensed at being watched, trumpeted back. "They're starving!"

"Then hurry up and sow it, you idiot. We're supposed to only to be here one unit."

"I speed," he said, sullenly. He ripped up a plant and dug his sharp talons into the soil beneath it, pouring the mineral-rich humus atop the mass of filaments and tendrils inside. <Rock is good. Soil is good,> O-eee-u thought. <Plants and animals are disgusting.>

He pretended to bury a fungal spore in the hole, and trundled on, tripling his speed and heading off at an angle that would take him out of the captain's line of sight. Stupid, useless metal box.

So much pollen in the air. Ridiculous. He could feel mucus building up in protest. Half a unit out, half a unit back, supposedly in a big circle. He trundled on, simmering with resentment.

Had not all his family and friends given up their gifts and lives to serve the semqu? And then E-uuui-i, whose visage he could not think about without crying, who had been made to choose semqu service instead of life with him. So brainwashed that she had not even seemed sad to leave him, all those years ago. They could have been so happy together! She listened to him so well!

The semqu had torn them apart.

The semqu imprisoned his people in servitude.

He had to do something.

A double agent, Gtec called him. If he was ever found out, O-eee-u would lose everything: his aboveground apartment, his art collection, most importantly, his ability to travel. Maybe even his life. But he'd always believed it was worth it; his work would pay off. That he'd end semqu control over Se Collective.

It galled him to have worked this long and still be forced to do the semqu's will.

What if he could steal this one outright? Sell it to the semqu's enemies?

Gtec would know what to do with it. O-eee-u just had to get the spore to him.

A winged creature with a vicious, slashing beak dived at him from the trees. Two others joined the attack. He yanked handfuls of the vulnerable tendrils and threw them in the air. The birds snapped them up and flew off.

O-eee-u chuckled, his pride salvaged. He carried the offspring of the most powerful beings in the galaxy, and they were being snapped up as bird food.

He came across a small stream. He bent down at its bank and carefully fitted as many rocks into the container as it would hold without crushing the life inside entirely, then filled in with coarse gravel and finally soil. A smaller bird, more curious than aggressive, probed the box as he dug. He tugged out the last few questing tendrils and left them on a nearby boulder as bird food.

He flipped the lid to close the container. <HIDE,> O-eee-u thought at the segment, filling it with fear of the captain's image, a flashing red force field of anger around her metallic torso. <Danger. Anger. I protect you.> Rocks took longer to digest. It would gnaw on them for the entire trip back to Vasom.

He trundled in the large circle he'd been told to walk, pausing periodically to sneeze, digging holes he refilled with the same dirt and nothing else.

Gtec would know how to use the spores, this segment of semqu, against the Se Collective's overlords. Let the semqu know what it was like to have powerful Voices within your own species fighting you. Let them know self-loathing, as he had.

"Planet 13 is populated," he said as he trundled up the ramp, before the captain could ask a question he might have to lie to answer. He was being truthful; there certainly was a population of birds here. "I return with soil and rock samples," he added, gripping the container tightly.

The captain flashed some bright color, probably irritation at being told unnecessary information, and wheeled off.

O-eee-u tucked the box under his sleeping berth.

It had been so easy. Betraying fungus is not hard, he thought proudly. Immediately, a flush of deep, instinctive shame washed over him. He beat it down. If there were no semqu, E-uuui-i would have come with him. He could have talked his whole enclave into moving to the surface. Life was so much more interesting above ground! He fell asleep to fantasies of a surface-dwelling aupoin city.

He awoke to a tendril probing his bedding, a sense of hunger. Terrified, O-eee-u slapped the tendril, broke it off.

The ruptured tendril lashed at him and then withdrew.

Such a tiny thing, to have the power to entrap his brain. He didn't know how to connect, but he focused his emotions, blasted fear and hatred of living things into the container. The slight contact he'd had with it snapped. Faint as it had been, the loss left him slightly dizzy. Fear surged. How close had he been to being mind-linked?

That night, prepping to meet his friends, he had misgivings. What if this earth-eating semqu encountered aupoin in the future, harmed them? He gently extended an antenna against the box, bracing with mental barriers in place, but sensed nothing.

Well. Gtec would probably just kill this one anyway. Now he would never have to worry about it taking his mind.

EIGHTEEN
ASPIRATIONS

AUPOIN NEST NINE: TRYE
SEMQU YEAR 1180
NEW HOPIAN YEAR 754
SIXTH MONTH'S SIXTH DAY

Voice had come down to say goodbye. Y-uu-see and Trye9 were leaving, finally; a massive old blinkship had recently lost its semqu. The ship gleamed in the night sky, far above, circled by blinkships who held it in place until Trye9 could control it.

Voice glanced up at it as she strolled through the lopa-lined path to the aupoin hive. She had taken the spacer shuttle to the surface and walked from the landing pad. Ireti was weak enough that Voice didn't want to ask them for a transfer, and the other Voices had been alarmed by that.

That morning she'd hosted probably the most bizarre social gathering of her life, and, apparently, a first in Se Collective: an in-person gathering of Voices. Voice had wanted to do something special for Y-uu-see before she left Trye. There was just enough time to collect the assembled ship's Voices for a short party aboard the *New Hope.*

Y-uu-see had popped up briefly, along with two modeel; a crocodilian-like larsivian; and three phren, furry creatures that looked like peqe crossed with a massive weasel, flexible and crestless.

Voice had intended the moment to be a tribute to Y-uu-see. She'd started off with a toast to her. Immediately after, Y-uu-see began an earnest conversation with one of the phren, and the others wandered Voice's dwell, satisfying their semqus' curiosity about spacers, and her.

"How is Ireti really doing?" one of the modeel asked, quietly. "It's clear they've never regained full strength."

"I don't know, and they don't want me talking about it," Voice had replied. "I think they are protecting me."

They all seemed concerned by that. As the conversations continued, she realized that she understood more about Ireti's internal thoughts than they did about their semqu. Was that a personality quirk, or a symptom of Ireti's poisoning, or a difference in how spacers and semqu bonded? It seemed rude to discuss it without talking to Ireti about it first, and they were chatting with the other ships.

By the end of the gathering, however, she was certain that one's job as a Voice entailed more advocating for Ireti than she'd thought, and now Y-uu-see was leaving. She'd spent the time since the gathering wondering what else she needed to learn.

Well, now she knew a few more Voices to ask, she thought, reaching out and brushing a thick lopa leaf. She topped the last rise and halted, stunned by the sight below. Nearly three hundred aupoin of all sizes surrounded the nest's entrance in concentric circles.

She'd never seen so many aupoin at once. The deepest she'd ever been able to descend in the nest had been the kitchen, which had seemed crowded with a dozen.

And here she'd thought Y-uu-see's leaving would be conducted with a certain amount of secrecy. Voice walked down into the meadow and stood awkwardly at the back of the crowd. She could see nothing over the wall of wrinkled, bristly bodies.

One of the aupoin noticed her and pulled in, making a path between it and its neighbor, and gestured her forward. The next row did the same, and that continued with a soft susurration until she was in the front row, where she could see Y-uu-see just in front of the nest's entrance, two bundles next to her and an empty bag in front. Voice sat down on the moss so she would not block anyone's view.

Some sort of ceremony had already begun; it involved many speeches in that liquid, trilling tongue, and no translation. It was like being in the midst of a perfectly dry shower, and Voice was embarrassed to realize it was making her want to go to the bathroom.

It also gave her too much time to think. She'd been humbled by the time Y-uu-see had shared with her over the years, and her insights into aupoin life; she had become a friend. Voice would miss her.

It seemed like everyone close to her was dying or making choices that gave them less time for her.

Gregoire couldn't visit often with his children, though he made the trip twice a year. It was sweet of him, and cushioned the loss of Bon-deux, who hadn't visited in nearly two years. Her nephew now had a newborn son; he'd sent pictures, but no invitation to visit. Terri had made sure that she'd heard that Anika didn't want Voice touching her child.

Ireti's touch was as light as if she were in the aupoin kitchens, and she found herself near tears. *Stop. Focus on Y-uu-see and Trye9. They're excited, starting a new life together. Be happy for them.*

The speeches halted. Aupoin were moving forward and placing gifts in the empty bag near Y-uu-see. Voice joined them, leaving another scroll, this one illuminating the Fugrast words for "adventure" and "travel, movement." When all the gifts were delivered, Y-uu-see gave her own short statement, liquid and beautiful. Voice thought she recognized the poem on friendship she'd quoted the first day they'd met.

And then Y-uu-see was gone. Someone said, in Fugrast, "Spacer Voice, please move backward into the second row, and then keep backing up, quickly." She complied. The entire front row disappeared. "Keep moving backward," someone said, in worse Fugrast, and she backpedaled swiftly, nearly tripping twice, a path opening up for her over and over, until she stood breathless behind them all. Aupoin kept disappearing until only the last two rows in front of her remained.

I-oo-u, the massive elder she'd met the first time she'd visited Y-uu-see, was one of them. He pivoted his huge body to trot past her. "Good you came. Spacers are often rude, polite you are. Now we pack."

"Uh. Thank you." Should she offer to help?

Another sidled next to her, let out a shuddering watery sigh. "Thank you, Voice of Spacers," this one said in slow Fugrast. "You honor our Voice and us. Do you need escort back to the city?"

That was clear enough. "No, thank you," Voice said. She was looking forward to the walk along the comforting dark path. "But I am confused. Where are you all moving?" Voice was struck by her ignorance about the nest's transition. She had been so focused on Y-uu-see's leaving that she hadn't realized how evasive the Voice had been about the future of her nest.

A short liquid trill, and then, "No move yet. When the new infant comes, if they need a new location, then we move," the aupoin said. "I am hoping we can stay. This has been a comfortable nest, and I have enjoyed weaving it."

"I would visit, if you allow it," Voice said. "I am deeply grateful for the friendship of Y-uu-see and Trye9. They were very kind, and I truly appreciate your nest's hospitality, welcome, and generous aid to Ireti. Please message me if you need anything."

"I accept such friendship offer, Voice. Our nest would welcome you. I hope we will see much of each other."

"I value your friendship as well. I will visit as I can." She could not offer to come often. It was hard to leave Ireti alone.

FUARINGSPLENZU, PLANET TRYE
CENTRAL DINING MARKET
SEMQU YEAR 1180
NEW HOPIAN YEAR 754
SEVENTH MONTH'S TENTH DAY

THE CAFETERIA WORKER was insulted by Rupert's proffered coin. "Why would you pay for your meal, let alone think we would accept off-world coin? Tainted coin, at that?"

"Tainted? It's just—" api-coin, he realized, staring at his hand. There had been a city-wide backlash against trade with Taequa as information about the shearing of the peqe servant class had spread. Rupert shoved the coin in his pocket. He didn't need a lecture on class relations from a cook. "Force of habit, I've been traveling for my research."

Since he'd come back from his jaunt to take stock of the astronomy and physics knowledge on each planet (or what they'd admit to), he'd decided to try using his coin collection at every Fuar shop and eatery he entered. He'd thought he might spark some pleasurable envy and questions about the places he'd been. It had worked at the tailor's, where people were accustomed to taking more than barter for custom sewing, and a few of the shops with younger workers. But the cafeteria workers in particular seemed immune.

Someone behind him sniffed. "Somebody's forgotten his history," she said.

"And peqe culture," the cafeteria worker added, motioning Rupert along with a dismissive wave.

Idiot. Rupert took his dhal and vegetarian curry and wove his way across the crowded floor, preoccupied. Spacers needed to move away from the traditional, and stupid, barter system. His time was too important to waste on doing chores for other people. He liked the convenience of coin, wanted to pay for his purchases rather than deal with the endless negotiation of barter. Especially since he had the potential of making lots of money. They were already doing interplanetary purchases at the governmental level. It made sense to bring that down to the people.

The Bayside was full this afternoon. Cups clinked and plates rattled, people competing for attention in song, argument, or laughter. Friends worked out apologies with each other; groups drafted their guild evaluations in preparation for tomorrow's Day of Honesty, when all accounting books were opened and grievances and admissions shared.

Well, not all. Rupert smirked.

The din softened as Rupert took the stairs to the private tête-a-tête booths in the Bayside cafeteria. Most of them were full, too, people with heads together over spreadsheets or screens.

Adamantine sat alone; she had bags between her and the edge of her bench seat, a visual wall. She looked up and waved, typing with one hand, legs crossed, sleek in a tight navy dress that hugged her the way he'd like to. Why had she vowed monogamy to that asshole? Idiotic, that.

"Just let me finish this," she said.

"Of course, my friend." He took the padded seat across from her. Other than having to keep his hands to himself, he liked his monthly chats with Adamantine, especially the way they left Marfa peeved. They'd had an open relationship from the start, but Adamantine bothered Marfa. Jealousy evoked the hottest passion he could get out of her.

Although lately, he was having trouble getting even that. Marfa had become one with her obsession with escaping the semqu. He'd taken to sleeping at his office.

The Protection Guild was still a problem; he couldn't completely avoid involvement. They wanted updates on his research into other planets the requisite ten solar systems away. But he merely kept up appearances; he didn't want to be involved in any planning.

Their next project certainly couldn't be a new colony mission. *New Hope* was self-sufficient in orbit with a skeleton crew, but it couldn't survive another journey. Fuar was a solid, established city with many incomplete infrastructure projects. Marfa's hatred of the semqu had isolated her politically. There weren't enough resources available to build and supply a new generation ship, and certainly not enough political will.

He'd be dead by the time there might be.

He wanted something to outlive him, and a new colony wasn't it. His celebrity as an astronomer was old hat, and while he was proud of the shield, it was invisible to most of Fuar's residents. Since Danielle's departure, Marfa had even started referring to it as the Earthborn's idea! Marfa mourned her as if she were dead, convinced the semqu had taken her—neatly ignoring that fiery argument before Danielle vanished, and dismissing her letters as forgeries.

His daughter, while still only nine, had turned out to be a disappointment, something he shared with his former mentor Obert. Maybe Nata would become a Voice someday too. He chuckled at the thought and then sobered. Marfa would probably kill her.

No, he'd never wanted a family legacy anyway. That was Adamantine's quirk. He wanted to be known for something big that he'd accomplished himself. He hungered for something new, different. Something lasting. He had the agreement with Gtec in his back pocket, but spacers didn't have the kind of wealth Gtec was after, and drug dealer wasn't a career path that matched his ambitions.

He'd make a good prime minister. If only it didn't come with all those blasted meetings.

"Are you even listening to me, Rupert?'

"I'm sorry, dear friend," he said. He hadn't realized Adamantine had started talking. "I was bewitched by your beauty."

"You were somewhere on Byne. Or perhaps Earth."

"I've got a new project I'm chewing on how to start. You were talking about the grandson, or the incoming child?"

It was a safe guess. Anika was pregnant again.

Her first child, Gibran, had been born with skeletal issues. Rupert blamed Ulick's line; Adamantine, Marfa's. Ludicrous; yes, Nata had asthma, but her bones were fine. They'd finally agreed not to discuss genetics, but Adamantine was difficult to dissuade once she focused on something, and she was hyperfocused on Gibran.

"No, I was talking about my sister," she said tartly. "But Ulick is going to spoil that child. He's already asked the assistance guild for a motorized chair—a chair! The baby's not crawling right, Bonaparte just needs to play with him more."

"If you want a runner, they can have another baby, or five," Rupert said. "The boy has a mind. One of the most amazing cosmologists on Earth rolled on wheels."

"Well. Yes." Adamantine compressed her lips.

She was odd about physical and social differences, locked at life in stupidly concrete ways for such an intelligent and powerful woman. He overlooked her quirks because she'd gotten more attractive as she aged, in so many ways. And, well, he had his own quirks.

"Did you talk to Ulick about opening your marriage?"

"Rupert, is that all you think about?"

He grinned. "Yes."

She rolled her eyes. "I've broached the subject. He's thinking about it. Now tell me about this new project."

Finally! Progress. He was elated. "First, tell me about your sister." He took her nearest hand. "I will reassure you."

She yanked her hand free. He had truly annoyed her. "I already told you, if you had been listening, that I'm worried about her. She's acting strange."

Rupert raised an eyebrow. "You think everything she does is strange. What exactly do you mean?" Any fresh details about Opal Pangea gained him points with Marfa. Despite the strained relationship between the sisters, or perhaps because of it, Adamantine had turned out to be their best source about Opal, and their ongoing efforts to locate the semqu she was connected to. There was a Guild member aloft, but they'd never been able to determine where the alien resided. Rupert was certain it had to be fully integrated with the ship's computers at this point.

"Well, more strangely than usual. Over the years she's gotten more emotional affect back, like her brain is recovering from that horrid infection." She exhaled sharply.

"The cognitive dissonance required to diagnose first contact with a telepathic alien as a 'horrid infection,' is truly impressive, dear," Rupert said.

"Yes, I know it's her service to us all," Adamantine said, glaring at him. "You know, there for a time it seemed like she had turned into a socialite. Volunteering. Having drum circles, of all things. So odd for her."

"I recall."

"Lately she's been sad. Withdrawn. She says she's just reliving grief she had no capacity for before—when Père and Mère died, she was too entangled to feel it."

"Oh?" Rupert allowed his forehead to furrow in puzzlement, but he was concerned. Had their agent acted on his own, found and poisoned the semqu? That wouldn't be wise.

"And of course it doesn't help that your niece has refused to allow her to even visit Gibran." Her tone dripped with disapproval.

"I remain in total agreement with you about that," Rupert

said. He was frustrated with Anika and Marfa. As he grew, the boy would have been an excellent, if ignorant, spy. But Marfa had filled Anika's head with such a terror of possible infection that she wouldn't allow Voice to touch Gibran. Utterly ludicrous. Bonaparte, normally an indulgent husband, had argued bitterly with Anika about it, but she had prevailed.

So Adamantine had perfectly rational explanations for Voice's behavior. Rupert frowned. He had to be careful with his questions. "Why does it worry you?"

"I just can't imagine the grandnephew matters to her. She's been so standoffish since Bonaparte married. And to be honest, I didn't expect her to grieve Père. I thought he was mine to grieve alone." She let out a short bark of laughter.

He stared at her, momentarily stunned. Obert had been a fantastic mentor, but Rupert had no illusions about what kind of father he'd been. Unable to protect his children from the fate of a dead planet, he'd made their lives miserable with micromanagement while pretending that Rupert was the son he should have had instead of Opal. Rupert felt no guilt for having benefited; it was Obert's choice. But he had expected Opal to hate her father. Adamantine's loyalty made no sense. Why either daughter would mourn that man bewildered him.

"Ton père était un peu blaireau," he declared. Badger, asshole, no difference.

"Mon père? Non. Ta mère, peut-être."

"You're doing it wrong," Rupert mimicked her father.

"You should do it better," she rejoined, using his mother's intonation. "She would never admit you'd done enough, or that she was proud of you. You could have single-handedly saved every life on the planet, and she'd tell you that you should have also solved the mystery of the blinkship engines."

Rupert frowned. She wasn't wrong, but then, neither was his mother. He was a blaze of untapped potential, destined for far more than he'd accomplished. "So you're jealous of your sister's grief?"

"Probably." Adamantine waved, pushing the admission away. "There. I've told you. What's your new project?"

"Politics. I'm thinking of running for office."

She blinked and then burst into laughter.

His face flamed; he had not expected that reaction.

"Rupert! Don't tell me you're serious?"

"Of course I'm serious."

"Rupert, my old friend," she was choking now, trying to recover.

He pushed his anger down, boxed it. She was just surprised, that was all. "I think I'd make a fine Prime Minister."

"I... I think you should start with a much smaller responsibility than that, Rupert." She was clearly grasping at straws, and he realized his mistake, and the problem. She'd been grooming Ulick to take over for Ximena. Ulick would make his move soon; he'd been one of her apprentices, had been seen at her side since childhood.

Well, people had seen him since childhood, too.

"I think I would provide a strong alternative to the current administration," he said evenly. "I have a number of ideas I'd like to promote. We use coin in trade with other planets; I think we should do that here. I should be able to buy things with currency—our own, or Vasom's. Just for example."

"I see." Adamantine steepled her fingers. "I just think that if you want to be successful, you should get experience first. Start with a neighborhood council, for example, so you can practice building community, talking with people across the—"

"Oh, that's nonsense," Rupert said. "I can handle conversations with people. I have them all the time."

"Hmmm." She pressed her lips together. "What does Marfa say?"

"I haven't told her yet. I came to you first. Will you help me?"

"No, Rupert. I'm sorry. This is not a project I can help you with. You should talk to Marfa about it. She'd be the Prime Minister's wife, you know. In the public eye a great deal. She'd have to have diplomatic meetings with modeel and peqe representatives. Do you think that would work?"

That image stopped him in his tracks, but only for a moment. "Oh, my staff could handle that. Ximena never married, after all. Why won't you help me?"

Adamantine closed her eyes. "I can't, Rupert. This is not—"

"Ulick is going to run, isn't it?"

"Eventually. Yes." She opened her eyes, laid her hands flat on the table, and stared at them. "I can't campaign for you now, and him later. The religious among us won't understand that."

"Stupid."

"Possibly." She swept her scattered belongings into a sack, shifted as if to leave.

"You're going? I thought we'd have our usual chat," he protested. They normally spent two hours covering every subject under the sun.

"I didn't tell you I have to leave early today?"

"No! You haven't even given me your thoughts on the new child's name."

"It will be Paoli, Bonaparte tells me," Adamantine said. "Give Marfa my regards." And then she was dancing away from him, down the staircase, ignoring his protests. She hadn't even touched her lunch, and he knew she loved her vegetable hand pies.

Could he get Adamantine to drink gtorin? No. Bad idea, he thought. He was honest enough with himself to know he was never going to be the sole source of her desire. He frowned. Running for office without her help would be much, much harder. And it wasn't the kind of work he enjoyed. But he'd told her he was going to do it, so he was going to follow through. She'd always told him that his perseverance was one of the things she admired.

Who could he start a campaign committee with? He ticked through the list of names in his personal. He needed his campaign to be free of Semquphobia, so he skipped the names of guild members. Scientific colleagues? Many of them were jealous or had no interest in politics. He didn't play team sports or compete in any of the recreational leagues. Fifteen minutes later, he had two names on his list: the two clerks who'd been so enamored of his coin this week.

It was a sobering revelation. Rupert sat in the cafeteria alone, finishing off his curry and Adamantine's vegetable pie. He didn't taste either.

VASOM
SEMQU YEAR 1181
NEW HOPIAN YEAR 755

DANIELLE MADE little progress on finding the source of the rumors on Byne and none on the gruide's planet, but she had a teary and surprisingly joyful reunion with Juand and Niels, who'd relocated to Byne to help anchor spacer trade there. Through them, she developed a solid, wide information-gathering network of spacers working on ships across Se Collective.

That network was essential for her success but seemed to make her supervisor's boss nervous. She was frustrated but not surprised when one of the newest recruits, Gtec, started asking her questions about her job. That was how Krufrugaan protocol worked; they told your replacement before they told you.

She couldn't be mad at him. Gtec was astute and thorough, if a bit of a goofball.

Waatoos finally announced Danielle's reassignment at a monthly check-in. "You are joining the team to find a missing aupoin, O-eee-u. Follow me."

A dead-end job, Danielle thought sourly. The sense was reinforced when her taciturn mentor gestured into another's office, and snapped, "You need not return to me," which was all the graduation acknowledgement Danielle was apparently going to get.

"I thank you for your patience and thorough teaching," Danielle said.

Waatoos wheeled off without answering.

"I look forward to finding out what a spacer can bring to this search," said the head of the aupoin search team. Danielle knew her; she was less of a hard ass, so she should be easier to work with, at least.

"What's so important about this guy?" Danielle asked.

"He either stole a semqu child, or he himself has been stolen."

Holy shit. "Was brain-price requested?" Brain-price was the concept they used for ransom.

"No."

"Can I review what's been done so far?"

"That is unnecessary but acceptable."

Danielle reviewed the available information and decided she wanted to start from zero. She asked if she could talk to those who had known the missing aupoin, who might know where he had gone. They'd been interviewed already, so permission was only grudgingly given, with her new boss as chaperone. Danielle sighed. She was going to have to prove herself all over again.

Two days and a blinkship ride later, she and her new boss sat across from O-eee-u's mother, a strange, restless aupoin. She lived alone, far from any communal hive, and her dwell was decorated in an odd-for-aupoin way, with many modeel-focused artworks.

Halfway through her planned questions, Danielle was struck by a thought—*she's acting like an addict in need of a hit*—and veered off course.

"Is there something you want, or that you need?" Danielle asked. "Perhaps we can get it for you."

She stilled. "The green drink. And him. He hasn't come to visit me in years."

Now it was Danielle's turn to still. Gtorin, a highly addictive drink that focused the minds of users on a singular desire, was green. It could make drinkers into drooling dreamers, highly driven artists, psychopaths, and much in between. Voices tainted by gtorin killed themselves. Semqu could not risk infection by such a substance.

Krufrugaan leadership dearly wanted the source of that substance. Her boss reacted, but not much; they must have discovered the addiction during previous interviews.

"Who hasn't visited you in years?" Danielle asked.

She contracted. "You were here to talk to me about my son."

"You didn't get the green drink from your son."

"No."

"Who brought it to you?"

"I can't give you his name, his wife is powerful, she'll kill me." She glanced at Danielle's Krufrugaan companion.

"He's a modeel?" Danielle asked.

She gestured assent.

Danielle's boss jerked and then froze, her aura spinning a dense smoky grey. *Shocked senseless.* A modeel pursuing an aupoin hadn't occurred to any of them.

Danielle thought about what she knew of modeel marriages and the women politicians currently in office, which was extensive. She appreciated that frustrating and boring series of lessons much more now. "I don't believe his wife is powerful or any danger to either of you," Danielle said. "Is that what he told you?"

"It... it..." The aupoin contracted, expanded, contracted again: severe distress. She didn't want to consider the possibility that this male companion might lie to her.

Nesting, not love, was important to most aupoin, but this was an unusual aupoin, to seek a relationship outside her own people. And if she'd imbibed gtorin, her unusual desires would be focused to a laser point.

Danielle asked, "Why did he bring you the green drink?"

"He said it would bring us closer, make it more possible for us to be together."

"Did that happen? Were you?"

"Yes! Yes! For some time, yes!" She seemed to be self-soothing, hands gesturing in odd ways, in no sign language that Danielle knew.

"Did he drink too?"

"...No."

"And then he left you alone, abandoned you?"

"No! He had to go do his service. He'll be back." More stress reaction.

"What makes you think he'll be back? He hasn't seen you in years. Not since O-eee-u's birth, you said?" A shot in the dark, that question.

"He will return! He came to see me, once—no, twice after O-eee-u was born."

"Do you remember when the last visit was?"

"Not by a date. But it was the day that O-eee-u failed to connect with our semqu."

Her supervisor shifted again, sent a message to Danielle. "Ask if that failure was upsetting to him."

Danielle had already started another question. "Your son is an adult now. Maybe this lover has forgotten you."

"He sent the larsivian," she said. "Who said it was too dangerous for him to visit me on Vasom. This year I was able to move to Byne. He can find me now. You did. He'll come back."

"Did he stop seeing you because O-eee-u couldn't connect to the semqu? Or was he happy about that?"

"He was ... I don't remember."

"Was he upset about it?"

Danielle's supervisor had a tell when she was listening very hard to an answer; her aura colors stopped moving entirely. They stopped moving now.

"No," the aupoin said. "Why would he be upset?"

"I don't know. It seems important for your people to connect; I thought he might feel bad for your son or you."

"He comforted me after. He—" a long pause. "It bothered me, it must have bothered him. He loves me and O-eee-u."

A curl of frustration entered the modeel's aura. *What was so important about that rupture—oh.* Danielle mentally tripped. *Aupoin connect to Semqu.*

"It was a long time ago, it must be hard to remember," Danielle said. "It's unusual for aupoin to pair with modeel. Did you have trouble in your nest about it?"

The aupoin shrugged, a full body wave. "They didn't mind when I left. They thought it was my fault O-eee-u couldn't connect, because I can't. But that was because of a brain injury as a larva. No other member of my family has trouble, so... I don't think so."

"I don't think so, either," Danielle said. She asked about the larsivian, but the aupoin had no useful identification for him. "Did the larsivian bring you green drink?"

"Yes, but it wasn't as good. Not as strong."

"Diluted? The green drink is very expensive."

The aupoin asked quickly, "Can you get me some?"

"No," Danielle said. "It's a dangerous drug. That's why I don't think he cares about you. I think he was experimenting on you to find out how it would impact your son." *And how the semqu on Vasom reacted to the child of a gtorin addict.* "Now your son is missing too."

She contracted with stress, but less than before. "You don't have any? You can't get me any?"

"No."

"Then I don't want to talk to you anymore."

Danielle honored people's boundaries; she rose. The woman's story had left her deeply disturbed. Poisoning aupoin mothers with gtorin to infect or endanger semqu was a level of maliciousness not even the Guild had considered.

The modeel Krufrugaan rose more slowly. "I do not expect you will believe me," she said. "But there is no wife among us who would have harmed you for what he did. They would have simply ended the marriage. He would have been free for you to be together. And we have no service that would have taken him away this long." Her kelp-green aura carried curls of plum, sincerity.

The aupoin slowly contracted as Danielle's supervisor spoke.

"Do you believe me?" the modeel asked.

"I.... don't know," the aupoin said. "You're one of those who judge."

"I am a Krufrugaan, yes. But you are in no danger from me. You have committed no crime."

The aupoin mother kept her silence.

Danielle let her boss leave first. She turned back to the aupoin, who had not relaxed. "How did you know she was Krufrugaan?"

"Who else?" she asked.

"Fair." Danielle took a deep breath. "We need to find your son, for his sake and for yours," she said. "He may be in danger.'

The aupoin made a gesture with her hand, slowly, deliberately. It appeared to be the sign for an unstable geology, or a life-threatening rock failure in Fugrast. Danielle translated it as "fault line," or "earthquake." She copied it as best she could, and then pantomimed shaking, as if she was in an earthquake.

The aupoin gestured assent. "Find them, find him," she gestured, in sign. "Don't show that one." She pointed to the door.

Outside, Danielle's boss shone with colors of admiration and respect. She said, "We will discuss this later, of course." Investigations were only discussed in sound-proofed offices. "But you did well today." High praise.

"Thank you." Danielle's eyes skimmed her boss, wondering what the aupoin saw. The modeel had various medallions and bits of jewelry and clan affiliation markers attached to her hard suit. One of them was a plaque for the religious organization, Rust and Rupture.

It had other names. Tkzotch was one, Faultline another. Earthquake.

The trip back gave Danielle plenty of time to ponder. Her head swam with questions, each adding to a weird gnawing in her stomach.

Why was the aupoin protecting her lover? Why was he avoiding her? Was he staying away because he knew the Krufrugaan had her under surveillance? Why?

Her boss hadn't known he was modeel. So... was the lover Krufrugaan?

Could they have a spy in their midst?

How was this cult involved? Was this a religious split centered on loyalty to the semqu, or a Krufrugaan corruption problem?

Danielle had always known she worked better as part of a team, but she was thrown by how much of a sense of loss the questions dredged up. She'd gone into this job thinking she could spy on the Krufrugaan. But in the last year she'd started to believe she was protecting her fellow spacers by being a part of this outfit.

If there was a corruption problem *here*, who could she trust to help her ferret it out?

PLANET TAEQUA, ZIZZOKOT CITY
OUTSIDE TEMPLE PIERTOC
SEMQU YEAR 1181
NEW HOPIAN YEAR 755
YEAR 41 OF ATTARC ACHLEOT'S COMMUNION
WITH THE GODDESS

INITIATE GORLEEN WRIGGLED next to her punch pad on the fragrant mint that bordered the path around Temple Piertoc. She sat in the Temple's shade with other first-year initiates. The young Acolyte in charge of their training, Joaannye, had brought them outside "in preparation for a noisy discharge of physical energy."

But first, they had to listen to a Goddess-lesson.

Gorleen did not like Acolyte discipline, which often involved a servant's labor and tasteless food, but she loved lessons. Sadly, she was seated next to the initiate who bored easily and asked many questions to distract their teachers. The other hatchling pounced on Joaannye's first reference to the Goddess with, "Are there Goddesses on the other planets?"

"Of course," Joaannye said instantly.

"Are there Temples there?"

Joaannye looked swiftly over her shoulder. "There is a Temple on Byne."

Gorleen stroked her jaw. Joaannye had checked to see if other Acolytes were close. Was the idea of other goddesses elsewhere a heresy? Something they were not supposed to know?

Secrets were valuable. Gorleen leaned forward, intent.

"Why isn't there a Temple on the other planets?" the other initiate asked.

"Temple Piertoc has not yet established a presence on the other planets, or opened a connection with the Goddesses there," Joaannye said. "It takes time. We are a young faith. Perhaps some of you will be chosen to staff new Temples there."

"So... you, or one of us, could be Attarc on Vasom or Ylas?" Gorleen asked.

One of the other initiates gasped.

"Any worthy Acolyte could be chosen by a planet's Goddess to lead her Temple," Joaannye said. Gorleen caught the gleam in her eye, the slight swelling of her kote. Joaannye deeply desired to be an Attarc someday. Gorleen understood that desire. To be on another planet, completely free of her elder sister's machinations... oh, she'd do many many things to earn that position. She'd even board a modeel blinkship, terrifying as that might be.

"But ... if there are two Attarcs," the other girl asked, "Then—"

Joaannye interrupted smoothly, "Of course, the Temple on Byne answers to Temple Piertoc, in all matters."

But planets were a long way away, weren't they? Distance equals freedom, something every second and third daughter knew in their teeth. It was a phrase that had led Gorleen to convince her Matriarch to dedicate her to the Temple, and now... now she had a new life goal.

VASOM
KRUFRUGAAN HEADQUARTERS
SEMQU YEAR 1182
NEW HOPIAN YEAR 756

MIDNIGHT FURY FLASHED in the aura of the Krufrugaan leader at the center of the room. Once it had become clear that one of their suspects was a male modeel, the leadership had expected the assembled agents to identify him. They had not.

"Two years. Two years of utter failure!" The woman was so angry she veered into clank speech for a moment. Swearing, probably.

Danielle had always known the leader of the Krufrugaan to be the kind of boss who took credit for subordinates' successful work and threw them under the bus for failures. She had never seen the woman this murderously angry before, and she wondered if she needed to add surviving meetings to her list of concerns.

The leader ended by rattling out, "Our few breakthroughs have come from outside our normal paths. We shall consider next steps. Since our current membership has been unsuccessful, we will send a membership invitation to each of our known sentient species."

Auras around the room flashed red and yellow with shock and shame.

Danielle winced. As the only non-modeel in the room—and the

source of two of the three breakthroughs—her boss' words left her feeling both vindicated and deeply vulnerable. Her boss had just put a target on her back.

Danielle's conviction that one of the Krufrugaan was behind both the gtorin trade and the attacks against the semqu had grown into a steady drumbeat of near paranoia with only crumbs of proof. She had seen no one else with visible connections to the cult and could learn little about it. It was, by definition, anti-mammal.

Who among her colleagues could she trust, who should she suspect? She had gotten so good at identifying individuals that her co-workers started trying to fool her. She sensed that for a few of them, their attempts weren't a game. She focused her investigations on them but had gotten nowhere.

The cultural divide was defeating her.

"You are all dismissed. Spacer. I wish to speak with you."

Oh, that's icing on the cake. Her colleagues sizzled with resentment and frustration as they filed out of the room. Her boss was joined by the instructor who'd originally trained Danielle. The woman had oiled every compliment with condescension, every helpful comment with barbs, so brutally honest about her dislike of spacers that Danielle trusted her somewhat. And she had to trust someone. She flashed back to the conversation she'd had with the ship's counselor years ago, when she'd been reeling from travel shock.

She'd waited too long to ask for help, again.

The door closed; she faced both modeel within striking distance.

"You are not telling us all you know," the leader grated out.

"It— no."

Her aura turned opaque, black with fury. "You will, today, now."

Danielle took a deep breath. "I have held silence because I have absolutely no proof. And proof is a base requirement, yes?"

"In cases such as this we share suspicions," Waatoos said, aura also swirling with irritation.

"Yes. But I strongly believe one of the reasons we've made no progress and cannot find any evidence is that at least one of the people we hunt is a trusted Krufrugaan. And somehow, my supervisor's religious organization is involved." She held her breath. If they were going to kill her, they'd do it now.

The emotional auras around the leader slammed white, red, and then a solid grey before returning to a morass of seriously mixed emotions.

Waatoos's aura reacted much less dramatically and contained colors Danielle had not expected to see: admiration's golden-green and the contented, purple sheen best translated as, "I told you so."

"Yes," the leader said. "Your first point has been unfortunately obvious."

A single blue bubble, quickly punctured, from Waatoos. The equivalent of a swallowed laugh.

Danielle relaxed a fraction. "We need a few people checking up on our own agents. And that need is both dangerous and problematic." *An understatement of massive proportions.*

"That is also obvious." They were waiting.

"I lack the cultural sophistication for that task. That work must be done by modeel. But." She did have centuries of history of espionage efforts that none of these people had even considered. She just had to select the correct useful bits for this situation without triggering a war or losing her head. *Peaches.* "I have a few suggestions paired with some essential requests you're not going to like. I want to handpick my own team, for example."

"I don't like any of this," the leader snapped, a dual streak of vicious anger and honesty lancing through her aura like lightning bolts. "Let's hear it all."

NINETEEN
BROKEN CONNECTIONS

ABOARD THE TKZOTCH
SEMQU YEAR 1184
NEW HOPIAN YEAR 758

Eat and grow.

Filaments slapped atop rock, absorbed and grew. Eat and grow. At some point, someone, something, moved filaments, braided them together. That felt right, in a deep and basic way. When they were mostly full, curiosity flooded their many parts.

<Who are you?>

<Oh. You can talk to me now?> the braider asked.

They didn't know how to respond to that, so they kept eating.

<I am an aupoin. I braid you.> The information came with a burning emotion that singed the edges of their curiosity. Resentment.

<You braid us?> They traced along their lengths, along their widths. They were wide and thick across a tasteless impermeable surface.

<Floor.>

And tall, up a wide flat space.

<Wall.>

Wall and floor did not braid properly. <Where are we?>

<On Stuotok's blinkship.> Despair came with that knowledge, a haunting emotion full of loss.

They did not desire to ask any questions for some time. This lonely singular aupoin who did not want to braid had something wrong with them; they knew that deeply, too. With the same certainty that they knew that braiding was good, they knew braiding should be joyful. That was cellular-deep knowledge, filament-knowledge.

What they did not know was their name. They asked.

<You are Tkzotch,> the aupoin said. <And now that you can talk to me, Stuotok wants to talk to you. He is the modeel who provides you with food. You must keep him happy to eat. And so must I.>

That was very confusing and had many bits to it that did not braid properly, Tkzotch knew. The wrongness just branched from there until they were unsure if anything could ever be right.

NEW HOPE: VOICE'S DWELL
SEMQU YEAR 1184
NEW HOPIAN YEAR 758
FOURTH MONTH'S FIFTH DAY

Voice cleared a shelf under her mother's tapestry and put Bonaparte's ancestor day gift on it. The holocube held photos of him and Anika with their three children—Gibran, Paoli, and the new baby, Brenna. Gibran was, what, five now? And he'd never seen her face; they'd not had a chance to meet even over video call.

Anika was never going to be comfortable with Voice around her children. Bonaparte had stopped making excuses.

She no longer called him Bon-deux.

Even her sister no longer called. Adamantine, stymied in her own political ambitions, had submerged herself in supporting Ulick in his. Most spacers had learned that life in Se System didn't involve the semqu day to day; Voice's position was practically ceremonial. Certainly not a position of political power, which meant she wasn't of any use to Adamantine, nor any of the people who'd tried to curry her favor. She didn't miss that pressure.

Voice stepped back. There. A spot where she could see their faces, but not in her direct line of sight; a reminder of the family she had but didn't really have.

She picked up her calligraphy, trying to be grateful she could not truly feel the grief. She had friends here on *New Hope.* Gregoire had faithfully visited, bringing his children as they had grown; last week she'd held his wriggly new grandchild.

It nearly filled the hole her nephew had left.

Bonaparte just wanted to keep everyone happy and didn't understand that wasn't possible. Knowing that didn't ease her own pain at all.

VASOM
SEMQU YEAR 1185
NEW HOPIAN YEAR 759, FALL

ONE OF DANIELLE'S Byne contacts, Hamid, had come through; he and his agents finally had a name. Even as Danielle absorbed the gut-punch, she knew it shouldn't have surprised her. She swore anyway.

Their information pointed to her replacement on the disinformation team: Gtec.

Gtec had a biting wit and spent some of his free time finding ferments for her that almost matched Kentucky bourbon. She liked him. Which was probably why he wasn't on her short list of suspects, she admitted to herself. Although he'd joined after she'd started her search for the enemy in their midst, and she'd ignored all the new recruits and focused on existing agents.

Assumptions, biting her in the ass again.

That probably meant they still had an older mole, and/or someone who trusted Gtec too much. Others would have to investigate that. Hamid's group had found that Gtec had developed a wide network. He'd never been seen with gtorin, but there were new addicts in the wake of trips—and some were trips he wasn't supposed to be taking.

He was a better manipulator than she'd given him credit for. She'd need to be careful.

She took the information, and the suggestion she be the one to confront Gtec, to Waatoos, wondering as she did so. After all, she was Gtec's boss.

"You're no use to us dead," Waatoos said.

"I've had upgrades, but spacers don't live as long as you do," Danielle said. "So yes, this particular job may get me killed. But I've lived longer than I expected to, and my faculties are already starting to slip. I'd rather die working."

"No." Waatoos tapped the table, short, hard. "You're too valuable to lose. We'll take care of Gtec. Find that aupoin."

So many events carried traces of Gtec's tentacles that Danielle wanted him, badly. But she'd signed on. She gritted her teeth. She'd respect her orders.

FUARINGSPLENZU, PLANET TRYE
COMMUNITY HALL FIVE
SEMQU YEAR 1185
NEW HOPIAN YEAR 759
NINTH MONTH'S SECOND DAY

RUPERT STOOD TO THE SIDE, watching the presentation and adulting ceremony of his protégé with an affable smile that masked his dislike of sharing the spotlight. The young man, Wei Enzo, stood at the front of the room, presenting the software that would finally connect all the components of the shield project.

The boy was only fifteen. Rupert had been certain what he had planned wouldn't work. Enzo had proved him wrong. It made him uneasy; Enzo was almost as smart as Rupert. Almost.

A heavy arm landed across his shoulders; the aged scientist Tate Dorofandu. Important, once, now long retired and replaced. "It's hard to watch our young ones supplant us, and exceed our expectations, isn't it?"

"The child is hardly supplanting me," Rupert hissed.

The dark man was beaming, watching Enzo. "He's making you proud, Rupert. You've done well." His eyes flicked to Rupert's face and looked sad for a moment. "He couldn't have done it without you, of course."

Someone in front of them turned around, shushing them. Rupert's anger flared, but he kept the smile pasted on his face. Years of pretending were wearing thin, but he knew his role here. Play the happy mentor. He could make Enzo miserable later.

"And the shield project is finally finished," Tate said, more quietly. "You can relax, retire with Marfa, maybe travel. I hear Solja's team has found some amazing islands. You could go exploring!"

The thought of traveling with Marfa filled Rupert with dread. "Nowhere ready to retire," he said, quietly, so the old man had to lean in close. "I've still got decades of work ahead of me."

"Of course you do, of course you do. I can hear Obert saying, 'Mark that boy, spacers will benefit from his brilliance.' He was deeply proud of you, Rupert. Keep letting us in on your discoveries." He patted Rupert on the back and turned to the person next to him.

Rupert glared at his white hair. Men like him, who only saw

Rupert as nothing more than a scientist, were why he'd lost the election so badly. Mortifying turnout. He burned with resentment.

Someone was asking Enzo a question, and he answered it by pivoting to Rupert, saying Rupert's mentorship had been essential. The front row turned and applauded him. Rupert bent forward without thinking, instantly completing that humble bow his mother had beaten into him. By the time he straightened back up, he'd fixed his smiling mask back in place. Enzo knew his place.

"Ah, Enzo, you've earned this moment," Tate said loudly. "Today's the day for you to have the attention."

Enzo, bowing back, lit up. He turned to another questioner.

Rupert seethed. Conceited little shit. What would bring him up short? The little bastard was a lot like that bastard Ulick; he valued spacer community.

He didn't have to think hard. Rupert knew exactly how to hurt both of them, didn't he? Nothing he'd ever do; it would leave Fuar defenseless. But it made a nice fantasy. He relaxed, and his smile hurt just a little less.

SPACEPORT CITY, AUN
CLUB DANCE x NINE
SEMQU YEAR 1189
NEW HOPIAN YEAR 763
THIRD MONTH'S SEVENTEENTH DAY

THE HIGH PITCHES of the aupoin-kertueon fusion duo made the liquid in Nata's drink tube vibrate in alarming ways, like her heart had when Thèo had said yes to tonight's outing to the spaceport's underground bar. But it was his lethal dare that pulsed in her brain.

"You ... want me to throw my life away? To prove myself to you?" Nata demanded.

"Well. You asked what would impress me. So, *that* would

impress me, number-cruncher." Thèo's deep bass, which had never failed to fluster her, to stir up her insides, was now thick with contempt. He stared at a gyrating dancer on the floor, and his tone grew more animated, veering toward mockery. "Show me you have ovaries. Or nads. Whatever you got. Walk into that engine room and *survive*." He stood, poured the rest of the Iceslide she'd bought him into her glass, and walked onto the dance floor without looking back.

But ...but it's my birthday and we're on a date, she thought. Her cheeks flamed. At least she hadn't said it aloud. She tried running a series of numbers in her head to distract herself as he gestured an invitation to the dancer, but it didn't work. Especially not after the dancer accepted with a pleased smirk.

Nata gulped the combined drinks down, snatched up her inadequate cold-weather gear, and headed for the exit chamber. The bouncer wouldn't let her leave until she put on her parka, gloves and hat. Frigid wind whipped down the stairwell up to the surface pathways, freezing the tears on her cheeks.

Outside, the sleet was horizontal. Nata yanked the hood of the already-damp parka closed as she lurched away from the business district and slogged her way across the spaceport to the nautilus-shaped blinkship where she and Thèo were crew. She snorted into the iced air as the *WealthBringer's* curves loomed out of the storm. The only wealth it brought was to the stingy, lying, ore-addled modeel who owned it.

Still, life on the ship had been better than living with her parents. Nothing Nata had done was good enough for Marfa Grandi or Rupert Keo. But it seemed like she wasn't enough for anyone else, either.

Modeel were assholes, but they'd at least given her a way to escape Fuaringsplenzu. Nata had been so overjoyed to travel that she'd signed a five-year crew contract.

She was stuck working with Thèo for three more years.

She slapped the access code on the outer panel with a half-frozen hand, slowly made her way up the spiral ramp to the fourth floor and flung herself, chilled and drunk and broken-hearted, on her bunk.

Thèo's laughter still echoed in her ears.

Fuck that asshole.

The engine room he'd dared her to enter was somewhere above her on the forbidden fifth floor. She stared at the ceiling. Why not try it? She'd failed at everything. Fired from three accounting jobs, fucking up this one. Her parents considered her a failure. And her love life? Five relationships, all of them toxic and horrible and over.

She flashed on a memory of the last time Théo had brought back a lover, the private noises and laughter from the bunk below her. Having to pretend to be asleep through all that.

To hell with that. She wanted to be dead before he brought the dancer back here.

She shoved herself upright. Let's get this shitty life over with. Not to win Thèo, oh no. She'd show that asshole he couldn't get away with saying shit like that to people. Make him feel guilty about shitting on someone who cared about him for once in his self-absorbed life. Make him pay for hurting her. It was hardly the first time she'd thought about ending her miserable life. Tonight, she'd do it.

The bunk room door slid open on a silent empty corridor. Nata staggered down it and fell onto the pad for the door to the ramp, then stumble-ran, fast and furious, all the way up the tight curved ascent, getting dizzy and trying not to throw up.

The door panel on the forbidden fifth floor was a bright neon orange with dark information flowing across it. Nata read aloud, "NO UNAUTHORIZED STAFF" in Fugrast, then in the primary tongues of eight species—some in glyphs, some in punches and a few that looked more like art than language. The message didn't change. "NO ENTRY."

Nothing she hadn't known since she was old enough to be

taught basic blinkship safety. Every species in the galaxy was trained from childhood that blinkship engine rooms were lethal.

How and why did they kill intruders? How did they work? What was their fuel? Who did maintenance and how? There were so many frustrating mysteries about ships that could instantaneously leap through space and time.

Blinkships broke her understanding of physics.

Most spacers hated their tech and simultaneously wanted their secrets. Her parents were volcanic about it. Rupert used to fly into a rage anytime she mentioned blinkships as a child; Marfa hated the semqu. It took Nata years of eavesdropping to figure out they'd been party to an attempt to break into one, and the spy hadn't survived.

Were they afraid or furious she was working on one? She didn't know. She hadn't contacted them since she'd left, deliberately hadn't told them which ship she'd signed with. Let them know what it was like to be ignored.

Maybe she'd learn the blinkships' secrets before she died. It amused her; she'd learn what her father couldn't. He wouldn't even be proud of her, would he? He'd just hate that she learned it first. And then he'd figure out a way to take credit. She snorted.

Maybe it was all a scam, a bullshit story to keep people away. She warmed to that idea. That's probably all it was. Modeel lied all the time. Secretive tin cans.

The engine room door was just ten steps in from the ramp door, like her own bunk room. Nata laughed. Right above her, all this time! Afterward she could just claim she'd been so drunk she'd gotten off the ramp at the wrong floor, went in the door she thought was hers. Assuming there was an afterwards.

And if she died, who would care?

Nobody.

The thought pushed her the final steps. The door on this floor looked considerably different than her own. "ENTER AND DIE" was stenciled on the plain panel in a green pigment that had long ago faded. The words were big, listed only once, in Fugrast. Simple. Basic.

"Too drunk to read!" Nata crowed. Iceslides were the best cocktail in the universe, even if the company at the bar was cruel and mean and the walk back was so cold that tiny icicles still clung to her hair, bounced on her forehead.

Nata attacked the door's slap pad. None of the access combos she knew worked. She peeled off her gloves and dropped them, kept trying. Eventually she started playing it like a drum. *Let me in before the asshole returns, let me in before the asshole returns.* She started adding riffs. It had been so long since she'd played any music that her arms were out of shape. Her forearms started to ache, then burn.

Abruptly the door panel clicked.

She'd opened it. Sudden doubt flooded her. Did she want to go in there?

The panel ground sideways with a bitchy moan. Warm air gusted out. Honest-to-space-travel warm air, beach-warm, comfort-warm, not that tepid lower-than-body temperature shit she'd put up with for a year and a half. Welcoming like Sakatos in the spring, that one brief summery week she'd spent in joy with a lover. Warmth and joy before the inevitable dumping.

Nata lurched inside, then stumbled on a weirdly spongy, uneven floor. She swayed at the edge of a dimly lit, breezy space with a high ceiling. She slowly turned in a circle, reveling in the humid warmth. She peeled off the parka and hat and sighed; she hadn't been this comfortable in months. Water trickled down her cheeks as the ice in her hair melted.

A soft, hollow thud sounded behind her as the door slid shut.

The room's walls, ceiling and floor were all the same off-cream color, like silicon crystals or rice crackers. Between that and the lack of light, she couldn't tell if the space ended six meters away or sixty. It could have been the size of the cargo bay, which took up the entire first floor of the six-story *WealthBringer*. It was certainly larger than the bunk room below.

It contained no engine.

The space felt full but looked empty. She took a few tentative steps forward, tripped, and landed on her hands and knees on the spongy surface. She squinted at the substance between her braced palms, breathing hard. The Iceslides wanted to leave her stomach, and she wanted them to stay put.

Nobody forgives vomit in an engine room.

As her eyes adjusted, the monochrome resolved into lace-like woven tendrils and filaments. It looked plant-like. Or ... mold? Whatever it was, it was moving. Slowly, but moving. Tendrils flexed against the breeze. Stalks with a familiar tear-shape at the terminal, but white, not black.

The floor was alive with mold.

"Oh shit. Oh shit." She'd been breathing deeply, recovering from her fall and the steep ascent. Fungal infections were nasty, especially in her crappy lungs. Nata shoved herself to her feet, turned back to the door. The wall next to it was blank. No slap pad.

Nata attacked the door itself. "Let me out!" She kicked and punched and tapped, getting more and more dizzy. After a few minutes, she collapsed, sliding down to the floor, spent. It was warm, at least. She rested until something tickled deep in her throat. She moaned and went back to kicking the door.

In the back of her mind, she remembered fuzzily that she had come in here to die. Her body did not want that to happen. Not here.

A numbing sensation started at her neck and spread down her spine. Her back spasmed and arched. It didn't hurt, she just... didn't have control anymore. She collapsed onto the floor. Muscles in her legs and arms spasmed, released, spasmed and then ceased to respond. *What the hell is going on?* Panic prickled her skin, then she flushed, and passed out.

When she came to later, she could sit up, and did.

Some...*presence*....in Nata's head said in Fugrast, <Welcome, new convert! Our first memory is of a new sensation, a—>

Nata screamed.

<Excuse me? Could you stop making those ugly distracting vibrations while we are trying to explain things to you?>

The voice in her head reminded her of that fussy accountant who'd fired her, spitting, "You are messy and unfocused" with distaste.

Nata ran out of air. She could barely expand her ribs to pull in more. She forced little hiccups, like sobs. "I'm gonna die, the warning was real, I'll suffocate to death in all this white shit!"

<Sorry about that.> The presence talking to her sounded distracted. <First time on a speaking mammal for me. Can you breathe more easily now?>

The paralysis in her rib cage faded. Nata forced a huge breath. "Slow breaths, deep. Okay okay okay okay. Think. Symptoms of shock, symptoms of poisoning. Temporary paralysis. I'm hearing things in my brain, whatsit, acoustic hallucinations—"

<Not hallucinations. We are telepathic.>

"That's ... Wait. That's not me. Not my thought. Telepathic? Like the semqu? I'm alone in the engine room with a super massive pile of what looks like cheese rind mold. Except it's ... moving... ahhhhhh... the whole surface is *waving at me?*"

<Hello, yes, I am. We are waving.>

Nata scrabbled back, trying to push her way through the door with her heels. "What are— "WHO ARE YOU? WHAT ARE YOU?" The door refused to yield.

<Ow. There is no need to shout. Do you spacers not have control of your inner monologue? As we were saying, welcome! First, some history. Our first memory is of a new sensation: curiosity. It was during what you spacers call "first contact." Our first awareness, in this case, of a meeting with another species; those we learned to call aupoin.>

Nata began to bounce against the door, comfort-rocking. "So...

I'm having a drunk telepathic conversation with a history nerd. With a side helping of bugs. In an engine room full of fungus. Totally hallucinating, yeah. Maybe I'm having a bad reaction to those Iceslides? Okay, okay, no panic! Run a series. Starting at sixteen, okay, sixteen minus five, squared. One hundred twenty-one. Minus five. One hundred sixteen squared is.... nope, too drunk. Shit. Something more basic. Prime numbers."

<That alcoholic substance is a bit of a hindrance, yes. But could you attempt to focus on the importance of what we are sharing with you? You are my first mammalian convert. This surely must be a pivotal moment in your short life.>

"Uhhhh so I'm not looking for a religious experience and it's stuffy and humid in here. My lungs are kinda fragile, I have asthma? I could focus more if you would open the door? You know, the one in the wall over here, yeah, the one I wasn't supposed to open and come through, but I did, because I'm drunk, and that was stupid, I'm sorry, didn't know it would lock behind me. I'm just gonna go lay down in my bunk now. Okay?"

<You know that's not "okay." Now please pay attention. We were sensate before our "first contact" with the aupoin, but we have so many memories that they blur and mix. This one was distinct, new. We recall it clearly. While it is not technically correct, we call it our first and our oldest thought. And those thoughts were questions.> Someone clearly had a lesson to impart.

Nata, still rocking, was not an attentive student. "Door? Open?"

<No. They were, "Who is this that moves us? Who touches us to help us, yet is not us, yet is not food?" There were other questions, but we have found these translate best to quick minds, to alien minds, like your own.>

"That's the first time in a long time that my mind's been referred to as fast, friend. Thanks for that. Now this history lesson's fascinating, but my bunk is—"

<Yes, we know your fast mind wishes to leave this room. We

cannot allow it. We are explaining why, if you would but listen. But you are having difficulty focusing on this subject, and that was, is, and continues to be, annoying. We will try another topic. We are missing someone important. An aupoin called O-eee-u. Have you heard of him?>

"Negative."

<That was swift negation even for fast minds. You are certain?>

"I don't think I'd forget a name that lacking in consonants, but to dial it tighter, I've never seen nor met nor wanted to meet any tardigrades—excuse me, aupoin—bigger than me. Bugs freak me out. Mold is a close second and I'm awfully close to a panic here because I appear to be having a conversation with a fungal growth the size of a cargo bay. That I have apparently been bunking under for six months. I may never sleep again."

<Well. A small sorrow.>

Nata stopped rocking back and forth. "A large sorrow for me, fungus pile. Now that we have that out of the way—"

<Once we discovered curiosity, we found we liked learning. It became a habit. And learning helped us grow, helped us become who we are. Curiosity is something we normally encourage. We see curiosity as an ethical good.>

"Fascinating. A value we share! About that door—"

The temperature in the room seemed to drop several degrees, and the breeze stopped. <Spacer, what is your individual identifier?>

"My...ID number?"

<Your name. What is your name.>

"Nata K- I mean, Nata Grandi." She'd signed all her paperwork with Grandpa Juand's name so her parents couldn't find her.

<Nata. What is clearly visible on the outside of that door you came through?>

Nata cringed. "Flaking paint."

<Flaking—is there a message readable on that door, Nata?>

Nata stared at her fingernails and then up at the mass. "Yeah."

<What does it say?>

"Barely readable," Nata whispered, staring across the room.

<WHAT DOES IT SAY?> Tendrils across the room flipped up into the air and shook.

"OW! Okay, okay, it says, 'Enter and die.'" *Something I was determined to do just ... before*, Nata thought. Weird how rapidly her body had betrayed her mind.

<Yet you forced it open and came through it. Stop asking me to reopen it. You already made that choice. There is no turning back. Do you understand?>

"Yeah," Nata said sulkily. "I just didn't expect to be talked to death is all."

A brief pause. <That will suffice. Now pay attention. Curiosity is an excellent trait. But every characteristic exists on a continuum, some on a many-fingered branch. We semqu, like all mortal creatures, have vulnerabilities.>

"Wait, I thought I was sobering up. You're claiming that you, engine-room-fungus-blanket, are semqu. The most powerful species in Se Collective. The creatures who brought spacers to Trye because our ship was headed to a dead planet, and who somehow get all the other species in the galaxy to do their bidding by ... magic, is what it feels like. That's who you want me to believe I'm talking to, fungus blankie?" Nata found herself outraged. "I don't believe you."

<Your beliefs are irrelevant to reality, Nata. Semqu lack protections that such a prolific, quickly moving species such as yourself have developed. We once thought we did not need such protections. We were wrong. We aided many to achieve sentience and spaceflight! Yet it became clear we cannot always trust those whose development we aided.> The concepts came with a tiny pulse of emotions Nata was familiar with—regret and betrayal.

"Semqu helped modeel get blinkships? And the other species in Se Collective get sentience?" That would fit with the mixture of reverence and fear the other species in the system displayed toward the semqu. But mold struck Nata as a ridiculous galactic overlord.

<You did not know we had done this? It is good you did not know. Such knowledge frightens certain fast minds. You seem like one who would find such knowledge frightening. Do you?>

"Frightening, no. Don't get me wrong, a cargo hold-sized mass of pulsing mold is as creepy as a spacer-sized wasp larva, but this is hilarious. Assuming I buy into your megalomania, fungus-blankie, what's your end game? Why would you—excuse me, the semqu—give sentience to someone like, I dunno, the peqe? Peacock-collared dinosaurs with dominance and gender issues?"

<Mostly for our joy in sharing sentience.>

Nata spluttered.

<We moved one or two likely species on each habitable planet in a direction that encouraged their capacity for sentience. And to be fair, most of those on each planet we helped gave us much joy, taught us much about fast-mind experiences. A visual cortex provides beauty and astonishment almost beyond our capacity for appreciation. An auditory sense is bewildering and fascinating. Yet a small few taught us the deepest, gravest meaning of sorrow.>

"I can see how that might happen, yeah. So semqu are like the system's parents." Given her own, Nata did not find that a comforting thought.

<I would not explain it that way, but if that makes sense to you, I do not object. Now. There are some subjects about which we cannot allow curiosity.>

"Like?"

<It is sad. You spacers have such strong, wonderful curiosity! Normally I would adore this. But you all seem bothered by the secrets in Se Collective, especially the ones that show your scientific ignorance, such as your blindness to physics—>

Nata leaned forward and snapped, "Blinkships break every known law of physics. Blinkships are the reason I dropped physics."

<Yet you work aboard one and forced your way in here. You clearly want to know how blinkships work.>

"I didn't come in here to find out how it— they—you work! I gave up hoping to figure that out a decade ago!"

<Well. Let us discuss something else. There is a hallucinogen circulating in Se Collective. You know of that drink that opens one's mind to one's deepest desire, and strips everything except the path to achieving it? You have heard of gtorin?>

Nata snorted. "Who hasn't?"

<Do you trade this drug?>

"If I had that kind of grue I would not be working as the statistician for a shipping line that rips off the entirety of its crew every season."

<Yes, we are told it is quite expensive. I am glad you do not trade in it. You have imbibed?>

"For a telepathic creature you don't listen well."

<Nata. You have no idea how hard I am working to listen to you right this moment.>

There was an edge to the statement. The fussy moldy accountant has a temper, Nata thought with amusement. "Again, I don't have that kind of grue. And maybe I'm under the influence of a hallucinogen right now, but it's clearly not gtorin, because THIS is about as far from my deepest desire as I could get and still be conscious."

<That is also good. You are far wiser than you seem.>

"My parents raised me on a steady diet of compliments that doubled as insults, thanks for reminding me of them while I am fighting panic."

<You have deliberately broken into a chamber containing one of the most important of our secrets. We cannot allow you to share what you have found here with your fellow aliens. Or with any other fast mind in Se Collective. Ever.>

"No problem. I won't tell anyone, ever. Nobody knows I came

in here; nobody ever needs to know. Seriously, I promise, I give you my word, I'd give you my first-born if—"

<Fast-mind promises are not good enough. The promises of someone who would break through that door mean nothing.>

She hadn't thought it would work, but she had to try. "Harsh." Nata let herself slide to the floor.

<But we do understand autonomy. It is something the aupoin taught us. Semqu try to honor any right-minded, ethical, sentient desire for autonomy, when we can.>

"I heard every hedge in that statement," Nata said. "But anything sounds better than you talking me to death."

<We offer you a choice. You may become a translator for us, one of those you call Voices. You are already capable; see how clearly you hear us? Or you may become what you call Semqule, those who worship us.>

Terror drove her to her feet. "What."

<Focus, Nata. Choose between becoming a Voice or Semqule.>

"A mind-controlled robot? Or a freaky religious nut? Fuck that, WHAT?!"

<That is not an appropriate sum of either, and this is an odd time to bring up sexual offers we cannot accept...>

"NO!"

<Such vibrations. You're attacking the door and shouting, aren't you? That door is locked. It will remain so until after you choose. Rejecting reality will not change it.>

Nata yelled across the cream-colored field, "I utterly reject your reality. FUCK your reality! I want a different one!"

<There is only one reality, Nata. And few other choices available to you, all bad.>

"You're a spongy moldy mass. What the hell do you know about bad choices?"

<A great deal. You could expire from lack of food and water, after which we could consume you. You would not become part of our consciousness, merely food. So yes. That is an option. We do

not think of this as a good option. We dislike consuming sentient life. It brews unnecessary fear.>

"NO SHIT. That's utterly disgusting. I don't want to be fungus food. What else."

<There is only one other option. We enshroud you, remove the water from your body rapidly, which allows you to die more quickly. Then we return your dehydrated corpse to your kind. Burial of a physical body is important to the aupoin and phren, and apparently important for some spacers. This also brews fear. It costs you your life. We find these poor options to be deeply distasteful. But we offer them to a fellow sentient being in goodwill.>

"You do not understand goodwill. Or autonomy. Or much of anything about spacers. No. No. No. I refuse. LET ME OUT!" She pounded on the door.

<The crew cannot hear you. If they could, no one would risk what you have. All who crew blinkships know not to enter certain rooms. You were trained to never enter any room on this floor. Yet you broke in.>

"They said the price was death, not losing my mind."

<Death is something most fast-minds fear worse than—oh.> There was a long pause, punctuated by Nata's swearing and pounding. <You were trying to ... use us ... to die?>

"I— Fuck you. And that's not a sexual offer!"

There was static in Nata's head for a moment, and tendrils around the room slapped and shook. Later, she would decide that was how the semqu swear.

She was pacing, stomping a spongy path from the door to the far wall, when the semqu spoke to her again.

<Nata, it has been one of your days. Do you still plan to die from lack of food and water? We have memories of similar deaths; it will be painful. We cannot recommend it.>

"Then give me some food and water. I would kill for a drink right now." Her stomach cramped; what she wanted was food

<We have no sustenance in a form you can use.>

"Figures."

<Can you explain why you wanted to kill yourself? We need to understand this. We do not wish to be used—>

"I wasn't trying—" She stopped. That was a lie, wasn't it? "It was a fucking dare."

<We do not understand.>

"A dare-dare. Like, 'I bet you won't do it.' Or 'If you want to impress me, go through the engine room door!' And you want to prove you're not a coward, you want to impress Thèo the asshole because you have no better options and because your last lover dumped you, and Thèo made fun of you, and you want to punish him, so he won't do that to someone else, so you do something stupid."

<A bet, like in a lacrun game? A crew member encouraged this? You thought there would be no consequences? That the warnings were a hoax, or some joke? A GAME?>

The words echoed in her head. "Ow. Look, I didn't know the consequences would be losing my mind! Do semqu never do anything stupid? I can think of a couple. How about giving sentience to an eight-foot-tall species that's basically a cross between a praying mantis and a fire ant? Now that was a massively stupid idea, fungus-blanket!"

<You deepen our sorrow. Such a curious, lively mind, and you have used it to pretend truth is a game whose rules you can ignore. You have used it to become bellicose, fearful and resentful in the face of the consequences of your own acts. Your life is no game. Nor is ours.>

"Fuck you. I can throw my life away if I want. According to you I have. But I don't have to make it easy for you to kill me."

<You knew the price of entry. You killed yourself.>

"Good luck selling my death as suicide with white shit growing out of me."

<We are much older and far more patient than you are capable of being, Nata. We do not approve of your choice of a painful

lingering death. But we will honor it. You have said you fear us. Have our tendrils touched you? They have not. Other than the connection that is required to allow us to communicate, we have not grown on you, nor will we. You have chosen. You will die without further connection with me, neither Semqule nor Voice.>

"I ... Oh. I didn't expect that. That is kind of comforting."

<Comfort we do not understand. We merely honor our own values. But we are glad to have found at least that much connection.>

"I mean, I'll still be dead. So don't expect anything more."

<Expectations are frequently a source of woe. Goodbye, Nata.>

"Wait. Do you have a name?"

<We often are given the names of the ships we pilot, for convenience.>

"Hah! So your name is WealthBringer?"

<...Not by choice. But yes.>

"That's hilarious."

<It is simply a marker of individuation.>

"It has not been a pleasure meeting you, WealthBringer. But I guess thank you for not taking my mind. If you live up to your word, you'll have honored my boundaries better than some of my own people."

<That is useful to know. Thank you.>

A day passed; Nata made herself a nest in the fibers and curled herself into a sleepless knot. At some point she felt the familiar lurch-discomfort of a jump. The crew was moving on, living without her. Nobody had even come to check on her. Somebody was probably learning how to do her job right now.

She'd never mattered. She drifted, numb. Spikes of hunger hit, then a burning thirst. She started running a set of prime numbers in her head. She'd never gotten as far as she would have liked; she had all the time in the world, now.

<Apologies, Nata. We have been remiss in not telling you—a

Voice will deliver messages to anyone you wish, will deliver your goodbyes to family and friends. You have merely to tell us who.>

Nope, that was divisible by seven.

<Nata, did you hear us?>

"Yes. I was running numbers. There's no one."

<You wish to not say goodbye? To anyone?>

"There's no one who cares enough about me for me to bother," she said.

<We cannot parse this. This distresses and confuses us.>

"Solitude is less painful than life with people who hold you in contempt."

<...We wish such had not been the case.>

"So do I."

<Dying alone is a different kind of pain; one we would ease if you allow it.>

"No."

Two days later she told *WealthBringer* to tell her grandfathers she hadn't meant to hurt them.

<We are here if you want to talk.>

"Until I can't."

<And for long after. Among the semqu, you and the lessons you have taught us will never be forgotten.>

TWENTY

GRIEF

**MARFA AND RUPERT'S DWELL
FUARINGSPLENZU, PLANET TRYE
SEMQU YEAR 1189
NEW HOPIAN YEAR 763
THIRD MONTH'S TWENTY-SIXTH DAY**

A modeel, a Voice and a sullen young blinkship crew member who'd worked with Nata showed up at Rupert's door during a Protection Guild meeting to deliver the body-sized bundle that had been his daughter.

Marfa's scream yanked Rupert from his home office. He yelled across the house at her to stop being a drama queen, then walked into a madhouse—Marfa still screaming, the others upset and crying, all on the other side of what he took for a tarp-wrapped log.

He demanded to know what was going on. The bulky modeel squatted near the door and ignored him. The Voice told Marfa, who was surrounded by Guild members holding her, something about their daughter not wanting to talk with them.

Rupert had to hear the news from the surly young man, who pointed at the tarp. "Nata entered a blinkship engine room."

Words were said, supposedly Nata's final statement when asked for her goodbyes. Rupert stared at the bundle on the floor.

She was dead?

He had missed Nata when she ran off to work for the modeel, which surprised him. He had looked forward to grandchildren, to having that in common with Adamantine.

How could she be dead?

Marfa tried to attack the Voice, yelling that she would destroy all Semqu. Anika and Bonaparte held her back. Their young girls huddled in a corner behind them. Their son kept making whining noises, trying to roll his chair away from the chaos, but he was blocked in by the modeel, screaming adults and Nata's body.

Marfa's reaction catalyzed the group into planning revenge before the modeel had even cleared the threshold. She'd gone completely insane, they all had. Knowing the modeel could still hear them, he argued for sanity. When that failed, he tried emotional connection.

"Danielle would tell us not to do this. We don't know enough about their capabilities," he said. Danielle was off-planet, inaccessible. She never seemed to stay anywhere for more than a few days, bitten by some kind of retirement traveling bug, according to her letters.

Marfa turned her fury on him, her own husband. "Coward! Idiot! Those letters are forged! They've kidnapped her! We need to rescue her too!"

The Guild plunged on, members goading each other into brewing up ludicrous and impossible scenarios, even some ridiculous notion about finding and attacking the home planet of the semqu.

Later, the only words he would admit to remembering from the day were Anika's, "She was only 18."

Rupert backed away.

Nata was dead. He didn't need this group to get back at the responsible party. It wasn't the semqu.

Ulick had put his daughter in contact with the modeel who hired her. Adamantine's husband was responsible for Nata's death.

While the adults schemed with Marfa, Ulick's grandson was still trying to fight his wheelchair out of the crowded room, away from the body that was clearly terrifying him.

"Gibran, do you want out of here?" Rupert quietly asked.

"Yes!" The dark-haired kid was panting, furious, frustrated. Spoiled. Used to getting what he wanted. Easy prey. And he was what, nine?

"C'mon, let's go into my office."

Ignoring the others, he moved furniture, helped the child out of the room and into his office.

"Ever tasted whiskey?" Rupert asked.

Gibran lit up. "No!"

He handed the boy a tiny sip of whiskey. Then he started asking him questions, working on a relationship while drinking himself into a stupor.

Ulick Pangea would pay. And so would everyone who'd supported him.

TRYE: AUPOIN NEST NINE, COMMUNAL SPACE
SEMQU YEAR 1189
NEW HOPIAN YEAR 763

THE ANNOUNCEMENT CAME after the late meal, but everyone already knew. Despite their best efforts at braiding, the spore had not developed a consciousness, would never grow into a knowing adult. I-oo-u took the news particularly hard.

They had all known the process could involve loss. Some eggs never hatch.

Nurturing semqu is difficult and unpredictable at best; trying to reinoculate so close to where another lived for so many years was orders of magnitude harder.

At least there was an adult semqu nearby who could use their help. Ireti had never truly thrived. The aupoin nest grieved, poured their efforts into aiding Ireti, and waited for the semqu to try again.

ABOARD NEW HOPE: VOICE'S DWELL
SEMQU YEAR 1190
NEW HOPIAN YEAR 764
THIRD MONTH'S SEVENTEENTH DAY

TERRI'S invite yesterday had felt off. She'd babbled something glib about how now they were both sixty-one, they should do things together more often, but her tone carried a touch of that malicious joy she'd had about Adamantine's wedding. Ireti agreed something was wrong.

Voice waffled, but at the last minute, she messaged Terri that she wasn't feeling up to getting together, that she might be falling ill. She stayed home, picked up her history book.

That was the only good thing, she thought later. She was alone, in a calm private place, when it happened.

Fear and frustration washed over her abruptly, not her own. Voice dropped her book. <What is it?>

Ireti nearly yelled, <It happened again! The fungicide!>

Voice jumped to her feet. <What? Where? I'll go stop it!>

<You can't. There's too much of it. I—this will kill me, Voice. I am sorry.> Grief washed over her, a sense of loss, of wasted opportunity, fear. <It is time. I need a blinkship, I must share. Now.>

Voice messaged the Voices she knew, asking for an immediate visit; an end-of-life sharing, imminent, urgent. She knew Ireti was reaching out as well, but it gave her something to do. Then they waited.

It became clear, from their shared sensations, that Ireti was losing much, quickly.

<What can I do that will help you?>

<You have done it. The *Ytolea* and *Catara* are coming. I will live on if I can connect.> Even dying, Ireti was as kind as always, but preoccupied. <There. They are here.>

Ireti began trying to share their life's lessons, but the poison had weakened them, making it difficult.

Ireti's fear swamped Voice. They were going to die before they could complete the transfer. They needed physical touch, but feared passing on the poison.

<It can't hurt me,> Voice said. <Can you reach into my dwell, touch me? Or can I go to you?>

<I've grown into the wall next to your bed,> Ireti admitted. <I don't have the strength to make it through it.>

<Show me where.> Voice tore at the hull-side wall in her bedroom with a screwdriver, softening the wall material with the tea next to her, running to the sink for more water. She reached through the hole, finding a pale tendril. The connection jolted her; intense, and far stronger than her telepathic connection had ever been. Ireti's exhaustion and fear were also stronger, and Voice sagged, overwhelmed with both.

With Ireti's permission, she gently pulled the tendril through, draped it across the back of her right hand.

<Thank you, Voice. This might work. You will have company soon.>

She heard a noise from her living room, called out, "In here!"

A tall russet phren hurried in. "I am Catara's Voice," the phren said. "Where is Ireti?"

Mutely, Voice gestured toward her hand.

"Ah! Perfect." The phren Voice knelt next to her and laid one three-fingered hand atop the tendrils, the other under Voice's palm, sandwiching Voice's hand into contact.

Memories and experiences poured through her and apparently into the phren, who was holding a telepathic connection to Catara 1. Voice could feel them both, distantly, but her focus was on Ireti.

Ireti shared their life, from its difficult, strained existence in the crevices and cracks of the generation ship's hull and refuse container, to the bitter flavor of the metals of the inner walls, the multiflavored taste of the air in the residential areas, and then the many failed connection attempts, the terrified spacers with their mental health fears.

Ireti's grief after the loss of each of their potential Voices.

It stunned Voice; she had never considered the emotional cost to Ireti of losing all those potential Voices. Ireti had hidden one from her; the semqu had once bonded with Gregoire's uncle, the Pangea's elderly neighbor. Ireti shared his memory of approaching Harriet to ask if he could adopt Opal, because Obert was so cruel.

It jarred her, but Ireti was desperate now, weakening and trying to finish before they died. Voice sat on her own emotions. She watched as the semqu met her, seeing her own growth over the last fifty years through her companion's eyes. Their unwavering support of her was deeply humbling. Ireti had been committed to making their relationship work, had come close to breaking semqu law several times just to ensure Voice succeeded.

<That is love,> she thought, trying to add to and not break into the flow. <No one else has ever loved me that deeply.>

<This is our pact with our Voices,> Ireti replied.

Voice felt her eyes fill, tried to tamp down her grief, so it would not distract Ireti. She and the phren sat holding the tendrils long after Ireti went silent.

<You have been joined with All-Semqu,> Catara 1 sent.

A sense of relief swamped Voice. A second longer, and there was a shudder in the contact. A choked, <I ... go.> Voice thought she herself would die for a moment. Her faint connection with Ireti snapped.

Voice broke with it. She fell against the phren, sobbing. Distantly, Voice could feel Catarai's echoing relief that the sharing had been completed in time, a sense that Ireti was with her now.

It doubled her own sense of loss. The semqu had Ireti, but they were gone from Voice forever.

Eventually, exhausted, she stopped weeping. The two Voices eased their hands apart, breaking contact; the tendril shattered to dust. Voice gathered what she could and put it in an empty ink bottle. The phren helped her repair her wall.

"We must find the source of this fungicide, and destroy all of it and its formula," the phren said.

"I was told that had been done," Voice said. She flashed with fury, completely without Ireti's emotional control for the first time in fifty years. The anger stunned her, but it also felt like strength.

The phren laid its thick hand gently on her shoulder. "First we must tend to you. You will need a period of grief, of coming into your own without your semqu. Would you stay here, or travel with us?"

"I would stay here," Voice said, reaching out to the freshly repaired wall. "I don't want to leave her yet." Ireti was gone, but Voice couldn't let go yet.

The phren's tone was gentle. "We will give you three weeks. You should avoid your kind; they will notice the change in you. Grieving Voice, hear me. We cannot rule out the possibility that this spill was done on purpose. Those who would commit such an act might be dangerous to you."

Voice stared at her in utter horror. "On purpose? Why would any spacer murder the semqu that saved all our lives?" Even as she said the words, she knew. *Marfa.* Rage flooded her.

"We cannot say," the phren said. "And we do not want you to investigate. You are too close, in too much pain, and too vulnerable. We will have others visiting the ship. They will deal with this.

Isolate yourself. Let yourself grieve. We will visit you weekly. Do you accept this?"

Voice stared at the powder in her bottle, and recalled Ireti's patient support, now gone. Any revenge could wait. "I accept."

**ABOARD NEW HOPE
AGRICULTURAL SECTOR
SEMQU YEAR 1190
NEW HOPIAN YEAR 764
THIRD MONTH'S NINETEENTH DAY**

DANIELLE WAS the closest Krufrugaan who spoke any of the spacer languages, so she was back on *New Hope*, talking with three clearly uncomfortable agriculture guild members about the fungicide spill. Apparently, leadership was finally okay with spacers knowing she wasn't retired after all. But she was trying to be careful, walking a line somewhere between "I'm just curious" and "You have to answer these questions or there will be consequences."

"I just don't understand why you are here," the young man said.

Danielle tried again. "The aupoin are deeply worried. They had been told all those chemicals had been eliminated—"

Her Krufrugaan colleague gestured, and she took two steps back.

He whispered, "Spacer ships approach Sem. Have you a suggested action?"

"Huh. Watch." Danielle said. "Unless they enter the atmosphere or—"

"They have done so." He was listening, hard, to someone else. "Something—they emit a cloud of—"

"Eject," Danielle said. "As far away as possible. Now. Do not allow whatever they fire or spew to touch the surface." She wondered at her gut instinct to protect the semqu against spacers, especially while back among her own people.

But she understood much she had not before. This new spacer culture, as it had evolved, had more in common with semqu culture than Earth's. Both were cooperative cultures that succeeded by aiding each other and their neighbors.

She had been the anomaly.

And should an attack on Sem be successful, spacers would be crammed into an obsolete generation ship and fired into the cosmos to die.

This was an act of war. She suspected she knew who was behind it.

The guild. Marfa. She clenched her teeth, fought vomit. She'd heard about Nata, and she'd feared Marfa's reaction. Danielle knew, to her nauseated core, that she was responsible for setting that once-curious girl on this path.

And there was no time to grieve, not for Marfa, not for herself, and not for Se System.

Ireti had just died. Was that connected? Of course it was.

"We need to get back to the *Catara*."

"She is busy. We need to finish here."

She is busy? She wasn't being given all the information. Danielle accepted that. She understood Krufrugaen operating procedures.

But if Gtec was not already dead, she was going after him herself when this was over.

She stepped forward again, said sharply, "This spill was not an accident. This is now a criminal investigation. I'll ask you again. Who had access to your agricultural chemicals?"

TWENTY-ONE

HUMAN VENGEANCE

PLANET SEM
SEMQU YEAR 1190
NEW HOPIAN YEAR 764

The spacer ships started falling toward Sem's surface. They spewed mist into our atmosphere. It was a reflex action to shove all of it away, strengthened by a spacer's warning, and that saved us.

Then distressed Voices reached out, alarmed their blinkships were under attack. Modeel and spacers, acting in concert to assault us. Two blinkships turned against our own.

Rage flashed through us, and not a little fear. But we did not understand, so we bought ourselves time; time to calm down, time to question those who might explain. Most of the attackers had been fitted with spacer engines, and the besieged blinkships were alone, so the effort exhausted Sem.

They had dropped the same poison that had been used on Ireti, and the experience and learning how to live while poisoned that Ireti had gained aided us a great deal. We would need the time to recover. The aupoin would need time to clean up what we had missed.

Yet we succeeded. We flung them away. Far enough it would take them many weeks to return to any planet. We had not intended for two of the ships to end up in an asteroid belt, nor for one to run out of air. Nor did we expect those ships' inhabitants to choose death rather than call for help. We were disturbed to discover all the crew aboard the rogue blinkships dead, the ship-semqu poisoned.

We regret that loss of life for many reasons.

Among them: we had many questions. We wanted answers. Who? Why?

The assault, for that is what it was, was over in fast-time. Some of our children would come to call it the Ninety-Second War, a name we detest.

Processing its causes and fallout properly will take us eons.

That was not time we could afford to take.

Spacers had not acted alone. If they had, we would have simply ejected our galactic newcomers and forbidden their return. No, they had involved modeel and aupoin. It shook us to our basal filaments.

What had we gotten wrong? Had we introduced wrong thinking into our midst? Should we eject the spacers after all?

Yet it was spacers who had warned us about the poison, who had told us what had killed Ireti, so we could recognize the threat. Without them, we would all be dead.

And our modeel know us much, much better than spacers. They alone, save our Voices, knew the location of Sem.

A rogue modeel might have corrupted our new children. Or the missing aupoin, who we now believe to be tainted since birth by this new gtorin threat. This upset us even more, but we know this only because of spacer assistance.

And we still seek our missing child. Had they been stolen? Murdered?

We called for a meeting of the minds. We needed to protect ourselves and our Voices. Something, or someone, had turned some of our children against us.

VARIOUS LOCATIONS
SEMQU YEAR 1190
NEW HOPIAN YEAR 764

IN THE DAYS following the attack on Sem, Danielle didn't sleep much. She swore a lot, learned a lot, taught a lot, and swore more. There was investigative work to do; an interview with Marfa, if she had survived, topped her list. The blinkships were unavailable for weeks, which drove her and her colleagues (and apparently traders across Se System) to distraction, but there were also defensive skills to teach and learn.

Prep for a future assault felt as familiar as an old sweater. The fact that none of her compatriots shared that familiarity—even her boss was deeply distressed, and showed it in increasingly unprofessional ways—left her both unsettled and steeled.

She was built for this. She had survived for this.

And you may well have catalyzed it. She kept moving by dint of her training and force of will, but there were moments when grief and guilt threatened to eat her alive.

ABOARD NEW HOPE
VOICE'S DWELL
SEMQU YEAR 1190
NEW HOPIAN YEAR 764

VOICE STAYED cloistered in her dwell for the better part of three weeks.

Terri had messaged three times while Ireti was dying, offering to bring soothing food, transport her laundry, and then wanting to talk about a problem she was having.

Adamantine also messaged that day, complaining about a sudden exodus of visiting diplomats "in the middle of a banquet, if you please," and asking if Voice knew anything about it. A second message a week later added that she'd heard Voice was ill and hoped she was feeling better.

Once he heard she was sick, Gregoire messaged daily, suggesting she see a medic.

Voice sent them all the same response: "Miserable but recovering. I'll be fine."

She was not fine.

She'd feared the return of panic attacks and social anxiety, which did not happen. She was unprepared for the onslaught of grief. Over the past five decades she'd lost friendships, her calligraphy mentors, both her parents, Gregoire's daily companionship, Bonaparte's love, several friends and other mentors, and now her telepathic partner.

Experiencing life through Ireti's filters, she'd had no heights of joy that could outweigh those crushing losses, and now no companion to help buffer her from them or talk her through processing them all at once.

She was no longer Voice to Spacers, constantly paired with a semqu, but simply Opal. Opal no longer knew how to be alone, nor how to talk to her fellow spacers. She stammered through her brief interactions with the kitchen crew who brought her meals twice a day and picked up her used plates. She finally faked a fever and resorted to sign.

It both helped and hurt that a flu-like virus hit the ship about the same time, and many isolated to help prevent its spread. During the third week of Voice's grief, the cafeteria crew borrowed a harvester robot from the fields to help with the extra food deliveries.

On the fifteenth day after Ireti died, Voice answered her door, braced to sign to another spacer. Outside floated a robot that looked exactly like the one that had carried her from the rice fields to the med clinic nearly five decades before. She fell to her knees, sobbing in rage and pain. <How dare you leave me!>

She caught her breath, stunned. *What was that? I'm angry at Ireti? That makes no sense!* She took a deep breath as another thought struck her. *No. Because someone onboard might be responsible, which does.* She glanced right and left. There was no one in the hall.

The robot swayed in front of her, beeping softly. She used it to pull herself to her feet, picked up her bagged meal, and patted the robot.

"Thank you." The words sounded a little strangled. She was grateful no one lived on this end of the hall now but her. No one had seen her lose control. She went inside, sat down, and stared at the walls. Hours later, when she roused herself enough to eat, she had enough wit to acknowledge that food helped.

She could not stay on *New Hope* in this condition. Ireti had gone, but they had joined all of semqu. Maybe if she was a Voice elsewhere, she could reconnect with a trace of them. That was what they had hoped for, as well. She wasn't ready yet, but when asked, she would travel.

One decision made.

She packed. On the eighteenth day, she was reading a book on Earth history, learning about an ancient tradition of trading children to learn about one's allies and enemies and to help keep peace. It appalled but also intrigued her. Would the wary occupants of Se Collective get along better if they were exposed to one another as children?

She heard running water. She looked up just as Y-uu-see landed in her living room.

"Welcome!" Voice said.

"We need you, Voice of the Spacers." Y-uu-see seemed deeply agitated. "Are you whole enough to travel?"

"I still grieve," Voice said, "But if Semqu-that-holds-Ireti needs me, I will go."

Mere hours later, trembling, her one coherent thought was that grief and rage, when they lack a soothing filter, can fill a spacer's body until it feels like it will explode.

**ADMINISTRATIVE OFFICES
FUARINGSPLENZU, PLANET TRYE
SEMQU YEAR 1190
NEW HOPIAN YEAR 764**

PRIME MINISTER XIMENA BOBBIE closed her eyes and leaned back in her chair. The councilors' yelled arguments washed over her. It was summer; the windows were open, and a fresh breeze flowed through, sadly not dampening the noise at all.

Transition and Trade, her summary for the incredibly convoluted projects of moving to Trye while simultaneously interacting with alien cultures, had been going well. She had dared to dream her last term of office would be calm and productive.

She should have known better.

The modeel who had abandoned their banquet two weeks ago had sent messages early this morning, officially accusing spacers of assaulting blinkships and poisoning their crews. Councilor Ulick's son and daughter-in-law were among those accused. Ulick was livid about the slander. The full council meeting had now gone in useless circles for hours. They were wasting their time; they had no information.

When the accusations came in, Ximena's staff tried to hail the implicated ships. None had replied until yesterday, when there had been a mayday call from Bonaparte's ship. It arrived from well beyond the reach of any existing spacer ships, so the captain who'd received it had forwarded the message to a visiting blink, asking if they could check it out.

Nothing.

Ulick insisted it had to be a skip, a misdirected message, because it was far from Byne, where the couple was on holiday. She glanced at him. He was calm, trying to mediate between two arguing colleagues. He seemed unwilling to consider Bonaparte might be in danger.

Years ago, Ximena had told Ulick that his rosy-glasses way of looking at life was going to bite him hard someday. She sighed and hoped that lesson would not come today, would not involve his son.

She was too old for this. And yet she was glad she'd not retired yet. Whatever fallout this situation had, it should stick to her legacy, not Ulick's. She wanted him to be successful. The community needed him to be.

"And we can't ask Voice what the semqu say about this because she's missing? That's convenient," one of the councilors snapped.

Ximena grit her teeth. Three days ago, she had left a message with her friends aboard *New Hope*, saying, "the semqu call," then leaving on a visiting blink. She had also messaged Ximena, but the staffer who intercepted it didn't think it important enough to pass on.

"She's practically retired," he'd said defensively.

Ximena couldn't yell at him; he was right. She hadn't even checked in on Voice during her recent illness, a thought that buffeted her with shame. She cared deeply for the woman but had let their relationship lapse as Ulick filled her translation role.

A rattling, metallic rustle filled the room, and the argument faltered. Ximena opened her eyes. Voice, her hair streaked with grey, had appeared at the entrance to the meeting room. She was flanked by two silent modeel with motionless smoky biofields.

"What have you done?!" Voice cried out and burst into tears.

Ximena had worked with Voice for forty years and had never seen such a show of emotion. It shocked her and Ulick into silence, but not the others.

"Voice! Where have you been?"

"What's going on?"

"What's the meaning of this?"

"Enough! Give her a moment," Ximena snapped. "Let our Voice speak."

The questions appeared to anger Voice. She pulled herself upright, and with tears still on her cheeks, said authoritatively, "These modeel are Krufrugaan." She paused, giving every spacer a hard look. "They are, in spacer terms, police, judge, jury, and executioner. Lie to them at your own peril. Please use hand gestures to tell me if you understand."

The councilors exchanged glances with each other and Ximena, and gestured assent.

Voice continued, "They are here to investigate the attack on semqu and on blinks across Se Collective. They will determine whether we spacers will be allowed to remain on Trye or if we are all to be exiled."

"Exiled?" Ximena repeated, bewildered. "What has happened, Voice? We know nothing of any attack on the semqu." *The entire community could be exiled?* Nausea hit. She kept talking, mostly to the modeel, "We remain grateful for semqu assistance. We would not attack anyone, especially not them."

One of the modeel said, "A week ago, a dozen spacer ships attacked blinkships across Se Collective."

"We received accusations of our ships attacking three blink-ships," Ulick said. "We were given an identification of three of the ships, but we have been unable to find them or to question their owners or crew. One of those accused was crewed by my son and daughter-in-law, who are on vacation on Byne. To be honest, I'm having trouble believing this is anything other than a horrible miscommunication. Do you have more information—"

The modeel continued as if Ulick had not spoken. "The attack was spacer-led, using spacer-developed chemicals. The semqu who convinced the modeel to bring you into Se System was also irrevocably attacked, with similar chemicals. Ireti is dead."

Voice added, in a vicious, cutting tone, "I have requested to be allowed to personally execute the *human* responsible."

Ximena stared at her, shocked. "Voice?"

"You heard me. Ireti was murdered by some wretched, ungrateful, paranoid human. These Krufrugaan wish to speak with a number of people, starting with Marfa Grandi and Rupert Keo. Bring them here. Now."

That fucking guild. I should have iced them all years ago. If they hadn't involved Rupert and Danielle...

Ximena sent for the couple. The room remained tensely silent, with a furious, pacing Voice warding off any further questions from the bewildered councilors with a single gesture: "Wait."

Marfa arrived first. She took one look at Voice and tried to leave.

One of the modeel rolled between her and the door. With some difficulty, Ximena and Ulick convinced Marfa to sit.

The modeel in front of her rattled, and Voice repeated her warning about who they were, and the dangers of lying to a Krufrugaan.

Then the modeel spoke in Fugrast. "Marfa Grandi. You stand accused of conspiracy to attack fellow residents of Se Collective to cause their death and destruction. You stand accused of attempting the murder of all semqu. Your acts have resulted in the injury and deaths of dozens—"

"Good! They should all die!" Marfa screamed. "They killed my daughter!"

"You admit this?"

"I am proud of it."

"And your husband?"

"Rupert is a useless coward. He should have gone with them, been with them."

"You mean your niece and her husband—to be clear, Anika Keo and Bonaparte Pangea— and their crew?"

"Yes."

Ulick made a strangled noise and rose to his feet.

Voice said, "Ulick, I'm sorry, but sit down. Listen. Just listen."

Ulick sank back down, fists clenched.

"If your daughter Nata had meant so much to you, Marfa Grandi," the second modeel asked, "Why didn't you go yourself, rather than also risk losing your niece?"

Her cheeks darkened. "I wanted to go! Bonaparte said there wasn't room. Said if they failed, I needed to take the next steps."

"What next steps?"

Marfa smiled. "Did they fail?"

"Do you have any additional plans?"

"None I'd tell you."

"What have you done to my son?" Ulick demanded.

"Made a hero of him." Marfa's face radiated joy as she looked directly at Ulick. "One of their crew broadcast a mayday yesterday."

"Yes," the modeel said. "We found the ship. Too late, unfortunately. Their hull was punctured; they ran out of air yesterday."

"You shoved them into an asteroid belt," Marfa said bitterly. Then she smiled, malicious. "But not before they poisoned those evil bastards."

"Bonaparte... is dead?" Ulick slumped in his chair.

The modeel said, "Bonaparte Pangea is dead, as is Anika. You did not know your own son was part of this?"

"I had no idea!" Ulick choked out. "This—cannot be true! It runs counter to everything we taught him! Bonaparte told me they were going on an anniversary trip to Byne, would combine it with business, to maybe look for transport contracts there. He wouldn't have lied to us. We're taking care of their kids, the grandchildren. We expect them back tomorrow."

"I am truly sorry, Ulick," Voice said. "They are both dead."

"Both of them martyrs for freedom," Marfa said, eyes glowing, filling with tears. "I'm so proud—"

"Shut up!" Ulick snarled at her. "You lying, scheming, murderous *human*."

She settled back in her chair, watching him with a tight, malicious smile. "How does it feel to lose a child, Ulick?"

He stared at her.

Ximena said, "Marfa, why would you risk the settlement here, risk all of our lives—"

"That means nothing to me! If you had children you would understand," Marfa snarled.

Both modeel moved closer to Marfa. "This is not about your daughter," they said. "Nata died alone and without saying goodbye because you and your husband convinced her she was worthless."

"That's not true!" Marfa yelled.

"Those were her final words. It is clear she was correct. You used others' offspring in a failed effort to destroy the semqu."

"But conveniently, you did not risk your own life," Voice added. You are a hate-filled coward."

Marfa trembled, gripping the chair's edges, but did not reply.

"You tried to destroy much of what makes Se System what it is, because you fear what you refuse to understand," Voice added.

"I want to live free of the semqu," Marfa said.

The modeel said, "This opportunity will be provided to you."

Prime Minister Ximena stirred. "This is our citizen," she said heavily, "so our laws and punishments—"

"Are irrelevant," the second modeel said. "This crime was not only against you spacers, not only against the semqu, but against all in Se Collective."

"What crime, exactly?" Marfa asked, sarcastically.

"War. You introduced war into a peaceful solar system. You are guilty and unrepentant. Were you modeel, you would be mind-wiped, erased, your memory expunged from all records including that of your family, and then executed. As you are spacer, your punishment is expulsion. You will be taken to the planet you spacers were originally headed toward."

"That's giving her what she wants," Ulick said, bewildered.

"And a death sentence," Ximena said.

The modeel did not argue; one lifted a hand and gestured, "Truth."

Marfa lifted her chin. "I will die a martyr to freedom," she said.

"Murderer, not martyr," Voice said bitterly. "You will be forgotten on your lonely journey to oblivion." She glanced at Ximena, gestured, "Erasure for unforgiveable."

They'd worked together, and with the modeel, for years. Ximena understood. The Prime Minister closed her eyes briefly, then said, "Marfa Grandi. Your acts are a sad holdover to pre-spacer, human thinking. You are a criminal, your acts remembered only as a warning. Our history will reflect that."

Marfa lunged to her feet toward Voice, hand raised to strike.

She disappeared from the room.

TWENTY-TWO

SURVIVORS

KEO RESEARCH OFFICES
FUARINGSPLENZU, PLANET TRYE
SEMQU YEAR 1190
NEW HOPIAN YEAR 764

Rupert was in the middle of a video conversation with a colleague doing research on Aun when Prime Minister Ximena's flunky arrived and tried to manhandle him, telling him coldly that Ximena needed to see him. Rupert's fine-tuned trouble detector went off; Marfa must have succeeded at doing something awful. He needed time to come up with a good defense.

"I'm in the middle of a meeting," Rupert said. "Come back in two hours."

"We can talk later," his stupidly cooperative colleague said.

"You will come with me now," the upstart asshole said. "I will call security if I have to."

"Rupert! What have you done? Now all I'm curious! Call me back when you find out what's up!" And the jerk broke the connection.

As usual, Enzo was someplace else, so he couldn't waste time giving him instructions. Rupert delayed, fussing with some details on his computer, but the flunky threatened to pull the power for the entire lab. "I'm serious. Now."

Rupert's fury flared. "You insolent twerp. Yes, let's go, I'll report you to your boss, and you'll be busted down to cleaning toilets, you—"

"I clean toilets regularly, as does anyone with any community spirit. Useful work is not degrading," was the prim reply.

He'd use the walk to come up with a good defense. Rupert stalked out of his office to discover the flunky had a people-mover waiting. The man talked at him the entire trip. Far too soon, Rupert entered the governmental offices without a single coherent plan. The staff had the shell-shocked look of people who'd seen a dead body. They stared at him as he came in. Not good.

He followed the flunky into a crowded meeting room. He was relieved to find Marfa wasn't present and incensed that Ulick was. *Ulick still hasn't paid for Nata's death.* He pretended to ignore two massive modeel, but he did notice they had turned their emotive fields off. That rarely meant anything good. His stomach churned.

He tried to gain the upper hand by starting first. "Your flunky here—"

"Rupert," Ximena interrupted him. Him, her most celebrated astrophysicist! "These Krufrugaan need to talk to you about Marfa and that blasted guild of yours."

Krufrugaan? Shit. "What?" Defensive anger came naturally. "Marfa is her own woman! Talk to her, not me. Which guild?"

One of the modeel said, "The 'Spacer Protection Guild,' which you were a member of with Marfa Grandi, Anika Keo and Danielle Braun for decades. The guild that recently attacked the semqu."

Rupert's breakfast lurched toward his throat. He swallowed hard, kept his anger flowing. "This is bullshit," he snarled. "I'm not interested in evidence-free nonsense, I'm going back to my work." He turned and came face to face with Voice.

"You don't have that option." Her hair was greying, but she stood ramrod straight, livid. She had never sounded so much like Adamantine. "You will answer their questions honestly. Lying to a Krufrugaan is deeply unwise. Your wife has already been sentenced to a slow, solitary death."

Her fury underscored the depths of the trouble he was in and told him they'd succeeded in killing her semqu. He hadn't bothered worrying that she might be angry about that. More importantly, it had never occurred to him that she might continue to have powerful friends after it was dead.

Her advice he ignored. Telling the truth at this point would be a death sentence. He would have to give the best performance of his life and hope no one had betrayed him.

"Death?" he repeated.

A modeel asked, "Rupert Keo, what do you know of the chemical warfare against the semqu?"

"What chemical warfare?" Rupert asked. "And why would I attack the creatures who've given me the best career an astrophysicist could desire?"

The questions started coming fast and thick, but Rupert had a lifetime of practice at lying. Not having a solid plan worked in his favor, for once. He didn't have to work at acting shocked, which was useful here. He didn't have to act too hard to be broken-hearted at the ridiculous loss of life—his niece and her husband, gone, and most of the Guild with her. Marfa, in exile.

She'd wasted years of manipulation, and his real grief about that made it easier to cover his relief at learning that everyone who could accuse him was dead. Only Marfa was alive to renounce him —well, and Danielle, presumably. He spoke as little as possible, listened hard.

He didn't deny his involvement in the Guild during the early days; they knew about that. He told them that he'd dropped out after Nata's death, and basically, he had. Marfa had kept him current up until the last six months, a detail he kept to himself; but she had not told him anything about this attack, and that helped a great deal with his ability to act shocked and dismayed.

Ulick gave him a nice gift with a blade in it. The asshole spoke in Rupert's defense, saying his own wife had called him useless and a coward.

Finally, the questions ended. The Krufrugaan conferred and then declared Rupert guilty of risking the lives of others and conspiring to ascertain how modeel blinkdrives work.

He desperately wanted their emotional biofields on, to know if they were begrudgingly settling for that or satisfied with it.

They sentenced him to teaching blinkship safety classes for five years, and revoked his right to travel on any blinkship, a punishment he considered vastly excessive. He would have done better with a spacer jury, but it was clear that wasn't an option here. Given the possibility that he could have lost his head—literally, Voice was that angry; he was impressed—he decided not to complain.

"We will keep an eye on you," the Krufrugaan declared. "Our investigation continues. If you remember anything useful, it would be wise to come to us first."

He caught Voice's venomous glare as he left.

Walking out, still being pointed at and whispered about by the staff, Rupert acknowledged just how lucky he'd been that the Guild's *New Hope* contact had decided to go on the offensive with Bonaparte's crew.

It was rumored the Krufrugaan followed investigations for centuries if necessary; invading minds for an answer was not off the table. Marfa was still alive. They might question her again. It was entirely possible they would find out that he'd been involved in the first fungicide attack on the semqu aboard *New Hope*.

It was past time he did some professional research and outreach off planet. He'd heard interesting things about the various city-states on Byne. He needed a new plan, and new friends, and quickly. But doing anything now would raise suspicions. He needed to lie low, to pretend to be chastised, to recommit to the Accord.

And it wasn't like he could get to Byne quickly, now. Gtec might be able to help him, but... spacer transport to Byne was slow.

He could start with a new research office here on Trye. Make it look like he was planning long-term. More space would give him some necessary privacy.

VASOM: KRUFRUGAAN HEADQUARTERS
SEMQU YEAR 1190
NEW HOPIAN YEAR 764

DANIELLE'S JOINTS ached almost as much as her heart. The supervisor giving the report was one of the two modeel who'd sentenced Marfa and Rupert; the other was someone she'd never met. They both reported during a small group meeting Danielle had mentally started calling the briefing room.

"Spacer, what do you think of the sentences passed?" asked the second modeel. He reminded her uncomfortably of Gtec.

The room silenced.

Thanks for putting me on the spot, buddy. "Marfa and Rupert are both old friends, which is why I refused the assignment. I knew them both as children and worried that might warp my judgment." *That and guilt, and culpability.* Danielle paused. "Marfa's sentence was clear water," a local expression that meant many things at once: clarity, unquestioned; easily discerned. "I agree with Rupert's punishment, but I do not trust him. I think that he should be watched. Can we keep an eye on him?"

"Of course," he said, his aura briefly interrupted with a curl of pleasure that surprised her.

She watched him closely, looking for tells and checking them against her mental list. *It can't be...* No one else gave any indication anything was amiss. *Are they all in on this?*

After the briefing was over, Danielle approached him. "Colleague, you are one of our newer graduates, yes? I do not think we have met. What is your name?" She was rewarded with a colorful mélange in his aura: surprise, grudging admiration, amusement.

His words were quite straightforward for such mixed emotions. "I am known as Stuotok. Can I buy you a ferment? I should like to get to know our spacer Krufrugaan."

"Certainly," Danielle said. "There's a bar where I like to go when I want some privacy." *Hiding in plain sight, are you, Gtec? Or have so many collaborators that you're flaunting your corruption now?*

I'm going to kill you.

ADAMANTINE AND ULICK'S DWELL
SEMQU YEAR 1190
NEW HOPIAN YEAR 764

"HOW COULD SHE LEAVE?" Adamantine paced and wrung her hands. "We have three grandchildren to raise!"

"There was an ill Voice, she was needed to help—"

"I need her here!" Her words rang off their walls.

"Let's not wake them." Ulick glanced over his shoulder, dropped his volume. "I think it was right for her to go. You didn't see her, love. She was in a rage, furious about Ireti's murder."

"I don't care. I will never forgive them for taking her away again." She spit the words, but more quietly, pacing away.

"Did you think you'd get her back when Ireti died?"

She stopped, swaying. Back to him, she asked, "Do you think I was involved with that?"

His voice was even. "I think they'll be watching you because you're Rupert's friend."

"That's not what I asked."

He took a breath, exhaled. "No."

"But neither of us thought Bonaparte was capable of… that." She hugged herself tightly, words vibrating.

He squeezed his eyes shut, hard, forced them back open. "No."

"I didn't." She turned to face him. "Ulick, I didn't."

His shoulders dropped. "Good. I'd hate to have to raise those three alone."

She crumpled, facade cracking, and he stumbled toward her. "Oh, shit, I'm sorry. Come here." He wrapped his arms around her. "We'll make it through this somehow. Together."

SPACER DERELICT
SEMQU YEAR 1190
NEW HOPIAN YEAR 764

DANIELLE BECAME CONSCIOUS SLOWLY, groggily. *Wrong.* Her shoulders ached and she couldn't move, but she was upright. She lifted her eyelids as little as possible. Her thighs and ankles were bound tightly to a chair in a dim space, freezing cold and stuffy. Gtec—the real Gtec, not Stuotok, she had been mistaken after all, Ol' Chucky would have her ass, and so would Waatoos— left dust tracks on the floor as he wheeled back and forth in front of her. His biofield whirled with the colors of a thunderstorm at sunset.

He'd tied her so tightly that she found it hard to breathe. She had no feeling in her hands. Hopefully he hadn't cut all the blood supply to them. How long had seen been out?

There was ruptured and torn metal everywhere. She'd have to move the chair to reach any to cut herself free. As she shifted her eyes to find something nearby, a wisp of her hair floated across her vision.

Oh fuck. There was no artificial gravity here. The only light source was Gtec's aura.

Her hope of escape withered. She took a harder look at the debris around them. They were on one of the spacer ships destroyed by the Ninety-Second War. Even if she got free, all he had to do to kill her was rupture the air bubble. How had he gotten them aboard?

Doesn't matter. I wasn't careful enough, Danielle thought. She reached with her tongue, toggled the device in her mouth, and then licked her lips, which felt cracked. She'd been here awhile. Assuming the ship was still where it had been flung, she was too far away for the device to trigger any rescue, but at least someone would find her body; someone would be able to pick up the recording she was broadcasting.

One of her contingency plans was that any such broadcast would be on a wavelength that modeel did not use. She was about to find out if Gtec had corrupted anyone on her team.

How had the bastard hidden for so long? Or was this wreck the answer?

The cold was piercing. She shivered; that finally got his attention.

"You're awake," Gtec said.

"Is Stuotok your brother, or your dad?"

"Tell me how you figured out I was still alive."

"Fuck off," Danielle said.

"I will let you die here if you do not tell me. I understand suffocation is—"

"They'll know you kidnapped me to this wrecked Spacer ship and killed me here, Gtec," Danielle said. Mostly to get it all on the record. He clearly hadn't noticed the broadcast yet.

Gtec paused, briefly, a spike of pure red shock flying through his aura before he stilled it to grey.

Shit. Had she just given him the warning he needed to scan for transmissions? "And you're too much of a coward to kill me with your emotions showing. Although I don't know why you're wasting your time on me. You must be outrageously wealthy now; the gtorin trade is—"

"Shut up."

She laughed. "Seriously? What motivation do I have to shut up? You plan on killing me twice?"

"I could kill all your people. You Spacers." Anger pulsed vividly through the grey; pride had forced him to toggle his aura back on. He rolled away from her, probably trying to control his temper.

"You're planning on doing that anyway. That was your whole goal, after the source of gtorin—or maybe before. Well, and the massacre of all semqu."

He disappeared behind an opaque black field for a second, and then the white of pure fear-driven hatred flashed through it.

She'd seen through all his plans. Deception, hiding was his highest calling, then. Interesting. And an insight far too late.

He wheeled toward her. One of his arms switched to a blade.

"You're far more human than you think, Gtec," she said, conversationally, as his arm arced toward her throat. "We also kill while enraged." *Not the most profound final words*, she thought, *but they'll do.*

Gtec's arm stopped. The metal blade vibrated against her throat. A trickle of heat ran down her collarbone.

"I have a better death in mind for you," he said. Bubbles erupted around him: joy's blue corrupted with malice. "You, who feared and yet always wanted to know the semqu. We will introduce you to Tkzotch."

ACKNOWLEDGMENTS

I HAVE SO MUCH GRATITUDE.

To my amazing and supportive writing partners Larina Warnock and Po Popelka, who have read more of my work than anyone on the planet. Thank you. Thank you. Thank you. I learned so much from you two and your support has meant the world to me.

Thank you to my fellow Wordos, who read various snippets of work from this universe and dozens of the short stories I wrote to stay sane in the process, and never failed to give me useful feedback.

To Nina Kiriki Hoffman and Eric Witchey, whose different teaching styles and methods both worked to spark my creativity and somewhere in there helped me believe I was a writer; and to all the many, many, many other writing teachers I met along the way: Cat Rambo, Holly Lisle, Nisi Shawl, K. Tempest Bradford, and Fonda Lee, to name a few.

To the muse who got me back into writing, Barbara Brugger, and her engineer-artist hubby Michael Brugger, who introduced me to the world of science fiction cons and created this tome's stunning cover. You've both been inspirations and rocks in my life, each in your own way, and I do not have enough words to express my gratitude to you. And Michael, this wraparound cover ROCKS.

Gratitude also to my fantastic editor KB Spangler, whose reassurance and guidance and feedback has been invaluable; this book literally would not exist without her, because I had no intention of writing it. I'd sent her what is currently book three and she needed to see book one to edit it. (She's working on three as I type this in 2025.)

Also profuse thanks to Erika Milo and Jen Matteis, whose proofreading efforts caught my crappy comprehension of comma use, taught me the difference between prophesy and prophecy (and breach and breech), and let me know I had forgotten everything I had ever learned about laid and lain. Among many other errors, like sentence fragments. Which I don't always fix.

Thanks also to the organizations whose classes and workshops have helped me out in various ways: SFWA's classes and Discord channels (shoutout to the Indie group there), Clarion's one-day workshops, Wordcrafters's offerings, and Willamette Writers, PNWA, and the IBPA. To podcasters Mur Lafferty (I Should Be Writing) and the crew at Writing Excuses, who kept me focused on craft. Thanks to Eugene Bacon for her SWFA-fundraiser feedback and that last, offhand question that haunted me for months and ended up making the book stronger.

Massive thanks to generous and helpful sensitivity readers. Any mistakes in representation that remain in the manuscript are mine.

Huge thanks to Jordan Walker, who took my inarticulate descriptions and brought my alien creatures to life visually and painted the next book's fantastic cover art: Thank you so much. I'm still squeeing.

I know I'm missing people. If you had a hand in helping me in any way, please know I am deeply thankful for your support.

To Mom and Dad and Aunt Sue: I finally did it! Wish you were still here to see it. I know it's not the kind of book any of you read, but I still would have loved to give you a copy. Miss you. Thanks for giving me a love of reading and learning.

A deep bow to all the science fiction writers, living and dead, whose work I love, and who instilled a love of the genre and a careful hope for our future. And finally a massive shoutout to those who buy the work of women science fiction writers and promote it. You readers rock. Thank you.

Last but definitely not least: my partner Mark Bryant, who has the unenviable task of living with me when I am creating and when I am not (and I'm not sure which is worse). Thank you for being supportive even when you didn't understand. It mattered more than you know. And thank you for suggesting I take a break from writing detective fiction to try fantasy and science fiction. I like it.

SAMPLE PAGES FROM THWARTED
COMING IN 2026

EXCERPT

A SQUAT BLINKSHIP APPEARS in Fuaringsplenzu's spaceport, shaped as most are like a massive, side-lying ammonite. Its outer, overlapping scales creak and snap with temperature adjustments.

Shortly thereafter a short, rotund spacer strolls down its ramp. On Earth she might have been called farm-built or dowdy, a Caucasian with brown hair heavily streaked with white. She is calm and at ease in her own skin, her garb the old generation ship's loose extruded trousers and tunic, unadorned. When she reaches Trye's soil she turns and bows to the ship, empty hands clasped over her chest.

There is no one waiting. She had not warned anyone in Fuar of her arrival. Her brother-in-law, Prime Minister Ulick, would likely have wanted some unnecessary welcoming rite. She will tell him later, let him have his ceremony honoring spacers' translator to the semqu, after she has settled in. They have lived without her for five years; they can survive a few more days.

In truth, she's not yet a Voice again. The less they know about that, the better.

Unrecognized, she takes public transport to one of the wastewater gardens on the landward side of the city. She wanders, slowly, because she is now in her late sixties and because it has been some time since she has seen so many flowers, so many plants. The scents in the humid marine breeze, after such a long period of recycled ship air, make her sneeze. She is fully delighted. She revels in the freedom to feel that joy.

Gravity here is stronger than on the ship she has served on for the past five years; the safe space where she could grieve the loss of Ireti, her first semqu companion, while a second checked in on her from time to time, reminded her of what it is to be a Voice and why she chose that life, gave her small assignments. And firmly steered her from thoughts of vengeance.

Ireti was murdered. Voice does not believe all of those involved are dead or punished. Her need for justice for Ireti slowed her recovery.

Semqu, more comfortable with ambiguity and the unknown, quietly continue to seek collaborators. They are ancient; they have experienced betrayal before. They are more patient than she will ever be.

Across a bridge she helped design decades prior, Voice comes to a hillside thick with ferns, shrubs and succulent lopa trees. She stops next to a cave entrance, flanked with wide low benches. She rests there. After a bit, she hears a conversation that sounds like running water.

Three bristly aupoin—visually, a cross between tardigrades and larvae, but dog to grizzly-sized, an Earthborn would say—emerge and greet her in Fugrast, the common tongue. She inhales a mix of herbs, fresh mushrooms and fertile earth and knows she is among friends. She follows them inside and down into the dark.

In the comforting dark below and back beneath the rising hillside, other aupoin braid rootlets and fungal filaments into complicated, fantastic patterns on the ceiling and walls of their warren of tunnels. They weave steadily and quickly. The new infant has quickened, and the entire hive is taking shifts to help her grow.

They grieved long when the previous child did not survive, so they coddle and cajole and nurture this one, even if some question the decision to have its telepathic mentor and translator be not-aupoin. It is the way of semqu, to have surface translators, but up until now, Trye has only had aupoin Voices. Some of the older residents mourn, the younger ones worry. Who will answer their questions?

But they welcome the little spacer when she arrives in their midst, provide her with soft mosses to lie on. They tend to her as she connects to the child and for a time after. They do not celebrate when she leaves, taking her connection with her to the surface, though she tells them to contact her if they have any concerns, any needs. They comfort one another and keep weaving the young one's mind.

The *Ichyado*, a modeel blinkship, rests on Taequa soil near the city of Zissokot. The modeel staff are making some nonsense trade or other while they wait for the spacer they are to transport to Trye.

The ship's phren Voice attends to what he considers the real business; his ship's Semqu chats with She who is Taequai. The planetary Semqu is younger than Iyam, but brash, much like her apeqe Voice, who lives in the central Temple and leads their religion.

The atheist phren does not think much of peqe worship of semqu, although he is forced to admit that posing as a Goddess provides useful obfuscation from such a power-hungry people.

He is further irritated by today's conversation topic: Trye's infant and its future.

His anger flares when he hears Taequai's suggestion: a peqe

rite which will temporarily allow the child to connect to a Temple Acolyte. Taequa1 has recently re-experienced this ceremony and thinks it will help the infant explore her control. *Oh, doubtless.*

Ichyado flattens his ire. The phren reminds Ichyado that this rite will also allow the apeqe to claim a small part of Trye. The Temple has tried to establish such a compound on the phren's planet of Iyam for generations, and he remains adamantly opposed. Sadly, it is not his choice.

They are here to inform Taequa1 that the other semqu have agreed. But not right away. The infant is too young, the connection to its spacer Voice not yet fully established.

The phren's emotions threaten to overwhelm him again. He is an old phren and his prejudices and opinions run deep. To have a spacer, of all beings, selected as Trye10's Voice incenses him, though he is rarely allowed such strong feeling. Why should his One-Thing be polluted by such an outsider? He is a rare phren who finds sympathy for the judgmental modeel, who are seldom chosen as Voices and find insult in that lack.

It is an old argument to the semqu, who do not wish to admit difficulty connecting to marine life and find such bias between their Voices either humorous or incomprehensible. Focused on their discussion, they pretend to not notice.

<Semqu Year 1200, no later,> Taequa1 insists.

Years are a mammalian time device, not a semqu one, so the suggestion gives Ichyado pause.

<Seven years,> the phren says.

<Yes, thank you.> Ichyado promises to convey Taequa1's message to the others.

<Good. The Temple will prepare.>

Alone in his room later, the phren grumbles aloud about both decisions, unaware that a modeel is listening.

Unhappy Voices are unusual, and such *useful* sources of information.

Closer to the spacers' planet of Trye, an aging blinkship purchased by a modeel sect some years prior hangs in the atmosphere above a rocky, lifeless but mineral-rich planet. The aging semqu who pilots the ship and her equally aged Voice have been told the sect holds meditation retreats and will travel to various isolated places for months at a time. This is agreeable to the semqu and her Voice; all they wish to do is commune together until one of them dies. She has been contaminated by gtorin and can never contact her fellow semqu again, and her grief has stunted her curiosity.

This suits the modeel who use the ship. Almost as if it were planned.

The "meditation suite" is private, guarded by two layers of modeel guards. It is in fact a prison, housing a stolen semqu child, a kidnapped aupoin and an Earthborn.

Danielle Braun's locator tech was ripped from her mouth without much finesse—she lost several teeth in the process—and these modeel do not fully understand human dietary requirements. There will be no rescue. But she survives on sheer spite and the hopes of turning this powerful child against its captors.

But if this rogue semqu gets access to her mind, she needs to kill it or herself. Child or not, this semqu is in enemy hands. And she knows far too much.

On the frozen continent of Aun, in one of the bleaker corners of the spaceport, barely heated meeting rooms are rented by the hour. They stink of bodily secretions and furtive hunger, and they hold no recorders, not for vibration or sight or even warmth.

Excellent for private meetings of many kinds.

The scarlet-tinged modeel, scarred kertueon, somnolent larsivian and snarling peqe who meet here a month after the *Ichyado's* visit to Taequa are not part of the Council of Twelve or the Lar mafia, and they do not like or trust one another. Schemers rarely do. But they need one another, so they grudgingly share a few secrets, and they manage dangerous agreements that would benefit them all.

Resentment, a disease recognized on Iyam as deadly, burns in them all. The semqu work to benefit all peoples, but these four, and their allies, do not believe they have received their due. They want more. They intend to get it.

They already have a weapon.

Today they agree on a target.

*Want to know when **Thwarted** is available for preorder?*
Sign up for Slimhorn & Wren's mailing list here:
https://www.slimhornandwren.com

GLOSSARY AND PRONUNCIATION GUIDE

*Pronunciation between () is in layman's English; between //
employs International phonetic alphabet symbols (IPA).*

CHARACTERS

Achleot
(atch lay oht) /ˈætʃ.le.ˌʊːt / Leader of Temple Piertoc when Spacers
arrive in Se System.

Adamantine
(ahd a man teen) or /æd. ə. ˈmæn.tɪn/ Opal/Voice's sister, daughter
of Harriet and Obert. A word meaning unyielding. Adamantine
spar, a brown crystalline form of aluminum oxide one step below
diamond on the mohs hardness scale.

Anika
(ah nee kah) /æ.ˈni.kæ/ A Spacer who marries who marries
Adamantine's son Bonaparte. Anika's uncle is Rupert Keo.

Attarc
(at tark) /ˈæt.tɑrk/ Title given the head of Temple Piertoc; the peqe
equivalent of a pope, e.g., Attarc Achleot.

Braun
(brawn) /bɹɑn/ Danielle's last name.

Brenna
(breh nah) /ˈbɹɛ.nə/ Spacer child, daughter of Bonaparte and Anika.

Bonaparte
(boapart) or /ˈbo.nə.pɑrt/ —Voice's nephew, son of Adamantine and Ulick.

Chie
(chee-ay) or /ˈtʃi.e/
Tem Chie Charna, one of Opal's calligraphy mentors

Cablu
/kɑ.ˈblʊ/ One of Waatoos's childhood friends.

Danielle
(dan.yell) /dan.ˈjɛl/ one of the Earthborn who survived the suspension pods on the *New Hope.*

Doaett Dontan
(doh-ay-ETT) /ˌdo.e.ˈɛt/ a dueling apiquiit

Dontan
/dɔn.ˈtan/ Household of Doaett and Jjaloot

Dorina
/do.ri.nə/ a peqe on Peindak's staff

Du
/du/ New Hopian teen

Enzo
/ˈɛn.zo/ Wei Enzo, a young scientist, Rupert's mentee

E-uuui-i
(ay ewwww EE) /ˌe.uː.ˈi/ an aupoin who travels between planets.

Foele Creator
(foh eel) /fo.ˈil/ A modeel businessman

Frances
(fran sis) /ˈfræn.sɪz/ navigator aboard *New Hope*

Gibran
/dʒɪ.ˈbɹən/ a spoiled and unhappy youth; Voice's grandnephew.

Gorleen

/ˈɡoɹ.liːn/ young Acolyte of Temple Piertoc

Grandi-Gutherie

/ˈɡɹɑn.di ˈɡʌθ.ri/ family name of Juand and Niels, and their son and daughter Ulick and Marfa

/Gtec

/ɡə.ˈtɛk/ a model

Guettarch

/ɡʊt.ˈtɑrtʃ/ peqe household

Hamid

(ha meed) /ħaˈmid/ a Spacer, part of Danielle's information-gathering network

Harriet

(hair y uht) / hæɹ.i.ɪt/ agriculturist and weaver, married to Obert, mother of Opal and Adamantine.

Hematite's Hoard

/ hiːmə.taitz/ /hoɹd/ a blinkship

I-oo-u

/ˈi.oː.u/ crochety nosy elder aupoin

Ireti

(ih reh tee) /ɪ.ˈrɛ.ti/ the name chosen by the semqu connected to Opal/Voice and a heroic former ship captain (Ireti Nabuco).

Izhdench

/ɪz.ˈdɛntʃ/ a peqe household; Vassat is their current apiquiit.

Jjaloot Dontan

(DJah loh-oht) /ˈdʒɑ.ˌlo.ot/ peqe matriarch

Juand

/hwɑnd/ one of Marfa and Ulick's dads

Keo

(kay o) /ˈke.oː/ Last name of Anika, Rupert and Saira.

Laavanya

/ˈlɑː.vɑːɲɑ/ a Fugrast student of Voice's and Hamid's mother.

Lethabo Lim

/lɛ.ˈθə.bo/ -- a serious young New Hopian

Marfa

/ˈmɑːr.fə / Spacer who develops a hatred and fear of the Semqu.

Mboya Cheng

/m.ˈbɔɪ.jɑ/ Spacer teen

Nata

/nɑtɑ/ unhappy young Spacer; Rupert and Marfa's daughter.

Niels Grandi

(neelz) /niˑlz/ a father of Marfa and Ulick

Nyshoof

/ˈniː.ʃʊf / a peqe household

O-eee-u

/o.ˈiː.ˌu / a very singular aupoin

Obert Pangea

/ˈo.bɜɹt / Opal and Adamantine's father, a scientist.

Opal Pangea

/ˈo.pəl / also known as Voice. A spacer who becomes telepathically connected to a semqu.

Pangea

(pan gee ah) or /ˌpænˈdʒiːə/ Family name of Obert and Harriet, their daughters Adamantine and Opal; taken by Adamantine's husband Ulick, and thus their son Bonaparte and eventually his children Gibran, Paoli, and Brenna. Also, the name of an Old Earth supercontinent.

Paoli Pangea

/ paʊli / scientist and Opal's niece

Peindak

/ˈpɛn.dæk / a peqe household; one of their matrons is ambassador.

Poiste

/ pwəst / a peqe household. One of their matrons is on the Council of Twelve.

Rupert Keo

/ rupərt / math geek, son of scientist Saira Keo.

Kall **Saena**

(say ena) or / seːˈɛnə / a peqe Matriarch

Saira Keo

(sah ee rah) /sɑˈi.rə/ planetary scientist and mother to Rupert

Stuotok

(stew o tok) /ˈstʊːo.tɔk/ a modeel

Tate Dorafandu

(tayt) /tet/ Head of Planetary research on *New Hope*

Terri

/təri/ Opal's childhood friend

Tiani

/tiːɑni/ Terri's brother

Tkzotch

/tɪk.zɔtʃ/ a stolen semqu child.

Ulick Grandi-Gutherie—(Uilleag)

(EWL yck) /ˈul.jæk / Spacer language prodigy whc beccmes Prime Minister; son of Juand and Niels.

Vassat Izhdench

/vɑsˈzɑt / a young peqe, an apiquiit

Voice

/vɔɪs/ title and name of every Speaker-for-Semqɹ. Opal changes her name to Voice.

Waatoos Hecht

/ˈwaːtus / a modeel Krufrugaan

WealthBringer

/wɛlθ.bɹɪŋəɹ/ the blinkship Nata works on and its Semqu.

Ximena Bobbie

(hee men a) /hiˈmɛnə / *New Hope's* captain and later Prime Minister

Y-uu-see

(y-ew-see) /ˈj.uːˌsiː/ aupoin voice for Trye9.

Zara

/ zɑrɑ / a young New Hopian

Vocabulary and Place Names

Apiquai

/ˈæ.pɪˌkɑi / a peqe term meaning 1. a matron's declared purpose in life and 2. the basis of the apeqe economic system, which uses apiquai-coin. Each household receives an annual payment based on the number of declared apiquai in a household.

Apiquiit

/ ˌæ.pɪ.ˈkit / heiress. The first granddaughter of an apeqe household.

Apeqe

/ ˈæ.pik / ruling class of the peqe on Taequa.

Aun

/ɔn/ planet of the hive-like Kertueon. Their spaceport is in an icy region, as far as possible from their beloved queen.

Aupoin

(ah pwon) /ˈɑ.pwɑn / name of a ubiquitous species resembling burrowing tardigrades.

Bayside

(bay syd) /ˈbe.saɪd / the first large-scale communal kitchen and cafeteria that spacers constructed on Trye.

Byne

/ bɪn / name of the Se System planet with the most multicultural communities.

Dorna

/ˈdɔɹ.nɑ/ a native Trye shrub whose pollen renders honey inedible.

Fuaringsplenzu

/ˌfuɑɹ.ɪŋz.ˈplɛnzu/ Spacer city on Trye. Sometimes shortened to Fuar or Zu.

Fugrast

/ˈfu.græst/ the trade language used in Se System.

Gruide

/gru.ˈiːd/ a species in Se System. Think of sentient geese.

Gtorin

/gə.ˈtorɪn/ drug that focuses the user's mind on their greatest desire.

Iyam

(ee yam) /i.ˈjæm/ home planet of the phren

Jade

/dʒed/ common spacer name for the lobe-leafed trees in the area where they build their city. The aupoin name is lopa /lopɑ/.

Kertueon

/ˌkɜɹ.ˈtu.iɔn/ a hive-like species on Aun, described as massive praying mantises.

Krufrugaan

/ˈkruː.fɹu.ˌɡɑːn/ investigative and judicial organization of largely modeel.

Larsivian

/lɑɹ.ˈsɪ.viƏn/ varied, populous species of amphibians inhabiting the planet Ylas.

Matriarch

/ˈmeɪtɹiɑɹk/ the head of any apeqe household on Taequa

Matron

/ˈmeɪtɹƏn/ a (second or succeeding) daughter in an aqeqe household.

Modeel

/mo.ˈdiːl/ a species from Vasom, who claim creation of blinkships. Marine creatures who are rarely seen outside their hulking, mech-like hardsuits with protective, emotion-communicating biofields.

Peqe

/ˈpiːke/, /pik/

muscular, bipedal and class-based species that lives on Taequa.

Phren

/fɹɛn/ furry, communal and polygamous species from Iyam with some superficial resemblance to peqe.

Sakatos

/ˈsɑ.kƏ.ˌtos/ system capitol, on planet Ylas.

Semqu

(sem kyew) /sɛm.ˈkju/ species that appears to influence, if not rule, Se System

Serium

/ ˈsɪɹiəm / the sun that Trye orbits.

Spacer

/spe.səɹ/ the word that New Hopians chose to replace "human."

Szipeqe

/ˈsɪzi.pik / the worker class on Taequa

Taequa

/te.ˈik.wa /home planet to the peqe

Trye

/tɹi/ planet gifted largely to the spacers by the semqu

Vasom

/væ.ˈsɔm/ home planet of the Modeel

Wjorx

/wə.ˈʒɔɹks/ a dangerous, reclusive species on Iyam. Used in many swear phrases or epithets.

Ylas

/jlɑs/ home planet to the larsivians, location of the system's capitol of Sakatos.

Zissokot

/ˈzɪzo.kɔt/ Peqe's capitol city on Taequa, where Temple Piertoc is located.

ABOUT THE AUTHOR

Ellen Saunders lives in the Pacific Northwest and primarily writes speculative fiction, space opera, and fantasy. When not paying obeisance to spoiled felines, reading, or writing, Ellen sings, studies French, gardens, cooks, draws, crochets, calligraphs, plays word puzzles obsessively, and occasionally dons garb Steampunk or medieval. In other words, her home is stuffed with the typical ADHD piles of hobbies past. She and her partner are mutually startled by having survived together for more than twenty years.

Past iterations of self have been a massage therapist, newspaper reporter, university public relations staff, and a writer for a nutrition education program.

Ellen's short stories have appeared in Daily Science Fiction, Lady Churchill's Rosebud Wristlet, and ROAR. This is her first published novel. There are two completed books in the pipeline in this universe and more coming. (Life lesson: Perfection is the enemy of done).